Praise for Elizabeth Dean and
It's in Her Kiss

"Dishy . . . There's no shortage of action in this girl's guilty pleasure."
—*Publishers Weekly*

"Deliciously over-the-top . . . Dean handles her romantic moments with a lusty appreciation for sex and love, but the real appeal of this pleasurable novel lies in her deft way with daffy dialogue and comic situations."
—*Bookmarks*

"A sudsy beach read . . . Dean's pages practically turn themselves."
—*Out*

"Dean's beach novel is an entertaining, fast-paced soap. With crackling dialogue from a politically correct mix of characters, Dean's book is a true page-turner."
—*Booklist*

"Comedic . . . romantic . . . perfect material for a light read."
—*Philadelphia Gay News*

It's in Her Kiss

Elizabeth Dean

KENSINGTON BOOKS
http://www.kensingtonbooks.com

KENSINGTON BOOKS are published by

Kensington Publishing Corp.
850 Third Avenue
New York, NY 10022

All Kensington titles, imprints and distributed lines are available at special quantity discounts for bulk purchases for sales promotion, premiums, fund-raising, educational or institutional use.

Special book excerpts or customized printings can also be created to fit specific needs. For details, write or phone the office of the Kensington Special Sales Manager: Kensington Publishing Corp., 850 Third Avenue, New York, NY 10022. Attn. Special Sales Department. Phone: 1-800-221-2647.

Kensington and the K logo Reg. U.S. Pat. & TM Off.

ISBN 0-7582-0090-0

First Hardcover Printing: July 2002
First Trade Paperback Printing: June 2003
10 9 8 7 6 5 4 3 2 1

Printed in the United States of America

To Alison Picard, my trusted agent

"One way or another, she's going to track each of us down and kill us in horrible, unspeakable ways if we don't make her believe in these shows we're about to pitch," I said to my creative group as we sat, shivering, in the well-chilled conference room waiting for the Dragon Lady to roar through the door. I figured that if I helped get everyone's heart rate fibrillating prior to the Dragon Lady's appearance, by the time she showed up no one would go into cardiac arrest.

Because there would be no time to perform CPR—or even to call the paramedics.

Here at Lesbian-TV, or L-TV for short, there was no time for anything other than work. Sometimes you might be able to grab a bite to eat. Sometimes you might be able to go to the bathroom. And sometimes you might be able to glance out of the windows of the refurbished, circa 1803, red-brick and black-shuttered four-story building that housed our offices, which overlooked Boston Harbor.

But there was no time for illness, no time for injury, no time for personal issues, and certainly no time for cardiac arrest.

You're here working one-hundred-and-twenty-five percent for me, Debbe Lee—known to her enemies and employees as the Dragon Lady—had told us as soon as the ink had dried on our two-year contracts. *Or you're dead. And if you're dead, we'll roll your still-warm body out onto the elevator, press the Down button, and have your office filled with a living, breathing replacement by the end of the workday.*

If we weren't making so much money—a healthy amount, by television-writing industry standards—and didn't have such excellent benefits, from health and dental to generous expense accounts to a small percentage of profit-sharing that commenced two years after the network's launch, I'm sure no one in their right mind would want to work for the Dragon Lady. It was an experience, to use legal terminology, that would certainly qualify as IIED; intentional infliction of emotional distress.

Even David E. Kelley wouldn't want to work for the Dragon Lady. And I'm certain that Chris Carter would beg for an alien abduction and gladly submit to the anal probe on a daily basis just to get away from her.

Okay. So our stomachs were constantly bubbling like hot springs, our heads incessantly throbbed like the speakers in a techno dance bar, and the entire staff at L-TV had essentially no life outside of 55 Water's Edge Way. We had three vending machines in our snack room—one filled with candy bars, one that contained only caffeinated beverages (including three racks of Jolt), and the other stocked with Tylenol, Excedrin, Mylanta, Tums, razor blades, pre-tied nooses, and loaded pistols.

Guess which vending machine had to be refilled the most?

So why did we keep coming back day after day? Why didn't we set fire to our contracts and run for our lives from the house of television-writing torture that Debbe Lee had built?

Because—damn—we had the potential to be rich! After all, a once-fledgling cable-TV network dubbed "HBO" regularly racked in a shelf full of Emmys each year, and even the lowly Fox Television Network had its own hits to brag about. Can anyone say *Beverly Hills 90210*? Or *The Simpsons*? And—hot damn—we knew we were being given the unique opportunity to break some serious television-networking ground.

Hand us the shovel, Dragon Lady! we wanted to collectively cry out to her. *We're ready to dig for TV gold!*

Just think—you could say what it was like to launch the next HBO, Debbe had told us. *You could be there at the Emmys accepting award after award for the shows that came from your minds. Shows that you gave birth to. Shows that were your babies.*

There's no doubt about it. Debbe Lee knew how to hit all the right response buttons in her creative writing team. But that wasn't too surprising. After all, she had hopscotched her way through the alphabet letters of the networks and had learned everything about the business from ABC to Z. She had single-handedly delivered some long-running, award-winning series to each of those major networks: *Fly Boys, PDQ 900, Gone to the Dogs, Racketeers,* and *Preston Avenue,* to name a few, and had long ago surpassed Oprah Winfrey in financial net worth and network clout.

Debbe Lee was that rare Type Triple A personality who could incite a riot in a monastery, an orgy in a maternity ward, or a string of four-letter words from the mouth of a minister preaching a Sunday sermon.

And I don't mean words like holy, or pray, or amen.

What Debbe Lee had told us—what had convinced us all that this woman's army was the best gig going yet—was that, flat out, we had the potential to realize the greatest dream any television writer could have. The amateur athlete sought the Olympic gold medal. The actor or actress yearned for the Oscar. The senator longed to be president. The author pined after the National Book Award. The newspaper photographer craved the Pulitzer Prize.

But what the television writer craved the most was to have total creative control over a show. Total. To not just write the words that would be spoken each week on a new episode, but to devise the plot, create and mold the characters, determine the setting, spark the conflicts, ignite the passions, and provide the raison d'etre.

Debbe Lee might be our Zeus—the god of all creation—but we were the lesser gods who had been given the power to breathe new life into the fantasy world of television.

They said no one could ever surpass CBS, ABC, and NBC, the Dragon Lady had told us during our first weekend retreat to Provincetown as a group. *And, well, hell, what did they know? And now* they *say that no one but a small percentage of the TV-viewing population will watch L-TV,* she had continued. *And, well, hell, little do they know that we're going to be showing them up with our own unique style of programming. Look at HBO. It's got sports broadcasts. So will we. We've negotiated for the rights to broadcast the gamut of NCAA women's sports—from basketball games prior to March Madness to lacrosse to field hockey to rugby to softball to you-name-it. If there are women playing a sport and there's a scoreboard, well, you can bet that we'll be there.*

HBO makes its own movies. So will we—everything from bios to action-adventure to romance to sci-fi. Our first, as you all know, is Fallen Gladiator, *which is loosely based on the lives of women gladiators who fought in Roman London. Filming has already started, with Mel Gibson directing and Angela Bassett, Meg Ryan, and Neve Campbell on board.*

HBO produces its own series. Can anyone say The Sopranos *or* Sex and the City? *Well, so will we—that's why you're here. You're the brains behind the next hit shows that America will be talking about at the corporate watercoolers and on call-in radio talk shows each morning. We will be the new must-see TV—every night of the week.*

Just like HBO, we'll make our own documentaries. And, just like HBO's lineup of Hollywood movies, we'll offer up solid inde-pendent films. And Playboy After Dark *is going to seem like a chil-dren's all-Barney, all-the-time video network compared to the pornography we're going to be able to air after prime time is over. Tell me we're not going to get a large male population watching women making love to women!*

So what is HBO? Huh? Debbe had asked us as her coal-black eyes had momentarily locked onto each pair of eyes in the room, which were all focused on her. *I'll tell you. It's everything. And that's what we're going to be, too. We're going to make L-TV stand for more than just Lesbian-TV. We're going to be known as Lead-TV. The leader. As in the one to beat. We're going to break new ground, and soon every network is going to be scrambling to try to catch up to us.*

It was a brilliant speech that the Dragon Lady had made to us back then, and it had inspired us all to rise to the challenge of breaking new ground. We had our heads held high when we left that retreat, and there was a swagger in our walk.

But now, sitting around the well-polished, maple-veneer oval conference room table in the subarctic temperature that the Dragon Lady seemed to thrive in, which reduced even the most well-layered writer to a hunched-over shivering mass, we were not a very highly confident group. We had spent the first few months after the retreat spinning our wheels in the infamous name-dropping TV series pitch game:

"It's *I Love Lucy* with the biting sarcasm of *Maude* and the great ensemble of *Seinfeld*."

"It's *JAG* meets *NYPD Blue* meets *Law & Order*."

"It's *ER* with a *M*A*S*H* feel to it."

"It's *The Monkees* on a *Gilligan's Island* type of thing."

"Think *Charlie's Angels*, then think *Xena: Warrior Princess*, then think *Sex and the City*."

"It's a fat girl's *Ally McBeal*."

No matter what ideas we had come up with at the time, it seemed that everything sounded like something that had already been done before. Which it had. Those initial months were followed by weeks in which we sat silent and stone-faced in our once vocal and exciting brainstorming sessions, staring off into space and thinking our own thoughts. Which all added up to: *Shit! Everything's been done before.*

Finally, when we couldn't stand the sight or the smell or the presence of one another and we just started automatically shooting down any idea that was thrown on the table for group consideration, I told my group to get lost for a week.

"I mean it," I said. "Get the hell out of here—out of these bad-karma offices—and get out into the streets. Take a trip. Sign up for a course. Follow someone around for a day. Just do something different. Open your eyes. Look around you. Notice people. Notice their lives. And then find the drama. Find the adventure. Find the humor. Find the relationships. And don't come back here until you have something solid, something good, something different to offer up.

"Something that will be big."

I had then pointed to the door of the conference room, and there was no hesitancy following that gesture. Like the burst of activity that erupts after a starter's pistol is fired at a track and field Olympic qualifier, the writers had practically scrambled over each other to get out of that room and exit the building as fast as they could.

Like rats fleeing a sinking ship, I had thought to myself, and then I pictured in my mind the *Titanic* rearing its big fat butt end high in the air before slowly slipping into the frigid North Atlantic waters.

As I sat in the empty conference room, the Dragon Lady had walked in.

"Was that a massive walk-out I just witnessed, or did you fire everyone?"

"It's creative rejuvenation," I had told her.

"We haven't even launched our first season, and you're telling me your writers need creative rejuvenation? C.J., that's supposed to happen after our shows have become hits and all the story lines have been done to death. Are these writers just not good enough?"

"Oh, they're good enough, Debbe. They just need to start thinking out of the box."

"I thought they already knew how to do that. Isn't that why they're here? Or did we spend months looking through stacks of resumes for people who aren't even qualified to be meter maids?"

"We hired the best, most creative writers, Debbe," I replied, trying to keep the edge out of my voice because I didn't want to stoke the fires of her razor-sharp retorts. "You know that. But you wanted award-winning journalists. You wanted savvy copywriters. You wanted National Book Award nominees. What you told me you specifically didn't want were professional television writers—those who already had a track record in the industry—because you felt they might be locked into writing for shows geared to a straight audience. This is a new venue for these writers."

"Then let's just fire the lot of them and hire professional television writers. Since they're all out of the building anyway—"

"Don't," I cut in. "They just need a little time to—"

"C.J., time isn't something that someone needs. Time is something someone has. That's why they say that people waste time. You don't waste something you need. You either do something with it, or you piss it away. Which appears to be what your staff is doing. What are they going to do now? Walk around Boston eating ice-cream cones? Stop in to see the penguins at the aquarium? Maybe take in a matinee? Get some free pussy? Whatever they're doing, I'm sure it's not a very effective use of the money I'm paying them."

"Trust me, Debbe. They're going to come back here filled with ideas."

Debbe sucked in air between her perfectly aligned white teeth and then raised her plucked-to-the-wire eyebrows. "I hope those ideas are going to be better than a show that—hmmm—how did I overhear it described in the ladies' room? As a show that has a Sandra Bernhard–like character in it?"

"What were you doing in the staff ladies' room?" I asked. "I thought you had a ballroom-sized lav next to your office."

"I've been known to frequent well-attended bathrooms," Debbe said as her full lips parted into a subtle smile. "You can pick up a lot of interesting . . . things . . . in them. You might want to try them out for yourself sometime, C.J. It might end that drought you've gotten so accustomed to enduring."

"Keep this conversation out of my personal life, Debbe," I warned her.

Debbe snapped her head back, and her long, arrow-straight

shiny black mane cascaded behind her shoulders. "Just a suggestion, my dear C.J. I do worry about you drying up completely. First it starts between the legs, you know. And then your brain cells just start shriveling up until all that comes out of your head is bitterness and regret."

I rolled my eyes. "Spare me the drama."

Debbe placed her hands on the table and leaned towards me. I was assailed by the scent of some expensive perfume I'm sure she'd had imported from Paris. It had probably traveled from Paris to Boston buckled in a first-class seat. Or maybe it had been the sole passenger on a Lear jet that had been given priority landing at Logan over Air Force One. "I'll spare you the drama when your writers give me a drama, C.J. And a comedy. And a few potential hit series. And, as to the suggestion for a Sandra Bernhard–like character—there's no such thing. As much as we'd like it to be true, Sandra Bernhard cannot be cloned. And, *please*, I don't want another *Ellen*. Nope, I don't. Unless she and Helen Hunt become an item, and then we can have *The Ellen and Helen Show*."

Despite my lousy mood and the fact that I couldn't slip a piece of paper between Debbe's body and mine at the moment, I cracked a smile.

"Ah. Good. It's nice to see I can still say a few words that will elicit something other than a frown on your face."

"You have your moments, Debbe."

"We had our moments once, C.J. Some nice ones, as I recall."

I shook my head. "Don't go there."

"Don't you?"

I toed the carpet and pushed my chair back from Debbe, adding distance between our bodies. "Not since you started taking nasty pills with your daily vitamins and I discovered that you were sharing our bed on a regular basis with—"

"I wasn't totally nice to you, was I?" she cut in.

"No. But you know that. We've had this conversation before. I'm sick of reruns."

Debbe took a step back from me and folded her arms across her chest. It was a move that she had perfected over the years, a move that lifted her ample breasts and afforded them a position for better public viewing.

I willed my eyes to lock in with hers. No matter how I felt about Debbe, no matter how much time had passed since we had shared our satin-sheeted bed, I always responded like a melting ice cube to the sight of her cleavage.

"It's just that sometimes I'm still attracted to your . . . your good-girlness, C.J.," she said. "Your morality. Your do-the-right-thing way of living. You're like Karen what's-her-name on *Knots Landing*. Krystle Carrington on *Dynasty*. Jo on—"

"Debbe, please stop comparing me to television characters. You know how that annoys me."

"Well, what annoys me, darling C.J., is seeing no one in this office during working hours, doing what I'm paying them to do. I hate pissing my money away, unless it's on me and what I want. So I just hope, for the sake of your career at L-TV, that your Girl Scouts return from selling their cookies door-to-door with a big payoff. I hope that what you'll then have to show me will impress the hell out of me. And I hope that the shows you'll be pitching will help me to forget that your group of top-notch creative writers was even considering such a dumb idea as a Sandra Bernhard clone."

We just have to pull it off, I thought as I drummed my fingers on the conference room table. Our first formal presentation to Debbe a month ago had degenerated into her flinging Finagle-A-Bagel bagels and tubs of Bread-and-Circus flavored cream cheeses at our storyboards, knocking them to the carpeted floor as she screamed that we all had to have been *ON LIFE SUPPORT* and *BRAIN DEAD* to have come up with *SUCH SHIT-FILLED IDEAS*.

This second meeting was less than two weeks away from the deadline to make our final programming decisions. Then we would have to scramble to hire actresses, producers, directors, set designers, and all the other essential personnel we would need to create our first season of Lesbian-TV programming, which would run from late September to early May. We already had a number of shows on board to fill the morning and early afternoon time slots: the requisite cooking shows, exercise programs, and real-people chat sessions.

But where we really had *to kick butt,* according to the Dragon Lady, was in our prime-time programming.

If you can't get the fat slobs at home who are sitting on their big butts to press two simple buttons to change a channel so they'll watch our network, she had told us, *then you should just pack your stuff in a box, go to the nearest T stop, and lay your hand on the third rail. That would be more interesting,* she had concluded. *In fact,* she added, *we could film that and get higher ratings than this crap you've just shown me.*

The Dragon Lady had certainly been spewing big fat snorts of fire on us that day, I recalled. No one in the conference room had been left without a third-degree burn somewhere on their ego.

"I wish the Dragon Lady would fry in hell," Meri Wiggins had muttered as soon as Debbe had slammed the conference room door.

"Cleanup on aisle three," Taylor Shoemaker muttered as she righted a storyboard, glanced at the cream cheese blob on it, and then dropped the board back to the floor.

"Hell is too good for that bitch," Chantelle Colby replied. "She'd think she was at a summer picnic."

"Bitch is too nice a word for her," Maria Hernandez piped in. "When I'm a bitch, I'm much nicer than she is."

"She's a venomous viper," Taylor hissed, then popped two Excedrins in her mouth and washed them down with a swig of Dr. Pepper.

"In my homeland," Samata Naroff began, "there is ways of how we deal with people, mostly those who do not like the politicians. We make them go—poof!—disappeared."

"If we did that to the Dragon Lady, it'd be—puff—disappeared!" Meri pointed out with a grin.

"How do you mean, 'puff'?" asked Samata, who had a puzzled look on her face.

"You know, like Puff the Magic Dragon," explained Taylor.

"That song used to make me cry when I was little," said Maria.

"Debbe Lee is no Puff the Magic Dragon," said Chantelle. "She's Godzilla."

"But Godzilla was not a dragon—am I correct about this?" Samata asked. "Godzilla was—"

"God of the Zillas," Meri said with a smile and a short snort.

"Okay, knock it off," I had cut in before the few remaining writers had had a chance to add their own comments and terrible puns—and things really got out of hand. "Debbe's the boss, and whatever she says goes. Remember, it's her name on your paycheck."

"Yeah, but she keeps signing the checks 'Debbe Lee' instead of 'Dragon Lady'," muttered Taylor. "Just who are we really working for? A woman or an overgrown reptile?"

"Are dragons reptiles?" asked Samata. "I thought they were warm-blooded."

"Well, she's certainly not warm-blooded," said Maria. "That is one freeze-dried c—"

"Button it up, everyone," I cut in as I surveyed the room. "We're just wasting time. Back to the drawing board."

No one—not even I—called Debbe Lee "Dragon Lady" to her face, although I suspect she had an inkling that some sort of unflattering nickname had been assigned to her. After all, you don't get approval to launch a controversial cable-TV channel, a handful of million-dollar backers, and a few big corporate sponsors to fall over one another to buy advertising time because you're a nice person. Or low-key. Or everyone's best friend.

While such big scores on Debbe's part had made veterans in the cutthroat television industry shake their heads with wonder, amazed at how she had been able to magically get so many willing partners on board so quickly, I had to agree with my writers on one comment. Puff the Magic Dragon she was not.

Debbe Lee was the kind of person who could interrupt a funeral to sell raffle tickets—and make a profit.

But you couldn't sell a hit show like *Everyone Loves Raymond* to the likes of the Dragon Lady. As she had once told us, *I don't give a rat's ass about Raymond. I'd much rather see* Everyone Can't Stand the Sight of Raymond *and then watch people trash him each week. But it's not just me who feels this way. TV-addicted Americans would rather see an overbearing, overweight gay man walking around naked on a tropical island beach, or an undereducated truck driver calling someone a rat or a snake, or people lying, cheating, stealing, murdering, raping, or backstabbing than Lassie rescuing Timmy from the well. Trust me on this.*

We did.

Today's presentation of L-TV's prime-time lineup to Debbe "Dragon Lady" Lee would be our second—and last—chance to sell our souls and save our asses.

Because, when you sign on to work for the Dragon Lady, there's no three-strikes-and-you're-out rule. You have to load up the bases with hit after hit, and start scoring big time.

Or, plain and simple, you're out of the ball game.

"**Two** things I'm going to tell you before you show me what you've got," Debbe announced as she cruised into the room with her harried assistant following in her wake. The assistant—a buxom, blonde, blue-eyed Swedish-looking number who had apparently replaced the leggy Latino twenty-something who had been caught a few days earlier on a security surveillance tape lap-dancing after-hours in Debbe's office with a woman from the accounting department—was juggling an armload of black vinyl notebooks, a dozen videotapes, a cell phone, and a laptop computer. As she turned around to nudge the conference room door closed with a shoulder, one of the videotapes slid to the floor.

Samata immediately rose from her chair and bent down to pick up the tape.

"Sit down, Saffron!" Debbe snapped at her.

Samata arose with the tape in her hand and turned to look at Debbe. "My name is Samata."

"My assistant doesn't need an assistant," Debbe told her.

"That is certainly your opinion," answered Samata. "But it appears she needs an extra hand, and I thought I would assist."

Debbe raised an eyebrow and showed Samata a smirk. "Samantha, I'm sure Abba here would like an extra hand—somewhere—

but you're going to have to pursue that on your own time. Remember what happened to Lucia. Now sit down."

Samata showed a half-smile to Debbe's assistant, then handed her the tape. "Abba, is it?"

The blonde shook her head. "No, it's Britta," she replied. She looked at the tape, then glanced at the bundle of items she was desperately clinging onto.

"Britta," Samata murmured as she gently slid the videotape on top of the precariously positioned armload. "I am Samata."

"Thank you, Sa—"

"Ladies, this isn't a lunch-date fix up," Debbe interrupted. "Simba, stop making goo-goo eyes at Abba and sit your butt down."

"Samata," muttered Samata as she returned to her seat.

Taylor leaned over the arm of her chair towards Samata. "Let it go," she whispered. "We'll mix up the cement and toss her into the harbor later on tonight."

I widened my eyes at Taylor in warning.

"Have you got your people under control, C.J.?" Debbe asked as she opened one of the notebooks Britta had handed to her and started flipping through it.

I nodded.

"Can't hear you," she said without looking up.

I took in a breath. "Yes."

"Good. Because the next mutterer will be able to mutter all she wants while she stands in the unemployment line." She glanced at Taylor. "Or in the lines at Home Depot, while she waits to purchase a bag of cement."

Taylor's face grew beet-red, and she immediately looked down at a pad of paper in front of her.

"Don't think for one minute—no, one second—that I can't see everything, hear everything, and know everything that goes on here, ladies. So I'd strongly advise you to—"

"We're all set, Debbe," I cut in.

Debbe was silent for a few moments as she tapped her red-lacquered fingers on the conference room table. Then she glanced over to Britta. "Set it up," she told her, then took slow, measured strides to the front of the room. "The first thing I'm going to tell you about is the non–prime-time programming that's already in place at L-TV. I'll take you through it quickly. The second thing I'm going to tell you is that if you can't sell me on each of your ideas thirty seconds after you start your pitch, it's a no-go. As are you and your short-lived career at L-TV. Let me repeat that. Thirty seconds. No more. You're not making opening arguments in a criminal trial or telling me a bedtime story. Are we clear?"

If anyone on my writing staff was unclear, she wasn't about to admit it.

And so, with each person in the room but Debbe Lee clenching their jaws to prevent their teeth from chattering—both out of fear and because we were all in the early stages of hypothermia—Britta dimmed the lights and pressed a button on the VCR remote control.

"Ya, here ve go," Meri whispered into a cupped hand.

We focused our attention on the large television that was set up at one end of the table.

Joan Jett's version of the theme song from *The Mary Tyler Moore Show* blasted into the room as the rainbow-colored logo for Lesbian-TV flashed on the screen with the tagline, "Watch how women do it." What followed was a fast-moving montage of clips from L-TV's daytime show lineup that dropped a few jaws, drew occasional cheers, and kept us spellbound—eyes glued to the set—as we tapped our feet or jiggled our legs in time to the music.

L-TV had everything. I mean *everything*. Anything that any viewer watched on other TV channels during the day, we had as well. We had soap operas. One show, which elicited the loudest whistles and catcalls, was *Provincetown*. This daytime soap featured scantily clad women cavorting on a beach, women dirty dancing in a crowded disco, and women opening bedroom doors and discovering their lovers in bed with other women—or some-times a man.

So, what, have you switched teams on me? asked a woman who had discovered her lover in bed with a Brad Pitt lookalike.

The woman in the rumpled bed ran her tongue up and down her male partner's fingers, then guided his hand underneath the deep-purple satin sheet that covered them. *I'm playing on both sides,* she answered. *You get to score more that way.*

As if you've ever had a problem scoring.

Do I detect a bit of nastiness in your tone of voice? Or perhaps it's jealousy. Why don't you join us, Cecilia? Do this, and I'll get you on the fast track in the firm. Don't, and you might as well kiss this house, your job, and our friends goodbye. Because I won't keep quiet about that secret you've so carefully guarded.

Organ music swells . . .

What secret?

. . . and stops.

Oh, didn't I tell you that your brother paid me a visit yesterday? He told me all about that overdose of medication that you gave your sister the day she went out horseback riding—and never came back.

The clip fades out after showing close-ups of each character looking suitably shocked, smug, or sex-starved.

The tape rolled on into clips from two other soaps that looked equally backstabbing, spiteful, and filled with beautiful, evil peo-ple, then launched into clips from a couple of cooking shows and then a craft hour.

Yes, I know you don't think it's possible to make a wreath out of wild rice, but wait until you see this! exclaimed a woman who went by the first name Angel, whose show was called *Angel Arts.*

Other clips followed: from a garden show, *Gardening with Gerry;* exercise programs that featured fitness kickboxing, self-defense, and weight lifting; home schooling shows; and a lineup of talk shows that focused on particular topics of interest—lesbian and gay politics, sex and relationships, and ethical and legal issues.

L-TV had its own home improvement show, called *Hammertime*, which featured a denim-clad, spiked-haired, tattooed muscular woman who was sporting a tool belt and a T-shirt that proclaimed, "I. M. Hammered."

I gotta tell ya, ladies and gay boys. It ain't hard to hang your own kitchen cabinets. Hammertime*'s gonna show ya how. Why pay for them other guys ta do the job for ya? All they're gonna be doin' is messin' up your kitchen and overchargin' ya. And most'a 'em is uglier than a cow's rump, so there ain't nothin' to keep ya entertained, boys.*

Heck, you'll pay as much for the hangin' as fer the cabinets. You got money comin' out the wazoo, then go ahead and pay while you sip your pina coladas by the pool. But if you ain't got no pool and yous tired'a payin' through the nose, then I'm here ta help ya.

All you're gonna need is a measuring tape, screws and a screwdriver, and a couple'a strong arms ta help out. So let's get hammered—okay?

L-TV even had its own home shopping network, which offered up gay-themed items—from rainbow flags to gold jewelry inlaid with rainbow-colored gems to household items for home entertaining to a wide variety of sex toys.

How much do you think you'd pay for this double-sided dildo, with clitoral vibrating stimulators for pleasuring two people? Hands-free! And remember, with your order we're also going to throw in a dozen double-A Rayovacs®, include the newest design in butt plugs, and ship everything to you for FREE—that's right— for FREE! And with everything you order, you get the money-back, no-questions-asked guarantee from L-TV. . . .

Before the evening news hours, when L-TV would be picking up a national and world news feed from CNN, there was a Hollywood gossip and movie review hour hosted by two lesbians and a gay man, called *Parlez à Trois.*

Hi, I'm Lance Lights.

I'm Candy Camera.

And I'm Amanda Action.

We're Lights, Camera, and Action, on the Hollywood scene.

On today's show, Sylvester Stallone's new movie is such a turkey they should've released it at Thanksgiving instead of during the summer. We'll review this helluva gobbler and tell you why the Italian Stallion should've gotten out of the acting ring before the Rocky *series ended. What do you have for us, Candy?*

Lance, I've gotta ask, what's up with Jennifer Aniston's new hair style? Isn't it the most butch do you've ever seen? She's been telling people it's for a new movie she's filming, but we all know that Aniston's feature-film career has been, well, Pitt-iful. Also, will Cameron Diaz' third trip to rehab be a charm? The latest on John Travolta's divorce. And what's up with the rumor that Deborah Harry is going to marry Jim Carrey? Now to you, Amanda.

Candy, if Deborah keeps her name, will the new couple be known as the Harry-Carreys? Sorry, but I had to say that. Today, if you've ever wondered how the stars survive months of shooting out of the country, away from family and friends, we'll share with you some of the on-the-set survival tips of the stars.

All this and more . . . on Parlez à Trois.

The videotape ended, and as Britta turned the conference room lights up to full brightness, we cheered. Loudly.

"Enough!" Debbe shouted, then crossed her arms over her chest.

Several pairs of eyes immediately focused on her chest as the room grew silent.

"This isn't a show I've decided to put on for your benefit," she snarled. "This isn't my time to entertain you. But I have done something very nice for each of you. I've given each night of the week, prime-time, a solid lead-in. Now the question that faces each and every one of you is, can you hold up your end of the bargain and give me a prime-time show that'll keep viewer interest glued to L-TV?" Debbe looked around the table. "Hernandez. Show me what you've got."

"Uh, Debbe, uh, I've got a—"

"Stop!" Debbe cut in sharply.

"Christ, that wasn't even three seconds," Meri mumbled. "I'm dead in the water."

Even though Maria was clutching a stack of papers in front of her in a death grip, her hands were visibly shaking.

"This is a presentation, not a shoot-the-breeze discussion," Debbe said. "Stand up, walk to the front of the room, and present to me, please."

Maria sprang up from her chair, fumbled around with her papers while Debbe crossed her legs and sighed audibly, and then made her way to the front of the conference room.

"The idea I, uh, have is for a—"

"Stop!" Debbe cut in again. "What are you trying to do? Ask me out on a date?"

Maria shook her head.

"What the fuck is the name of the show?"

"The name of the show—"

"Christ! What is wrong with you people? You're not in third grade. You don't have to phrase your answer to a question in the form of a complete sentence. I ask. You answer. Bing, bing. Just like that. Do you have a show for me? Yes. What's the name? Blah blah. What is it? A comedy? A drama? A fucking quiz show? 'Debbe, it's a comedy about two women who are barkeepers in competitive bars in Seattle. What keeps the interest going is that each week the barkeeps and their patrons compete in a different event—from the common, like a softball game, to the unusual, like who can steal the most dangerous animal from the zoo.'" Debbe glanced at her watch. "Bing bing. Thirty seconds. So let's go, Hernandez."

Maria nodded, then took a deep breath. "*One Big Happy Family* is a real-TV, docudrama-style show in which an experimental community of one hundred diverse people is thrown together for a year. Only twenty houses will be available for them to live in, which means that five strangers initially need to group in living situations that they are comfortable with. For the first month in this community, the people will have an equal amount of resources to survive for one month. In addition, each home will be given supplies that others will eventually need. One house, for example, will have a surplus of medical supplies. Another house will have a surplus of household staples—coffee, tea, sugar, flour, rice. After the initial month, all ties to the outside world will be severed, and the community then has to learn to pull together as a whole as well as in their five-person 'family' units. The show seeks to discover whether or not people can put aside their differences, prejudices, and judgments of others in order to work together for the good of the community. The goal is for everyone to live together as one big happy family."

Maria finished her presentation and held her breath as she looked at Debbe.

"Green light," Debbe responded. "Good work, Hernandez."

Maria nodded and smiled.

"Now sit down," Debbe ordered. "I'm not going to hand you an award. What about you, Wiggins?"

Meri sprang up and marched to the front of the conference room. "*Tragic Endings* is a biography-styled show that explores the tragic deaths of well-known female personalities. But there will be a different twist offered in this series, with reenactments providing vivid details of the last, tragic moments of these personalities. We'll show Patsy Cline's airplane crash in vivid detail, right up to the moment when the plane slammed into the side of a mountain. We'll show Princess Diana's fatal car crash. We'll get to see all of the gory details of Sharon Tate's murder at the hands of Charles Manson. We'll show Billie Holiday's drug overdose. Karen Carpenter's—"

"Meri, aren't you the comedian in this group of writers?" Debbe interrupted.

Meri shrugged her shoulders. "I guess. Sometimes."

"That's a pretty gruesome show you're suggesting."

Meri sighed. "Yeah, well, I just thought that people would—"

"Love it," Debbe finished. "People love all that tragic ending stuff. The more fatalistic, the better. And I like the reenactment idea. I hope you're planning on having lots of blood and screaming and tears. Have you ever thought about doing a segment on the victims of the Boston Strangler? What about that woman who played Aunt Bea on the Andy Griffith Show? I think she killed herself by putting a plastic bag over her head. And then there's the whole world of literary tragedies—Virginia Woolf filling her pockets with rocks so she sank like a stone in the ocean, Sylvia Plath sticking her head in the gas oven, Zelda Fitzgerald drinking herself into oblivion."

"I can certainly—" Meri began.

Debbe held up her hand and nodded. "Green light." She looked around the room. "This is more like it, people. Okay, Shoemaker. Tell me what you've got."

Taylor stood up and walked to the front of the room. "The name of the show is *On Again, Off Again.* The focus is on relationships in the lesbian community and how our former partners rarely leave our social circle. How they become friends, as well as, sometimes, partners again. How some relationships are short-term. How some are—"

"Stop!" Debbe cut in. "Shoemaker, did you go off your Paxil?"

Taylor blinked and looked at Debbe. "Excuse me?"

"I can't think of a more uninteresting show than what you're proposing. Are you suffering from depression? Angst, perhaps?"

"Well, um, maybe I'm not really explaining it very well. You see, so many of the rela—"

"I don't want any background, Shoemaker. I want to know what the premise of this show is."

"Well, I'm trying to tell you—"

"Not fast enough, you aren't."

"Okay. Uh, well—"

"Quicker! Quicker!" Debbe cut in.

I watched Taylor fumble with the index cards she was holding in trembling hands.

"Faster! Faster! Let's go," Debbe urged her, slapping her hands together.

I shut my eyes.

What the hell are you doing, C.J.?

I lifted my mouth from Debbe's breast and peered down at her. *I'm making love to you.*

What? In slow motion? You've been doing the breast thing now for three or four minutes.

So what's wrong with that?

You did the kissing thing, and then you did the neck thing, and then you did the fondling-my-breasts thing. Enough already. I want to come, C.J. I want to come now!

I thought that's where I was taking you.

Not fast enough. Like this, she said as she grabbed my head between her hands and roughly pushed me down her naked body, until my face was positioned between her legs.

I stuck out my tongue and slowly started to taste her.

Debbe pushed my face hard into her moistness, squeezing my nostrils shut. *Hard, C.J. Hard and fast. Fast, fast, fast. Come on, let's go . . .*

"Time's just flying away here, Shoemaker," Debbe said as I blinked my eyes and returned my attention to the meeting. "Forget about whatever the hell the name of your show is. Do you have anything else?"

"If I might assist," Samata said.

Debbe turned to her. "Oh, Cassandra to the rescue again. I bet you go to the dog pound each week and take home a stray, don't you?"

"The name is Samata. Sa-ma-ta," Samata pronounced slowly as she stood up and walked to the front of the conference room. "I have heard Taylor present this show idea, and it is a good one. She is forgetting to tell you something very important. *On Again, Off Again* follows several different couples as they endure ups and downs in their relationships. Some people are nice, some aren't. Some couples seem to be meant for each other, some aren't despite the love—or the lust—they might have for each other. Some couples go to counseling, and so on. The most interesting facet of Taylor's show, however, is that the audience gets to decide for the couples if they should stay together. If the secret about an affair should be discussed, for instance. It is the audience who will make or break these couples—and how many of us haven't wanted to tell the characters on the television, 'Stop what you're doing!' or 'Don't be with her. She is such a shit and you can do better!' This is the chance for people to do that. If you do not like the name of the show, Debbe, that can certainly be changed. But the idea of the show is quite unique."

Debbe sat silent in her chair as she regarded Taylor and Samata. "And so this was your idea, Taylor? The way that Samata has explained it—that was your original idea?"

Taylor cleared her throat. "Well, uh, sometimes it's hard to really determine where the original seed of a creative idea came from. We all work together as a writing team and—"

Debbe held up her hand. "Nice save, Sa-ma-ta. Did I get that right?"

Samata nodded.

"She just saved your nice, white ass, Shoemaker," Debbe said. "Now sit down. Samata, what do you have for me?"

"Murder, Debbe," Samata said with a smile. "Plain and simple.

The show is called *The Body Farm*. I have so enjoyed the novelist Agatha Christie and her works, and I was greatly inspired by her book *And Then There Were None*. Picture an old farmhouse in the middle of nowhere, on acres and acres of land. Ten people are sent to the home. The one who survives is the winner of, say, a large sum of money. The murders are not real, of course, but the plotting of the murders is, as are alliances that may be formed by the cast. How the murders are committed is entirely left up to the cast, but only we the audience can see who is being murdered and who the murderer is. If an attempt to murder someone is viewed by another cast member, then the murderer is considered to be dead."

Debbe nodded. "I love it. Murder sells—we all know that. Green light. And now for you, Chantelle. Are you going to impress the hell out of me?"

"I hope so, Debbe," Chantelle said as she stepped to the front of the room. "The show is called *Can't Let Go*. It's a show about a mentally unstable woman—we all know she is, at least. Each week, she attempts to stay one step ahead of the police, who are trying to nab her for a crime for which she was framed because of her mental condition, and the psychiatrists who are trying to get her committed. She's a woman who you love and fear at the same time, because you never quite know what she's capable of. But the main point is that no matter where she travels, she succeeds in gaining trust before she starts acting obsessively, needy, wacky, and dangerous. Little by little, as the show progresses, we get glimpses of the crime she was framed for and we realize that she's on the track of the people who really killed her long-time lover and their child."

Debbe nodded. "Kind of like a *Fugitive* and a *Fatal Attraction* pairing."

Chantelle aimed an index finger at Debbe. "Exactly."

"*Can't Let Go*. I like it," Debbe said. "Have we got a strong actress being considered for the lead?"

"We're holding auditions even as we speak," Chantelle replied. "Nicolette Sheridan and Mariel Hemingway look to be strong contenders and their names might help. But we're also looking at a good crop of unknowns."

Debbe stood up. "That's more like it, people. It looks like we have a good prime-time lineup and that you've all kept your jobs. Congratulations! Now get back to work."

Three

drinks are usually my limit, especially on a weeknight. But we were all still flying high from the day's green-light signals we had each received from Debbe Lee on our proposed prime-time shows and since each writer wanted to pay for a round, it looked like I was only halfway to achieving what would be my new weeknight alcoholic consumption limit.

"Okay, now I'll tell you guys the part about the day that I liked the most," Meri said, then sucked on a lemon slice, tore off the pulp with her teeth, and tossed the rind on top of the pile of drying lemon rinds we were communally building in the center of our table. Her voice returned me from my own reflections on the workday to the table we were clustered around, which was tucked in a dark corner, set back from the bar, stage, dance floor, and main arena of table-and-chair clutter in Alley's McBeal, a lesbian pub located several blocks from our office. A few scattered groups of patrons were circled around their own tables, and a short line of elbow-drinkers nursed beers while watching the Red Sox on television.

Meri wiped her mouth with the back of her hand, then smacked her lips. "What I liked the most, C.J., was when you called the Dragon Lady back into the conference room and said, 'Uh, Debbe, we have one more show for you.' "

"You got that right," Chantelle said as she nodded, then drained her margarita in two swallows and upended the glass on the table.

"Why do you do that?" asked Maria as she picked up a napkin and placed it around Chantelle's glass.

Chantelle shrugged her shoulders. "Because I can? Anyway, the look on Debbe Lee's face was like, 'Are you talkin' to meee?' Who knew our own fearless leader had a show to pitch?"

"It's an awesome, awesome idea," said Taylor as she leaned back in her chair. "And the way you introduced it was great. Just great. You said, with this air of nonchalance in your voice, 'I thought you wanted *six* prime-time shows, Debbe. You've got the five shows you've just green-lighted for weeknights. But what about Sunday night? We've got to go up against the networks with something solid—something as good as *The Practice* and *The X-Files.*' "

I stared at Taylor. "Did you memorize my speech? That sounds like, word-for-word, what I said."

Meri tossed a crumpled napkin at me from across the table and flashed me a grin. "And you thought we didn't pay attention to you, C.J. We hang on your every word!"

"You're the best, C.J.," added Taylor. "You're the best boss I've ever had."

"You got that right," Chantelle agreed.

"You're all drunk," I said.

"You got that right," Chantelle echoed.

"How many times a day do you say that phrase, Chantelle?" Maria asked.

Chantelle shrugged her shoulders. "Probably a lot. And I say it because I can. Loosen up there, girlfriend. And anyway, we were talkin' 'bout our C.J. and her new show for Sunday night on L-TV."

"You got that right, Chantelle," Meri laughed, then stuck out her tongue at Maria.

Samata raised her cocktail glass. "And so may I please you to present," she announced as Meri then rapped her index fingers against the table in a simulated drumroll. "That is good, Meri. And so I am here to present for you, the Dragon Lady, a new show for L-TV called *Madame President.*"

"I don't think I said that," I told her.

"*The West Wing* meets *The American President*!" Maria exclaimed. "A widowed senator from New Hampshire runs for the White House and wins—and then comes out while in office." Maria smiled and patted my hand. "What a winner, C.J.!"

"You got that—" Chantelle began, then stopped when Maria whirled around in her chair towards her.

"And the fact that you got Stockard Channing to sign on to play the first woman president—" Taylor began.

"The first woman *and lesbian* president," I corrected her.

"You got that right!" Chantelle exclaimed.

"Chantelle, you are really starting to annoy me," Maria said.

"You got that right!" Chantelle grinned at her.

"Would you just—"

"Hey, Maria, don't you remember the name of your show?" Meri cut in. "Isn't it called *One Big Happy Family*? How, like, unlike that are you behaving right now to your other worker-family members?"

"Exactly!" exclaimed Chantelle. "You got *that* right!"

"Ironic, is it not?" Samata asked. "I wonder. Are we all extensions of our own shows, or can our shows be what we would like to have in our lives, but do not?"

"Does that mean that you'd like to commit murder someday, Samata?" Taylor asked. "That maybe on our next working retreat—say, to a farmhouse somewhere in upstate New York—you're going to systematically knock us all off in the middle of the night?"

Meri held a cupped hand in front of her mouth. "Attention. Paging Dr. Naroff. You're wanted for a psych consult at the L-TV infirmary. Stat."

"Samata raises an interesting point," I said. "Perhaps I aspire to be president of the United States."

Maria turned towards Chantelle. "And isn't your show about a woman who's obsessive and compulsive? Who can't let go? Kind of like someone who says 'you got that right' over and over and over again."

Chantelle nodded. "You got that right!"

Maria stared at Chantelle, then burst into laughter. "Okay. *Now* I think you're funny."

"And there she is, everyone—Maria Hernandez is finally back from her recent visit to stick-up-the-ass land," Meri announced.

"Where is my T-shirt from your trip, Maria?" Samata asked.

"That's funny, Samata," Meri chuckled.

"Even possible murderers can have senses of humor," Samata said as she raised one eyebrow at Meri.

Meri returned an eyebrow raise to Samata. "May I remind you that my show is called *Tragic Endings?* Need I say more?"

"C.J., the fact that you got Stockard Channing to star in your show was the icing on the cake," Taylor cut in. "Debbe didn't know whether to be pissed off at you for interrupting her grand exit from the room or overjoyed at your idea. And who knew she was a Stockard Channing groupie from back to the days of the movie *Grease?*"

"I just got lucky, I guess," I said, then quickly drained my margarita glass.

"I loved Rizzo in that movie!" exclaimed Maria. "She was hot, hot, hot!"

"Give me Olivia Newton-John in those skin-tight leather pants any day," cooed Meri. "She was the one that I wanted!"

Taylor laughed. "You could see Debbe Lee's face going through all these contortions after you told her about your show and then announced that Stockard Channing had signed on to star. Like Jim Carrey's face. She didn't know what to say. And then Britta was just left standing in the doorway of the conference room, not knowing whether to come or go."

"She is pretty, is she not?" Samata asked.

"The Dragon Lady?" Meri queried as she raised both eyebrows at Samata.

"She's talking about the Swede," Taylor said.

"Her name is Britta," Samata corrected her.

"She's certainly blonde," Maria replied. "Blonde and white and, well, blonde."

"She certainly is white," agreed Chantelle.

Meri sighed. "She's a blonde-haired, blue-eyed babe. Very easy on the eyes, if you know what I mean."

"You have got that right," Samata agreed. "She is like a flower in the springtime, coming up early through the snowfall." She paused. "May I have another of these drinks, please?" she asked as she pointed to her empty glass and then hiccuped.

"This round's on me, I think," Taylor said as she looked over to the bar and waved her hand at one of the waitresses who was idly leaning against the counter. "Six margaritas, is it?"

"I'm still holding with my ginger ale," Maria told her.

"Oh, come on and have some fun, Maria," Meri coaxed as she ran a finger around the salted rim of her glass and then stuck her finger in her mouth.

Maria smiled. "I am having fun."

"*Now* you are," Chantelle pointed out. "Your evil twin, Skippy, was here a little while ago."

"But that's all you've been drinking tonight," said Meri. "Why not join us in at least one drink?"

"Somebody has to make sure everyone gets home all right," Maria said.

"Well, I'll be designated driver next time," Meri told her. "We'll all take turns taking care of each other, okay?"

Taylor nodded. "That's what I've been thinking about, Meri. We've been together now as a group for—what—six months? And we've got a monster for a boss. Not you, C.J. I know you're our boss, but you're not a monster. You're great. But you know who I mean. You all know who I mean."

Four heads nodded in unison.

"I have to abstain from that vote," I said.

"I know," Taylor said. "But the point is, we've got to stick together. We've got to be solid, you know? That's the only way we're going to get through this upcoming season. We've all got to get along, no matter what. We can't turn on each other."

All eyes turned to Maria.

"What?" she asked, then immediately looked down at her empty glass of ginger ale. "I'll tell that to Skippy," she mumbled, then looked up. "I'm with you guys. I am. I promise. I just get cranky sometimes. I don't mean to take it out on anyone—on you, Chantelle."

Chantelle held out an open palm to Maria.

Maria gave her palm a gentle slap.

The waitress arrived with a tray of drinks and began replacing the empty glasses. Taylor dropped a twenty on her tray, and then slipped a five into the waitress' apron pocket.

"To being solid," Chantelle toasted as she raised her cocktail glass in the air.

Five margarita glasses and one tall glass of ginger ale clicked together. We each took a sip, then picked up a fresh lemon slice from the dish the waitress had laid down on the table with our drinks. In sync, we ripped the pulp from our slices, chewed and swallowed, and then tossed the rinds onto the table.

"You know, this job couldn't have happened to me at a better time," Taylor said as she leaned her elbows on the table. "I had just been dumped. Since I was living in my ex's house, and she, of course, wanted her new lover to move in, I was also going to be homeless. Needless to say, I had sold the house I had been living in so we could live together and had moved from Chicago to New York just to be with her. So I'm thinking, as she's telling me all about her wonderful new lover, where the fuck am I supposed to go now? Should I stay in New York, or should I go back to Chicago? And then I heard about L-TV and sent in my resume. Relocation was no problem for me. But these past months have been like starting over again, you know? All my friends live in Chicago. The friends I made in New York were couple friends. So this job and you guys—"

"You're not going to get all weepy on us now, are you, Taylor?" Meri cut in.

"If the girl wants to cry, let her cry," Chantelle said. "I hear what she's saying. You go on, girlfriend."

"I have cried many nights since I have been here," Samata said. "Even though it has been years. My family is back in Egypt, you know, and so it is hard for me many times. When I teach at Columbia University, it is not so hard because there is always someplace to go where many people are, too. But in this city, and with such a demanding job, it feels sometimes when I go home to my apartment very empty."

"I find that emptiness scary," said Maria.

"Who said I was going to cry?" Taylor asked.

"Well, you were getting awfully serious," Meri commented.

"I just said I had been having a hard time, Meri," Taylor replied. "Haven't you ever had a lousy breakup?"

Meri rubbed her chin. "I'm pleased to announce that every one of my breakups has been lousy. Even damn one of them. I've had . . ." Meri paused as she set her glass on the table and began, one at a time, to raise the fingers on each hand until ten were showing. "I've had ten lousy breakups from relationships. Count 'em—ten. And I did not break up with even one of those women. I've always been dumped. But it's not worth it to piss and moan over someone who dumps you. Someone who kicks you out without a moment's notice. Someone who cheats on you. Someone who says, 'You know, we just want different things.' Or the big kicker, 'Uh, let's just be friends, okay?' What's that supposed to mean? Like we weren't friends to begin with, or we weren't friends while we were lovers? Anyway, why be sad over that? Why be sad when you can be mad. I get treated like that, and I get mad."

"Yes, it is good to get mad as well," Samata nodded. "I have two lovers since I am in America. The first was—how do you say it—a nighttime job?"

We stared at Samata.

"Huh?" asked Chantelle.

"You met her on a job?" Meri asked.

"No." Samata shook her head. "It was we go to bed and then—"

"Bye-bye, baby?" Taylor asked.

"A one-night stand?" offered Maria.

Samata slapped a hand against Maria's arm. "Yes! That is it."

"Oh, well, if I counted those as well," Meri muttered, then looked up at the ceiling and began to raise her fingers.

"Jesus, Meri!" Taylor exclaimed. "How the hell many women have you slept with?"

Meri sighed. "Well, now, that's the thing. If you ask how many relationships I've been in, that's one thing. But if you ask how many women I've slept with, well—"

"You must be a very satisfied woman, yes?" Samata asked.

"Not necessarily," Maria answered. "Just because someone's had a lot of lovers doesn't mean she's as good as she thinks she is."

All eyes turned to Maria.

Maria shrugged her shoulders. "What can I say? I'm Latino. I'm a sucker for a smooth-talking woman. And, believe me, there are a lot of smooth talkers out there. A lot of fine dressers. A lot of women who are out to impress, if you know what I mean."

Chantelle let out a short grunt. "I know what you're saying 'bout those smooth operators, girl. They'll be talking up a storm to you in the bar, whispering in your ear with their hot breath and leaning into you so they can brush against you—just so—right across your breasts. And your knees get weak and you get chills—"

"I got chills, they're multiplying!" Taylor suddenly sang out, then tossed back her drink.

"And I'm losing control," I piped in.

"Because the power you're supplyin'," Chantelle added.

"It's electrifying!" we shouted together, then burst into laughter.

Meri held up ten fingers. "Christ," she said, then drained her cocktail.

"So you've had twenty women in your life, Meri," Taylor said as she put an arm around Meri's shoulders. "There's no shame in that."

Meri pressed her hands to her face. "Double that, Taylor."

Taylor raised her eyebrows, then removed her arm. "Christ, Meri, you're a slut!"

"You've slept with *forty* women?" Chantelle said in a voice loud enough to turn the attention of others in the bar to our table. "Who are you, Wilma Chamberlain?"

"Oh, God!" Meri said as she dropped her head to the table.

"I mean, that would make sense if you were, say, sixty fucking years old and came out when you were twelve," Taylor began.

"Taylor, I don't think you're helping the situation," I said.

"C.J., my point is that if she's only—what—thirty-two, and let's say she came out when she was sixteen, and then—oh, yeah—didn't you say you had relationships, too, Meri?"

Meri let out a grunt.

"How long was your longest relationship?" Maria asked.

"Seven," Meri mumbled without raising her head.

"Months?" Taylor asked.

"Years, asshole," Meri said as she raised her head from the table.

"Were you monogamous?" Chantelle asked.

"Always and forever."

"I'm asking you seriously, Meri," Taylor said.

Meri glared at Taylor. "And I'm answering you seriously. Believe it or not, in all of my relationships I've been monogamous. My lovers have played the field, but not me."

"Then you sure as hell rebound pretty fast," Maria said.

Meri nodded her head. "Yes, I do. I guess I'm not really fond of sleeping alone."

"That is the same feeling I have," said Samata, "but I always am ending up alone in bed."

Taylor picked up her drink, drained it, and then rubbed her hands together. "Okay, so then, you take away seven years from the first equation I offered, which means that you've been with, like, four or five women a year."

"But she said she has been in other relationships," Samata pointed out.

Taylor nodded her head. "That's right. So that brings that per-year number of women slept with even higher."

Meri showed everyone a broad grin. "Damn! I'm good, aren't I? I bet nobody else here has been with that many women, have you?"

"Perhaps we have forty, all together," Samata suggested.

"Then why the hell am I single!" Meri exclaimed, then dropped her head back down to the table.

"Perhaps it is because you have been with too many women," Samata offered. "You might try being with less women."

Meri raised her head. "How the hell am I supposed to subtract lovers if I've already been with them?"

"What I say is, perhaps it is not such a good idea to go around saying to people, 'I have been with forty women.'"

Meri rolled her eyes. "Samata, I don't go around telling women that."

"Face it, Meri. You're a slut," Taylor proclaimed in a matter-of-fact tone of voice.

"I am not a slut!" Meri exclaimed, once again drawing attention from others to our table.

"Don't we all just want to be loved?" Maria asked. "I mean, isn't that what we're all looking for? A love that will last—that will last forever?"

Chantelle sighed. "I hear that, girlfriend."

"Me, too," Taylor agreed. "What about you, Miss Love Machine?"

"Fuck you, Taylor!" Meri exclaimed.

"No way! I want to be special," Taylor replied. "You'll have to find someone else in this group who's ready for a go with you."

"I don't think that's such a good idea," I said.

"Neither do I," seconded Chantelle.

"If you have been with forty women, Meri, then perhaps you are a good lover, yes?" Samata asked.

Meri sighed. "Oh, yeah, Samata. I'm Doctor Feelgood. That's why none of my lovers decided to stick around."

"In my opinion, sex is nothing without love," Maria said as she sucked on an ice cube. "When you make love with someone you love, well, there's no way that anyone, no matter how good in bed they are—no offense, Meri—"

"You know, I'm not as good as you all are thinking I am," Meri replied.

"Well, you probably do not fumble as I have done," Samata said. "It is embarrassing—yes?—to be out to dinner in the bedroom."

We stared at Samata.

"I think you mean out to lunch, girlfriend," said Chantelle.

"How come your scripts are so well-written, Samata, but you are out to lunch in conversations?" Taylor asked.

Samata shrugged her shoulders. "I guess when I write I can see what I say. When I speak, it just comes out."

"I think it's kind of cute," said Meri.

"Watch out, Samata," Taylor muttered. "She's setting you up for number forty-one."

"I am not!" Meri protested, then waved her hand towards the bar.

"You know, I had a point I was trying to make," Maria broke in. "About sex being nothing without love."

I nodded. "I agree with that."

"Me, too," Chantelle agreed.

"I'm in on that," Taylor said.

"As am I," Samata agreed.

"And I am, too," Meri said.

"So, Meri Mistress of the Mattress, how many of the women that you've slept with did you love?" asked Taylor.

"You know, I don't think it's any of your business who—"

"Excuse me, Miss Vagina Breath, but you were the one who brought it up to begin with!"

Chantelle held up her hands. "Enough, you two! Taylor, I think you need to back off from Meri. As I recall, you were talkin' 'bout solidarity in our group. Who the hell cares how many women she slept with? Anyway, if you want my nickel advice on this whole situation, I think you're still burnin' from your ex and takin' it out on Meri. My guess is that your ex had bushels of lovers and she'd flaunt them in front of you. Am I right about this?"

Taylor stared at Chantelle.

"Paging Dr. Chantelle Colby for a psych consult to—"

"Shut up, Meri!" Taylor snapped as she kept her eyes locked on Chantelle.

Chantelle wagged a finger at Taylor. "Don't you be starin' at me like you're gonna bite my head off, Shoemaker. You want this group to be solid, then get honest with us, girl."

"What do you know about anything?" Taylor muttered.

"I take that as a yes, then," Chantelle said, then reached a hand across the table to Taylor. "We've all been there. I swear to God, we all have. We're all smart women. We're all smart women who've made stupid choices, aren't we?"

"I have a Ph.D.," Samata said, "but it is certainly not in love. Or lovemaking."

The waitress then arrived with our drinks, and Maria immediately grabbed one of the margaritas from the tray and drained it in one swallow. She placed the empty glass on the tray and then picked up another and brought the glass to her lips.

"Slow down, there," I cautioned her.

"I'll come back with two more drinks," the waitress said as she placed the rest of the drinks on the table and whisked away the empties.

"She's an asshole," Maria said, then placed her second cocktail on the table, grabbed a lemon slice, popped it in her mouth, and chewed.

"Who?" Taylor asked.

Maria swallowed, raised the second margarita to her lips, then handed it to me. "Don't let me drink that, C.J.," she said.

I took the drink from her and replaced it with the glass of ginger ale the waitress had placed on the table. Maria flashed me a smile, took a sip, then expelled a long breath of air. "Okay, gang. You want me to 'fess up? You got it. First, you're the one and only. And then, well, there's this ex that she wants to get back with. And then, well, you're the one and only when the ex dumps her yet again. And then she's going to stop drinking. And then she says she'll get a job—she swears. But until then, you support her and let her do whatever she wants because if you say anything, well, that's another argument for sure and the weekend's ruined because you're left at home crying and wondering what to do and wondering whether she'll come home or not." Maria looked around the table. "And then I wonder if she's even thinking, 'Where's Maria? When is she coming home?' Like tonight, for instance. Does she even care where I am or who I'm with? If I don't come home. . . ."

"Is this an ex, or someone you're with right now?" Meri asked.

Maria showed us a sad smile. "On again, off again. Yesterday we were on. Who knows what today is. And now there's the added . . ." Maria paused, then looked down at the empty margarita glass in front of her. "I shouldn't have had that drink."

"Honey, are you all right?" Chantelle asked.

Maria sighed. "Let's just be solid, okay? I really need you guys. I really, really do."

"We all need each other," I agreed.

"But it is not just on the job," said Samata. "I think it is good if we are friends as well."

"To friends," Meri said as she raised her empty margarita glass.

"To friends," we said in unison.

"So, C.J.," Taylor began as she turned to me. "What's your love story?"

"My love story?" I asked, then paused. "It's . . . it's love means never having to say you're sorry."

"Uh, uh," Chantelle grunted as she wagged a finger an inch in front of my face. "You aren't getting off that easy, girl. Now you've heard all about our personally unfulfilling and loveless lives. It's your turn."

"When you say it that way, Chantelle, it really makes me feel better about myself," said Meri.

"Then maybe we should change the subject," I suggested.

"We will," Maria said. "After we hear about your love life, C.J."

"There's not much to say," I answered.

"Well, you've heard more about our love lives than we have about yours," Meri said. "You know I'm single—"

"And a slut," Taylor cut in.

"And you've heard that Taylor's still pissed off about being dumped," Meri added without missing a beat. "You know, Taylor, angry women don't attract lovers."

Taylor glared at Meri. "Good. Then that means you won't be making a pass at me anytime in the near future."

"And I am single and I am very lonely, that is for sure," Samata broke in.

"Ditto," Chantelle said. "But when I go home, it's not to an empty apartment but one that's filled with my sister and her kids and her boyfriend of the week. I think she belongs to a club. You'd think I wouldn't be lonely living in such a full house, but I'd give anything to have someone waiting at home for me who would greet me with a hug and a kiss and a 'how's your day.' "

"And you?" I asked Maria.

Maria ran a tongue over her teeth, then took a deep breath. "I'm a single woman in a couple, if that makes sense."

"And her name is . . ." Meri prompted her.

"Jesse," Maria answered. "And I've decided that this is her last chance to work things out with me."

"Good for you," Taylor said.

Maria shook her head. "There have been too many broken promises. Too many lies. Too many times my trust has been shattered by her. I'm a . . . I'm a very committed person in a relationship. I want to build a future with someone that's strong enough to last through the good times as well as the bad. So this last time when I took her back and we decided—well, let's just say that this is her last chance with me. And no matter what happens with Jesse, I know now that I can make it without her. If it comes to that."

We sat in silence for several moments.

"Someone say something," Maria said. "Please."

Chantelle broke the silence. "If it's what you want, girl, then I hope it works out for you. But if Jesse isn't going to treat you well or give you what you want, then you won't be alone. You'll have us. Each of us."

Maria smiled at Chantelle. "Thanks."

"And now it is your turn to make the big confession," Samata said as she looked at me.

I looked around the table. "Okay. Uh . . . my name is C. J. Jansen and I'm single."

"Welcome, C.J.," said Meri. "And how long have you been a member of the lonely hearts club?"

"That would be a few years now, Meri," I answered. "After a string of not-so-great relationships, I met the woman of my dreams. I fell hopelessly head-over-heels in love. But apparently I was the only one who felt that way in the relationship. So, end of relationship. End of story. Now, well . . . at first it was hard. I mean, I tried everything to get her back. And I thought, if I gave us being apart a little time, that she'd come to see that I was the best person for her. So I held out for her, for quite a while. I got used to being alone. It's not so bad. It really isn't. I think . . . well . . . I think maybe I should just shut up."

"Go on," Maria prodded. "I want to hear what you think."

"Me, too," said Taylor.

I picked up a lemon slice from the plate and stared at it. "I think maybe there's only one person we're supposed to fall in love with in our lives. And so if things don't work out with that one person, then you make a decision for yourself whether or not you want to be with another person or other people just for companionship or—"

"You're in love with your job, C.J.," Taylor cut in. "Face it. It's not that you've made some grand decision about whether or not you'll find true love again. I think you're just telling yourself that it's never going to happen. Or maybe you're afraid you'll get burned again. For whatever reason, you've taken yourself out of circulation. You've been twenty-four, seven with your job since I've known you."

"Ah, another interesting observation from Dr. Shoemaker," Meri responded as she rubbed her chin with a hand.

"You could be right, Taylor," I said.

"Maybe you should get out more and meet other women," Maria suggested. "And then, who knows, maybe you'll find some-one else who you'll love just as much or even more than—what's her name?"

I nodded. "Maybe you're right, too, Maria. Anyway," I said as I rubbed my hands together, "that's my love story."

"Girl meets girl, girl loses girl, girl falls in love with her job," said Meri. "It's just the same old story."

I grinned. "Same old, same old. See? My love story's pretty boring. So now who's buying the next round?"

$\mathcal{F}our$ minutes past three in the morning—at least that's what the alien-green glow emitted by my bedside alarm clock revealed to me in the darkness of my bedroom—and strange things were happening all around me. Every time I raised my head from the pillow, I heard the sounds of a factory in full assembly-line production. It sounded like car after car was being put together, an endless number of doors being bolted loudly to their frames and then slammed shut. Or perhaps I was wrong about that. Maybe Army tanks were being built from the ground up and then were rumbling out of huge warehouses fully assembled, making their way down an airport tarmac and then tipping their long snouts in the air as they grinded noisily up metal ramps into the bellies of massive airplanes that would take them to faraway lands to fight for freedom.

Except I didn't live anywhere near a factory or an airport. I lived in a two-bedroom Cape-style house with attached garage in Lincoln on a half-acre of landscaped property that was surrounded by conservation land.

And yet, there were those sounds again. Those hammering, banging, clanging sounds.

I groaned and dropped my head to the pillow. The noise of ocean surf crashing on a shoreline rushed through my brain.

Factories in production. Surf on a shoreline. It didn't make sense to me.

I tried to ease off my shoulder onto my back, but I couldn't move in that direction. Someone else was in my bed, tucked firmly next to my back.

"Hey," the someone else mumbled.

"Hey," I replied.

"What time is it?"

"Three and change," I said. "Who are you?"

"Meri."

"Meri? Meri Wiggins?"

"Um. Who're you?"

"C.J."

"C.J.? C.J.!" Meri exclaimed, then pushed her body away from me and sat up. "Oh, my God! My head!"

"Mine, too. I think we had too—"

"I'm going to throw up!"

"Not in my bed you're not," I exclaimed as I bolted upright and the factory noises resumed. I threw back the covers, tossed my legs over the side of the bed, and let out a loud groan.

"I'm really going to throw up right fucking now!"

I grabbed Meri's arm and pulled her out of bed. "This way."

Meri stumbled after me into the bathroom.

"Are you going to be—"

"Just go," she commanded as she dropped to her knees in front of the toilet bowl, lifted the lid, and coughed.

I quickly exited the bathroom and closed the door. I set my sights on the rumpled bedsheets and edged towards them, but as the sound of retching escaped from the bathroom, urging my stomach to respond in kind, I shifted direction.

I made my way out of the bedroom and down the hallway, then flipped on the light at the top of the stairs. My eyes screamed in pain, and I immediately flipped the light off. After several seconds the fireflies disappeared from my line of vision, and I was able to ease my way carefully down the stairs and then inch towards the kitchen. I fumbled around in the dark for a few minutes, reacquainting myself with the location of coffee filters, mugs, and spoons. I emptied a bag of coffee beans into the grinder, pressed down on the top, and groaned at the sound.

I immediately leaned over the kitchen sink, threw up noisily and painfully, and then rinsed my mouth out with shaking hands. I splashed cold water on my face and then retched once more. My knees gave out and I sank slowly down to the kitchen floor, where I laid my face against the cold linoleum.

"I need coffee!" Meri shouted from upstairs. "And aspirin! And I need a new fucking head!"

I raised my head. "Two out of three!" I yelled, then dropped my head back to the floor. "By the end of the week, for sure."

A half hour later, Meri sat across from me at my kitchen table. We were working our way through a second mug of strong coffee and were finally able to tolerate a small amount of light provided by an overhead chandelier. A plate of dry toast sat between us, untouched.

Meri placed her mug on the table and leaned forward in her chair. "C.J., are you sure we didn't . . . uh . . . do anything last night?"

I nodded. "Look at us. We're wearing what we had on in the bar last night, minus shoes and socks."

"But I might've tried . . ."

I shrugged. "You might have, but I sure as hell don't remember."

"We were in your bed, though, and—"

"I think we just passed out, Meri. There's nothing wrong with two friends sleeping in the same bed."

"Because it's not that I'm not attracted to you, C.J. I mean, I am. You're a really—"

"Meri—"

"It's just that I remembered something now."

"What?"

"Well, I think I've done it before with my clothes on. When I've been drunk. And I didn't think I had at the time—done it, I mean—but then I think I remembered that I had. I think."

"Meri, look at me."

"C.J., if I've been at all out of line, I—"

"*Look at me.*"

"C.J.—"

"Meri, noth-ing hap-pened. Have you got that? I would know. Believe me, I would know."

"You would?"

I nodded. "I would. Remember? I told you in the bar last night that it's been a long time for me. So I'd know if the drought had suddenly ended."

Meri stared at me for a few seconds, then flashed a smile of relief and sat back in her chair. "Yeah, I guess you would. I just panicked, C.J. I thought I might have gotten out of line with you. I mean, you're my boss and we all talked about being solid last night and I don't think being solid means screwing around with each other and then I thought, 'Oh, my God, here I am in that same old scenario again, in bed and not remembering who or what the fuck—' "

"I know, Meri," I cut in. "*Relax.* Okay? You have nothing to be upset about. Believe me, we'll laugh about this one day."

"You mean some day next year, when my head stops pounding and the nausea finally passes?"

I grinned. "Yeah. When that time rolls around, we'll go out for drinks and have one big laugh about this."

Meri rolled her eyes. "Drinks. Ha. How the fuck many margaritas did we have last night?"

I shrugged my shoulders. "I don't know, but it's going to be my least-favorite drink for quite awhile."

"I'll drink to that," she said as she raised her mug towards me, then swallowed some coffee. "Now can we try to figure out how we got here last night? Did you drive us home?"

I shook my head. "No. I checked. My car's not in the garage. Or in the driveway. It must still be back at work."

"Then who?"

"It must've been Maria. She was the only one who wasn't drinking. Or maybe we called a taxi."

"To take us from Boston to Lincoln? That's pretty pricey, don't you think?"

I shrugged. "It must've been Maria, then. I still have a lot of cash in my wallet. I guess we'll have to call a taxi to get into work this morning."

"Work? Uh, how about we call in sick today?"

"That's probably not a good idea. We've all got a lot of work to do. The launch of the new season's not that far away. And I'm sure Debbe will be on the warpath if even one of us doesn't show up for work today after yesterday's meeting."

Meri looked down at her rumpled clothes. "I can't go into work like this."

"There's still time for you to call a cab and go home to change. It's not even five o'clock. You could probably even sleep for a couple of hours. Coming into the office a little late, maybe around ten, wouldn't be that bad."

Meri nodded. "I could do that. Or you could just let me shower here and give me a change of clothes, and we could ride in together."

"We could do that, too."

"Let's do that."

I stood in front of the fogged-up bathroom mirror in my underwear blow-drying my hair while Meri showered.

"God, this feels good," Meri shouted from behind the shower curtain.

"How much longer are you going to be in there?" I asked as I shut off the hair dryer and cleared a circle on the mirror with a face cloth. "Lobsters take less time to steam."

"What day is it now?"

"Meri, get the hell out of there and let's get going."

"Yes, boss!" Meri shut off the water, slid back the shower curtain, and held out her hands. "Towel?"

I tossed her a clean towel.

Meri ran the towel down her arms. "Nice bod, boss."

I glanced in her direction, then quickly looked away.

"You can look, C.J. There's no harm, no foul in just looking."

"I suppose," I said as I rubbed gel in my hair, then toweled off my hands.

"What suppose? Come on, take a look, boss. I've got a pretty nice body."

"I'm sure you do," I said as I loaded a toothbrush with paste and began to vigorously brush my teeth. "It's . . . just . . . I haven't . . . so long . . . out . . . of touch . . . not . . . interested . . . any . . . more." I spit into the sink, then palmed water into a hand and splashed it into my mouth.

"Not interested anymore!" Meri exclaimed. "How can you *not* be interested? I mean, look at you. You have a great body. And you're at least two decades shy of menopause. You have a lot more orgasms left in you, girlfriend. Come on. Look at me. I'm nudie-kazoodie over here, just waiting for you to take a peek. Maybe seeing a naked female in your shower will get you revved up again. You need to start using your brain less and thinking about your body more."

"I really don't need to look, Meri," I said as I worked foundation into my face. "And if I really wanted to see a naked woman, which I certainly have no desire to do, I'd just pick up a *Playboy*."

"Oh, yeah. A *Playboy* will keep you warm at night."

"I told you last night at the bar. I'm not interested in getting involved again."

"Last night, if I recall, you said you didn't want to fall in love again. That doesn't mean you can't ever experience sexual fulfillment again. I mean really, boss. You are one hot-looking woman."

"Hot is not the look I'm going for," I said as I rubbed lotion on my arms. "I couldn't care less about how others see me."

"Really? So is that why you've been spending the past few minutes getting your hair looking just right and rubbing lotion on your body and putting on makeup?"

"It's my morning routine, Meri. I'm not doing this to attract anyone."

"Okay, sure. Yeah. I believe that."

"Believe what you want, but being attracted to someone or having someone attracted to me is the last thing on my mind."

"Fine, fine. Enough about you and your celibacy. What about me and my naked body over here? I'm getting a little chilly and my nipples—yes, I'm sure you remember what they are—my nipples are hard. Come on, take a glance at me and give me your honest assessment about my body."

"Oh, for God's sake, Meri, fine," I snapped, then turned and gave her body a quick once-over. "Yes, you have a nice body. Are you satisfied?"

"Satisfying me is going to take a little more of your time than just tossing me a glance, C.J."

"Don't go there, Meri."

"Come on. I want you to look at my body—really look at it. Let your eyes linger. Take it all in."

"You're a persistent son of a bitch, Meri."

"Come on."

I turned to face Meri. My eyes landed on her breasts and stayed there for several seconds, then wandered slowly down to her navel and then to her tuft of blond pubic hair. I cleared my throat, then sucked air between my teeth. "Okay. Well. Nice. Yes, nice. No wonder you've had so many lovers."

"Yes!" Meri exclaimed. "You do have a libido, boss!" She grinned, then did a quick shoulder shimmy that jiggled her breasts.

I laughed. "If being a television writer doesn't work out for you, Meri, you could always be a nude dancer in a club."

"I think I did that once," she said as she toweled the rest of her body. "Not all nude. Just bare-chested. I met up with this cute young thing at a Pride parade one summer and we went to a men's club afterwards. It was hotter than hell in the club and all the men had their shirts off, so I said 'what the hell' and we both stripped to the waist."

"I agree with Taylor. You are a slut."

"You both are sluts," a voice said.

Meri and I turned to see Maria leaning against the bathroom door jamb.

"Hey, Maria," Meri said, then tossed the damp towel in her direction. "Care to join us?"

Maria locked eyes with me and shook her head. "I'm really disappointed in you, C.J."

I crossed my arms and leaned against the bathroom counter. "There's no reason for you to be disappointed, Maria. Nothing happened. Believe me. Nothing happened."

"Nothing happened," Meri echoed. "We just crashed together."

"Uh, huh."

"No, not 'uh, huh,' " Meri said as she placed her hands on her hips. "No period. Nothing happened."

"How'd you get in here anyway?" I asked Maria.

"Your front door is wide open, C.J. Anybody could walk in."

"Including you," Meri said as she stepped out of the shower. "Hey, Maria, so what do you think of this body? Hubba-hubba, or what?"

Maria tipped back her head and placed a hand on her hip. Silver hoop earrings flashed under long, dark, wavy hair. "Your breasts could be bigger and perkier, Meri. You need to tighten up your arm muscles. Your abs need work, and—"

"Nasty, nasty, nasty," Meri cut in.

"Well, chica, don't expect me to add to your already inflated sexual ego," Maria snapped as she wagged a finger at Meri. Then she turned to me. "So? How much longer are you going to be? I'm going into the office now. You can ride with me and make it on time for the meeting."

"What meeting?" I asked.

"The meeting that the Dragon Lady called you and told you about. Like she called the rest of us. She left a message on my answering machine. Probably left one on yours, too. But I don't imagine you've had a chance to play your messages back since I dropped you two off here last night. You've obviously had other things to do."

"Like passing out and then throwing up," Meri said as she rubbed her fingers through her wet hair.

"What time is the meeting?" I asked.

Maria glanced at her wristwatch. "Exactly twenty-eight minutes from now."

"Twenty-eight?" I echoed, then tossed the hair dryer under the counter and pushed past Maria. "We've got to get dressed, Meri."

"And if any of us is late," Maria called out as she followed me into the bedroom, "I believe the exact wording of the message Debbe left was, 'Don't expect a good job recommendation from me.'"

"Fuck! Throw me some clothes, boss," Meri said. "And underwear, too."

"I don't think C.J. wears thongs," Maria sniffed as she sat on the edge of the bed and propped her arms behind her.

"Boxers or briefs, C.J.?" Meri asked.

"Bikinis," I replied.

"That'll do," Meri said.

"Tick, tock, you guys," Maria said as she stood up. "I'll be waiting in the car."

"You are coming now in the nick of time, thank goodness, C.J.," Samata said as I rushed into my office several minutes later with Meri and Maria in tow. "The Dragon Lady has been pacing up and down the halls so menacing and we have been covering for you. I told Britta you were handling some last-minute details with the planning of your show, C.J., and so that is why we are all here waiting for you."

"No, the real reason we're huddled in here is that basically we're all chicken shit and don't want to face the Dragon alone," Taylor said.

"Yeah. We figured that there's strength in numbers," added Chantelle.

"Thanks," I said as I dropped my briefcase on the floor. "How late are we?"

"Twenty-three minutes and counting," Maria answered.

Meri rolled her eyes. "Will you knock off with the timekeeping, Hernandez? That's all you've been doing the whole time driving in here. 'We're two minutes late. Now we're three minutes late. Now it's four minutes late. What does it matter how many minutes late we are? Late is late."

"Then we *are late,*" Maria snapped.

"You two look like shit," Taylor remarked as she handed me a cup of coffee and nodded at Meri.

Meri flashed her a smile. "Thanks, T. You are as lovely as I remember you last night, all liquored up, vomiting on the sidewalk outside the bar."

"No more coffee," I told Taylor as I walked behind my desk.

"Oh, like you're a beauty queen, Taylor," Chantelle said as she took the coffee from her.

"You don't have my hair, Chantelle."

"Straight and soggy isn't my style," Chantelle replied.

"Okay, everyone. Knock it off," I cut in. "Let me listen to my messages first."

"C.J., there's no time," Maria cautioned.

"And she would know all about time," Meri added.

"I think we should be hushed," Samata said as she nodded towards me.

I pressed the flashing message button on my phone, then punched in the numbers of my password and listened. "Debbe," I told the group as I held the receiver in my hand. "Where are you, blah, blah, blah.'" I punched a number on the keypad and listened. "Debbe. 'Where the fuck are you, blah, blah, blah.'"

"This can't be good," Taylor mumbled.

I punched a number again, then listened. I started jotting down notes on a pad of paper. After several seconds, I replaced the receiver.

"You're not going to believe this," I said as I tucked the pad under my arm. "But three big-name actresses want to play the president's love interest in *Madame President*."

"Who are they?" asked Chantelle.

"Sally Field, for starters."

"We like her. We really like her," said Taylor.

"Marlo Thomas."

"She's no spring chicken," Maria pointed out.

"Neither is Stockard Channing," I replied.

"But she supports a lot of women's causes," Chantelle said. "Always has. I could see her drawing an audience."

"Who is the third?" asked Samata.

I grinned. "Meryl Streep."

"Get out!" Meri exclaimed.

"And get this," I continued. "According to her agent, if we give her the role, she would prefer that her salary be donated to a worthy charitable organization such as one that does breast cancer research or a group like Mothers Against Drunk Driving."

"She's one class act," Maria said.

"I'll say," Chantelle agreed.

"Well, this is the best news I've had yet today," I said, then looked around at the group. "We certainly aren't the prettiest bunch of writers, but we'll have to do. Let's go down to the conference room and see what Debbe wants."

I led the writers down to the conference room, opened the door, and turned on the overhead lights. Out of the corner of my eye I caught Debbe sitting in a chair at the head of the large table, drumming her blood-red lacquered nails against the polished surface. Britta sat next to her wearing a wide-eyed frightened expression on her face. I stopped in my tracks.

"Well, well, well. And so it is that the workday can finally begin, now that the head writer of L-TV's creative group has graced us with her presence," Debbe snarled. "But who is this motley crew of—what are they—homeless people you've brought in off the street? Or, wait, some of them do look familiar to me. Have I seen them anywhere before? Ohhh, yes. It's all coming back to me now. They're the writers working under you, right C.J.? Toiling, toiling, toiling. Looks like you all had a hard night. I imagine you were up until the wee hours fussing over your programs, am I right? Or perhaps you all got together for some sort of group love-in."

The writers stood as still as statues behind me, not daring to move to take a seat in the room.

Debbe rose slowly from her seat, then pushed against the chair with the backs of her legs. The chair sailed into the wall behind her, hitting it with a thud. "Do you know how absolutely *fed up* I am with you, C.J.? And this bunch of idiots you call your creative team? When I call a fucking meeting, I expect you to show up on time. When I say six, I mean six. Not—what time is it, Swede?"

"It's six, um, forty," Britta answered.

"Six um forty is not six o'clock," Debbe said as she paced slowly towards me. "Six um forty is . . . um . . . forty minutes late." Debbe strode behind me, clearing a path between me and the writers, then kicked the conference room door shut with the toe of her black leather spike-heeled shoe. "Sit down, would you please," she said to the group, then grabbed me by the left arm and squeezed hard. "Did you have some sort of party without me, C.J.? You know I don't like things going on without my knowledge."

"Drinks after work," I said as I wrenched my arm out of her grasp, then turned my back on her and pulled out a chair.

"Drinks after work, and then what?" Debbe asked as she stepped behind my chair and then placed her hands on my shoulders. She pushed down hard, and this time I couldn't squirm out of her grasp. "It appears we've all had some sort of group shower this morning." Debbe slowly scoured the group with her dark, almond-shaped eyes. "Am I paying you so little that you can't even afford hair dryers? I count three wet heads in this bunch, though I can't really tell what's going on with your hair, Chantelle. How about wearing a shirt that isn't wrinkled, Shoemaker? Samantha, that clothing style went out in the sixties, man. Peace," Debbe said as she held up two fingers in a victory sign.

"My name is Samata."

"Well, I don't like it, so I'm going to call you whatever I want," Debbe responded, then turned her attention to Maria. "Hernandez, are you putting on a little weight, chunky girl? And Chantelle, our token African American Toni Morrison clone—can't you do that bead thing and look a little more ethnic? And what can I say about Meri Wigglebottom? Our resident sex maniac?"

"This is why you wanted us all to be in here at the crack of dawn?" I cut in. "To insult us? I would think you'd—"

"This is how I *respond* when you're *late* to a meeting I *call* at the crack of dawn," Debbe snapped, then leaned her face down close to my right ear. "And don't ever—*ever*—interrupt me again, C.J. Don't ever try to make me look bad or show me up or think you can do better than I can at building this channel. You work for me, C.J. And la-di-da about your grand idea for a show." Debbe flicked her tongue quickly in my ear, then looked up at the group. "I bet you thought C.J. was pretty damn special coming up with that idea, didn't you? *Madame President?* I bet you thought she showed me, huh? Well, I don't take too kindly to people stealing ideas, and that's exactly what your clever little boss did. She tried to take credit for something that she and I discussed months ago."

"Debbe, what the hell are you talking about?" I asked.

"You see," Debbe continued as she released her steely grip on my shoulders and began to slowly walk behind each writer's chair, "C.J. and I were once lovers. Yes, that's right, Meri-maid who once tried to get me into bed. We were. I bet she never told you that, did she? I mean, who would want to admit that they were in their current position of power simply because they had slept their way into that job, right?"

"Debbe?" Britta interrupted in a soft voice.

"Can't you hear me talking, Greta?"

"Your flight is leaving in an hour, and you still have to get to the airport."

"Ah, yes. The real reason for this meeting. I guess I must return to the business at hand." Debbe crossed her arms and grinned at us. "But I was having such good fun. Weren't you, C.J.?"

I slowly released the death grip I had on my pen and laid it gently on the table. I raised my head and met Debbe's eyes. "Yes, Debbe, it's always great to stroll down memory lane with you and learn your point of view about our five-year relationship. I am always so moved by the depth of your feelings, and I'm so glad you chose to share them with the group."

Debbe clapped her hands together and grinned. "What a dramatic, dramatic performance. Sure to win an Oscar, C.J. The woman scorned. So tragic, so tragic, don't you think everyone? Perhaps you can include C.J.'s monologue in your *Tragic Endings* show, Meri."

The room gripped onto silence for a few moments.

"Well, then," Debbe broke in as she beamed a smile that displayed her perfectly aligned, brilliantly white teeth. "Yes, I am off to New York shortly, to make my rounds of the morning talk shows. This is the big publicity push, girls. This is the official start of the media hype for L-TV. And you can be assured that each of your shows will be mentioned. Be prepared for the momentum to build. Be prepared to see this new cable channel and all its offerings hyped in every available media outlet. And be prepared to feel more pressure than you've ever imagined. It's do or die, chicks." Debbe lost the smile and suddenly slammed a palm against the surface of the table, causing us to flinch. "So you damn well better get your shows spit-polished to perfection. I will accept nothing less than the pinnacle—*the pinnacle*—from each of you.

You don't attain it, you fall short, and you're out. Pressure, pressure, pressure. That's the name of the game. Making our mark, and making it right. Good and right.

"You've got your shows, now get the stars. Big names, if you can. Names like Sally Field, for instance. Or Meryl Streep."

I stared at Debbe.

Debbe caught my stare and locked eyes with me. "What do you think of those names, C.J.?"

"I think I've heard them already today."

"Oh, really? From where? Like maybe your answering machine? Funny how I know everything that's going on around here, isn't it? I bet you thought you'd come trotting into this meeting whenever you wanted to and then lay those surprise names on me, just like you did with that show you claimed to be yours. Well, then. Who's surprised now?"

"So you accessed my phone messages?" I asked.

Debbe grinned at me and then winked. "No secrets, C.J. That's how I stay on top of things." Debbe pushed her way between Chantelle's and Taylor's chairs and draped an arm across their backs. "There are no secrets from me, ladies, and there *will be* no secrets from me at L TV." Debbe tossed back her shiny black mane and laughed. "Hey, that rhymes, doesn't it?" She then strolled towards the conference room door and reached for the handle. She paused, then turned to face us. "Make no mistake about this, you bunch of losers. I know all of your access codes and all of your passwords. I read your e-mails on a regular basis and listen to your phone messages. I know you have given me the nickname Dragon Lady. I kind of like it. It shows I have strength and power and am to be feared. But don't ever—*ever*—use it in my presence. And I know all about your private lives. My, but we do have some grand things we're keeping from one another. Right, Maria?"

Maria stared at Debbe.

"I know something they don't know," Debbe chanted in a singsong voice.

Maria looked away from Debbe.

Debbe grinned, then turned towards Britta and snapped her fingers. "Come, come, Swede. Let's go."

Britta flew up from her chair, gathered a large jumble of notebooks in her arms, and joined Debbe at the door. Debbe then reached out to Britta, placed a hand behind her neck, and pulled her towards her. She cemented her lips roughly on Britta's for several seconds, then broke her hold and licked her lips. She turned to Samata.

"What do you think of that, Egypt? I'm kissing your girlfriend. Right in front of you. Yum, yum, yum."

Debbe then set her sights on me. "Get your act together, C.J. Or you and your crew will be swept out with the trash."

Debbe pulled open the conference room door, gestured for Britta to exit ahead of her, and then patted Britta on the buttocks as she passed by. "Oh, what I could do with that nice set of tight buns." Debbe chuckled, then turned to face us. "So long, everyone," she said as she tossed us a wave of the hand. "Oh, and have a nice day."

"**Five** items I have written down on my notepad, which I wish to discuss now that the dust is settling," said Samata shortly after Debbe had exited the conference room and each of us had sat back in our chairs, expelled a deep breath of air, and visibly relaxed.

"I have just one thing I want to ask," Chantelle cut in as she turned to me. "What the hell were you thinking, being in a relationship with that . . . that . . . disgusting, racist, mean-spirited, venomous—"

"Was she good in bed?" Meri asked.

"She wasn't always that way," I replied.

"Good in bed?" Meri questionned.

"Why is that *always* the first thing you think about, Meri?" Taylor snapped.

"Why else would anyone be with Debbe?" Meri offered in defense.

"She's filthy rich?" Maria suggested.

Chantelle nodded. "You got that right. Poverty does have its downside in a relationship. Money is the number one cause of—"

"You can be poor and be rich in love," Samata broke in. "And sometimes that is worlds better. My family did not have riches like the wealthy in my country. And yet there were three generations living under one roof in my family's household. We did not have much in the way of material possessions. Not like here in America where so many things mean so much and you are told you have to have them. But that was not bad for us—I mean, we did not feel bad—because we had much joy and laughter and love. You cannot buy such things with money."

Maria nodded. "My family was like that, too, when I was growing up. But maybe it's a cultural thing. You're talking about Egypt, Sam, and I'm thinking of how things were for my family in Puerto Rico."

"Perhaps you are right about this," Samata agreed. "American ways can be so dollars and cents."

"And not always make sense, either," Meri grinned.

"I meant Debbe wasn't always the type of person she is now," I continued. "When I first met her, she wasn't rich. She was quite sweet to me and very devoted. She was romantic and loving. In the beginning."

"Aren't they all?" Taylor sniffed.

"She was a giving and kind-hearted person," I went on. "Or at least I once thought so."

"What changed her?" Maria asked.

I shrugged my shoulders. "Your guess is as good as mine. I don't know if it was how her last job at network television ended or simply because she fell out of love with me. But once she left the station, everything seemed to be different. Over time I noticed there was a hardness to her, a sharpness, a bitterness. She wouldn't talk to me about anything, we just started having surface-level conversations only. You know the drill, 'How's your steak? What did you do today? I think I heard it was going to rain. Did you put out the trash?' And then she started spending more and more time away from home. Nights. All night sometimes. I'd wake up alone in bed and wonder where she was, if she was all right, what I should do if she didn't come home. Whenever I confronted her about how she was treating me or the ways in which she was acting, I'd run up against a stone wall."

"Sounds like it was the beginning of the end, C.J.," Meri remarked.

"Not really. Because when she started talking about getting back at the networks and she came up with the idea for L-TV, things started to get better for us. For a while. We took a nice trip overseas to Europe, and it was like a second honeymoon. She acted like she was very devoted to me again, and we recaptured some of the passion and intimacy that had been put on hold."

"Jesus, C.J., it's like you're talking about my ex," said Taylor. "First we're good. Then we're bad. Then we're good again. Then we're—"

"No, I think she's talking 'bout mine," countered Chantelle.

"I think we've all been there," Maria offered.

"Been there, done that," agreed Meri.

"Shouldn't you say that about fifty more times?" asked Taylor.

"Please to shut up, everybody," Samata cut in. "Go on please with your story, C.J."

"That's about all there is to the story, Sam. Because then it really was the beginning of the end. We got on the plane to return home, and from the moment we entered U.S. airspace, Debbe was back to being the way she had been before we left. Brutish. Rude. Materialistic. Selfish. Sarcastic. Mean. She started bringing lovers into our home after that."

"What scum!" Chantelle exclaimed.

"I'd be lying in the spare bedroom, listening to her making love to someone else, and my heart felt like it was being squeezed like a sponge. I didn't leave for quite a while because each time it happened I thought that would be the last time. And that's what she told me, too."

"I know that feeling, C.J.," Maria said.

"Ditto," Taylor added.

"And then," I began, and suddenly my voice got caught in my throat. I blinked my eyes a few times and let out a sigh. "I didn't think . . . I didn't think it could still hurt," I said. "Sorry."

"What are you apologizing for?" Maria asked as she laid a hand on top of mine.

I gave Maria a smile, and then slowly slipped my hand out from under hers. "Anyway," I said as I ran a finger under my eyes, "that's water under the bridge. So? Did you have some things you wanted to discuss, Samata?"

"Yes, please, I did," Samata replied. "And that is one of the things I wished to find out about. Your relationship with Debbe. You did not say anything last night in way of identifying, and now I understand your reluctance to have the conversation about past lovers turn to you."

"It's not like I was trying to keep you guys from finding out," I said. "It's just that I thought you might respond to me differently if you thought that I might be emotionally linked to Debbe. And it's not true what she said, that sleeping with her got me the job."

"I didn't believe that for one minute, girl," Chantelle said.

I smiled and raised a finger in the air. "But wait! What *did* get me the job was her screwing around on me. When she finally asked me one day what it would take—how did she say it—to 'get the hell out of my life' I think were her exact words, I jokingly told her, 'How about a house in Lincoln, a Lexus—loaded—and L-TV's creative director?'" I grinned. "Two out of three ain't bad."

Meri laughed. "Way to go, boss!"

"What happened to the Lexus?" Chantelle asked.

"She ran out of money. Between sinking her life savings into L-TV and getting rid of me, Debbe Lee is maxxed out."

"Now? She's maxxed out now?" asked Taylor.

I nodded. "Oh, yeah."

"How is she paying our very good salaries?" Samata asked.

"On a wish and a prayer," I answered. "In reality, on borrowed money, Sam. That's one thing the American lending system is very good about. Keeping its borrowers in perpetual debt. And Debbe is way in debt, up to her gills. Her beautiful mansion by the sea, this station, her cars, her vacation home in Florida, her hired hands, her jewelry, and her designer wardrobe. We're talking about nearly a million dollars. If L-TV flops, Debbe Lee is bankrupt. She will go from being viewed as one of the world's richest women to the little match girl."

"Now that's a pretty temptation, isn't it?" Meri asked. "We all walk out of this job now, and the Dragon Lady doesn't have the dough to hire new writers and get everything ready for the new season. Ha, ha, she's busted!"

"As tempting as that may sound," Maria cut in, "I think it would be shooting ourselves in the feet. I don't know about anyone else here, but I can't afford to lose this job. It's not just the salary. I need the benefits. Health, dental—you guys know the great perks we're getting. Which means I can't afford to do anything that will sabotage the success of L-TV."

"Nor can I," added Chantelle. "And I don't want to do that, either. If L-TV is a success, do you know how much that increases our marketability, should we choose to leave? Debbe Lee may be a rotten person, but she's a very savvy businesswoman. I'd rather ride on her coattails than be taken to the cleaners by her."

Taylor nodded. "I've got loans I need to pay off myself. And if I don't, I wind up being the little match girl myself."

"I agree with Chantelle," Maria said. "If we pull together and make L-TV the success we all want it to be, all of us benefit in the long run. Whatever happens—good or bad—goes on our resumes. It may be hell working here, but we've got great shows that're going to be hits. We can't walk away from that."

"Speaking of shows," I said, "I just want you all to know that I didn't steal the idea for *Madame President* from Debbe. That show is one-hundred percent my idea. I have never once had a conversation with her about the premise of the show, nor did I even come up with the idea until after the network decided to cancel *The West Wing* last season. That's when I started to toy with the idea of a show that was based on a woman president." I rapped my knuckles against the table. "I don't steal ideas. I never have, and I never will."

"You are a woman of honor, C.J.," said Samata. "I believed

Debbe Lee was telling a lie the moment those words were spoken."

"We all know that show is yours, C.J.," Taylor added. "The minute Debbe accused you of doing that, she made herself look bad. Made her seem cheap and petty."

"Which she is," Chantelle said.

"You are an awesome boss, C.J.," Meri added. "Because you have morals. You treat the people who work for you really well. You're fair and honest. Like I told you last night, you're the best boss I've ever had."

"Is this the afterglow talking, Meri, or how you really feel?" asked Chantelle.

"What do you mean by that?" Meri demanded.

Chantelle spread open her hands in front of her and shrugged her shoulders. "Hey, I wasn't the only one who saw you and C.J. arrive together this morning looking like . . . well—"

"That is too one of the items on my list about which I wanted to speak," said Samata. "I believe there is to be no sex between us because of what we agreed last night, am I correct?"

I stared at Chantelle. "You really think Meri and I . . . you really think—do any of you really think—that I would sleep with someone who works for me?"

"Well, no," answered Maria. "But then again, yes."

"What she means is that isn't there always going to be that temptation between lesbians?" Taylor picked up. "We end up sleeping with our friends because our inner circles are so small. So you two got a little drunk last night. And you said it's been a long time for you, C.J., and—"

"And I also said that I believe there's only one person we're supposed to fall in love with," I snapped. "I don't sleep around."

"But Meri does," countered Taylor. "And with the booze—"

"I never should've opened my big mouth about my past lovers," Meri moaned. "Just because I've slept around in the past doesn't mean that I can't change my ways. That I can't be a different per-

son. I mean, it's not often that I can be in the same bed with someone and not do anything."

"You two were in the same bed!" Taylor exclaimed.

"Nothing happened!" I shouted. "Geez. What kind of person do
you think I am?"

"I think we are all just a little frightened," offered Samata. "This
job is difficult, yes? And so we are finding a solace in each other's
company, in a shared experience. To keep our relationships with
each other when we all are working so closely—so intimately—together, at a level of friendship will take hard working like dogs. If
we ally ourselves with another in a way that is more than—"

"If we fuck around with each other, this group is going to fall
apart," Taylor cut in. "I believe that's where you were going with
what you were saying, right?"

"That is correct, Taylor," Samata nodded.

"You don't have to worry about that at all," I responded. "Not
with me. And none of you should be getting involved, either. With
people in this group, I mean."

"I hear you," said Chantelle. "But I know what Taylor is talking
'bout. There's always going to be that temptation there."

"We just can't act on it," added Maria.

"But it is okay, is it not, to get involved with another at L-TV
who is not in our group?" asked Samata.

"Your personal lives are your own business," I told the group.
"But my recommendation is to be careful if you want to get involved with someone here. Debbe seems to know everything
that's going on—"

"Because she's been reading our e-mail and accessing our
phone messages!" Maria cut in. "That really burns me up. Can she
do that? I mean, aren't we entitled to some privacy?"

I shook my head. "Not when you're on company time, using
company phones, and the company e-mail system," I answered.
"As invasive as it may seem, when you're here everything you say
and do can be scrutinized. Think about all the workplace violence,

guys. There's a lot of crazy stuff that goes on or could go on. Debbe has to protect each of us, and that means—"

"But she's not doing that to protect us, C.J.," Chantelle countered. "She's doing that to control us. To manipulate us."

A chorus of agreement chimed in from the rest of the group.

I nodded. "I know, I know. But remember, you're on her turf. You're her employees. And because of that, your privacy is going to be compromised."

"And she has invaded your privacy, has she not, Maria?" asked Samata. "When Debbe said—I believe I remember but let me refer to the notes I have taken—that there was a grand thing that you are keeping from us, to what was she referring?"

Maria bit her lip and looked away from Samata.

"Is there something you want to tell us, Maria?" Taylor asked.

"Something we should know?" added Meri.

"At least let us know if you're all right," Chantelle said.

Maria ran her fingers through her long hair, then shook her fingers free. "Yeah, yeah, I'm fine. I'm just afraid, now that Debbe knows, that she'll think of some way to use this against me. And it's hard enough for me now as it is. I just don't know what I should say."

"You don't have to say anything," I told her. "We don't want to pry. I think we're just concerned."

"I know," Maria answered. "I know you guys are concerned—will be concerned, too, I hope. Not the Dragon Lady, though. Debbe will find some way to make this an issue, and she's not going to let up with me. I just know it. It's going . . . well . . . you're going to find out anyway, even if I don't say anything. It's not like I'm trying to keep this from you, but I wanted to tell everyone . . . I wanted to say something when . . . well . . . I guess I'm going to have to tell you guys eventually. It's not as if I can hide it."

"What is it?" Meri asked.

Maria sighed. "I'm pregnant."

"Oh, my goodness," Samata exclaimed. "There is to be a birth?"

"Not for a while, Sam," Maria answered. "But, yes, there will be a birth. I will be having a baby."

I raised my eyebrows. "And so that's a good thing, right?"

Maria shrugged her shoulders and showed a sad smile. "It was supposed to be a very, very good thing. But Jesse . . . well . . . Jesse's always going to be Jesse. We thought . . . we wanted this so much. For a long time. We'd try, and it just wouldn't work. And we'd try again and again and again. It was so frustrating. And so expensive! Things started to get worse between us. I can't tell you how many times we've broken up and then gotten back together over this one issue. Or at least I thought it was this one issue. The first time Jesse left me . . . well . . . Jesse told me she really, really wanted to raise a family together. To bring children into a home that was filled with love and happiness. Jesse grew up with two alcoholic parents, and there wasn't much love and happiness there for her. But Jesse is an alcoholic, too, and she can't seem to stop drinking for very long. Or hold a job. Or stay away from an ex who broke her heart and now loves to play with it like it's a yo-yo. She also can't seem to find love and happiness within her. Jesse is . . . well . . . she's really a good person inside but she's not the easiest person to give your heart to.

"Anyway, when she came back this last time—months ago, now—and said she really wanted to work on things and start a family together, we tried again. And just like that, I got pregnant. And now . . . now Jesse has left. She left weeks back. I lied to you guys last night. She's not coming back. It's done. We're over."

"And you're going to have a baby," Meri said. "That she wanted."

"I wanted it, too, Meri. And I want it now."

"So that's why you didn't have anything to drink at the bar," Taylor pointed out.

"And why you wanted me to stop you when you were about to drink that second margarita," I added.

Maria nodded.

"And is that why you've been so snappish towards me lately, Maria?" Chantelle asked. "Because of being pregnant?"

"No. You just drive me nuts, Chantelle," Maria snapped, then broke into laughter. "Yeah. I get so tired and cranky sometimes. Your emotions, well, they just go all over the place when you're pregnant."

"Do you think you should be working?" I asked.

"Oh, for God's sake, C.J., I'm pregnant not debilitated. Women have been doing this for years, you know."

"Does that mean you're going to give birth in the woods and then return to work the same day?" Meri asked.

"I think we have a good maternity leave policy, don't we?" I asked, then scratched my head. "Actually, I never really paid much attention to that part of the health plan."

"I did," Maria answered, "and it's pretty much standard." Then she turned her attention to Meri. "I could be training for a marathon right now and it'd be okay. I could also probably give birth in the woods and return to work with a baby sucking on my breast. But I think I'll opt for the hospital and drugs."

"Well, that's a relief," I said. "I'm glad you're not one of those everything's-got-to-be-natural, give-birth-in-a-tub-of-water-with-Native American–chanting pregnant women."

"I did consider a midwife for a time," Maria said.

Meri shook her head. "I wouldn't—not after reading that best-seller *Midwives*. You just never know what can happen."

Maria laughed. "I read that book, too. But after I had made the decision not to use a midwife. It helped me to feel better about my decision."

"Is everything okay with you, then?" I asked.

Maria nodded. "I'm fine, C.J. You just have this roller-coaster thing going on inside you when you're pregnant. And I do get very, very tired at times."

"So how are you to be having this baby by yourself?" Samata asked.

"That's a good question," Maria answered. "Before I met Jesse, I never gave a second thought to having a baby. I would've been happy just being with her, growing old with her. There wasn't any biological clock ticking inside me when I hit my thirties."

"I think most lesbians know how to disconnect the clock," Meri replied.

"And replace it with wiring that increases the urge to own cats," Chantelle added.

"Please to go on, Maria," Samata cut in.

"Well, the more Jesse wanted to raise a child, the more I found myself wanting to do that, too. We decided I would be the one to carry the baby to term because I simply had better genetic programming than Jesse. The harder it was for me to conceive—and it was hard—the greater the desire became for both of us. But when Jesse left after I became pregnant—"

"What a kick in the teeth!" Meri exclaimed.

Maria nodded. "That it was. Then I was faced with a difficult decision. Should I keep the baby and be a single parent or . . . or have an abortion? I spent a lot of time thinking about what I should do. It wasn't just an emotional decision. I had to break out the calculator and see if I could really do this on my own. It'll be tight, for sure, and I'm going to have to make some big changes in my lifestyle pretty soon. But I *want* to be pregnant. I *want* to have this baby. But I'd be lying if I said I wasn't scared. I *am* scared. I'm alone and I'm pregnant."

"You're not alone, Maria," Taylor said as she reached an arm around the back of Maria's chair. "You have us. All of us. We can be there for you. We're going to be solid, remember?"

"I know a lot about babies," offered Chantelle. "My sister's been cranking them out for years. I get up a lot of times in the middle of the night to help with the feedings. And I'm a terrific diaper changer."

"My sister-in-law is a nurse at Beth Israel," Meri said. "I can get any medical information you want if you just ask."

"We'll throw you a terrific baby shower and get you all the things you need," Taylor suggested.

"We can each assume a turn at babysitting," offered Samata.

"And you can take whatever time you need for doctor's appointments and things like that," I told her.

Maria smiled. "Thanks, you guys. This is exactly what I needed to hear."

"Well, anyone else have a deep, dark secret to share with the group?" Meri asked.

"I do not have a secret, really," answered Samata. "But information I would like to share and then advice I would like to solicit."

"Shoot," Chantelle said, then caught Samata's blank expression. "That means go ahead and say it, Sam."

Samata shook her head. "This language still gets the bug in me. Shoot is something you do with a gun, yes? And then recently I hear in an old Hollywood movie the word shoot used like it means regret. 'Shoot, I cannot go to the ball game today.' Is that a correct way of using this word?"

I nodded. "It is."

"Okay, then, I shoot now. I asked the lovely Britta, via e-mail yesterday prior to our departure to the bar, if she would like to join us there or perhaps, if she could not do so, to be my guest for a drink or dinner at another time. She did not show up last night, and I was greatly disappointed. But when I opened up my e-mail this morning, I was overjoyed to find that she had replied to my e-mail. She said she would enjoy to have dinner with me this week. Perhaps Friday, she suggested."

"Way to go, Sam!" Meri cheered.

"I think that's great," Maria agreed.

"Where are you going to take her to dinner?" Taylor asked.

"First you have to find out what she likes to eat," Chantelle pointed out. "She could hate fish, for instance, or be a vegetarian."

"A Swede who hates fish?" Meri chuckled. "And I think a vegetarian would be a stretch as well."

"Just because she's Swedish doesn't mean she only eats Swedish foods," Taylor offered.

"What are Swedish foods?" I asked.

Everyone grew silent for a few seconds.

"Thank you, C.J., for asking that stumper of a question," Samata broke into the silence. "For it is now that I can finally get a word in through the edge."

"Meatballs!" Meri exclaimed. "The Swedes eat meatballs. Swedish meatballs."

Chantelle rolled her eyes. "Where the hell is a Swedish meatball restaurant?"

"If you think about it," Taylor cut in, "there aren't any Swedish restaurants. I mean, there's Italian and Vietnamese and Chinese and Japanese. And German. And Mexican. And French. Maybe the Swedes don't have good food."

"That is really not the issue which I want to address," Samata said. "If you would please to bear with me. My purpose in bringing this up is to wonder about Debbe kissing Britta before she left the room today. I see this and I think perhaps Britta does not know I am asking her out on a date. She wants to be friends maybe. I certainly do not wish to tread on the same ground as Debbe Lee, if Britta is her girlfriend."

"Samata, that was not a kiss you witnessed between Debbe and Britta," Maria said.

"But their lips—"

Maria shook her head. "Trust me, Sam. That wasn't a kiss. That was all about control."

"And power," Meri added.

"And hurting you, if Debbe had accessed either yours or Britta's e-mail before the meeting," Chantelle offered.

"But their lips—"

"Sam, I could come over there right now and put my lips on yours," I said. "Would that truly be a kiss?" I shrugged my shoulders. "By all definitions, it probably would be. My lips would be touching yours. And since I have great affection for you, there would be some emotional basis for that kiss. After all, friends kiss friends all the time. Family members kiss family members. But what you're asking about is a kiss that comes from deep within the heart, from a different place."

"Yes!" Samata exclaimed and flashed me a brilliant smile. "It is to this kiss that I am addressing. Is this, I am asking, the kiss that was between Debbe and Britta this morning?"

"No!" the group shouted.

"So I am not to assume that Britta is involved with Debbe?"

"Hardly," Meri sniffed. "Did you see Britta's body posture during that kiss? She was arching her back away from Debbe. I think if she hadn't had her hands full, she would've pushed her away."

"Or given her a quick right cross," Taylor grinned.

Chantelle raised an eyebrow. "Think that leaning back wasn't noticed by Debbe, Sam? She knew she had Britta in a position of vulnerability. It was her mean-spirited way of inflicting hurt through her position of power. I don't think Britta was too happy about it, either."

"She could definitely sue Debbe for sexual harassment," Maria pointed out.

I shook my head. "No. That wouldn't stand up in court for one minute. Look at some of the sex shows we're offering at L-TV. Look at the fact that both Debbe and Britta are lesbians. Do you think anyone would believe the work atmosphere here isn't already sexually charged, and that what happened was just a natural extension of the sexual tension?"

"True," Taylor agreed.

"So it was not a real kiss?" Samata asked.

Meri shook her head. "If it had been a real kiss between two people who really, really were hot for each other, Sam, Britta would've dropped everything she was carrying the second their lips pressed together. She would've then wrapped her arms around Debbe and stayed in that embrace for as long as she could. Debbe's kiss would've floored her—"

"If what was in her kiss was a true, honest expression of passionate interest," Maria cut in.

"And Britta felt the same way about her," Chantelle added.

Samata slapped a palm against the table. "Yes! That is the real kiss to which I speak. And you say that was not in her kiss today?"

"No!" the group chorused the reply.

"Maybe that's a kiss you can share with Britta," I suggested. "But it certainly wasn't the kiss that Debbe forced her into."

"That is good, that is good," Samata said. "So. I look down my list now of five things. We have addressed all of them I believe. C.J.'s past involvement with Debbe—explained. C.J.'s television show—it is hers. C.J. and Meri and their night together—nothing happened. Maria's secret—revealed. And Britta's kiss—understood. I am done now. That is the five things which I wished to discuss."

I looked at each of the writers. "Then if that's all we have to discuss, we're done. Let's meet back here in an hour to see how Debbe does on national TV."

I had just settled into tackling the massive pile of paperwork on my desk when Maria rapped her knuckles lightly against the open door to my office.

"Do you have a minute, C.J.?"

"Sure. What's up?"

Maria entered my office and closed the door behind her. "I wanted to tell you that I was sorry I didn't let you know I was pregnant before today."

I gestured to a chair in front of my desk, and Maria took a seat.

"You have nothing to apologize for, Maria. And Debbe was way out of line putting you on the spot that way in front of all of us."

"Yeah, well, she was just being true to form."

I grinned. "That she was."

We looked at each other for a few seconds.

"I can't tell yet," I said.

Maria smiled. "You could if I showed you my belly." She stood up, raised her shirt, and turned sideways. "See?"

"Oh, yeah. Look at that round belly. Huh! You really do have a bun in the oven, don't you?"

Maria rubbed the palms of her hands lightly against her belly, then dropped her shirt and sat down. "It's so exciting, C.J. Amazing. To have this start of life inside you. To know that someday I'll be able to hold what is slowly developing in here. To watch my child grow."

"It sounds pretty amazing. And you're all right, health-wise?"

Maria nodded. "I am. But I wanted to ask you for a little time off. It's not anything medical. I need to find a cheaper place to live. Then, when the baby's born, I can find a bigger place. But for right now, I thought I'd put my furniture in storage and look at rooms for rent. I found a few places advertised in the paper that were very reasonably priced and want to make appointments to see them on the same day, sometime next week, if that's okay."

"Sure, that's fine. But won't storage fees be expensive in the long run?"

"I have it worked out with what I can afford in rent and storage. It'll be less than what I'm paying now in rent at my apartment."

"Well, that's good."

"Okay." Maria stood up. "Then I'll let you know what day I'll be taking off."

"Sure, but . . . well, oh, I don't know if you'd even be interested."

"Interested?"

"Yeah. Uh, the basement in my house was nearly finished to be an in-law apartment before I purchased it. Right now there's a completed bathroom, a partial kitchen, a small bedroom, and a small living area where I've stored a lot of my stuff. All that stuff can be moved. So you could probably fit all your furniture in and not pay for storage. And we could work out something in payment if that would make you feel better. But it's not being used and I don't need the money."

"You're asking me to move in with you?"

"Not really *with* me. There's a separate entrance. But, yeah, you'd be in my house. We could even save you some extra money by sharing the commute into work during the week."

"I don't know, C.J. I mean, it's certainly a sweet offer. But you saw how the group reacted to Meri spending the night at your house. What will they think if I'm staying in your house?"

"You wouldn't be staying in my house. You'd be renting an in-law apartment in my house."

"I don't know, C.J. It's probably not a good idea. The rest of the group might think I'll be getting special treatment from you because of such an arrangement. And I know I'll be asking for special consideration throughout this pregnancy."

I shrugged my shoulders. "Well, I just thought I'd let you know. It's certainly available for you to move in whenever you'd like. I'm not doing anything with the basement except lifting weights a few days a week down there. You can think about it, you know."

"Okay," Maria said as she walked to the door. "I'll think about it. See you in the conference room in a few."

"**Six** minutes past the hour," Katie Couric announced as she faced the camera.

"What is that woman doing with her hair now?" Chantelle asked as we settled into chairs in the conference room shortly after 8 A.M.

"I liked it when it was short," Meri commented.

"There's the Dragon Lady herself," Maria said as the camera panned back to reveal Debbe Lee, who was sitting in a chair across from Katie.

"She appears much smaller now, does she not?" Samata asked.

"She's the size of a Barbie doll—a Bitch Barbie," Taylor chuckled.

"Coming soon to a toy store near you," Chantelle added.

"Wearing a belittling smirk, Bitch Barbie comes with such accessories as a whip," Maria quipped.

Taylor held her index finger and thumb out in front of her. "What was the comedy routine that Kids in the Hall used to do? 'I'm squeezing your head,'" she said as she pressed her fingers together.

"Quiet," I ordered.

"First there was *Friends,* a long-running hit NBC series about six single twenty-something heterosexual friends who shared love and life with each other," Katie continued as she spoke to the camera. "Then there was *Sex and the City,* an HBO series about four single heterosexual women in search of Mr. Right in New York City. Then there was Showtime's *Queer as Folk,* about five gay men and their tales of sex, love, and friendship.

"And now there's a new show—or, I should say, a new network—on the block. It's call letters are L-TV, which stands for Lesbian Television, and I'm here today with the president and CEO of L-TV, Debbe Lee. Good morning, Debbe."

"Good morning to you, Katie."

"Debbe," Katie began as the camera angle shifted to show both Debbe and Katie on the screen, "tell us about your network and some of the shows that you'll be offering in the fall."

"Well, Katie," Debbe began as she crossed her legs and leaned back in the upholstered studio chair, "L-TV is a new cable network offering programming by, for, and about lesbians and their friends and family. We'll be featuring everything from cooking shows and talk shows to soap operas to sitcoms and dramas that will compete with the networks and other cable channels during prime-time hours."

"Interesting," Katie commented. "But from what I also understand, Debbe, L-TV will offer many shows that parents may find offensive to children. Shows that will be similar to the Playboy channel on cable in that they will show nudity and sexual acts. And, like HBO and Showtime and other cable channels, even though your shows will display a rating prior to airing, there will certainly be shows that contain violence, language that might be deemed offensive to some, and scenes depicting sexual acts between women that—"

"And men," Debbe grinned. "Yes, Katie, we're going to have it all."

"But don't you think that L-TV is going to have a very limited audience, since it's geared towards lesbians and current statistics show that only ten percent of the total U.S. population is comprised of lesbians and gay men?"

"Oh, Katie, there will be a much larger percentage of the U.S. population that will be watching L-TV and our outstanding shows,"

Debbe said as she casually propped an arm on her chair. "We've already sold several shows overseas, and I can promise you that our channel will draw a very large heterosexual male population of viewers as well."

"That will be for the titillation factor, though, won't it? But if you draw males to the shows you're offering, wouldn't that be defeating the overall purpose of L-TV—to gear shows to lesbians and, as you say it, to their family and friends in a positive—"

"The overall purpose of L-TV is to offer new shows to the viewing public," Debbe cut in. "Plain and simple. I don't care what the sexual preference is of those who watch our network. Just so long as they watch. And they will, of that I'm certain. In fact, several cable companies have informed our marketing department that they will be adding L-TV onto their high-end viewing packages. I think some companies are even calling it their Rainbow Package," Debbe laughed. "You do know about the rainbow colors as a gay symbol, don't you Katie?"

"I do, Debbe. But don't you think—"

"Has anyone else noticed that every question Katie is posing begins with the word 'but'?" Meri asked. "She's coming across as quite negative."

"What? Did you think she'd embrace L-TV?" Chantelle answered. "Remember, she has children of her own. She's being a parent right now, and I don't think there are going to be a lot of parents—heterosexual parents, that is—who are going to think L-TV is a good idea."

"Then this will be a difficult sale to make, yes?" Samata asked.

"It sure will," I answered. "But in America, controversy and being controversial are what pays the bills. People are going to start to get quite vocal about their opposition to L-TV, which is only going to generate interest."

"Think back years ago to Anita Bryant and her outspoken views on homosexuality," Meri said. "Florida orange juice companies took a big hit from that."

"And just where is Anita Bryant now?" Chantelle asked.

"In a gay relationship?" Taylor suggested.

"So we're using the old negative publicity tactic to sell L-TV—is that right?" Maria asked me.

"Publicity sells," I told her. "Good or bad, it sells. Think about it. John Rocker spouts off about his opposition to gays and ethnic populations, and the next game he pitches is sold out. The Clinton administration's Lewinsky scandal makes headlines and lead stories on news reports for months. The more scandalous, the more outrageous—"

"The more you get Dr. Laura and the religious right and Rush Limbaugh against you," Taylor cut in. "And then the more people want to find out what's going on. I bet the first week we're on the air, our ratings will be sky-high."

"That's right," I agreed. "And then we'll keep the viewing public tuned into L-TV with the quality of our shows. Who will want to watch some of the lame and tame shows on network television once they see what we're offering?"

"Certainly you couldn't put all of these prime-time shows you've just told us about on the air without an awful lot of help, Debbe," Katie was saying.

"Yes, Katie, help is good, and I have very, very good help at L-TV," Debbe replied.

"Here we go," Taylor said. "Now comes our moment to shine."

"Tell us about the rest of the people at L-TV, Debbe."

"While certainly each of the offerings at L-TV has been my creation and mine alone," Debbe began, "I have a wonderful staff of writers who will be providing the scripts for those hit shows. And of course there's our marketing and advertising departments, a legal staff, and numerous other support personnel who will ensure that my vision at L-TV comes through to the American viewing public and makes its mark."

"Debbe, I wish you great success in your network and will be following the ratings to see how your shows do this fall. Matt? Back to you."

"Thank you, Katie. Today's segment on men's health focuses on one of the leading—"

"Shut that thing off!" Meri shouted.

Taylor picked up the remote control and hit the power button. Then she tossed the remote on the table. It bounced once, then slid off the table and dropped to the floor.

"Am I to write this correctly?" Samata asked as she stopped writing on a pad of paper and waved her pen in the air. "It is what she said, 'certainly each of the offerings at L-TV has been my creation and mine alone?' "

"Remember to also write down that there's a staff of writers—that's us, we're the staff—who will be providing the scripts," Meri hissed.

"What a goddamned piece of shit!" Chantelle cursed. "She's a fucking goddamned—"

Maria held up her hand to silence Chantelle. "Forget about us, Chantelle. C.J.? She didn't even acknowledge you."

I stretched my arms up and arched my back, then relaxed my body and sighed. "Oh? Yeah, I guess you're right. She didn't even acknowledge me."

"And she took full credit for all of our shows, C.J.!" Meri exclaimed. "Those aren't her shows. Never were. They came from us. After a lot of hard work and—"

"Yes, Meri, your show is your show—in theory," I said as I shook my head. "As are all of our shows. But now they're Debbe's. They're the property of L-TV, and that means they are hers to do with as she wants."

"But to take credit for them?" Maria asked. "I mean, that's going way beyond . . . I mean, it's a flat-out lie."

"I know," I agreed. "I don't know what to tell you."

"Well, that's it. I quit!" Meri shouted, then stood up from her chair and stormed out of the conference room.

"I can't believe this!" Chantelle muttered. "I can't fucking believe this."

"I . . . uh . . . I should probably take a look at my resume," Taylor said as she stood up. "Update it. Send it out. See what's out there. Sorry, C.J. But this is absolutely ridiculous. These shows are no more our babies than . . . than . . . this chair is mine," she said as she pushed her chair under the table and left the room.

"Now what, C.J.?" Maria asked.

"Are you going to quit, too?" I answered.

Maria shook her head. "I told you earlier. I need this job. I can't afford to lose the healthcare coverage. If I leave and take another job somewhere else, my health benefits won't kick in for a few months. I can't risk that."

I nodded.

"I will be staying as well, C.J." Samata said. "I would like to see how L-TV fares and perhaps if this will open an avenue up to me somewhere else in the near future. Plus, I must tell you that I send my family back in Egypt a large portion of my paycheck. They depend upon this, and I must not let them down."

Chantelle met my eyes. "I hate this, C.J. I really, really do. But I'm a slave to the paycheck as well. My sister's ne'er-do-wells don't put food on the table or keep the phones and lights working. I'm just going to have to suck it up and get on with the work on my— on the show."

I nodded. "Okay. Let me see if I can talk Meri and Taylor down from the ledge before they jump. I was going to suggest that we stay and watch the rest of the shows Debbe will be on, but I don't think her tune will be changing."

"I hear that," Chantelle muttered as she gathered up her things and exited the conference room.

"I must to go make a few calls about the location for *The Body Farm,*" Samata said as she got up from the table. "Please to excuse me, C.J."

"Thanks, Samata."

Maria and I sat in the conference room in silence as minutes ticked by.

"What are you going to do, C.J.?" Maria finally broke into the silence.

"What am I going to do," I echoed as I twirled a pen on the table.

"C.J.?"

I looked up to see Britta standing at the entrance of the conference room.

"Debbe just called to say that she's on her way next to the Regis Philbin interview. Should I call the rest of the writers back into the room to watch?"

"No, Britta. I think we've seen enough of Debbe in one day."

Britta raised her eyebrows. "You're not going to watch her? But she left me with specific instructions to—"

"I'm sure she did, Britta," I cut in. "Why don't you just tape the shows for us, okay? We're a little too busy now to sit around all morning watching television."

"But Debbe said she'd fire me if—"

"She's not going to fire you, Britta. But if she does, I'll hire you, okay?"

"But—"

"Don't worry about it, Britta. And don't let her intimidate you. She's just a person, okay? And this is just a job. We're not saving lives here. It's not brain surgery we're doing or heart transplants or finding the cure for cancer. Keep the job in perspective and her idiotic tantrums in perspective, and you'll get along okay. Let her step all over you, and she'll throw you out in the next trash pickup. You've got to stand up to her. That's the only way she'll keep you around. The woman loves a good fight. She always loves a good fight. That I know."

"Good for you, C.J.," Maria said.

Britta clasped her hands in front of her and swallowed. "I've never been treated this way in any job I've ever had, C.J. Debbe Lee is . . . is not a very nice person. And I was so embarrassed—no, horrified—when she grabbed me and kissed me in front of everyone."

"Don't worry about it, Britta," Maria said. "Debbe embarrassed herself by doing that. Not you."

"She's a horrible person, don't you think?"

I nodded. "Yes, she is. But everyone else here is nice. Focus on everyone else, and you'll enjoy your job a lot more. Things . . . well, hopefully things won't always be this way."

Britta smiled. "Maybe I'll try to get fired just so I can work with you, C.J. And I probably should've joined you guys for drinks last night. But Debbe kept me late and—"

"Next time," I cut in. "You'll join us next time, Britta."

"Thanks, C.J. I guess I'll set up the recording in Debbe's private conference room."

Britta left, and Maria and I let the silence cloak us again.

"Now what, C.J.?" Maria asked. "Do we just go on like it's business as usual? Or do we sit down with Debbe when she gets back and tell her how we feel so she doesn't do that to us again?"

I slowly drummed my fingers on the table as I thought about Maria's questions for several seconds. "I think I should sit down with Debbe, but I don't think the writers should be there when I do," I finally answered. "It'll seem like we're ganging up on her, and the way Debbe handles any criticism that's directed at her is to try to wriggle out of it as quickly and effectively as she can. Which might mean that she'd ax everyone just out of spite. I don't want to do anything that'll put your job in jeopardy, or the jobs of any of the other writers."

Maria shook her head. "I don't know, C.J. Maybe you should've never asked Debbe to make you creative director here. First you have to deal with how badly Debbe treats you in your relationship with her. And then you have to continue to see her every day and deal with her all over again, though in a different capacity."

I let out a short laugh. "Seems like I'm still in a relationship with her, doesn't it?"

"Well, they say that you spend more time with your coworkers than you do with significant others. I remember . . . well . . . you can't believe how jealous Jesse would get when we had our initial meetings after I was hired. 'You're always working. You're always with your coworkers doing *something*,' she'd say. She'd even accuse me of having affairs with people in our group. And then the weekend trip to P-Town was a day-long argument all on its own. 'Oh, yeah, and I bet you *worked* the whole time you were there,' she said. 'Like you didn't go to any clubs or have a little fun in the sun.' "

I nodded my head. "You know, until I was involved with Debbe, I had never been in a relationship before that had had so many arguments. But because I had never really fallen head over heels in love with previous people I had dated, for a long time I thought that was simply part of the territory. That if your positive emotions were running that high for someone, then it stood to reason that your negative emotions would be as supercharged as well."

Maria nodded. "That's exactly how I felt, too. Until I had met Jesse, previous lovers had made me feel content, safe, secure. I had always been grounded with them. But I had also felt that something was missing. They were nice to me and we always had nice times together, but . . . And then I locked eyes with Jesse's one night at a Latino festival, and my heart did that flip-flop thing."

"Beware of the flip-flop. Always beware of the flip-flop."

"Hey, you never think that during the flip-flop."

"Only afterwards."

"When your heart's been flopped on its flip."

I laughed. "You know, my friends even told me Debbe was going to break my heart. They knew she was playing the field when she was with me. Did I listen?"

Maria cupped a hand around an ear. "Huh? My lover's cheating on me? My lover's a loser? I can't hear you!"

I grinned. "I know. Friendly advice often falls on ears deafened by heart palpitations."

Maria smiled, then rubbed her belly. "And my friends have told me deciding to have this baby on my own isn't the smartest thing I've ever done."

"They'd rather you have it with Jesse?"

"No. They're happy that Jesse's out of my life, but they'd rather I was with someone who would love me and parent with me."

"Well, maybe that will happen."

Maria shook her. "No, no. It's not going to happen. Who wants to be with a pregnant woman? Can't you just see me in a bar? Or can you imagine the personals ad I'd write? 'Latino lesbian looking for long-term life partner to help raise a child. Forget about long walks on the beach, movies, and quiet nights in front of a fireplace. Expect little sex and even less sleep.' "

I smiled at Maria. "What's wrong with that?"

Maria laughed. "Okay. I'll get right on posting that ad. Anyway, C.J., I'm not looking for my next ex-partner, if you know what I mean. Finding a relationship matters less to me than staying healthy and having a healthy child."

I nodded. "Yeah. That should be your primary concern."

"It is. The next time I fall in love, I'm certain it will be when I look in my baby's eyes."

I smiled. "That's nice."

Maria returned the smile.

"Here it is, C.J.," Meri announced as she marched into the conference room, then slapped a piece of paper down on the table in front of me. "I've given you two weeks' notice."

I lost the smile and sighed. "Meri, why don't you sit down for a minute. We need to talk about this."

"Talk isn't going to change my mind, C.J. My decision is final. No offense against you, but I'm outta here."

"No offense taken, Meri, but I'm afraid it's not as easy as you think to leave L-TV."

"Oh, yeah? Well then watch how fast I can pack up my stuff!"

"Meri, don't take your anger at Debbe out on C.J.," Maria cut in.

"I'm not taking it out on you, C.J."

"But you're yelling at C.J.," Maria pointed out.

"Butt out, would you?"

"And now you're taking it out on me," Maria snapped.

"Calm down, Meri," I said. "Why don't you sit down and let me explain."

"Explain what? There's nothing to explain, C.J. Debbe's rotten to the core, and I want out of here."

"I'm sure you do," I replied. "I'm sure you're not the only one. But then watch how fast Debbe takes you to court for breach of contract. When she's done with you, you won't have a box to pack your things in—let alone anything left to pack."

Maria stood up. "I think I'd better let you guys hash this out without me. I'll talk to you later, C.J."

When I walked into my office suite after talking with Meri, my assistant ripped off her transcription headset and immediately rose from her chair clutching a handful of pink telephone message slips. "C.J., the phone's been ringing off the hook," she huffed as she circled around her desk. "I'm trying to get through with typing up the contract you wanted me to prepare for Ms. Channing, but I keep getting sidetracked by all these reporters' calls."

"What reporters, Janice?"

"Oh, the *Boston Globe, Los Angeles Times, New York Times,* they're all written down," she said as she waved the message slips in front of me. "They want you to comment on some of the things Debbe said in her interview on the *Today* show."

"What things?"

"Well, they know you're the creative director, and they want to know how you feel about what Debbe said. Whatever she said, I don't know. I didn't watch the show. I don't know what's going on and," she said as she held a hand up in front of her, "I don't want to know. I've told you once, I've told you twice. I'm union. I have set hours. And I don't get involved in office politics. Been there, done it. Divorced my husband, put two kids through college, and I can't wait until I can retire from this rat race so I can garden to my heart's content. So as I've said, I've been trying to get through that contract you wanted and I know that we're under a deadline and so I'm trying my damnedest to make sure—"

"Jan, just get me every person who's contacted me," I said as I returned the slips to her.

"But, C.J., we have to have Ms. Channing's signa—"

"Start with the *Globe,*" I cut in. "Right now, this takes priority. I need to return these calls as soon as possible. Then you can get back to the contract."

"Okay, but I don't think we have a whole lot of—"

"Put that first call through as soon as you can," I cut in. "And when I'm done returning those calls, get hold of Meryl Streep's agent. We're going to have another contract to get out. And yes," I called over my shoulder as I headed into my office, "I know you leave on the dot of five. Just do the best you can. That's all I ask."

I closed the door behind me, clenched my fists tight for a few seconds, then released them.

"You want to play hardball, Dragon Lady, then you've got it."

That afternoon, the writers were waiting for me when I walked into the conference room.

"Great. I'm glad you're all here," I said. I walked to the head of the table, then held up a piece of paper. "First, I don't accept your resignation, Meri." I ripped the paper into pieces and let them flutter to the table. "You signed a contract, and you're obligated to stay through to the end of your contract. Quite frankly, it's not worth it to fight it, so just stay put. Taylor, I'd advise you to stay on as well, for the same reasons. As to how Debbe completely ignored the lifeblood of L-TV—namely, us—get used to it. You've seen it time and again and you'll keep seeing it. What you weren't prepared for is for her to have gone public with her conceit, and while you may feel degraded, devalued, and I'm sure there's another word that begins with D-E but I can't think of it right now, I don't feel that way about you. And that's really all that matters. You work for me, you report to me. And I'm the one who reports directly to Debbe."

I placed my palms against the table and leaned towards the writers.

"I've let matters go along the course they have for too long.

Enough is enough. You're soon going to find out that it's best if you let me fight your battles for you. Because I will. Just don't let Debbe get under your skin. If you let her start to rip this group apart, then she will have won. And that's what she wants. She always wants to win. *Always*. So if you walk out of here because you're miffed you're not getting the accolades you need and public pats on the back that you think you desire from her, then she's going to make certain that you owe her. For starters, you'll owe her the money that's due you for the term of your contract. And then you'll have to give up the right to take any credit for your shows. Oh, and forget about being able to get another job, because Debbe will always be one step ahead of you. She'll make sure you don't get any job offers, no matter where you go."

I leaned back from the table, then slowly circled the room.

"So don't be stupid. Don't be defensive. Don't be volatile. Don't be vengeful. Don't be angry. Remember the line from that song in *West Side Story*? I know you want to explode. I know you want to retaliate. But be cool. *Be cool.*

"I have taken action. You will soon hear what I've done because I don't like, any more than you do, not getting credit for our work. Just be cool. Keep working on your shows. By the end of next week, I want a report on my desk from each of you about the status of your shows. This includes stars signed, scripts written, production schedules detailed, and so on. Let's stop letting our emotions get the better of us. Do what you were hired to do and let the rest fall off your backs. I will protect you. You can be assured of that. I *will* protect you."

"**Seven** newspapers, and seven lead stories on the arts pages screaming in my face, C.J.!" Debbe shouted as she pounded a fist, heavily weighed down with gold, white gold, and diamond-jeweled bracelets, on a thick layer of newspapers that littered the top of her elegant black marble desk. "*This* is what I return home to after working hard to promote L-TV in the national media so I can ensure the careers—the very *futures*—of your staff? Do you know how many hours I spent *wasting my fucking time* in airports because of delayed or cancelled flights? I mean, it's not *rocket science* landing planes, is it? Some dodo sits at a control panel and says, 'You go *here*. You go *here*. You go *here*.'" Debbe paused and sucked air between her teeth. "But I digress. Do you know how much *infinitely timed* coordination, how much *hard work*, by our publicity department went into arranging this trip? How much *pushing, cajoling, begging,* they did to get me on the shows? Hell, press agents for Mel Gibson and Julia Roberts combined wouldn't have been able to have gotten this much publicity for those stars' new films. And it was nonstop, C.J. *Nonstop*. No time for spas. No time for relaxation. No time for *me*." Debbe paused for a moment and then propped her elbows on the desk and leaned towards the upholstered chair I sat in on the other side of her desk.

"Cat got your tongue, C.J.? You've got nothing to say to me? You know, I didn't fly from the east coast to the west and hit a total of *ten shows* in three days just so I could come back here to find out that my baby, my dream, my L-TV has been *stabbed* in the back by its own creative director." Debbe tapped her fingernails on the newspapers and narrowed her eyes at me. "What is *wrong* with you? What were you *thinking?* Were you once again going over-board, overreacting, making everything in the world *about you?* Are you PMS? Are you *nuts?* Are you trying to get back at me be-cause of our own personal history?" Debbe focused her fiery eyes on me, waited a few seconds, and then stood up and stamped a spiked-heeled foot on the lush carpeting on her office floor.

"Damn you, C.J.! Damn you, damn you, damn you! What is it that you want from me? You got everything you asked for when we split up—all but the Lexus. I didn't think you *deserved* anything I gave you—I've never given anything at any time to someone I was kicking out of bed—but I still was nice enough, *kind enough,* to comply with your wishes. Far be it from me to turn my back on someone who was clearly so *emotionally needy,* on someone whose life was most certainly *bottoming out.* So we didn't work out. *So what?* C'est la vie, you know? But you *had to have* the white picket fence and the dream of happily ever after, didn't you? Didn't you?" Debbe slowly clenched and unclenched her fists as she stared at me.

"Okay. Fine. That was all ancient history. And so I gave you everything you wanted but the luxury wheels. And then I thought things were going well here for you and me. It had seemed that we'd been able to put aside our past differences and focus on the present. Or so I had thought until I came home to this," she said as she swept a hand dramatically over the newspapers. She paused for a moment, then slowly wagged a finger in the air. "C.J., if you're pissed about not getting the Lexus in the big kiss-off, then I'll order you the damn Lexus. I'll get it for you—do you hear me? What color do you want? What model? Just tell me what you want!"

Debbe stared at me for a few beats, then placed her hands on her hips and expelled a loud sigh.

"What? You're not going to say *anything*? You're just going to sit there while I go on and on? *Fine.* I'll go on and on. And I'll probably make a hell of a lot more sense than you ever will trying to explain this . . . this stupid fucking stunt! This kind of publicity is going to kill us, C.J. *Kill us!* The last thing we need—"

"Is a lot of press?" I cut in. "But Debbe darling, didn't you tell me that the lifeblood of any new launch is how much buzz you can create? Didn't you tell me that negative publicity was as good as— maybe even better than—praise because the more controversial you can make something, the better?"

"Finally, she speaks," Debbe said as she slowly walked around her desk, folded her arms over her chest, and then leaned back against the edge of her desk a few feet from me. "So *this* is what this is all about? You're getting involved in the publicity of the show by trying to create *buzz*? You're actually trying to *help* L-TV—and not hurt me or the channel?"

I stared at her, then shrugged my shoulders. "What do you think I'm doing?"

Debbe considered my question, then showed me a smile. "Oh, no, dear C.J. You've got something else up your sleeve."

I stayed silent while Debbe tapped her foot on the floor.

"Okay, C.J. I *know* what this is about. Really I do. I didn't *acknowledge* the writers. I didn't *mention* their names or sing "Glory, Glory, Hallelujah" in their honor. That's it, isn't it? Your little bunch of lesbian scribes took offense and went waa-waa-waa to you. 'Oh, poor us! So unappreciated!' And so C.J., the do-gooder boss who hates to see anyone unhappy, any little birdie helplessly fluttering on the ground with a broken wing, came to their rescue. C.J., at some point in your life you're going to have to realize that you can't make everyone happy. You can't fix every little skinned knee. You can't wipe away everyone's tears. You can't mend a broken heart. You just simply don't have that power."

"Oh?" I answered. "My feeling is that if *you* have the power to cause such unhappiness, Debbe—all the skinned knees and buckets of tears and broken hearts—then I believe I have power to undo whatever harm you do to others. And you know damn well what you did. You pulled a stunt of your own. You took credit for the writers' shows. On national television. And you made certain that they'd be watching when you made your declaration of ownership over their creations. You knew what you were doing, and what I can't figure out is why you'd want to do something so unprofessional and potentially damaging to L-TV when our launch date is so near and so critical. You took a terrible risk. You almost lost two writers. If it wasn't for me, the production of at least two of *your* shows would be in jeopardy right now."

Debbe raised her eyebrows, threw back her head and laughed, and then clapped her hands together. "What a delight you are, C.J.! It's times like this that I find myself getting *so wet* for you, that I want to throw you on the floor and fuck you *so hard* because you get it! The light finally dawns on Marblehead, so to speak."

I stared at Debbe.

"Well," she said as she turned and began to sort through the newspapers on top of her desk. "Which is your favorite headline, C.J.? I liked . . . let's see," she muttered as she licked her fingers and thumbed through the newsprint. "Oh, yeah. The *Los Angeles Times* was good. 'No Pussy-footing Around: Cat Fight at New Lesbian Cable Channel.' A couple of the alternative papers had good headlines as well. Here's one: 'Hot Licks Exchanged at Lesbian TV.' Ummm. I *like* hot licks. And what was the other?" Debbe laughed as she held up a newspaper. "'We're Here, We're Queer, We're Screwing Each Other!' " Debbe peered over at me. "Did you help write any of these headlines, C.J.? Because they're magnificent. They truly would be your best work."

I frowned at her. "What do you mean the light finally dawns on Marblehead?"

Debbe dropped the newspapers, stared at the newsprint on her fingers, and then carefully pressed a long-nailed, polished index finger on her desk intercom. "Britta? Come in here with that hand sanitizer. *Now.*" Debbe clicked off, then turned to me. "You can't be serious, C.J. That you don't get it after all?" She paused for a moment as she held her hands out from her body. "Or maybe you can. Ah, Britta, my buxom assistant," she said as Britta opened her office door. "Be a love and rub that sanitizer on my hands. I seem to have gotten dirty with these daily rags, thanks to C.J.'s hard work." Debbe extended her hands to Britta.

Britta lifted the cap to the bottle she was carrying and squeezed a few drops of liquid on Debbe's hands.

"Now rub it in, Britta."

Britta stepped back from Debbe. "You can do that yourself."

"But why would I want to do that when you're here to help me? And why would you refuse to help me? In fact, if you rub in that sanitizer, I'll give you a hundred dollars. Just like that. For what? A few seconds of your time. A hundred dollars would go far in your little world of thriftiness, wouldn't it, Britta? A hundred dollars would help to pay off any remaining nasty debts you've rung up without my knowledge—oops! I wasn't supposed to say anything about your love of playing the horses, was I? You see, C.J.," Debbe said as she turned to me while she held out her hands to Britta, "I met our beautiful Britta late last summer at the flat track in Saratoga Springs. Britta, weren't you chambermaiding and hustling and dealing—and what else were you doing when I helped you escape arrest that day at the track?"

Britta glanced quickly at me, then glued her eyes to the floor as she stepped closer to Debbe and began to rub her hands.

"That's nice," Debbe smiled, then turned to me. "Yes, our beautiful, model-lookalike Britta was going to be arrested by the big, bad cops that day. Until I stepped in, that is. Yes, it was certainly a winning day for me. I made thousands at the track in less than an hour—what a streak!—and then I got to play the role of the knight in shining armor and come save this fair damsel in distress. After I had played Prince Charming and palmed enough money in their hands for the cops to look the other way, gorgeous Princess Britta told me how much she was in debt. Lord, C.J., she owed a bundle to some very shady individuals there. *A bundle.* I was positively floored. *Floored!* I mean, it's amazing the enormous amount of debt can be racked up when you're addicted to gambling. I think Saratoga Swede here had lost enough at that point in her life to build a new dorm at Harvard. And, you know, some people will do just about anything to keep playing. To keep chasing after that elusive dream of riches beyond belief. Right, Britta?" Debbe leaned close to Britta's ear and whispered something to her that I couldn't hear. Britta's body immediately stiffened and she drew back from Debbe. Debbe grinned at her and then at me.

"And so I paid off those individuals who wanted to do nasty things to Britta," Debbe continued. "I cleared Britta's lingering account with them—a debt that surely would've resulted in her painful, tortured execution and her naked body later being found by some hiker in a dense forest, partially devoured by wild animals. And then, after a few nights of amazing sex, where Britta repaid my generosity by letting me do whatever I wanted to do to her and she did whatever I asked her to do to me, I offered her a job here as my assistant. Of course, the poor thing has to attend Gamblers Anonymous meetings three times a week, per her contractual agreement with me. That's why you couldn't join the writers for drinks on Friday, wasn't it, love? You had to go stand up in front of a bunch of other losers and say, 'Hi, my name is Britta and I'm addicted to gambling.' But she's turned her life around, C.J. She really, really has. Isn't it wonderful the things I can do for others? Britta is my humanitarian project this year. Just like you were one of my previous projects, C.J. That makes me a very giving person. And you thought I didn't have a heart."

Debbe clasped Britta's hands in hers, and then pulled Britta towards her. Debbe buried her face in Britta's long blond hair and then ran her tongue along Britta's neck.

I met Britta's eyes for a second. Britta then lowered her eyes, squeezed them shut, and pulled herself out of Debbe's grasp. She turned and walked out of the office.

Debbe smiled. "You will convey to Summo that Britta is spoken for, won't you, C.J.? I so hate to see someone as innocent as Summo get her heart broken. But right now Britta is my pet project, and I haven't tired of her yet." Debbe grinned. "Do you see *now,* C.J.? It's about *control,* darling. It always has been, and it always will be. You can't be in my position, you can't possibly do the things I've done and the things that I do now, you can't open the doors you need positively blown off their hinges, without control. *All* the control is preferable. But taking as much control as you can is sometimes the best you can do, given a situation where you're facing off against others who want the control as well."

"So you're saying—?" I began, and then stopped. I glanced at the newspapers on Debbe's desk.

Debbe followed my eyes and nodded. "Sweet C.J. Dear sweet dumb C.J. I know that you live in this little Walt Disney world of yours, in a world of pots of gold at the end of rainbows and four-leaf clovers and golden rules and morals and do-the-right-thing philosophies. But don't you see, C.J.? I thought you did, by pulling this stunt. You don't get anywhere in this world without screwing someone. You thought you were screwing me, didn't you? You thought you could play my game, C.J. You thought you could get back at me." Debbe shook her head and showed me a sad smile. "But—and I'm *so sad* to break this news to you, C.J.—you simply *can't* play my game. You are not equipped. Because my game has no rules. My game has no goals. And my game has no referee, no guiding force to dictate the way the game is played. My game is a fluid free-for-all. I make the rules. I break the rules. I change the rules. This is the mantra I live by. Make, break, change. Make, break, change. You will never, ever, get the better of me, C.J."

Debbe stepped towards me, slowly dropped to her knees and kneeled in front of me, and then took my hands in hers before I could pull out of her grasp.

"Don't you remember all those nights when I brought women home, C.J.? I made the rule that I could do that. And you tried to talk to me about how that made you *feel.* You wanted to *process* it, didn't you? As if I cared. Honey, if I had cared about you the way you thought I had, I wouldn't have done that, right? And I made the rule that I would scream as loud as I could whenever I came with them, so you'd hear me. Do you remember those long, long nights you spent by yourself in the room next to our bedroom, listening to me loving other women?"

I clenched my teeth and wriggled my fingers to remove myself from Debbe's grasp.

But Debbe gripped my hands tightly in hers, refusing to release me, and then pulled one of my hands close to her mouth. She began to slowly lick my fingers.

"And you stayed, didn't you, C.J.?" she asked, then flicked her tongue lightly and rapidly against a finger tip. She stopped and looked up at me. "You accepted my rules, and you lived by them. And so that's what I thought you had learned in talking to each of those newspaper reporters. I *enticed* you into giving those interviews. I *manipulated* you. Because I know you, C.J. You're like so many of the millions of stupid people in the world who can be lead like lemmings over a cliff because they feel some sort of righteousness to stand up for what they believe. That is your *downfall,* C.J. It's not, quote, *a good quality."*

I stared at Debbe and then shook my head. "But you weren't like this when we first met."

Debbe released my hands, then made a fist and knocked it lightly against my nose. "When are you going to stop focusing on the past, C.J.? You are so pathetic. You keep saying, 'But you weren't always like this, you weren't always like this,' and every time you do that you deny that *I am* like this. I really always was. You just never allowed yourself to see it. But sometime soon you'll need to shake off your shield of misunderstanding about our relationship and the way you felt it should've been or ought to have been and see it for what it really was. You'll need to take a long look, a long, intense review of those tapes of our past together and look for those red warning lights that would've let you know years ago the type of person you had chosen to be with. Because they are there. Believe me, they were there. Because I *put* them there. It was you who denied who I was. Not I who changed."

Debbe stood up, stretched her arms, and then let out a slow, luxurious yawn. "You make it so easy for me, C.J. Sometimes I feel bad," Debbe flashed a quick grin at me, "but for only a second. Never longer. Because I can't feel bad. I don't have time to feel bad. Feeling bad takes away from the control I have over you, over everyone here. And do you know how I get that control, C.J.? Through the weaknesses of others. You are weak. Britta is weak. Each member of your staff is weak. They think that they can simply walk off this job if I offend them. But they can't. Because I have something I can use against everyone here. I have hired weak people who I can easily manipulate. And I have you to thank for that, because you helped me hire them."

Debbe patted the top of my head. "So go ahead, C.J. Try to play my game if you'd like. But your time would be better spent doing what I want you to do. Because you will never win. You will never wrestle the control out of my grasp."

Debbe walked around her desk, and then sat in her black leather chair. She pulled open a desk drawer, opened a flat gold cigarette case, and lit a cigarette with a gold desk lighter. She tossed the lighter onto the newspapers, then blew a long, thin stream of smoke through her lips.

We regarded each other in silence.

"What do you mean when you say that I helped you to hire weak people?" I asked.

Debbe smiled. "Your staff, as talented as they are profession-ally, are weak emotionally. They were not in the top of the resume pool, but they showed sufficient talent and a certain moldability that was critical to me. I weeded through all of the resumes myself before you even got to see them. Then I showed you the resumes of those people who I believed would be adequate writers, who would get the job done, but who also could be easily manipulated. Every writer that you chose was the writer I wanted you to choose. I made sure of that."

"So you tossed out resumes of qualified writers who—"

"Believe me, C.J., the staff you hired is made up of the *only* people who could last in this job." Debbe paused. "Why is this so hard for you to understand? I repeat: It's about control, my darling. If I want the writers to do what I want them to do, then I've simply got to have a way to get them to follow my rules. And I can only do that if there is something I can use against them. Take Britta, for example. She has a gambling problem. This is always a card I will be able to play with her, to force her compliance with my way of doing things. You saw how quickly she responded to me once I aired that skeleton in her closet, didn't you? Well, everyone else on your staff has a similar skeleton—a deep, dark secret that they'd prefer not to be made public knowledge."

"How the hell did you—"

Debbe smiled. "Once again, C.J., you underestimate me. Do you think I learned nothing when the network forced me out years ago? I had tried to go up against someone who was an even better manipulator that I, and I fell ass over teakettle into her trap. She kept her job; I lost mine. Never again, my dear. I vowed that that would never again happen to me. And so I hired people who knew how to dig, C.J. I did that to protect myself and to ensure that I wasn't going to ever be faced with anyone walking off this job at a critical time because they didn't see things my way." Debbe placed the tip of the cigarette against one of the sheets of newspaper and watched as the paper blackened. "What better way to force compliance than to know some deep, dark secrets? Samata, for instance, had a terrible time leaving her homeland. She was quite homesick. And then a beloved family member died when she was over here. The poor thing took it so hard—blamed herself, in fact—that she washed down some pills with a bottle of vodka. She had her stomach pumped and was hospitalized for a week."

"*So?*"

Debbe ran a tongue over her lips, then took a long drag of her cigarette. She exhaled. "Think contract, C.J."

I thought for several seconds while Debbe continued to blow smoke around me.

"Oh, Lord, this is taking far too long. If you look at the writers' contracts, C.J., there's a clause in there about mental instability. I can force Samata out of her contract if I want to because of her suicide attempt. But she won't be able to squirm away on her own without being forced to repay me every dime I've ever paid her because of that episode." Debbe smiled. "As much as you might like to think that you did such a noble thing, talking the writers out of walking off the job, you really didn't *prevent* any writers from leaving. Because not one of them would've been able to walk out of here without having to repay me every cent I've paid them. So tell me, C.J., who in your group can afford to do that?"

I shook my head. "You are one sick individual."

Debbe tossed her head back and laughed. "It's called business savvy, C.J. Now let me guess who of the writers were huffing and puffing about leaving. I bet Meri was the first, right?"

I stared at Debbe.

"Right. Now let me tell you a little bit about this cunt-obsessed woman. Years ago, when she was a camp counselor, she had a relationship with a camper. Who, naturally, was underage. That's a bad thing, isn't it? Of course it is! And naturally there's a clause in the contract about sexual indiscretion. So Meri really wouldn't have gotten very far off these premises without this secret affair with a minor becoming public knowledge."

"But that was years ago!"

Debbe shrugged. "Doesn't matter. Priests sexually abuse altar boys and then are prosecuted decades later. This is no different. In fact, I dare say that the public would take an even dimmer view of such a blatant example of lesbian recruitment."

I stood up. "I don't want to hear any more. You've made your point."

"Yes, I can well imagine you don't. It must blow your mind, C.J., to realize that not everyone can be so good and so pure as you'd like them to be. And so it's probably best that I don't tell you that Taylor cheated on a critical exam in college—in reality, she really wouldn't have earned her degree if this had been discovered—

Chantelle helped her sister scam food stamp money, and Maria, our resident pregnant lesbian, killed someone when she was living in Puerto Rico."

I sat down.

Debbe snuffed out her cigarette in a crystal ashtray, then waved her hand in the air. "But don't worry, C.J. You don't have an ax murderer on your writing staff. The lovely Latino knifed a man— some friend of the family—who had been sexually abusing her younger siblings. It wasn't self-defense, but she was never brought up on charges. Shortly after that, she left Puerto Rico."

I closed my eyes and sighed.

"What a world we live in, huh C.J.? Not everyone is who they appear to be. Except for you, darling. You . . . well . . . my snoops extraordinaire couldn't find a damn thing on you. Apparently you've never done a bad, bad thing in your life. Never even stole a paper clip. Or maybe you have been a bad girl and you've just been really good at covering it up. At any rate, I'm not too worried about ever losing you. You will always be here with me, C.J. Not because you can't let me go, but because you can't ever imagine leaving your writers here alone with me. You've appointed your-self their little protector, and that you're going to do, C.J. I expect you to protect them from having any of their dark secrets exposed to the world. And since you know what I have on them and they don't know that you know, it's important that you make sure everyone toes the line. Just the way I want them to. No one is going to fuck up L-TV. And no one is ever going to fuck with me again.

"So trot on back to your staff, C.J. Tell them that I am *infuriated* by what you did and that I admit I was very, very wrong not to praise them like they were the greatest thing since sliced bread. Make them feel worthwhile and valuable and all those other things you're good at doing. Let them believe you scored one against me. And then get your programs going. We've got deadlines to meet."

I slowly rose from the chair and leaned over Debbe's desk. "I'm not going to answer for you, Debbe. I'm not going to make up lies or tell lies on your behalf. I'm not going to play games with my writers. Especially games that you devise."

"Suit yourself, C.J."

"Maybe I'll let them know how they were hired and what secrets you're holding onto."

"Again, it's your call," Debbe said as she busied herself clearing the newspapers from her desk. "But my guess is that if you do that, their focus will shift from their shows. They'll be more preoccupied with making sure their past indiscretions aren't publicly revealed than on working. Sometimes, C.J., honesty is not the best policy. Look at how far it's gotten me, love. You may not like who I am or how I operate, but you can't deny that I *am* successful. So it's up to you what you want to do. Success is at your fingertips. You can either hold onto it, or you can turn your back on it. Stick with the plan to make L-TV the best it can be, and I'll be on your side. But do anything to fuck this venture up, and you can be certain I will make your life a living hell. I will not forgive and I will not forget. You got that, darling? Now run along. I've got more important things to do than to sit here chitchatting with you."

$\mathcal{E}\text{ight}$ weeks later, L-TV was well into its regular season programming and things around the office had settled into a predictable, albeit hectic, routine. But despite the constant deadlines and pressures, we were all walking around on a cloud because of L-TV's astounding success. Both the October and mid-November Nielsen ratings showed that a large percentage of prime-time viewers were tuned into each writer's show. Although we hadn't been able to best the networks' weeknight offerings, we were consistently landing in the top five most-watched shows each weeknight and had turned so many heads with our ratings—both in the gay and lesbian community and the heterosexual TV viewing base—that cable subscribers had continued to sign on in large numbers for cable-TV broadcast packages that included L-TV.

Debbe Lee had informed us at one of our recent staff meetings that our advertising agency had been quite chagrined when our legal department had informed them that they couldn't steal MTV's popular promotion line from the past and proclaim instead, "I want my L-TV." But, in her typical underhanded fashion, Debbe effectively obliterated a paper trail between her office at L-TV and a lesbian-owned business which, at our expense, mass-produced I WANT MY L-TV! bumper stickers, with the L-TV rainbow logo, and sent thousands of the stickers to every store on their mailing list for free distribution. On my ride into work each day, I could usually count a handful of cars sporting the stickers.

L-TV had successfully weathered what many pundits in the industry had predicted would be the curiosity factor for the first few weeks of premieres of our prime-time lineup, and we had not only held onto our viewer base since we launched in mid-September, but had gradually increased it from week to week. Like many cable networks, we often repeated episodes so new viewers had the opportunity to catch up with each show's story lines, and oftentimes these repeated episodes stole some of the audience from new network prime-time offerings. On Sunday afternoons, during the hours that coincided with gay and lesbian tea dances, we aired back-to-back episodes of each of our prime-time offerings. A marketing analysis of this effort revealed that gay and lesbian bars were, indeed, airing L-TV during this time period, and those establishments that advertised this to the community reported larger-than-normal crowds.

The walls of the office corridors at L-TV were now lined with framed, poster-size promotion stills from each of our shows—daytime as well as evenings and nights. Our soaps were doing well, and the cooking and home improvement shows had even scored big with viewers. Each week, the marketing department taped new banners on the stills that let everyone know what our market shares had been. L-TV's legal department was swamped with requests for licensing T-shirts, magnets, key chains, and other merchandise that promoted our shows and the cable channel. The administrative assistants for each show were kept busy answering mail that arrived each day in large plastic bins, and the phones in the reception area were rarely silent for more than a few seconds.

Like many of the cast members of the popular *Survivor* series on network television, which was now in its eighth reincarnation, the real people-actors on *One Big Happy Family* and *The Body Farm* had become overnight celebrities. Media talk shows debated the activities and alliances formed each week on *Family* as well as soundly criticized promoting murder as merry mayhem on *The*

Body Farm. Each murder "victim" ousted from the *Farm* usually made the network morning talk-show rounds, and a few had even signed advertising deals with gun manufacturers like Remington and Colt or the renowned Swiss Army knife line, with their pictures appearing in *Field & Stream* and other outdoors magazines under the advertising tagline, "If I'd only had _____ (a Colt, a Remington, a Swiss Army knife, etc.) at *The Body Farm,* I'd be alive today." It was the type of unpredictable marketing fallout from L-TV's success that had people like conservative Republican and NRA-head Charlton Heston in a quandry; he didn't know whether to support us for our seemingly pro-gun stance or condemn us for being queer. And although Samata was overjoyed at the success of her show, she would often ask at our weekly staff meetings, "They are aware, are they not, that these people are to be alive? That they are not really murdered?"

Can't Let Go had created its own cult following, assisted by the schizophrenically good first-time acting of a buff, former personal trainer who went by the stage name T-Rex—her real name was Tina Rexalli—and a waiting list of guest stars that appeared each week. *On Again, Off Again* and *Tragic Endings* did fairly well against competitive network shows, but most significantly *On Again, Off Again* sparked a lot of dialogue and debate within the lesbian community. *Tragic Endings* appealed to a large gay male audience, who never seemed to tire of retellings of the tragic deaths of female superstars like Patsy Cline, Judy Garland, and Marilyn Monroe.

Debbe Lee had arm-wrestled a number of prominent personalities in the gay and lesbian community to introduce the shows each week—gratis—in order to catch viewers up with the latest happenings. Melissa, Ellen, Harvey, the Indigo Girls, and k.d. were soon joined in doing these honors by Madonna, Susan Sarandon and Tim Robbins, Bono, Steven Spielberg, Angie Dickinson, and Cher; the waiting list of celebrities who were ready to volunteer grew.

Like each of the writers, I had a framed still from my show in my office. *Madame President* was now the highest-rated show at L-TV, due in large part to Stockard's acting, scripts that had been well researched and polished by a crack team of second-tier L-TV writers, and Meryl Streep's steamy guest appearances as the president's lover. The picture that hung in my office showed Stockard standing in front of the American flag in an Oval Office set, clad in a bright blue designer-label skirt suit, looking suitably presidential, with Meryl sitting on a couch next to her. Stockard's hand was resting on Meryl's shoulder, and the look of adoration and love being exchanged between the two was amazing. Sometimes I found it hard to believe that the show and the characters I had created for it were only make-believe.

The first kiss that the two had exchanged in a previous week's episode had made the front page of nearly every gay and lesbian newspaper and magazine. The straight media had, at first, resoundingly criticized the kiss, saying that "it desecrated the sanctity of the Oval Office." Apparently the media had been quick to forget other well-known White House indiscretions, or maybe they had simply accepted them as being par for the course for heterosexual male behavior. But when L-TV's marketing department had issued press releases about Meryl's decision to donate her payment for appearing in several shows to the fight against breast cancer, the critics were immediately silenced. After all, who wanted to take on the Academy Award–winning actress or appear to be belittling the good cause that she was supporting?

And the critics also stayed silent, thanks to the president and first lady's surprisingly vocal support of the show. "The First Lady and I are quite pleased with *Madame President*," the president had said at a press conference when asked about his feelings about the show. "In fact, the first family makes time in our schedules each week to watch this fine show together and to discuss the particular sensitivities that women bring to politics and political decisions. Stockard Channing, in her role as president of the United States, is first and foremost a woman who shows herself to be a positive role model for women everywhere. The fact that she's gay has so little to do with who she is as a person and how she leads the country that perhaps it's time for everyone to look beyond lifestyle and peer deeper into each person's heart and soul. While the First Lady and I may not watch everything that L-TV offers its viewers, we applaud its use of the rating system to warn parents of mature show content that may be unsuitable for younger viewers. And we support wholeheartedly the ability of this cable TV show to exercise its right to free speech and to show, in a multitude of positive ways, the people in the gay community."

That's what having a democrat in the White House will do for alternative lifestyles and artistic expression.

I blew a kiss at the poster, rubbed my eyes, then glanced at my watch. Although there was nothing on my desk that needed my immediate attention and Janice had made her punctual five o'clock exit over two hours ago, I grabbed the top trade magazine in the stack that Janice had piled on a corner of my desk, leaned back in my chair, and threw my feet on top of the desk. Ever since my last conversation with Debbe and her revelations about the writers, I had been reluctant to join them for another afterwork round of drinks at Alley's. While this hadn't been difficult to do in September and early October, as we had all been working more than sixty hours a week on our shows, once things had lightened up my staff had wanted to get together again outside the office. Thus far I had refused a handful of their invitations, and I wanted to continue to keep my distance. Knowing what I knew now about each of them had made me wary to spend time socializing together. It felt awkward for me, knowing what I knew about each of them, like passing a room, glancing in, and seeing a friend standing there naked. As much as I tried to forget what Debbe had confided to me, or even to overlook these indiscretions from the past, it had had an effect on me, tainting my view of each person. Being the honest person that I am, I felt that my trust in them had been violated, and I really didn't know how to deal with that.

Although no one had come right out and asked me why I was backing away from spending time with them outside the office, I knew it was a question of time before one of them would ask me what was going on. Disappearing into work and using that as an excuse would only go so far; with the upcoming Thanksgiving and Christmas holidays and the shows for the rest of the year already in the can, I really had no good reason to refuse a drink. But going home would send the message that I was available, so staying glued to my desk seemed to be the best option.

I worked my way through the magazines, reading and discarding, until the pile was gone. I glanced at my watch again, gave myself another thirty minutes before I felt it was safe to leave, and started working through my e-mail.

"Let's go," Meri said as she entered my office without knocking. "We're heading to Alley's, and we're not leaving without you."

I glanced up and saw the rest of the writers clustered around my door.

"Not tonight, Meri," I said. "I'm working my way through a ton of—"

"It is time to work no more," Samata cut in. "Britta is waiting for us already at the bar."

"Yeah, come on, boss," Taylor said. "You know what they say. All work and no play makes you—"

"A very bad friend," Maria finished.

"We're not going there without you," Chantelle said. "So turn off the computer and let's go get drunk."

"I really can't go, guys."

"You're refusing us again?" Meri asked. "Each week, it's the same old excuse. Work, work, work. I think you're avoiding us, boss."

"I'm not avoiding you."

"Yeah, right," Chantelle nodded. "Hey, remember when you considered us your friends and we talked for hours and laughed? Those were the days, C.J."

"And remember how we all shared our deepest, darkest secrets?" Taylor asked.

"I don't like secrets," I said. "Anyway, I'm really beat. I'm just going to work for a bit more, then head home."

"Then it appears we will have to do something by force," Samata said, then turned on her heel and walked away.

I sat behind my desk, staring at the writers, who returned the stare.

A few seconds later, the fire alarm sounded.

Samata returned to my office. "I believe we must all vacate the building now, yes?" she asked.

"Good one!" Chantelle exclaimed as she held up her hand to Samata.

Samata slapped Chantelle's hand, then grinned at me. "Please to let me save you from the devastating fire, C.J. It is ripping through the building even as we speak."

I sighed, then turned off the computer.

"Smart decision," Maria commented as she unhooked my coat from the back of the door and held it open for me.

Maria killed someone when she was living in Puerto Rico . . . knifed a man, I heard Debbe's voice in my head.

Maria smiled at me, then shook my coat. "Come on, Madame Boss with the hit show. I'll help you on with your coat."

I slowly walked towards Maria.

I killed someone, I heard her say. *Knifed him in the back. So watch out, C.J. You may be next! Come a little bit closer to me, would you?*

I stepped in front of Maria and held out my hand for the coat. She shook her head and held open the jacket for me.

Cheat, cheat, never caught! I heard Taylor chant.

I looked at Meri. *I like young girls,* she told me. *But you knew that, didn't you?*

Please to accept that I tried to kill me, Samata added.

I looked at Chantelle. *I had the greatest scam going, C.J. You want me to show you how?*

I turned my back to Maria. *Now this won't hurt a bit, C.J. A bit of pain for a while, a pretty massive blood flow, but then you'll be sleeping like a baby.*

I whirled towards Maria and yanked my coat out of her hands.

"Geez, C.J. Can't a girl be gallant with you?" she asked.

"A pregnant girl, no less," Meri added.

I slipped on my coat. "Sorry," I mumbled. "I thought you were handing the coat to me."

Maria furrowed her eyebrows and peered at me. "Are you okay?"

"Of course she's okay," Taylor answered. "She's blowing this popsicle stand and going out with her friends. We're going to give you a much-needed dose of reality, C.J. We're taking you away from the games and lies and deceptions of the Dragon Lady."

"Welcome back to the real world, C.J.," Chantelle grinned.

"I'm buying the first round!" Meri proclaimed as she hit the switch on the wall and doused my office lights.

"Then my first round is six drinks," Taylor responded.

Maria grabbed my arm, and I stiffened.

"Are those your gloves?" she asked as she pointed to the floor.

Let's jump her now! Chantelle cried out. *We've got to get rid of her before she reveals what she knows about us.*

I slowly bent down and picked up the gloves.

See, if you wear gloves, C.J., there won't be any fingerprints on the knife, Maria advised. *Remember O.J.?*

"I'll . . . uh . . . meet you guys there, okay?" I said as I slowly slipped on the gloves.

"I will be riding with you," Samata told me as the writers walked out ahead of us. "There is something of which I need to speak."

I started the car, then let the engine warm up while I buckled my seat belt and fiddled with the CD player. The underground parking garage was nearly vacant at this hour, and its damp chill seemed to infiltrate every muscle in my body, making me shiver. I secretly gave thanks for not having Maria sitting in the passenger seat next to me.

Margie Adam's luscious voice and piano playing filled the interior, and I began to relax.

"I am so very sad, C.J.," Samata said as she locked in her seatbelt buckle.

I turned to her. "Why? Your show's doing great and, oh, is it because you're so far away from your family?"

"No. That does not make me feel so lonely anymore, now that I have friends and a good job that I love. It is my relationship with Britta."

"You're in a relationship with her?"

Samata nodded. "This you would know if you were meeting us for drinks and not continually working. We are being on the sly for the past several weeks. And that is what I wish to speak of. Britta has being involved with Debbe Lee. This she has told me. I do not know if you know this."

I opted for silence, hoping that my lack of response would help Samata to continue.

"Is this information hurting to you, C.J.?"

"No—no! I'm over Debbe. Really I am. I put her and our relationship in the trash can a long time ago."

"And then you put it out on the sidewalk with the garbage so it could be picked up?"

I smiled. "And then I put it out with the garbage."

"That is good. But now, C.J., Britta is finding it hard to get away from Debbe. She does not love her; she says she loves me. And I so adore and love her. But she feels that if Debbe found out about us, she would lose her job. Is this so bad? But then she tells me that her life would be made very difficult. And it is this that I don't know how to handle. How is this, to be with someone who is also being with someone?"

I shrugged my shoulders. "It's certainly not easy."

"That is for certain. Britta comes to my apartment every night, and she is upset. Distraught. She says there are some things that she cannot tell me. That she is not the person I am seeing. She is afraid I will not love her if I know of her. But I cannot imagine that she could be telling me anything that will be making me love her less. I love her now, and when she is also being with the big boss. She says she must. And that is something I do not understand as well. But this I accept."

"Why do you accept it?"

"Because I know that this is not always going to be. It cannot, because we love each other. This is a love that grows every day, like a garden in summer bloom. At some point, my lovely Britta will find the courage to get away from Debbe. I want this, but this also concerns me. She says that Debbe's reach is far. Do you understand what this means?"

I nodded, then flicked on the car heater. "It means that if Debbe wants something, she'll do anything to get it."

"But she cannot make Britta be with her, no?"

"No, she can't, Sam. But she can try everything she can to break you two apart."

"I have thought of this. She could fire me, for instance. And then I would not be here at L-TV. But no matter where I am, Britta could be with me. She could quit her job. I have told her so. But Britta tells me no, that Debbe has a control of her. How can this be?"

"You're asking me a lot of questions, Sam."

"I know I am. But you have been with Debbe. Maybe there is something you know that could help me with this dilemma."

I sighed. "All I can tell you is that you don't want to cross Debbe, Sam. You really don't. Not now. Not ever."

Samata rubbed her hands together. "But I do not wish to let go of Britta. And she does not wish to let go of me."

"Then maybe you need to say to Britta that she should tell you everything about her," I suggested. "That she needs to not keep any secrets from you. Maybe if you knew what she was so afraid of—and she knew that you knew, if that makes sense—it would make things better. Or at least help you to understand."

"Do you know what this is, C.J., that she is so afraid of?"

"Please don't ask me that question, Sam."

I felt Samata's eyes on me, but stayed silent. "Everyone is so afraid of Debbe Lee," Samata said as she clenched her hands into tight fists. "So afraid. Like she is military police. Britta is afraid of her. You are afraid of her. But yet you sometimes stand up to her. Why cannot Britta do the same?"

I released the parking brake and shifted the car into drive.

"Please to stay, C.J."

I put the car in park and set the parking brake. "Sam, I don't know what I can do to help you. I don't know what to tell you. I guess you just have to stick it out, maybe until—"

"There are calls that come to my apartment, C.J. In the middle of the night. It is Debbe Lee—I know it, though there is no voice on the other end. Just silence, and then it is hung up. But I do not want to be afraid of her. I *will not* be afraid of her. It is hard for me, being in my homeland, and being gay. I had to fight very hard. And then I come to America. It is not supposed to be hard in America."

"I think it's hard being gay anywhere," I responded. "But it's not about you being gay, Sam. It's about your choice of a partner. Britta is simply not available, not in the way you want her to be. Not now. Who knows when, if ever?"

"I have not known love like this, C.J. Love that hurts. That aches. That pains like an open wound. I have not in my life felt pain like this."

"Never?"

Samata shook her head.

I stared at her. "Well, haven't you ever—I don't know—lost someone close to you? Maybe someone in your family?"

Samata smiled. "Years ago, when I was a child, my beloved great-grandmother died. But she had been sick for so long that my family celebrated her death. We gave our prayers and joys to the peace she was now finding."

"What about being here in America? Didn't—did you ever lose someone in your family after you came here?"

Samata shook her head. "No."

"No?"

Samata stared at me. "Why do you think this?"

I shrugged my shoulders.

"I have been very happy in America, C.J. Sometimes I have been lonely, but lonely is a temporary condition. It comes and goes. I have really been very happy. Now I am sad like I have never known before. It makes me want to do something to be rid of the sad."

"Like what?" I asked as I sucked in my breath and held it.

"Perhaps purchase airplane tickets and take Britta with me somewhere new. Somewhere that Debbe could not find us. We would be lambs."

"Huh?"

"We would be lambs. You know, being somewhere new without anyone knowing of us. Like fugitives."

"Oh! You mean that you'd be on the lam."

"Yes! Or maybe I would go to Debbe Lee and tell her to let Britta go. Tell her that she loves me, not her, and please to leave her alone so we can be happy. I wish to do something like these things. I would do anything to be with Britta. Even if it means to lose this wonderful job and leave behind my lovely friends."

I released my breath. "Well, you can't really leave L-TV, Sam. Not with your contract."

"This I know, C.J. I will not do anything that would make things difficult for you. I am a woman of honor. Perhaps this is why I find this situation so disturbing. I want to do the right thing, but there is nowhere really to find the correct answers on this."

I placed a hand on Samata's shoulder. "Maybe now isn't the right time to be involved with Britta."

"This advice is too late."

I nodded. "It appears to be. Then I don't know what to tell you, Sam. Hang in there, I guess, would be about the best I can say right now. I don't know how you do that. But you're kind of in a hopeless situation."

"That is for sure, yes?"

"Yes," I agreed as I released the parking brake and steered out of the garage.

"Well, it's about fucking time!" Chantelle shouted over the music that was blaring at Alley's after Samata and I had worked our way through the crowded maze of women towards the back table that the writers had taken over. "We thought you were both blowing us off."

"Or that maybe Samata had *murdered* you," Maria joked with a smile, her eyes showing mock horror.

I stared at Maria.

"It's a joke, C.J.," she said in response to my blank expression.

"I know that," I replied as I pushed in front of Samata and slid into the open chair next to Taylor.

Samata circled the table and sat in the chair next to Maria.

"Did you lose your sense of humor over these past few weeks, girlfriend?" Chantelle asked as she slid a clean mug across the table to me.

"What's a sense of humor?" I asked.

"It's what we all had before we signed our contracts with L-TV," Meri answered.

"I hear that!" Chantelle replied.

Meri leaned into me. "Let's see, boss. We have a pitcher of beer, a pitcher of tequila sunrise, and a pitcher of virgin sunrise—no tequila—for the preggo chick. Name your passion."

"Beer," I said as I peeled off my coat and draped it over the back of the chair.

Meri poured me a beer, then raised her mug in the air. "Everyone—a toast. To our boss, and her number one show at L-TV!"

"Hear, hear," the group responded in unison.

I raised my glass. "And to all of you, for doing so well with each of your shows."

We clinked our mugs together, then drank.

"And to Maria, who is now in her fifth month!" Chantelle declared. "You go, girl!"

"Five down, four to go!" Taylor declared.

Maria raised her glass. "I am healthy, the ultrasound shows that the baby is healthy—it's a girl, by the by—and if all goes well, I'll be giving birth around the time the TV Guide Awards are given out."

"You should name the baby T.V.," suggested Meri.

"Well, that's stupid," Taylor scoffed.

"Not if those are just her initials," Meri countered. "It would be like C.J. You could name her Teresa . . . uh . . . Vivian."

Maria stared at Meri. "You do know that I'm Latino, don't you, Meri? What kind of name is Teresa Vivian for my baby?"

"Is the sperm donor Latino?" Meri asked.

"Yes," Maria replied.

"This baby is going to be one hot mama!" Chantelle grinned.

"What do your initials stand for, C.J.?" Taylor asked.

"They don't stand for anything," I replied. "That's what my parents named me."

"Just initials?" Taylor asked.

"Not initials. It's my name."

"So you could just name the baby T.V.," Meri told Maria.

"But remember that if you do that, she will be constantly asked what the initials stand for," I added. "Believe me, I've heard that question so many times growing up—my parents heard that question so many times—that when I was young they were actually thinking about giving me names to go with the initials."

"Why didn't they?" Chantelle asked.

"Because I told them I liked C.J. I thought it sounded cool. And anyway, that was already my name. Giving me something new wasn't going to change what anyone called me."

"I haven't even thought of a name yet anyway," Maria said. "I haven't had time."

"Perhaps we could all help you to naming this child," Samata suggested.

"Aren't there baby-naming books?" Taylor asked.

"Yeah, with like a million names," Chantelle replied. "I think my sister has one lying around the apartment. I'll give it to you, Maria."

"Just don't pick Debbe," Meri said. "No matter how you spell it, just don't pick the name Debbe."

"Yes, I agree, Meri," Samata replied. "The baby would be cursed with that name."

"Speaking of cursed, how long is Britta going to be in the ladies' room?" Meri asked.

"One stall, two closed due to overflows, and a long line," Maria answered. "Trust me. She's going to be there awhile. I begged my way to the head of the line when I went. Having a big fat belly and walking like a duck has its advantages."

"I have told C.J. about Britta," Samata announced to the group.

"So what's your take on the situation, C.J.?" Meri asked.

I shrugged my shoulders. "I think Sam and Britta should be careful."

Taylor nodded. "My thoughts exactly. Who knows what Debbe might do."

"I think Sam and Britta should say, 'Screw you' to Debbe," Meri said. "Debbe can't stop them from being together."

"Well, Britta needs to officially end it with Debbe," Taylor offered. "And since she's not willing to do that—"

"She is being willing!" Samata immediately countered. "But she is being scared!"

"Of what?" Chantelle asked. "Debbe Lee's just a person. A rotten, lousy one. But she's just a person. And I agree with Meri. Relationships don't come along every day. You've waited a long time to find the woman of your dreams, Sam. You and Britta make a great couple. Debbe's just playing her games with Britta. Stand up to her, Sam."

"I disagree," I said. "I think now might not be the right time to challenge Debbe, to force her to—"

"Don't tell me you're on Debbe's side," Maria cut in.

"I'm not on her side," I answered. "I'm not on anybody's side. I just think that—"

"Sam and Britta should let themselves be pushed around, manipulated, *bullied,* by Debbe?" Maria asked.

"That's not what I'm saying," I argued.

"You can't be careful when you're in love," Chantelle said. "You're just in love. That emotion is complicated enough. But Taylor's right. Britta needs to sever the ties with Debbe."

"How is she to be doing that?" Samata asked.

"She needs to say, 'Debbe, it's over between you and me. I love Samata and I'm going to be with her,'" Maria offered.

"I can say that to Debbe," Samata said.

"It shouldn't come from you, girl," Chantelle replied. "It has to come from Britta. That way, Debbe knows that it's how Britta feels and not just how you feel."

"But she is not ready to do this thing, to make this speech," Samata answered.

"Then leave it at that and just accept it," Taylor advised. "Or just walk away from this relationship."

"This I will not do," Samata answered.

"No, you shouldn't," Maria agreed.

"Britta needs to break it off with Debbe when she's ready," I said. "Maybe now's not the right time. You know, L-TV's just getting going and Debbe's—"

"Why are you supporting Debbe?" Maria cut in. "It's as if—oh!—you're jealous, C.J. Aren't you? You're having a hard time with Debbe being involved with—"

"I am not!" I shouted, momentarily silencing the table and some of the bar's customers who were standing near us. I took a sip of my beer, then set down the mug and placed my hands on the table. "I'm sorry," I said, lowering my voice. "I didn't mean to get so defensive. I'm not jealous about Debbe wanting to be with Britta. Believe me, she cured me of that feeling by her aversion therapy technique while we were in the relationship. If anyone has a bone to pick with Debbe—if anyone would want to see Debbe's heart broken into a million pieces—it would be me. Believe me, I would. You don't know for how long after we had broken up that I prayed for Debbe to want to get back together with me—for her to realize that she loved me—just so I could break her fucking heart when she came crawling back to me."

"I hear that fantasy," Chantelle replied. "Umm, I hear that."

"But her involvement with Britta has nothing to do with love," I continued. "It's about control. It's always about control with Debbe. If Samata and Britta weren't involved, Britta would really mean nothing to her. But she can control Britta now, and that's what this is all about. And that's why I don't think it's a good idea to challenge Debbe on this or to push Britta into doing something that might be like striking a match near an open gas can."

Maria opened her mouth to offer a rebuttal, but Samata quickly put a hand on her arm to silence her and then stood up to greet Britta.

Britta met my eyes, then quickly looked away and took a seat next to Samata. Samata kissed her on the cheek, then took her hand. "I have been missing you," she said.

"Okay, lovebirds," Chantelle grinned. "You two may live for loving each other, but the rest of us are now living for industry recognition. We want people to like us—really like us. So tell us what the TV awards schedule is, C.J."

"I want at least one of us to win an Emmy," Taylor said.

"Oh, that'll be C.J., for sure," Meri replied. "*Madame President* is going to be the drama series to beat."

"Well, remember that new category—the best reality series of the year," Taylor said. "I think *One Big Happy Family* is going to go all the way."

"Thank you, Taylor," Maria smiled.

"And what of *The Body Farm?*" Samata asked.

"If no one really gets murdered, then how real is that?" Meri grinned.

"Anyone of us could be up for the new series of the year award," Chantelle offered.

"And then there's all the supporting actress and best actress awards," I added. "T-Rex could very easily win something for her role in *Can't Let Go.*"

Chantelle held up a hand with her fingers crossed. "I'm hoping, C.J."

"Just getting nominated is good enough for me," Taylor said.

"So what are the awards that we could possibly be up for?" Meri asked.

I cleared my throat. "The Golden Globes are given out at the end of January. The Emmy nominations are announced shortly thereafter. Then there's the Screen Actors Guild Awards, and the *TV Guide* Awards in early March—"

"When I'm due," Maria cut in.

"And then there's the People's Choice Awards," I continued. "The Emmys are given out in September."

"Slammin'!" Chantelle exclaimed. "We could win award after award. I guess that means I should start looking for my own place to live. I'll need room for all the awards."

"Do we be keeping our awards, C.J.?" Samata asked. "Or will the awards be going to L-TV?"

"You're the ones who run your shows," I said. "Your awards are yours, as far as I'm concerned."

"Then I'm going to sleep with my awards," Meri grinned.

"And where are all your babes going to sleep?" Taylor asked.

Meri raised her glass in the air. "I'm pleased to announce that I'm now working on my second month of celibacy, folks. And, you know, it's not all that bad."

Chantelle rolled her eyes. "Oh, yeah? Well then try it for a few years, hot stuff. Then you can tell me how you feel."

Meri took a drink, then set her mug on the table and ran her fingers up and down the outside of the glass. "It's just nice spending time with myself. It's weird, but I'm really getting to know me. I never really gave myself that chance before. I was always with someone." Meri looked around the table, then shrugged her shoulders. "Make fun of me if you want. But it's a new thing I'm trying out, and it feels pretty good so far."

Taylor clinked her glass against Meri's. "Good for you."

Meri smiled at her. "Thanks. I want . . . well . . . I'd like to have what you have with Britta, Sam. I'd like to know what it feels like to really be in love with someone. I'd like to . . . uh . . . I don't know. Be myself. And get to know someone else. So I'm kind of taking this time to get to know me. Maybe I could actually have a long-term relationship some day."

"Will someone pinch me?" Taylor asked. "Because I've got to be dreaming this."

Meri reached over and pinched Taylor on the forearm.

"Ouch!"

"See what you've been missing by not going out with us, C.J.?" Chantelle asked. "The lives and loves of the L-TV writers!"

"A new L-TV series," Taylor joked.

"Welcome back, C.J.," Meri said as she smiled at me.

I think you're all wrong about these writers, I voiced in my head to Debbe. Then I looked at Britta. *I will not tell a soul what I know,* I silently assured her.

I know you won't, C.J., I thought I heard her voice reply. *I know I can trust you.*

"*Nine* days is all I have left now, C.J.," Maria told me as we left behind the heat of the bar and walked out of Alley's back entrance into the bracing chill of the autumn night air. We headed into the parking lot behind the bar. Britta and Samata had been the first to leave earlier in the evening, followed by Taylor, who was giving Meri a ride home, and then Chantelle, who was taking the last T home. Since I had volunteered to pay for the last round of drinks and the bar had been so crowded that the waitress was taking some time to make her way to our table, Maria said she'd keep me company while I waited to pay the bill.

"Nine days?" I asked as I turned up the collar to my leather jacket and felt around in my pockets for my car keys.

"Weren't you listening to me when I was telling everyone—oh!—that's right, you were in the ladies' room then," Maria said as she hunched her shoulders and snuggled her hands deep into her coat pockets while she blew out big white puffs of air. "It's . . . a bit nippy . . . tonight, isn't it? C.J., could you slow . . . down . . . a little?"

I turned around and saw that Maria had stopped a few feet behind me. I glanced down at her belly, and she flashed me a quick smile.

"Here comes the soon-to-be mama duck, bringing up the rear," she grinned between quick exhalations of air. "I'm waddling for two now, C.J. No wonder some of the best female athletes in the world don't have any breasts. I can't imagine lugging around the extra pounds while doing an aerobic workout, let alone walk less than a hundred yards from a building to a car." She slowly walked up to me, then placed her hand on my arm. "Do you mind?" she asked. "Some of the rain from last night has frozen, and I'm afraid I might slip and fall."

I shook my head as a shiver ran down my spine at her touch. *That was the hand that took the knife that stabbed the man that— oh, shut up!* I told the voice in my head.

"Thanks, C.J. Whew! If this is how it is for me at five months, I can't imagine that I'm going to be able to walk and breathe at the same time at nine. Shortness of breath isn't supposed to really start until my seventh month."

"Just take your time," I told her. "I'm not in any hurry."

"Good."

We stood together in the chilly November night.

"Look at the stars, C.J.," Maria said as she looked up at the sky. "I think the fall is my favorite time of year in New England. Everything seems so fresh and clean."

I nodded. "I like the fall."

"Have you always lived in New England?"

"Massachusetts, born and raised. I traveled a bit after college— even lived in San Francisco for a while—but I couldn't wait to come back here. I remember sitting in a diner out there one morning after a long night of bar hopping and thinking to myself, 'I want pumpkins. I want sweet, crisp apples. I want to see the leaves change colors. And I really, really want a white Christmas.' So I gave notice at my job, made a few phone calls to line up interviews in the Boston area, packed my bags, and left two weeks later. San Francisco was beautiful—I'd go back for an extended visit in a heartbeat—but it just wasn't in my blood to become a full-timer."

"I've heard that about native New Englanders. That you miss living here so much when you're gone that you can't wait to come back."

"How do you feel about being away from Puerto Rico?"

Maria sighed. "I miss the island. It has such beauty. But it's nice to have two homes and to have enough separation between the two so that I don't feel, well . . . uncomfortable. And my family is . . . let's just say that they've never really embraced my lifestyle. Sam and I talk about that a lot—about how different things are now that we're living in America. Not that Puerto Rico isn't part of America. It's just a different way of life, a different culture there."

"Do your parents know that you're pregnant?"

Maria shook her head. "No. Eventually I'll have to tell them. They won't like it, of that I'm certain. And they'll like it even less that I'm choosing to do this on my own." Maria paused. "Or maybe they won't. Maybe if they feel I'm not trying to create a lesbian family, they'll be more accepting. But I do want to find someone, someday. Someone who can love me and my baby. Someone with whom I can make a family."

"I know. I'm sure you will."

Maria squeezed my arm. "I don't know about that, C.J. Being pregnant, or having a baby, isn't a real draw for a partner."

"Maybe not for most lesbians. But some, I'm sure, will find both you and your baby attractive. Loveable." I looked at Maria. "I think it really is true what they say about pregnant women. You've got this wonderful glow thing going on. If I can see it, then certainly other women can, too."

Maria leaned into me. "You're sweet, C.J. You always know how to say the right thing. You're always so considerate of the feelings of others."

"Oh, I don't know about that. I have my witchy-bitchy days."

"Well, I've never seen them."

"Debbe did, when we were together. But no matter how mean or nasty I tried to be to her, I could never score a hit to her heart."

"Who can?" Maria sighed. "I guess we can start walking now."

"So what's this about nine days?" I asked as we made our way slowly through the parking lot.

"Oh, that. Well, the room that I'm renting in that house I found awhile ago—it seems I have to be out in nine days. Wait. What time is it?"

I turned my arm and glanced down at my watch. "It's past one."

"Then I only have eight days left. The woman who owns the house has a big family, and I guess they're all coming to stay with her over the holidays. She says that one of them might even move in with her, and so she's going to need the room back. She was nice about it, but she really didn't give me much notice. I only found out about this two weeks ago, and I've been looking around for a similar situation since. But I can't find anything. And I can't afford an apartment right now. I'm spending most of my paycheck each week putting baby things on layaway. And anyway, I'm going to have to find somewhere else to live once I have my baby. A room in someone's house just isn't going to do when that happens. But I'm getting ahead of myself. I wanted to ask . . . well . . . the reason I brought this up to you . . . you see, I was wondering if—aw, hell, C.J. I'll just come right out and ask. Could I take you up on your offer to stay at your house? I really hate to ask this of you, and I'll understand if you say no. But Taylor and Meri both have studios. Samata has Britta staying with her all the time. And Chantelle's living with her sister and her kids. Chantelle said maybe we could look for a place together once I have the baby, but I really don't think she wants to live with anyone, and she's certainly had her share of sharing a place with another person's children. My feeling is that after the first of the year, she's going to start looking for a place of her own. She says she just wants peace and quiet and to not feel like she's got to take care of anyone else, which I totally understand." Maria stopped, then turned to face me. "But I'm stuck, C.J. Plain and simple. I wouldn't ask you this if I felt I had other options. I promise I won't be a burden to you. I can have this baby on my own. I won't put you through having to deal with me and a baby living in your house. I just need a place now.

And for the next couple of months, maybe. And then I'll move out."

"I don't think you should say you'll move into my house and then a short time later move out. Doesn't that sound a little silly?"

She turned away from me and started walking. We concentrated on working our way slowly over a small patch of black ice.

"I don't have much, C.J. I mean in the way of furniture. So it's not like a moving van would be pulling up to your house or I'd be trying to fit a bunch of stuff into your place. What little I have is in storage. I'll just keep everything there but my bed. Where I'm staying now is furnished. And I won't disrupt your life. I think you said I could stay in the basement, and that's where I'd stay. I'd have to use the kitchen, maybe. Or I could get a hot plate and just heat up stuff I need downstairs. If there's a bathroom, then—"

"Maria—"

"I'll pay you, too, C.J. I can't pay much more than what I'm paying now for the room. I know your basement is probably much bigger than my room is. But I could do things around the house. Help you out."

I stopped and turned to her. "Like what would you do? Build me a stone wall out in front of the house? Sheetrock an addition? Put on a new roof? Slap on a fresh coat of house paint? Maria, I don't want you to do *anything* around the house. For God's sake, you're pregnant."

"That doesn't mean I can't do things, C.J."

"Well, you seem to be having a hard time walking and breathing at the same time."

"Okay, there's that," Maria agreed. "So maybe I'm not going to set any world records vacuuming or . . . or replacing your roof or repaving your driveway. But I can do some other things. I can cook. Can I ever cook, too! I can make anything. I love working with vegetables and cheeses. I eat very healthy now—no Big Macs or greasy pizza pies."

"Maria—"

"And I'm quiet, C.J. I don't play loud music. I don't talk on the phone a lot. At night I watch a little television and read. Mostly I've been reading my baby books. *What to Expect When You're Expecting* and stuff like that. It's amazing how many books there are on the subject. You'd think women just started having babies a few years ago, like this was some sort of new trend or something, and now all these—"

"Maria—"

"And I've talked to the writers about this, C.J. About my asking you if I could take you up on your offer. They think it would be a good idea. I thought, you know, that they might have a problem if I moved in with you. Like they might think I'd get special attention or something from you at the office. But they were absolutely fine—"

"Maria, could you please shut up for a minute?"

"Sorry, C.J. Okay. I understand that—"

"Yes."

"Yes?"

"Yes. Yes, Maria, you can move in with me whenever you'd like. You can come and go as you please. You can even take your stuff out of storage, because there's nothing down there now in my basement except my free weights and a small workbench. But there's carpeting on the floor, it's dry and warm, and it's not so far underground that you don't get nice light from the windows."

"Are you sure?"

"I'm sure."

"Really?"

"Really."

"Oh, C.J., this is so great! I'm so happy!"

"There's only one thing I request."

"Yes, yes. I can pay you."

"No, you're not paying me. No money. I don't like money being exchanged between friends."

"But I don't want to—"

"However," I interrupted her. "I will take you up on your offer to cook. You can be the house chef. I haven't had a home-cooked meal since I visited my parents last Christmas. Unless you count peanut butter and Fluff sandwiches, scrambled eggs, or heat-until-the-cheese-is-bubbly frozen meals."

"C.J., I will be an awesome cook for us! Thank you, thank you, thank you!" Maria threw her arms around my shoulders and gave me a hug.

A spicy, exotic scent, mixed with stale cigarette smoke from the bar, filled my nostrils, and Maria's long, dark hair tickled the end of my nose. I felt the hardness of her belly pressed against mine and immediately pulled out of her grasp.

"I'm sorry," I said as I reached down to lay a palm on her belly.

Maria smiled. "I won't break, C.J." Then she slid her arms across my shoulders, turned her head, and nestled her body against mine. "Thank you, C.J. I can finally relax now."

A thousand questions raced through my mind, all shouting out at the same time, but I wasn't paying attention to any of them. Instead, my eyes wandered up to the sky. I saw the Big Dipper shining down upon us, and I slowly released a smile.

"So what ya be wantin' me ta do here, I'm gatherin', is ta make this here space liveable and comfy, right?" The muscle-bound, rough-and-gruff woman who was the host of L-TV's *I. M. Hammered* home improvement show—a bull dyke whose real name was Betty Larson but who had been known to deliver a knockout punch to anyone who called her Betty and not by her nickname, Lars—stood in the middle of my basement, surveying the nearly empty space. A cigarette was propped behind a multi-pierced ear, while a lit one dangled from her lips.

"Yes, I'd like this to be very homey," I told her. "Maria Hernandez will be moving in—maybe this week. I know that doesn't give you much time, but—"

"Time ain't the problem, C.J. You tell me ya need a new house built for ya, and I'll have it up and runnin' just like that," she said as she snapped her fingers together so loudly I jumped at the sound. "I'm jus' thinkin'—and stay with me on this one, will ya—that ya got a pregnant chick comin' ta live here, right? She's 'bout ready ta pop, so I'm thinkin' she's gonna want a place for the crib and stuff. Right?"

"Well, I actually hadn't thought that far ahead. She just has to be out of the current place she's living by the end of—"

"See, so here's what I'm thinkin'," Lars continued. "Ya got this here big open space, right?"

"Right," I agreed. "And the free weights can move—"

"Button up, C.J., 'cuz I'm accountin' for them weights. But just as an aside, so ta speak, you ain't really doin' much with that amount a weight on them bars. But hey, you're just a writer sittin' at a desk. The way I understand it, writers don't even hafta lift pieces a paper no more or crank 'em 'round in a typewriter. I mean, that's at least some small form a exercise, right? But computers is takin' over the world. Takin' it over, I say. Now me. I'm lifting bags a concrete and cartin' two-bys up ladders day in, day out. So I'm hearin' ya 'bout the damn dinky weights, okay?"

I started to open my mouth to reply, but thought better of it and just nodded my head in response.

"Right. So's the way I'm seein' it here, I'm gonna build ya a separate *room* for them weights. So's you don't go disturbin' the chick and the little chicklet when it comes. Babies need their sleep, y'know, and you can't be just clangin' the weights without givin' no thought to that."

"Well, a room would certainly be—"

Lars slapped a measuring tape in my hands and pointed to a corner of the basement. "Go on over there and measure that wall."

I went to where she had pointed.

"Mark off ten feet, then go out 'bout another ten."

I did what she told me to do.

"Good. Now that there's gonna be your workout area. Long as them little bitty weights is all ya got and ya don't go gettin' no treadmill or nothing—I mean, is that the stupidest thing going yet? Just walk the fuck out the door and get yourself some fresh air. And don't get me started on them stationary bikes. If somethin' has

132

wheels, then it's meant ta move, right? But fools just sit on 'em and don't fuckin' go nowhere."

"Yeah, they are pretty—"

"Anyway, that there space'll suit ya just fine for your little work-out do-das. Now, for the rest of this here area. I'm gonna take that half-bath and make it inta a full bath, with a shower-bathtub combo. A stall's just not gonna do for a pregnant mom. They like their baths and they get tired a standin'. Their back aches 'n stuff. Take it from me. My sister popped out one, then twins, just like the governor. And if you thought Swifty was the size of a house before she had her twins, then my sister was a fuckin' *development*. Anyway, then I'm gonna put up a half-wall, like a divider, y'know, 'bout here," she said as she pointed. "That'll separate a bedroom area from a little den-like area for Maria. She can watch her TV here. You might wanna get her a nice rocker for the den. Mothers love ta rock. And this window here. I'm gonna make it bigger and longer—you got the room—so's she can have some natural light and not feel like she's in a dungeon. And right there's where I'm gonna put a door for her own entrance. It'll be a slider. That'll give her more light. And then here," Lars said as she strode to the bedroom area she had just described, "I'm gonna make like a little nursery arrangement. I'm gonna put a nice guide in the ceiling and hang a long drape for privacy for her little tyke, so she's can make it dark for the baby to take a nap."

"Well, that really sounds nice, Lars."

"Course it does," she said as she snorted air in, cleared her throat, then wiped her nose with the back of her hand. "Now, ya can't put no full kitchen down here, less ya wanna go file papers with the damn zoning board and try to duke out an in-law apartment with 'em. A bunch a fools, all-a them. And from what I know 'bout this hoity-toity little town a yours, they're bein' particular 'bout stuff like that. I doubt it'll be worth your effort. But ya can get Maria a mid-size fridge and a microwave and a little hot plate—I'll build ya a shelf and update your 'lectrical to accommodate them things—and she'll be as snug as a bear in a den in the winta."

"This all sounds great, Lars, but remember that she's moving in by the end of—"

"C.J., I know when you tol' me she's movin' in. I can *hear* what you're tellin' me. I'm tellin' ya what I can *do* with that there time frame. Now, ya give me more time, and I can do fancy moldings and such, but ya ain't doin' that, are ya? So I'm gonna give ya what I'm tellin' ya. I got a crew that's just dyin' ta do another job 'fore the holidays and the bills start pilin' up. You happy with my estimate?"

"Yes, but I didn't think it included everything you're—"

"C.J., I *base* an estimate on what I'm gonna do. I ain't gonna screw ya. Now, I gotta get goin' with this job here so's everythin' can be ready. Get the hell outta here, let me work, and I'll let ya know when you can come down. Okay?"

I nodded my head. "That's fine. Whatever you—"

"Oh, and brew a big pot a coffee and just give me the whole damn thing. And I don't want none a that vanilla bean or hazelfuck crap. Just give it to me hot, black, and strong. Long 'bout noon, I want six large pizzas with the works and a case a Coke. No diet or caffeine-free hoo-ha. Just the real fuckin' thing. And at 'bout five, we want Kentucky Fried dinners. The family-size portions, too. And none a that cole slaw. Vegetables are a waste a time, and don't get me started on vegetarians. Or them damn PETA people who go 'round saying don't fish 'cuz the little fishies feel the pain of a hook. Yeah, right. When a damn trout goes flippin' and floppin' inta a card shop ta buy a Hallmark 'cuz it's got so damn much feelin', then I'll maybe think 'bout givin' up my cabin in the woods in Maine. Hey, you like venison? 'Cuz every year I go up ta Maine and try to bag me a buck. I'll give ya some meat next time I do."

"Well, I don't think I've ever—"

"Anyways, 'bout the Kentucky Fried. Bag the slaw. Get a double order a mashers, double up too on them buns, 'n gravy for six. And then we like a gallon a milk each. Don't even try to get us that two percent watered down cow syrup. We want whole, or nothin'. If we had our way, we'd suck it right outta the cow's teats. That'll take us through the night. I bet you think we're eatin' like fuckin' pigs, but on a job like this, we actually lose weight. Keep the eats and drinks goin' on this schedule, and there won't be no problems. Hop to it, now. Time's a wastin'."

Two days later, while I was making the noontime six-pizza-and-case-of-Coke delivery to Lars and her crew, I surveyed the basement in astonishment. Already the space had been transformed into a luxury apartment. I made a slow, full circle, taking in the paneled walls, new windows, and slider to the backyard.

"Now don't go freakin' out on me, C.J., 'cuz we're not there yet," Lars shouted over the sound of hammering and power-sawing from her crew.

"Lars, this is amazing!" I yelled at her.

"Oh, fuck," she replied in a booming voice. "This here's still a mess."

I shook my head. "I disagree. This is incredible!"

"Hey, shut the fuck up!" Lars bellowed over the noise. Hammering and sawing immediately silenced. "Come 'n get your grub. Take it outside so's ya don't go making any more of a mess in here. And take a pile a them napkins with yous as well."

Lars' crew, which consisted of five hard-bodied lesbians, obediently lined up single file, took a pizza and two Cokes each, flashed me quick, shy nods and mumbled thanks, and then exited through the slider.

"And close the fuckin' door behind you. You ain't livin' in no barn!"

Lars looked at me and shook her head. "Ya try ta teach 'em a little class, but it's a losin' battle, I tell ya." She lifted the top of the remaining pizza box that I held in my arms, then opened her mouth and engulfed a half of a slice down her throat. She chewed a few times, then swallowed. "Ya hired the best, C.J. But then, you know that. Like everyone else does now, too. I love my show on L-TV—don't get me wrong—but it takes me away from this, y'know? I like doin' the jobs more than describin' 'em. And some a the things I do on the show, well, they ain't really my cuppa tea, if you catch my drift. I mean, ya gotta give the people what they want, right? But them gay boys is all wantin' to add stupid stuff to their homes. Leave it up to the homos to need things for their damn curios. 'I need a little space for my antique tea cups,' " Lars said in a high-pitched, lispy voice as she waved a limp hand in the air. " 'Can you show me how to build *a cabana* for my swimming pool? I need a wet bar. What can I do to display my blown-glass paper-weight collection?' " Lars snorted. "I need, I need, I need. And the chicks all want hot tubs or *li-brar-ies*," Lars enunciated with a sneer. "But if I had my druthers, I'd be buildin' all the time. Construction's funny, though. Ya can't depend on it. Ya go from bein' busy beyond belief ta comin' to a screechin' halt. That's when I'd be hittin' the beers. Hittin' the beers big time. Give up the beers, though, and then what d'ya got ta do with your time? Jus' sit 'round feelin' sorry for yourself. That's when I met Debbe Lee, and we started talkin' 'bout the show. She saved my butt, that woman did. Give me some business, too, 'til tapin' of the show started and I could start gettin' a paycheck. She said as long as I could stay off the booze, she'd keep me on at L-TV. Has it written in my contract to keep me clean 'n sober, and I've done that. Go off the wagon, though, and I'm out on the streets. She's a hard-talker, that girl. Tough. I like 'em tough. She's a fighter, she is. Don't take no lip from no one."

"Well, she's certainly—"

"Anyways, I can't stand around here listening ta you go on all day, C.J.," Lars cut in. "Not if I'm gonna keep on schedule. Thanks for the grub. Now get the hell outta here."

When I pulled into the driveway a few days later after work, with bags and boxes of Kentucky Fried dinners stashed in my back-seat and all the windows open despite the chilly night air so I could keep the nauseating greasy smell out of my nostrils, Lars' van and the beat-up pickup trucks of her workers were gone. I pressed the garage door button, waited for it to rise, then drove into the space. I hefted the dinners into my arms and walked into the kitchen.

On the counter was a stack of receipts. Next to it was Lars' neatly typed invoice, citing the estimated price she had given me, and a handwritten note.

C.J.

We're done. As you can see. Here's my invoice for the work. I also need payment for the receipts. Them's for the appliances and stuff. I just went ahead and bought em, cuz Maria said go ahead and buy em. She says she'll pay me, but I don't want her to. I think you should. SHE'S GONNA HAVE HER HANDS FULL WITH TAKING CARE OF HER BABY!!!! And I also checks with her and found out about where she's storing her stuff. Figured she shouldn't be carrying nothing big and such, so my crew's and I went and got the stuff and brung it here for her. The receipt for the storage fee is there, too. PAY THAT!!!! We set it all up, kind of home like, but you need and help her move it where she wants it. SHE'S NOT SUPPOSED TO LIFT NOTHING!!!!! Don't make her do that. Recommend me to your friends, would ya? I left ya my business cards. Okay. That's all. DON'T LET HER LIFT NOTHING!!!! And if you ever want to lift more weight and get some muscles on that thin body a yours, call me. I ain't going to charge ya. IT'S FREE ADVICE!!!!

Lars

P.S. I also put a safety bar in the shower. SHE NEEDS THAT!!!! But don't tell her it's a handicapped bar. It's what it's really called, but she ain't handicapped and pregnant chicks take offense whenever you say that. IT'S A SAFETY BAR!!!!

P.P.S. Tell Maria that there rocking chair in her living room is hers. I been making that awhile ago and don't have no need for it. IT'S HERS, NOT YOURS!!!!

P.P.P.S. I have a friend at the phone company that installed the phone jack downstairs for Maria.
YOU'RE ALL SET!!!!

I went outside, dumped the fried dinners into a trash barrel, then flicked on the lights in the kitchen, the living room, and the dining room as I made my way to the basement door.

The smell of fresh-cut lumber wafted up as soon as I opened the door. I walked down the stairs, then flicked on the light switch at the bottom of the steps.

Track lighting illuminated a basement that had been transformed by Lars and her crew into a luxurious living space. Empty chest-high bookcases lined the living room, designed to form a separation between the living room and the bedroom, where Maria's bed, end tables, and lamps had been set up by Lars' crew. They had also built a breakfast bar and then laid a wide strip of linoleum between the bar and the sink to make a separate kitchen area. The refrigerator had been plugged in and was humming invitingly. A new microwave was set up on the marble countertop, with a packet of instructions and warranty information next to it. Behind the sink were rows of elegant Spanish tiles that served as a back splash. Open shelves were placed low above the countertop for kitchen supplies, and Lars had built a spice rack and a wooden pantry for dry and canned goods. Cardboard boxes of varying sizes, each marked KITCHEN, were tucked into a corner.

I stepped out of the kitchen and walked into the living room. In the center was a rocking chair with a red bow stuck on it. Other pieces of furniture were neatly arranged. I surveyed the area, then touched a button on the wall near the sliding door. An outdoor floodlight went on, revealing a sloped brick path that led to the door from the backyard. Small accent lights lined each side of the path.

I switched off the outside light, then walked into the bathroom. New off-white tiles gleamed, reflecting off a large mirror over the sink that was lit by halogen bulbs. There was an oversized medicine cabinet and large towel rack next to the sink.

The new bathtub and shower sparkled.

I considered taking over the space myself and letting Maria move into the rest of the house.

I walked back into the living room, then ran my fingers over the back of the rocking chair. I tried to picture Maria sitting in the chair. I imagined her slowly rocking back and forth while holding her baby in her arms. Maybe she would be singing a soft lullaby to her. Maybe she would be gazing out at the backyard while the baby nuzzled gently at her breast. Maria's long dark hair would be—

I sucked in a quick breath of air and suddenly realized that I had been holding my breath. I drew my hand back from the chair, extinguished the lights, and then exited the basement.

After I had finished my heat-until-the-cheese-is-bubbly, serving-for-one dinner, I lit a fire in the fireplace, sat in a wing chair, and picked up my copy of the book *What to Expect When You're Expecting*. Samata had presented all the writers with copies of the book earlier in the week, at the conclusion of one of our meetings, because, as she had told us, "We must to know what Maria is to be going through. And we must to also be supporting her, and we can only do this by reading about her being with child."

Chantelle had taken one look at the book and sniffed, "Been there, done that. Thanks but no thanks, Sam. I've been through this enough times with my sister. I could've written the book myself."

Samata had looked hurt at Chantelle's comment. "But every woman is to be different," she argued. "I have read of this in here."

Maria took the book from Samata and said to Chantelle, "I know it's probably too much for me to ask you, but I was wondering if you'd attend childbirth class with me. I really don't want to go alone, and since you seem to know so much about—"

Chantelle had immediately raised her hand to silence Maria and then held out her hand for the book. "I mean, I don't know *everything,*" she said. "And I'd be honored to go to class with you, girl. It's just that my sister doesn't need any more kids. Hell, I don't even think she wants the ones that she has. And sometimes I think she resents how much I help her, how much she needs me to help her. But you really want yours, Maria, and I'll help you in any way I can. Just don't start calling me Dad, okay?"

Samata had beamed. "So this is to be good now," she said. "We will all understand. And now I volunteer Britta and myself to organize a shower."

"And I'll boil water," Meri chimed in with a grin.

"What can I do?" Taylor asked.

"You can deliver the baby," Meri answered.

Taylor shook her head. "No way. I'll babysit then. After all the blood is gone."

"You do know about diapers and spit-ups, right?" Chantelle asked.

"I'll help Sam and Britta organize the shower," Taylor quickly answered.

I had started reading the book one night as I was eating dinner, and I soon discovered that there was much in the book that wasn't meant to be combined with digestion. Each chapter that detailed the nine months of pregnancy outlined physical and emotional symptoms an expectant mother might experience, and as time progressed in a pregnancy I found some of the symptoms to be a bit unsettling. I read about nausea and vomiting, vaginal discharges that were described in great detail, with frightening names like leukorrhea, a seemingly endless state of constipation, flatulence, and bloating, occasional nosebleeds, leaking from the breasts, and hemorrhoids. I had pushed away my half-eaten dinner that night and questioned why anyone in their right mind would willingly get pregnant.

But once I had made eating dinner a separate activity from educating myself about Maria's pregnancy, the book had made for pretty interesting reading. The more I read, the more I marveled at how Maria could go into work each day and, too, work in such a stressful job, launching a new series on a new venture cable network. I was amazed at Maria's ability to hold herself together despite all of the emotional and physical pressures of the job.

But then again, women did this all the time, didn't they? I had asked myself.

Just not in my house, I had answered.

"**Ten** people are coming here for dinner?" I asked Maria as I surveyed my dining room table, which she had set earlier in the day in preparation for our Thanksgiving dinner tomorrow. A dried flower arrangement graced the center of the table, adding festive fall colors of yellow, burnt orange, and maple-leaf red. Candlesticks flanked the arrangement and, at each place setting, forks, spoons, and knives of two sizes rimmed both corners of a stoneware plate. "This table looks nice, Maria. But ten? I thought it was just going to be the writers. And that we'd just eat in the living room. In front of the football games."

"It's Thanksgiving, C.J. Not a nacho party."

"Okay. But ten?"

"Sam asked Britta to dinner, of course," Maria replied from the kitchen, where she was heating chopped onions in a skillet.

I watched Maria as she stirred the skillet with a wooden spoon. She had moved into the basement a little over a week ago, thoroughly impressed with the arrangement Lars had created for her and then overwhelmed with guilt when I repeatedly refused her insistence that she pay rent.

"But C.J., don't you know what a living space this size would cost me to rent in your town?" she had asked.

"I don't know, and I don't want to know," I had answered.

We had argued back and forth for hours. But once she had reconfirmed that the only payment for living in my basement would be to cook for us, she had asked me to carry her kitchen boxes upstairs and had outfitted my kitchen with a multitude of cooking utensils, mixing bowls, and other appliances that I never knew were integral to making great meals.

Since then, we had shared breakfasts and dinners together and had fallen into a comfortable and pleasant routine of commuting back and forth to work in one vehicle, now that we had several episodes of our shows in the can and wouldn't resume taping new shows until the new year. We got up early and lingered over breakfast, sharing the *Boston Globe,* and then enjoyed dinners she had prepared. After dinner, we sometimes took a walk together around the neighborhood if the weather was nice. Then I'd throw a few logs in the fireplace and we'd settle into the living room and listen to music and read until we went to bed.

We got along great, enjoying each other's company outside the office. Initially our conversations had been about work and people at the office, but then we had started conversing as friends. I shared things from my life and I learned more about hers, and one morning I woke up and realized that I no longer cared about the things Debbe had revealed to me about Maria or any of the other writers.

The heat from the stove top rose in steaming wisps, and Maria's face was flushed. She had clipped her long hair back from her face, but a few strands danced in front of her eyes.

"What?" she asked as she looked up and met my eyes.

"Nothing."

"Nothing?"

"Well, you've got that pregnant woman's glow thing going on."

"Oh, for God's sake, C.J., I have a hot kitchen glow going on. Not everything is about my pregnancy, you know. And I wish you'd stop reading that book. Lately that's all you've been doing. Now stop staring at me and see if you can find those folding chairs you said you have in the garage."

"I will. That's on my list of things to do. So Britta's going to come tomorrow?"

"That's what Sam told me. I guess Debbe has other plans. Or maybe Britta came up with a good enough excuse so Debbe didn't push it with her. At any rate, they'll both be here."

"Well, that'll be nice for them to be together for the holiday."

"I guess. But Britta really needs to break it off with Debbe. She's still going back and forth between Sam and Debbe."

"I know. But that's not going to be easy for her."

"Still, she should. Debbe's been talking up some trip she wants Britta to make with her, to some time-share she has in Aspen."

"Ah. I remember Aspen. Nice town house. Great skiing. Expensive shops. But too many sexy snow bunnies in tight jump-suits for Debbe to look at. Which, of course, she did the entire time we were there. I was just one snowflake in an avalanche of competition."

"Yeah, well, Britta does not want to go. And Samata wants her to go even less."

"How's Britta going to get out of that?"

Maria shrugged her shoulders. "All hell will break loose at some point, I'm sure. Sam is getting more and more nudgie about the whole thing. And you know that Chantelle is bringing T-Rex, right?"

"Seriously? She's going to bring Miss Buff, star of her show, who was just on the cover of *Entertainment Weekly*, to *my* house?"

"Yes. They apparently have started dating," Maria said as she began chopping vegetables on a cutting board.

"Dating?"

Maria nodded. "To quote Chantelle, 'You've got that right, girl-friend.' They went out for coffee, did movies one night, dinner out another time."

"Really? And so how is it going?"

"Well, Chantelle's walking around on a cloud, even though she tells me it's just a casual thing. That she doesn't want to get involved with anyone right away, after being single for so long. But you can see it in her eyes, C.J. She's smitten."

"So have they, you know—"

"Slept together?"

"Yeah."

"Not yet. But Chantelle tells me T-Rex kisses better than anyone she's ever been with."

"Well, she does have those full, lovely lips."

"And a lot more," Maria grinned.

"I'll say," as I cupped my hands beneath my breasts. "Hubba hubba. You'll have to find out if they're real from Chantelle, when she gets to second base."

"Oh, they're real."

"Really? Wow! And so how do you think T-Rex feels about our Chantelle?"

"From what I understand, she's on the same cloud as Chantelle."

"Good for them! So we have you, me, Sam and Britta, Chantelle and T-Rex, Meri, Taylor—"

"And Taylor's ex."

I turned away from the table and walked into the kitchen. "Taylor's ex? I thought she had nipped in the bud that request to get back together a week ago."

"Hand me that loaf of bread, would you, C.J.?" Maria asked as she rubbed dried herbs between her palms and sprinkled them into the skillet.

I picked up the loaf from the counter and handed it to her. "The last I heard—well, didn't Taylor say that she had told her ex that she didn't want to get back together after all the e-mails and then the phone calls?"

Maria nodded. "Can you believe it? Taylor waits around for this woman to change her mind and come back to her, but she rebuffs Taylor time and again. And now Taylor's over her—way over her—and out of the blue begs her to get back. 'It was all a big mistake,' she tells her." Maria let out a quick snort. "Like we've never heard that line before."

"So I assume her ex got dumped by the woman she had left Taylor for."

"Same old story, isn't it?" Maria asked as she started to slice the bread into cubes. "But get this. Now Alana, Taylor's ex, says she's willing to move to Boston to start over with her. In fact, she hopped on a plane and flew out here a couple of days ago so she could talk to Taylor face-to-face. She's staying at some hotel in Boston. Remember how Taylor told us that she had relocated from Chicago to New York just to be with Alana? Taylor's feeling like Alana has never been this serious with her before, saying she'd leave her life in New York behind for Taylor. But it's too little, too late, is what Taylor says. The woman broke her heart into pieces, and is now saying anything to get Taylor back."

"So why is she invited to this dinner?"

Maria picked up a wooden spoon and stirred the vegetables that she had dumped into the skillet. "That was Taylor's idea, thanks to Meri. Taylor kept telling Alana no, that they couldn't get back together. Right? But Alana kept asking why. Taylor kept telling her why. Because you were a shit. Because you were an asshole. Because you cheated on me. Because you broke my heart. Et cetera. But Alana kept yeah-buting her with everything she said. 'Yeah but, that was just a fling. Yeah but, I felt our relationship wasn't going anywhere at the time and we weren't happy together.' Yeah but, yeah but, yeah but. Finally, Meri says to Taylor, 'Why don't you just tell her that you've fallen in love with someone else? That you're not interested in getting back together because you have someone in your life now and you're not willing to end that relationship.' "

"Okay," I said as I picked up a few bread cubes and popped them in my mouth. "That's a plan, except—"

"Right. Except Alana then said, 'Well, who is this person?' when Taylor told her. 'Can I meet her? Can I see who my competition is?

If I see you and her together and I see with my own eyes that your heart is taken by someone else, then I'll get back on that plane and never bother you again.' "

I reached out for more bread cubes, but Maria immediately slapped my hand lightly. "Do you want your stuffing now, or at dinner tomorrow?"

I looked around the kitchen at the bowls and plates that were filled with food in various stages of preparation. "You're telling me we're not going to have enough food for ten if I take three more cubes of bread?"

"That's not the point, C.J.," Maria said as she wiped her hands on her apron and turned to face me. "I want you to taste the best, the most awesome turkey stuffing in the world. All you're doing is eating bread. But woman, when you taste my stuffing, you will regret that you even thought to eat one cube of bread that could've instead melted in your mouth as Hernandez' infamous stuffing."

I rolled my eyes, then grabbed a handful of bread cubes and tossed them at her.

Maria picked up the wooden spoon and waved it playfully in front of my face. "You play with your food now, C.J., and you will not sit at that magnificent table eating what I have prepared. I will force you to sit outside and eat one of your heat-up dinners."

"Okay, okay. So who is Taylor bringing to the dinner to make google eyes with so Alana will leave her alone?"

"Meri."

I stared at Maria. "Taylor and Meri are going to pretend they're an item? Oh, this should be interesting. They get along like cats and dogs as it is."

"Which only will serve to cement a relationship in Alana's eyes, don't you think? I mean, how many relationships do you know started out from the words, 'Oh, I can't stand that person. There's no way I'd *ever* be with her.' "

"That's true."

"So, C.J., we'll all have to play along with this charade."

"Alrighty then. Meri and Taylor are together. Not for real, but we're going to pretend they are. Because we want Alana out of the picture. For real. T-Rex and Chantelle are an item—does everyone know about that?"

"Yes."

"Okay. And Britta and Sam are celebrating their first holiday together. Oh, honey, isn't it great when the kids come home?"

Maria laughed. "Yes, dear. They do grow up so fast though, don't they?"

I held up my hands. "So we've got you, me, Sam, Britta, Chantelle, T-Rex, Taylor, Taylor's ex, Meri." I counted out the names with my fingers. "Wait. That's only nine."

"And I invited Betty."

"Betty who?"

"Betty Larson."

"Lars? You call Lars Betty?"

"Of course I do. That's her name."

"Yeah, but—"

"But you can't call her that. I know. I don't know why she lets me."

"Maybe she likes you."

"Maybe she does."

"Do you like her?"

Maria turned down the heat on the burner and then placed her hands on her hips as she faced me. "Oh, yeah, C.J. I like my women to be manly. Rough and gruff and tough is what I'm looking for. Why do you think I moved in with you? When I heard you were lifting weights in your basement, I couldn't wait to get over here so I could see just how butch you were."

I raised an arm, pulled up the sleeve to my sweater, and flexed a muscle.

Maria batted her eyelashes at me. "Oh my, C.J. Please stop. You are making me so hot. I am on fire."

I lowered my sleeve and grinned. "Maybe that's why Lars built me a separate workout room in the basement. So you wouldn't see me flexing my big muscles and go ga-ga over me instead of her."

"She really is a pussy cat, you know?"

"Lars? A pussy cat?"

"She's sweet," Maria said as she took handfuls of the bread cubes and tossed them into a large bowl.

"Have you seen the way she eats? We might not have enough food to fill her belly."

Maria turned to me with a smile on her face. "My goodness, C.J., I think you're *jealous* of Betty. But you've had your chances with me, woman." Maria stepped towards me and raised one eyebrow. "I wait alone in my bed at night, *hoping* and *praying* that you'll come down those basement stairs and take me in your arms. That you'll lift me up out of bed and onto your white steed, and we'll go galloping off into the sunset."

I chuckled. "Obviously you're not reading your pregnancy book but immersing yourself in romance novels instead."

"Obviously. I can't remember the last time I made love. So I can only fantasize about it through the pages of novels. But now, just think, I finally have the woman of my dreams, my muscular bull dyke who even made me my very own rocking chair."

I put my face close to Maria's and began to chant, "Betty and Maria, sitting in a tree—"

"Don't go there, C.J., or I'll have to sit on you. And my weight class is rapidly changing from lightweight to heavyweight."

Later on that night, after Maria and I had had an early dinner together and then sat in front of the fireplace reading before Maria had said she was tired and going downstairs, I went down to the basement to retrieve the folding chairs from the garage.

The lights were on when I descended the stairs.

"Maria? Are you up?"

"Yes."

"Is it okay if I get the folding chairs now?" I asked as I rounded the corner at the bottom of the stairs.

"Sure."

I looked around the living room area, then saw Maria lying on the floor. Her hips were turned to one side and her knees bent towards her chest. "Are you okay?"

"I have a bit of a backache. I think I did too much standing today while I was cooking."

"Is there anything I can do?"

"I'd love a backrub, especially on my lower back, but I don't know how to do that. I obviously can't lie on my stomach for very long. Maybe if you could just rub here," she said as she placed a hand on her hip. "Do you mind?"

"Not at all," I said. "That's what the book—"

"I know the book says that backaches are common at five months," Maria snapped, then paused. "Sorry, C.J. I'm just . . . my body is just becoming a bit foreign to me."

"That's okay," I said as I kneeled on the floor next to her. I placed my hands on her hip and began to slowly knead her hip muscle. "How's that?"

Maria closed her eyes. "Nice. Yes. That's nice. I'm sure that will help."

I massaged her hip slowly, pressing my fingertips into her nightgown. "I don't think I want you doing anything else tomorrow," I said. "Let me take care of everything. You can just sit in a chair and direct me."

"Most everything's ready," she murmured. "I just have to stuff the bird early tomorrow morning. You can help me do that. We have a big bird."

"I know."

"It will be a nice dinner, C.J."

I smiled. "I'm sure it will. I'm really looking forward to it."

"Me, too. I haven't had a big Thanksgiving dinner for quite awhile."

"Me neither."

I continued massaging her hip and lower back for a few minutes. "Do you want me to massage your other hip now?"

151

Maria nodded, then slowly opened her eyes. "I need to turn over. Can you help me?" She reached up and threw an arm around my shoulder, then lifted her upper body towards me.

I ran my hand across her swollen belly, then behind her back, and gently pulled her towards me.

Maria turned her body first to lay on her back, then stopped.

I looked down at her.

Maria tightened her grip on my shoulders and locked eyes with me.

I stopped breathing as I looked into her deep brown eyes.

Maria reached up with her other arm and gently touched my face with the palm of her hand.

I moved the hand I had placed behind her back up her body, ascended her back, and then placed it on her shoulder. My fingertips touched her hair, then began to play with a few strands.

Maria took a breath in, then pulled me down to her as she rested her back on the floor.

My lips touched hers lightly, making a gentle contact that caused a surge of energy to journey from my toes to the back of my head. My fingers traveled to her neck and stroked her soft skin. I breathed in, then pressed my lips against hers.

Maria responded with the same pressure against my lips, then pulled my shoulders down so my chest touched hers. She opened her mouth, and my tongue met hers.

We groaned at the same time.

I lowered my body so it laid against hers. She ran her fingers through my hair as I let her tongue explore my mouth. Then I chased her tongue with mine and slowly slid it into her mouth.

I tasted peppermint and some other flavor, a flavor that I slowly sucked into my mouth. Maria ran her hands across my shoulders, then up and down my back. I lowered my hand to her neck, to the top of her breastbone, then slowly searched for a breast. My hand cupped over her fullness, and she placed one of her hands on top of mine and pressed my hand into her. I felt the hardness of her nipple against the palm of my hand.

Maria moaned and raised her hips towards me, and my knee fell between her legs. I pressed my hips against her thigh and began to breathe harder. She started to move against me, and I matched her rhythm, a slow pressure that tightened my stomach muscles. I groaned again, and she responded to the sound by increasing her rhythm against me.

Our lips parted as we began breathing harder. We opened our eyes and looked at each other.

"Your kiss . . ." she breathed.

"Yours," I answered, then kissed her again.

We slowly ended the kiss.

"I was just coming down here to get the chairs," I whispered between breaths.

"I was just stretching out my back," she replied.

"Maybe I should get the chairs."

"You could."

"I could. Is that what you want me to do?"

"Is that what you want to do?"

"I don't know. I like this."

"I like this, too."

"Maria, you are so beautiful."

"C.J., don't get the chairs right now, okay?"

"Okay."

Maria pressed a hand against my shoulder and turned her body towards me.

I let her guide me to the floor. She raised herself up on an elbow, then looked down at me. She lowered her lips to mine, and her hair enveloped my face. I closed my eyes and drank in her taste as the rhythm of our bodies pushing together became more focused, more passionate, more intense. My muscles tingled and I heard my heartbeat pounding in my ears. Moans of pleasure rose from our throats. Her hand explored my breasts, my stomach, my thighs.

She arched her back and pressed hard against me. I could feel the warmth between her legs through my sweat pants. Her fingers found the band of my pants and then wriggled inside them.

I pushed my knee hard against her, which elicited a throaty gasp from her. I spread my legs as she found my wetness, and I went in search of hers.

Time held still as we explored one another, experimented, touched, tasted, moved.

"Is this okay?" I asked as I slowly slipped two fingertips in and out of her wetness.

"Yes," she breathed in my ear. Then she pushed her hips against me and urged, "Go inside me. I want you, C.J."

I did and, as I entered her, she pushed her fingers inside me.

"Oh, God," we cried out together.

"You . . . feel . . . so good, C.J. So good, so good, so good."

I ran my tongue up and down Maria's neck, inhaling her scent and blissfully licking the salt of her sweat. My house could've been burning down at that moment, firefighters could be pouring water on the fire and sinking their ax bits into the roof for ventilation, and I would've called out to them, "Be right with you in a moment."

"I can't remember . . . this . . . ever feeling . . . like this," I panted as my lips found hers.

We locked in a deep kiss as our bodies rocked together. I held her fingers tight inside me while she gripped mine. I felt myself rising up off the floor, lifting into the air, ready to take flight.

Then time resumed its passage as our passion exploded in unison.

Moments later we exchanged quick kisses and then fell apart. We lay next to each other on our backs on the floor, holding hands, as our breathing slowly found its normal rhythm.

"Well," she finally said.

"Well," I replied.

"That was . . ."

"It was," I agreed.

"You were—"

"So were you."

"Wow."

"Wow."

"But—"

"I know. I mean, I don't know. If you know what I mean."

"I do."

I stared up at the ceiling for a few moments. "You know, I was just coming down here for the chairs."

"I know. And I was just stretching my back."

"I don't have a steed, Maria, and it's way past sunset."

"Damn."

"I'm afraid Betty isn't going to like this."

Maria giggled, then nudged my shoulder with hers. "Let's not tell her, okay."

"Okay."

I slowly sat up, then turned to face Maria. "Now what?"

Maria shook her head. "I don't know. I guess you help me up."

I started to laugh.

"What?" she asked.

"Well, isn't this where, on the show *Sex and the City,* that the narrator says something like, 'And just like that, we made love.' As if that somehow explains everything."

Maria grinned as she turned on her side and accepted my hand for leverage as she started to pull herself up. "And just like that, the folding chairs for the Thanksgiving dinner became a nonissue."

I laughed. "And just like that, the pregnant lesbian came."

Maria released her grip on my hand, clapped her hands together, and rolled back onto the floor. "Just like that," she began, but a string of giggles interrupted her. She let out a few more giggles, then rubbed her eyes. "They always do that, don't they, C.J.? But it never really *does* explain anything, does it?"

"No," I replied as I once again helped Maria to her feet. "So how do we explain what just happened?"

"To whom?"

"To us."

"Just like that," Maria began, then took my hands in hers. "I like you, C.J. I have for awhile. You're a good person. I've learned a lot about you this past week. And you're attractive. So attractive."

"Thank you."

"You're welcome. I wanted, well, I . . . I can't explain what happened. I just . . . I wanted you, C.J."

I smiled. "I wanted you, too, Maria. You are so beautiful. *So beautiful.* And I like *you.* You're a good person and you're very brave to have this baby on your own. I admire you."

Maria reached a hand out and touched my face. "It's been a long time for me."

I nodded. "For me, too."

She sighed. "I don't know what this means. What we've done. What it should mean. If it should mean anything."

"Neither do I."

"Because I really don't want a relationship with anyone."

I nodded. "Neither do I."

"You can't depend upon a relationship," she added. "And they're so much work."

"You're right," I agreed. "They're a lot of work. And then you put all this energy into someone—"

"And they don't care."

"That's right. They don't."

"I don't want to do that again."

"Neither do I."

"I don't want my heart broken."

"Me neither."

"I mean, you go through this period that's wonderful, with great sex and anticipation and excitement—"

"The honeymoon period."

"Right! And you start thinking, 'Oh, this person is the one for me.' "

"And so you start fashioning your life around this person," I continued. "You start thinking in terms of we. 'We are going to do this. We are feeling this way. Wouldn't we really enjoy doing such-and-such on vacation.' "

Maria nodded. "And then you start talking about living together."

"Ah, the big step."

"Yeah. You start thinking, 'Let's blend your stuff with my stuff and make it *our* stuff.' "

"And so then you move in together, and what happens?"

"The inevitable," Maria answered.

I nodded. "Eventually the fairy tale ends."

"Not happily ever after."

"No, never."

"See, I think that's the mistake that a lot of lesbians make," Maria said as she went to her rocking chair and sat down. "Why can't we just date for a while, really get to know someone well, without thinking that the minute you make love to someone that you're going to spend the rest of your lives together?"

"It's too much pressure," I answered as I sat on the floor in front of her. "We let passion and physical intimacy rule our decision-making."

"And that's a big decision to make," Maria said. "The rest of your life. Straight couples don't do that. They take a long time to get to know someone before they walk down the aisle."

"But we pack up the U-Hauls in a matter of weeks—"

"Days, even."

"Right, and then fuse like we're both made of Velcro or something."

"That's right," Maria agreed. "I mean, what's wrong with getting to know someone and being true to that person *before* you decide to live together? Before you decide that someone is going to be the person you're going to spend the rest of your life with?"

"There's nothing wrong with that."

"I know." Maria paused for a moment. "C.J., maybe we could just take the time to get to know each other. I've liked getting to know you so far. And I really liked tonight."

"I'd like that. And I liked tonight, too."

"So let's make an agreement, right here and right now, just to forget about making those grand decisions. Let's wait years before we decide to live together. Let's not even think about that. Let's just get to know each other. Let's just see where this is going. What do you think of that?"

"I'd like that, Maria. I really would."

"It's mature, don't you think?"

"Very."

"I like making mature decisions. Ones I make with my head, not my heart."

"Me, too."

"Well."

"Well."

I slowly rose to my feet. I walked towards Maria, leaned down to her, and kissed her. "I guess I'll go to bed."

"Me, too. We have to get up early and stuff the bird."

"Yes, we do," I said, then walked towards the stairs. I paused at the bottom of the steps. "Maria, you do know that we're already living together, don't you?"

"I know, C.J. So I guess we won't have to deal with that issue."

"That's a relief."

"C.J.?"

"What?"

"I really like you. Let's not hurt each other, okay?"

I nodded my head. "Deal. See you in the morning."

"*Eleven* minutes late, is what you are," Lars said as she threw open my front door while I hurriedly came up behind her.

Samata started to step up into the hallway, then stopped. "Please to forgive, but Britta wanted to bring fresh flowers," she told Lars. "There is few places open on this American holiday of turkey and football." Samata extended a wrapped bouquet of flowers to Lars.

"Well, don't be givin' 'em ta me," Lars snapped. "Give 'em ta Maria, 'cuz she's the one that's been slavin' over a hot stove for us."

"Please to—"

"Come on in," I told Samata and Britta as I elbowed my way past Lars

Lars leaned back against the wall, then grabbed one of my biceps and squeezed it hard. "Well now looky here, C.J. I guess you've been liftin' them weights, ain't cha?"

Samata flashed me a puzzled look as she walked past me while Britta followed close behind.

"Lars, just chill, would you?" I whispered to her after Samata and Britta had walked past us. "It's not, well, polite to scold people when you greet them as invited guests."

Lars closed the door, then turned to face me. "I'm jus' bein' re-

159

spectful to the time, C.J. If ya say be here at such-and-such time, then I am."

"Well, actually, you were a half hour early."

"With a case a Coke."

I nodded. "Yes. Thank you for that. Now why don't you go in and sit down?"

"I mean, ya did say eleven, right?"

"Yes. But we're not eating until about one."

"Oh, geez, really? Then I'm gonna dive inta that bowl a chips, 'cuz I'm starvin' already."

Lars hitched up her jeans and strode past me into the living room, where a fire was blazing in the fireplace, a Thanksgiving Day parade was on the television, and Meri and Taylor sat side by side on the couch.

"I'm gettin' a Coke," Lars announced. "Say somethin' if ya want one."

No one answered, so Lars strode through the house to the garage, where her case of soda was chilling.

"What is up with her?" Meri asked when Lars was out of earshot.

"Britta and I have made her angry, yes?" Samata asked as she took Britta's coat from her.

"No, you haven't," I assured her as I took their coats from them. "That's just her way. Maria wanted to invite her to dinner, because of all the work she did in the basement. According to Maria, she's a pussycat."

"Oh, really?" Taylor said. "What breed?"

"The snarly kind," Meri answered with a grin.

"Be nice to her," Maria said as she joined us in the living room, wiping her hands on a dish towel.

"She just took Sam's head off when she answered the door," I told her as Samata handed her the bouquet. "She's pissed that people weren't here at eleven on the dot."

"Well, thank you Sam and Britta for the flowers, they're lovely— she's just trying to help out," Maria answered, then raised her eyebrows at me. "C.J., do you want to help me with something in the kitchen?"

"I can help," Taylor offered as she started to get up from the couch.

"I got it," I answered as I tossed the coats to her. "You can hang these in the hall closet." I walked into the kitchen, turned the corner, and was immediately enveloped in Maria's open arms. I kissed her, then hugged her close to me.

"You feel so good, C.J.," she murmured in my ear, sending shivers down my spine.

"You, too. How are you feeling?"

"Like I'm missing you every second you're away from me. Come in here and visit me every five minutes, okay?"

"I think our guests will get suspicious."

"Oh? We have guests? For how long?"

"Probably all day."

"Damn them. Make them leave, C.J."

"I'm afraid I can't. The smells of your cooking are just too much for them to bear. Now they expect a meal."

"An entire meal? I thought they were just here for chips and beer and maybe one football game."

"No. I think they're even planning to stay until after dessert and coffee are served."

"Good Lord! Whose idea was that?"

"Yours."

"Oh."

"Seriously, Maria, I don't want you to be doing as much today as you did yesterday."

"I won't. Most everything's done. And anyway, I think I've figured out a way to cure a backache."

"Really?"

"Yeah. It's very . . . um . . . satisfying."

"Well, I do have to bring the folding chairs back down to the garage after everyone's gone. Maybe you could tell me then just how your backache was cured."

"It's a deal," Maria said as she squeezed my shoulders, then put her lips on mine.

"Do you guys want any—hello!" Meri exclaimed as she walked through the doorway and caught us in our embrace.

Maria and I quickly broke apart. Then Maria grabbed Meri's arm and pulled her around the corner and into the kitchen. "Don't say a word, Meri," she said as she wagged a finger in front of Meri's face. "Don't tell anyone what you just saw."

"Or we'll have to kill you," I added.

Meri stared first at Maria, then at me. Then she rubbed her hands together and giggled. "I know a secret, I know a secret," she chanted.

"Shut up," I said, but with a smile on my face.

Meri grinned, then shrugged her shoulders. "Hey, I don't give a shit. I think you guys would be great together. I really do. You're two nice people who've been scorched by your ex-lovers. You deserve a lot better, and I think you two are the best."

"Thanks," Maria said. "But you know that we made an agreement that night in the bar about not getting involved with—"

"Who gives a shit?" Meri cut in. "I don't. And I really don't think anyone else will. Sam's got Britta now, and Chantelle's gonna get her kicks with T-Rex."

"And now you and Taylor are an item, I hear," I said.

"Very funny, C.J. But in all honesty, I'll do anything to get Alana out of Taylor's life. It's making her crazy. So don't sweat this thing between you two, okay? Just enjoy yourselves. And I'm sure everyone will be very happy for you."

"Not Debbe," I pointed out.

"Hell, she's not happy for anyone who's happy. But if you guys want to keep this a secret for awhile, then my lips are sealed."

"Thanks," I said.

The doorbell rang, and I immediately pushed Meri out of the kitchen. "Go answer that damn door before Lars does."

*   *   *

An hour later, nine of us were sitting in the living room sipping drinks and munching on snacks.

"Maybe she won't show up," Taylor said as she glanced at her watch.

"I wouldn't have a problem with that, honey bun," Meri said as she tossed an arm across Taylor's shoulder and pulled her towards her. "Then I'd have you all to myself."

"Knock it off," Taylor grumbled as she pushed her body away from Meri's.

"Oh, that's a convincing gesture of love," Chantelle observed. "I'm sure Alana will truly believe you two are together if she sees you doing that shit, Taylor."

"Hey, I'm trying," Meri answered with a shrug.

"When Alana shows up, *then* Meri and I can get all lovey-dovey," Taylor told Chantelle.

"Oh, so that's the two," T-Rex said to Chantelle.

"That's the two what?" Lars asked.

"Don't you think we should practice a little smooching, honey bun?" Meri asked.

"Stop calling me honey bun," Taylor snapped.

"Lambchop?" Meri suggested.

"Not that either."

Lars looked at me. "C.J., I know ya told me ta be polite and all, but I don't think it's too polite for them two ta be fightin' on this holiday."

"We're not fighting," Taylor told Lars.

"Must be my hearin's goin' then," Lars responded with a snort.

"Let's kiss and make up," Meri grinned as she turned towards Taylor.

Taylor leaned back in the couch, placed a hand on Meri's chest, and locked her elbow. "Meri, get away from me!"

Lars sucked air between her teeth. "Sure seems like fightin' ta me."

"We're not fighting!" Meri and Taylor yelled at her in unison.

"Geez. Okay. But I'm gettin' a little confused here."

Maria took a seat next to Lars and started to explain the situation to her.

"Maybe you two should practice kissing," Chantelle suggested. "I mean, you *are* going to kiss when Alana shows up, right?"

Taylor rolled her eyes. "I'm not kissing Meri. That wasn't part of the deal."

"Well then how is your ex going to think you two are together if you won't even let Meri near you?" Britta asked.

Meri cupped her hands over her mouth and blew air into them. She inhaled, and then asked Taylor, "Is it my breath, dear heart? Maybe I shouldn't have had that onion dip."

"Taylor, if Alana believes there is to be a fight in paradise, then she will certainly be pushing hard to get back together," Samata pointed out.

"She's right," Maria said. "I think you two should start practicing acting like you're lovers."

"I'm not doing that in front of you guys," Taylor said.

"She doesn't like to be watched," Meri explained as she dunked a chip into a bowl of salsa. "Even when I make love to her, we have to have all the lights out."

"Meri, shut up!" Taylor snapped at her.

"You'll just be acting, that's all," T-Rex pointed out. "There's nothing to it. Watch. I can kiss Maria like we're lovers and—"

"Kiss someone else," I told her.

"Well, then, Britta," T-Rex said.

"Please to not do so," Samata answered.

"You can kiss me, sexy," Lars said.

Meri stood up and walked over to T-Rex. "I'll volunteer."

"Like hell you will," Chantelle said as she rose from her chair and stepped in front of T-Rex. "You've kissed enough women in your lifetime already."

"Kiss *me*," Taylor told T-Rex.

"Why won't ya kiss me?" Lars asked T-Rex, then shrugged her shoulders and took a swig of her drink.

"Go ahead, T," Chantelle told T-Rex. "You can kiss Taylor."

"Hey, that's my woman!" Meri cried out.

"Oh, for God's sake, Taylor, just kiss Meri and get it the fuck out of the way," I said.

Taylor glared at me.

"Don't give me that look," I responded. "You want to get rid of Alana, don't you?"

"Yes."

"Then you're going to have to show her that you and Meri are more than just friends," I said.

"It don't sound like they're no friends ta me," Lars observed. "They sound like a couple a battlin' bitches."

"I'm not a bitch," Taylor told Lars.

"Ya kinda arc," Lars countered.

"I agree with Lars," Chantelle said.

"See?" Lars said to Taylor. "If you're gonna be doin' this pretend thing like Maria tells me, then ya gotta do it. Jus' like C.J. says. Get that damn kiss over with."

"Well, why can't we just hold hands and stuff?" Taylor asked. "Why do I have to kiss her?"

"Because a kiss is to be passion in a relationship," Samata answered. "Without a kiss, what is there?"

"The kiss *is* the relationship," Britta agreed and then leaned her head towards Samata and kissed her.

"Watch this, Taylor," Chantelle said as she pulled T-Rex to her and then kissed her.

"This is gettin' interestin'," Lars said as she watched T-Rex and Chantelle. "Not like any Thanksgivin' I ever had before."

"Can everyone please stop talking about kissing?" Taylor asked. "And kissing? This is getting to be like a soft-porn show."

"I kinda like it," Lars said.

"Kiss me, baby," Meri grinned as she moved her face close to Taylor's.

"You must to be kissing Meri," Samata told Taylor.

"Just pretend, Taylor," I said, then stood up. "Watch. I'll kiss Maria. That is, if it's okay with you, Maria. Can I kiss you?"

165

Maria stood up and let out a loud sigh. "Well, alright, C.J. If you think it will help the situation."

I nodded. "I think it will, because Taylor knows we're not involved."

Maria and I stepped towards each other, then began to exchange a long, deep kiss.

"Well, now, I call this a party!" Lars exclaimed.

"Go for it, C.J.!" Chantelle called out.

"That's what I'm talking about," T-Rex said. "*That's* a kiss."

Maria and I ended the kiss, then exchanged a smile.

"Terrific acting," T-Rex exclaimed.

"Oh, yeah, that's acting all—" Meri began.

"Shut up and kiss Taylor," Maria told her. "Taylor, wipe that frown off your face and kiss Meri."

Taylor stood up, then shrugged her shoulders at Meri. "So?"

"Are you ready?" Meri asked.

"Go ahead," Taylor told her.

Meri stepped towards Taylor, then turned her head and met Taylor's lips. Taylor placed her hands against Meri's hips and tried to pull back, but Meri threw her arms around Taylor and pulled her close.

"This is a strange, strange party," Lars said, then tipped her head back and finished her Coke.

"So Alana, how long are you planning to stay in Boston?" Maria asked as she passed a bowl of mashed potatoes in her direction.

"Well, uh, probably for a couple more days," she answered as she took the bowl from Maria, then glanced across the table at Taylor.

Taylor noticed the glance and then slipped her fork onto Meri's plate. She sampled a bite, then kissed Meri on the cheek. Meri responded by whispering something to Taylor, who then giggled and blushed. The two then dropped their forks on their plates and exchanged a long, deep kiss on the lips.

"You two!" Chantelle exclaimed as she raised her glass of wine and took a sip. "You are just meant for each other. Like two peas in a pod. I can only hope that T-Rex and I find as much happiness together as you have."

T-Rex nodded. "You guys have so much passion. Even after all this time together."

"Exactly how long have you been together?" Alana asked.

"Sometimes it feels like forever," Meri sighed. "Being with Taylor . . . well . . . I just know I've found my soul mate."

"Me, too," Taylor agreed. "It's never been like this for me before. *Never,*" she said as she locked eyes with Alana.

"Britta and I talk about your wonderful relationship often," Samata said as she passed a basket of rolls around the table. "Britta is always telling me, 'Taylor and Meri are a couple of lovebirds. Why cannot we be more like them?'"

Britta nodded. "I say that to her all the time."

"We hear that all the time," Meri said as she draped an arm across Taylor's shoulder. "Even from perfect strangers. Remember that time in P-Town, love?"

Taylor stared at Meri for a few seconds, then cleared her throat. "Of course I do."

"Remember those people who came up to us in the restaurant?" Meri asked. "They said—remember, hon?—that they'd been watching us through the whole dinner, wondering if they could recapture our passion in their own relationship."

Taylor nodded. "I remember. And I also remember those long walks on the beach, and making love until the sun rose."

"Taylor is the love of my life," Meri said as she met Alana's eyes. "We have so much fun together. And the sex—I mean, wow!"

"Aw, geez. Are we gonna talk 'bout sex now?" Lars said through a mouthful of food. "I'm eatin' here."

"And we've been eating, too," Meri said with a grin. "All night long."

"I don't want to hear about it," Alana hissed through clenched teeth.

"I, too, do not think that is appropriate for the dinner table,"

Samata told Alana. "But when you have two friends who you love very much and they find love that is true with one another, then everything becomes quite special, does it not? That is what I too respect the most with them. It is their deep, deep love."

Alana watched as Meri covered Taylor's hand with hers, then looked down at her plate.

Taylor stared across the table at Alana. "It's hard to watch, isn't it?" Taylor said to her. "But that's what I went through whenever you—"

"Maria, this stuffing *does* melt in your mouth," I cut in. "I believe I'll have another helping. In fact, why doesn't everyone take more food?"

"Well, I'm glad that's over with," Taylor sighed as she flopped down on the couch and leaned her head back against the cushion. "It was all too much for me."

Meri sat down next to Taylor and rested her head on Taylor's shoulder.

"I agree," Lars grunted as she slowly lowered herself onto the braided rug in the middle of the living room floor and then rubbed her hands over her ample belly. "I'm stuffed."

"I meant that Alana is gone," Taylor said as she raised her head. "Which means we're through," she said as she nudged Meri away from her.

"That she is," Lars said. "She done high-tailed it right outta here soon's we cleared the dinner table."

"For good, I think," Chantelle added as she sat across the couch in a chair, cradling a coffee mug in her hands.

"She didn't even want a slice of pie," Maria pointed out as she sat on the ottoman next to the chair I was sitting in. "Didn't eat much of the dinner, either."

"Her loss," T-Rex told Maria as she tossed another log on the fire. "That was a great meal."

"She came here for Taylor, not the dinner," I pointed out.

"And left here with empty-handed," Samata said as she sat on the floor next to Britta. "It is to be convincing to her that you are not available, Taylor. That is enough, yes?"

"Yes," Taylor agreed. "And you all helped out a lot with the things you said."

"Academy Awards for everyone," I declared.

"Thank you, thank you, thank you," Chantelle gushed. "You like me! You really like me!"

"Does anyone remember any other acceptance speech in the history of the Academy Awards besides Sally Fields'?" T-Rex asked.

"Who can top that?" Maria asked.

"You know, Meri, you're not such a bad kisser," Taylor told her.

"Is that a compliment?" Meri asked.

Taylor nodded. "Yeah. And that's all I'm going to say. I don't want you to get a swelled head or anything."

"You did good, my friend," Meri smiled at her. "Despite all your initial protests, you could've won an Oscar for your performance. I don't think Alana's going to be bothering you anymore."

"I hope not," Taylor said. "Although there was this little vengeful part of me that wanted to tell her to move here, gather up all her stuff and leave her job and her friends behind, like I did for her, just so I could dump her."

"You're not that kind of person, Taylor," Maria pointed out.

Taylor nodded. "I'm not. But I have to admit that I did fantasize about it."

"Don't we all," Chantelle stated.

"I'm with ya on that, woman," Lars agreed. "Women is somethin' else, ain't they?"

"I know," T-Rex laughed. "What is up with them anyway?"

"What do they want?" Meri asked.

"Everything," I said.

"And nothing," Chantelle added.

"Whatever they be wantin', it's never enough," Lars said. "Ya never spend enough time with 'em or enough money on 'em or you're dog-tired and they wanna talk and—"

"Process," Britta corrected her. "Women want to process."

"Endlessly," Maria added.

"Or not at all," I said. "You want to talk about things, and she doesn't. There's never a problem in her eyes—"

"Or it's always *your* problem," Maria cut in. " 'Why can't we just be together?' she asks you. 'Why do you always have to talk about things?' Why can't you just be satisfied?' "

"That's all Debbe used to say to me," I agreed. "Like I was supposed to be happy that she was bringing home women all the time."

"Debbe Lee, you mean, right?" T-Rex asked.

Lars propped herself up on an elbow and stared at me. "You were with her?" she asked.

I nodded. "For a few long, painful years."

"Hmm. She's a handful, ain't she?"

"Oh, yeah," I agreed.

"And now you're workin' for her?" Lars asked. "Don't that beat all?"

"No, there is much more that beats all," Samata said. "Like she is to be wanting Britta to be with her, to be going with her to this skiing place over Christmas. Fa-la-la. I am tired of this being in two places. It is time to end it for good."

Britta sighed. "Let's not talk about this now, Sam."

Samata shook her head. "This is what has been saying. Women do not want to talk about things."

"Well, not now," Britta said as she looked around at us.

Samata tightened her lips. "Not now. Not ever, it seems. I wish you to break off this relationship with her, and it goes on and on."

Lars sat up. "Let me get this straight. You're with Debbe, and you're with your friend there too?" she asked Britta.

Britta nodded.

"Well, now. This here's quite an interestin' group." Lars shook her head. "But ya can't be bein' with two people, woman. That ain't right. That ain't fair. Ya gotta make up your mind."

"This is what I have been telling her," Samata said.

"It's not that easy," Britta sighed.

"Sure it is," Lars boomed as she slowly raised herself up off the floor. "Ya say ta Debbe, 'I got myself another woman.' Jus' like you all been doin' today ta convince that Alana chick that Taylor don't be wantin' ta be with her."

"Then I'll lose my job," Britta told Lars.

"How the hell's that gonna happen?" Lars asked her. "It ain't about the job. It's about who ya love."

"I happen to like this person," Samata said as she looked at Lars.

Britta sighed. "Debbe . . . well . . . Debbe—"

"Is a vengeful person," I finished for her.

"So ya lose the job," Lars said. "Ya get another. And ya get ta be with your woman here. It seems pretty simple ta me."

"Debbe would make it hard for me to get another job," Britta explained.

"Now how in hell she gonna do that?" Lars asked. "She ain't the world, and there be a world a jobs out there."

Britta looked at me.

I shrugged my shoulders.

"I can't . . . well . . ." she began.

"Oh, here it comes again," Samata said. "The wall of stone is to be erected. End of discussion, right?"

"Sam, please—"

"Please to let's just get over this wall, once and for all," Samata shouted. "Tell me! Tell me why it is to be so hard to not end it with Debbe and to say goodbye to the job. The job you hate! You tell me you do not even like to be working with Dragon person. You do not be liking to be with her. You are like a slave with her master, Britta. 'No, no, I cannot say anything to make the master upset, Sam,' is like to be what you are telling me."

"Sam, that's not fair," Britta said.

"Oh, but you to be fair with me?" Samata yelled, her face reddening. "You know, this makes me too angry. This has pushed me to the edge. No! You will not go to be with Debbe anymore. The next time you do, you will not be coming back to me!" Samata stood up and looked at me. "I am so sorry to have be . . . to be loss of my temper, C.J. Especially on this holiday and this lovely time to be together with everyone. But I see nothing but heartache ahead for me. I do not need to be broken in the heart."

Maria stood up and went to Samata.

"I am to be apologizing to you, too, Maria. For this lovely dinner that you have worked so hard to prepare, I have ruined now."

"You haven't ruined anything," Maria told her.

"You need to let out how you feel, Sam," Meri added. "And you're with friends. We understand."

"We hear you," Chantelle nodded.

"Sam, it's my fault," Britta said as she stood up. "You're right. I'm not being fair to you. I . . . I think it's time that I tell you something."

"Please to not break up with me here, in front of everyone," Samata said as tears welled in her eyes.

"Oh, honey, I'm not going to break up with you," she said as she went to her. "I love you. It's *you* I want to be with. And I will. *I will*. I will because . . . because I . . . I've done a bad thing in the past, and Debbe knows about it, and she wants to use it to embarrass me and to keep me, you're right, to keep me as her slave. She's been holding this over my head long enough."

"Geez, and I thought you writers had the easy jobs," Lars said as she cracked her knuckles and joined T-Rex by the fire.

"You have done a bad thing?" Samata asked Britta.

Britta nodded, took a deep breath, and then explained her summer in Saratoga Springs to everyone.

"Shh, shh, shhh," Samata soothed Britta after she had finished her story. "I do not be caring about this that you have told me. Not at all. It is tiny potatoes."

"It's nothing," Meri agreed.

"It's in the past, Britta," Chantelle pointed out.

"Not according to Debbe," Britta sniffed. "She drags this out every chance she gets. It's driving me crazy."

"Hey, then, I must be a slave ta Debbe Lee, too," Lars said. "Jus' like you, she's done got it written in my contract 'bout me bein' a alkie. If I fall off the wagon, I'm finished at L-TV. But I ain't gonna be scared a her. No way. Like I tol' ya, it's a job. I can get another."

"You're all slaves," Britta said as she wiped her eyes. "Isn't that right, C.J.?"

All eyes turned to me.

"I heard what she told you that day in her office, C.J.," Britta continued. "I had the intercom on. Debbe Lee's got something written in everyone's contract that she's going to use against each of you if you ever try to walk out. If you ever try to get another job somewhere else. She told C.J. everything after she had gone on all those talk shows and never gave credit to the writers and you guys were furious with her."

"That's when we got all that bad press and Debbe was fit to be tied, wasn't it?" Maria asked me.

"C.J. was the one who talked to the reporters," Britta said.

"You were?" Taylor asked.

I nodded.

"You go, girl!" Chantelle exclaimed. "That was brilliant!"

"And that's the time when I handed you my resignation, C.J.," Meri added.

"Oh, yeah, Debbe knew about that, too," Britta said. "So she decided to tell C.J. things that would make her talk you guys out of leaving or thinking about leaving. Things that would make C.J. keep you guys on the job. So everything at L-TV would go on."

"What's she talking about, C.J.?" Maria asked.

"I do not gamble or consume beverages like an alcoholic," Samata said. "I am a clean person."

"But you were hospitalized, Sam," I said. "For your . . . you know."

Samata stared at me. "For what was I hospitalized, C.J.? I went once for the emergency room, when I twisted an ankle playing softball. I cannot play this game, although I know many lesbians do. For this I received an x-ray and an ice pack. For this I was not hospitalized."

"You . . . uh . . . tried to kill yourself," I said.

"You did?" Britta asked Samata.

"This is not true," Samata protested. "I have never to be trying to kill myself. This is wrong, what is told to you."

"And Chantelle," I said as I turned to her. "Debbe says she knows about the . . . the food stamps."

"What food stamps?" Chantelle asked.

"About the . . . uh . . . scam that you and your sister took part in."

Chantelle stared at me. "C.J., I *support* my sister. I buy most of the food. I pay nearly all of the bills. I provide everything I can for those kids. We have never—I repeat, *never*—taken government assistance for anything. Nor has my sister."

"Well, that's what Debbe told me."

"She's wrong," Chantelle told me. "I'd never do anything like that. I got my pride, girl. And even though my sister's life is fucked up, she tries really hard. She's got her pride, too."

"What did she say about me?" Meri asked.

I sighed. "That when you were a camp counselor, you had a relationship with an underage camper."

"I'd believe that," Taylor commented.

Meri delivered a swift punch to Taylor's arm. "Nice, Taylor. Except I never went to camp nor was I ever a camp counselor. The great outdoors and I have never had a relationship. We never will."

"No, you just have relationships with any and all available females," Taylor grumbled.

"C.J., what did Debbe tell you about Taylor?" Meri asked.

"This should be good," Taylor said as she looked at me.

"You cheated on a test in college?"

Taylor shook her head. "No, C.J., I didn't cheat on any test in college. Or high school. Or junior high. Or grade school. I don't break rules. I never have, and I never will. I don't even have a speeding ticket, let alone a parking violation."

Maria laughed. "Well this certainly is interesting. Everything Debbe Lee has told you about each one of us is wrong. And she's led you to believe what she's told you, hasn't she, C.J.?"

I nodded.

"Okay, then, tell me what Debbe told you about me," Maria said.

I sucked in a deep breath. "That you killed someone."

"She did what?" Chantelle exclaimed.

"Is she predicting her own demise?" Maria asked me.

"No," I answered. "She told me that you killed a friend of the family who was molesting your siblings."

"That's it?"

I nodded.

"You mean she didn't tell you about the family that I brutally murdered as well?" Maria shook her head. "This woman is positively crazy. How could you believe anything she told you?"

"Because of me," Britta answered. "Because what Debbe told C.J. about me was true. And C.J. saw with her own eyes how this devastated me. How it embarrassed me. How was C.J. to know what was true and what wasn't true after that?"

"Well, deep down inside, you must not have believed her, C.J.," Maria said. "Because I'm living here with you, and I don't think you would've let me through the door if you had thought I had really done what she told you."

"She's a fucking liar and a manipulator," Chantelle hissed. "A food stamp scam—ha! She's the scam. She's the fraud."

"I was with a seventeen-year-old once," Meri said, then burst into laughter. "When I was fifteen!"

"Why am I not surprised about that?" Taylor asked.

Meri wiggled her eyebrows at Taylor. "Sometimes it's fun being bad. You ought to try it sometime, Miss Goody Two-shoes."

"I got a D on a test once," Taylor told her.

"That's not being bad," Meri said. "That's being dumb. You should've cheated on it."

"So how'd I do it?" Maria asked me. "How did I kill someone?"

"With a knife," I answered.

"Colonel Mustard was murdered by Maria Hernandez in the study with a knife!" Meri exclaimed.

Maria shook her head. "I think the next show I'll pitch on L-TV will be about a devious television network executive and all the enemies she makes in her climb to the top of the ladder. Of course she gets murdered—"

"Of course," Chantelle chimed in.

"But did one person do it?" Maria asked. "Or did all of her enemies conspire together in a plot to commit the perfect murder—one in which everyone has an alibi and backs up each other's alibi so no one can be singled out and charged with the crime?"

"Nah, ya can't kill her," Lars scoffed. "Ya can't kill that there main character. 'Cuz everybody's watchin' the show jus' 'cuz a how mean and bad that there character always is ta people. People like that, them bad ones, they never get taken down. They always take everyone else down. That's what makes them shows good. Ya keep thinkin' they're gonna get it, but they never do. It's jus' the way it is. Them kinda people always lands on their feet."

We sat in silence, considering Lars' words.

"**Twelve** days without seeing me—how will you stand it, C.J.?" Debbe Lee asked me as I sat in a chair in her office.

"I'll manage just fine," I told her as I opened my notebook and screwed off the cap to my fountain pen. "Now what did you want to talk to me about?"

"How's your staff doing?"

"Fine."

"Fine?"

"Yes."

"And how are you doing?" she asked as she opened a gold box on her desk that contained her favorite brand of imported cigarettes and slipped one into her mouth.

"Fine."

"Fine?"

"Yes."

"How's Maria's pregnancy?"

"Fine."

Debbe lit her cigarette with a slim jeweled lighter, then blew smoke across her desk towards me. "Do you know any words other than fine?"

"Yes."

"So her living with you is working out—would you say, fine?"

"Debbe, what is this meeting all about?"

"Are you in a hurry to get somewhere?"

I glanced at my watch. "Well, I would like to enjoy this Christmas break. You did say the offices would be closing at noon today, right? I've got a lot of shopping to do."

Debbe smiled at me. "And what are you planning to buy me, love?"

"You have everything you need, Debbe," I said as I closed my notebook and recapped my pen. "If you don't have anything else to talk about, I'm taking off." I stood up.

"Sit down, C.J.," Debbe snapped at me.

I paused for a moment, then sat down and stared at Debbe.

Moments passed. "What?" I finally asked.

"Aren't you going to ask me how I am?"

I sat in silence.

"Well, now that you ask," Debbe said as she tapped ashes into a crystal ashtray, "I'm not doing so well. It seems that Cleopatra has finally prevailed in her attempts to get Britta away from me. I'll have to go to Aspen alone this year."

"Oh, that's a pity. But I'm sure you won't be alone there for very long. You never were."

"C.J., that's not the point. The point is this. I happen to have fallen in love with Britta."

The sudden laugh that escaped from me at her admission sounded like a bark. I shook my head. "Debbe, you don't know what love is."

"Don't be hurtful, C.J. You know, I do have a heart."

"Well, something's got to move the blood around in your body. The heart would be that organ."

"Oh, you're still so bitter. Still so bitter."

"Rightly so, Debbe."

"Are you still in love with me?"

"No. God, no."

"Then why all the animosity towards me?"

"Because you broke my heart. Over and over and over. And yet you kept telling me that you loved me."

"I did."

"You didn't."

"At the time, I did."

"No, you didn't. Because if you had known anything about love, you wouldn't have deliberately hurt me the way you did. That's why I don't think you know anything about love."

"So I had a wandering eye."

"No, Debbe, it was more than a wandering eye. Looking is one thing. Acting is another."

"But I always came back to you, C.J."

"And like a fool, I kept letting you back into my heart. That's my own damn fault. I let you treat me like I was some sort of port you could just sail in and out of whenever you felt like it."

"I don't want to do that anymore."

"Good. Because it's a lousy way to treat anyone you say you love."

"I love Britta."

"Britta's not yours to love, Debbe. She loves Samata."

"Britta broke my heart, C.J."

"Oh, for God's sake, Debbe. Stop lying to me, and stop lying to yourself. Britta was just another one of your playmates. She was just someone you wanted to control. I've heard the way you've spoken to her and I've seen the way you've treated her. Everyone has. Do you remember that day in your office? You were downright cruel to her. Who could love you with that kind of treatment? But, fortunately for Britta and unfortunately for you, you've discovered that you can't control her. She loves Sam, and Sam loves her. Game over. You lose. Go find someone else to play with."

Debbe leaned across her desk. "I love Britta. And I want you to help me get her back."

"I'll do no such thing."

"I can fire you."

"Really? And just who will keep *Madame President* going? Need I remind you that it's your number one show? And why is firing me or anyone and everyone on the L-TV staff the card that you always pull out?"

"Oh, it's just one of many I have, C.J."

"Well, it doesn't scare me. Nothing you can do will scare me."

"Since when did you become Braveheart?"

I stood up. "I'm not going to do anything to help you get Britta back. You made your bed, now lie in it."

"Alone? I think not. So maybe I'll reveal to all the world about her gambling problem."

"I don't think she has a problem, Debbe. From what you've told me, she's attending her meetings and not gambling anymore. So that's in the past."

"Then I'll reveal what I know about all the writers."

I smiled and leaned across her desk. "So do it, Debbe. Stop using threats and just make good on them."

Debbe sprang up from her chair in an instant, grabbed the front of my sweater, and pulled me towards her. "Don't you fucking talk to me like that!" she hissed in my face.

"Let go of me!" I gasped as I clasped my hands around hers.

Debbe released her grip on me, then sat down. She picked up her cigarette and inhaled. "So how far along is Maria now?" she asked. "Five months?"

"Six," I said as I readjusted my sweater. "You know, I just bought this."

"How good a driver is she, C.J.?"

I stared at Debbe.

"You know, traffic is terrible out there. People rushing to and fro. Drivers driving recklessly. She should be careful, you know?"

I sat down.

"So I have your attention now, huh?"

"Leave Maria out of this discussion."

"C.J., I don't have everything I need. I want Britta back."

"Needing and wanting are two different things, Debbe."

"I need and want Britta."

"Then talk to Britta."

"I did."

"Then there's nothing I can do."

"Let's see. Maria attends childbirth classes in the city, doesn't she?"

"What the fuck does Maria have to do with Britta? Leave Maria out of this. She has nothing to do with Britta choosing Sam over you. For that matter, leave all the writers out of this. They've got nothing to do with Britta wanting to be with Sam and not you. And, by the way, I hate the way you use these ridiculous threats. It's really juvenile."

Debbe stared at me, then extinguished her cigarette. "I want Britta on that plane with me, C.J."

"Debbe, I can't make Britta do what she doesn't want to do."

Debbe tapped her fingernails on her desk.

"If you want her to go with you so badly, then tell her you'll reveal her gambling problem."

"I have."

"And?"

Debbe narrowed her eyes at me. "Like you, it didn't seem to bother her. She just said to me, 'Go ahead.'"

"So there you have it. If you can't scare her into going to Aspen with you, I don't know what I can do."

"I can do something to her foreign lling. Maybe I'll fire her."

"That won't make Britta go to Aspen with you. It will make Britta want to be with Sam."

"Then I can threaten to hurt her."

"Which would be a terrible thing to do. And, once again, I reiterate that these threats are really annoying."

"But she'd get on that plane with me to keep Sumo safe."

"That's right. That's the only reason she'd get on that plane. It wouldn't be for you. And after your trip, she'd come home to Samata. You want her to want you, Debbe. But she doesn't. Get over it and get on with your life."

"Are you and Maria involved, C.J.?"

"That's an abrupt change of topics."

"Is she sharing your bed with you?"

"Maria is renting the basement in my home, Debbe."

"Do you have someone in your life now?"

"What does it matter to you?"

Debbe sighed. "It doesn't. I don't want to be with you."

"The feeling's mutual."

"I know. And Britta doesn't want to be with me, either." Debbe stood up and walked to the large picture window behind her desk. She looked out. "Everyone has someone, C.J."

"Not everyone."

"I'm alone, C.J. I'm alone, and I don't want to be."

"Debbe, I'm not your therapist."

"This time of year—it's hard, you know?"

I stood up. "Debbe, you've built yourself an empire here at L-TV. You're getting the recognition and respect in the industry that you've always wanted. You've got money and you've got looks. I'm sure there's someone out there for you."

"I don't want someone. I want Britta."

"Well, you don't get someone by manipulating them into a relationship."

"How do you find someone, C.J.?"

"The question isn't how you find someone. The question is, how do you hold on to someone once you've found them. That's what you need to figure out. From what I know about you, that's what you can't do. Because once you have someone, all you want to do is hurt them."

"I bought Britta a lovely piece of jewelry, C.J."

"You can't buy love either, Debbe."

Debbe turned to me. "Aren't you full of helpful advice."

"I'm only telling you the truth. It's something you've never enjoyed hearing."

Debbe turned away from me. "You can go now, C.J."

I watched Debbe for a few moments, then turned and walked out of her office.

I didn't want to cry.

But sitting in the parking lot outside the shopping mall an hour after I had exited Debbe's office, looking at shoppers scurrying in and out of the entrance and listening to the Salvation Army bell ringers urge spare change out of pockets that were going to be parting with considerably more in the seasonal spirit of sharing material wealth, I thought back to the last Christmas I had spent with Debbe.

We had decided to spend Christmas together in the home we had shared. No parties with friends, no separation in order to spend time with families. Debbe had convinced me that this was what she needed—or had she used the word wanted?—to rekindle her relationship with me. She had vowed never to cheat on me again, had told me she adored me and wanted to be with me for the rest of her life, and I had believed her.

This time, I had told myself, she really means it.

And so I had baked and roasted and peeled and chopped and sautéed a wonderful Christmas Eve dinner for us. I had set the table, finished decorating the tree, and wrapped her presents and set them under the tree.

I had put a bottle of champagne in the fridge to chill, then showered and dressed in silk loungewear she had bought for me on a trip to Paris.

Hours later, I was still waiting for Debbe to show up. I turned the oven to warm, salvaged as much of the dinner as I could, and set it aside. I finally fell asleep on the couch and woke up on the dawn of Christmas Day to an empty house.

I spent the morning cleaning up the kitchen and taking apart the table I had set. I tossed our dinner in the garbage, and then sat down on the couch, waiting for my last Christmas with Debbe to reach its painful conclusion at the chime of midnight.

Tears rolled down my cheeks at the memory as I sat in my car watching the people come and go, but not really seeing them. My stomach still clenched with the anger I had felt at the time, an anger that had been laced with fear, wondering if Debbe had been in an accident, an anger that had been kept seething with jealousy over wondering whose bed she had slept in on Christmas Eve.

How can something go on hurting for so long? I wondered. I had packed my bags, left Debbe, grieved the loss, read self-help books, gone to a therapist, and allowed my friends to rally around me. I had finally, mercifully, reached a point in my life when I could no longer remember what I had ever seen in Debbe that had made me fall in love with her.

But, I realized as I pulled the keys out of the ignition and slowly exited my car, I had never been able to forget what Debbe had done to me, had done to my heart.

And, as I locked the door and started to walk to the mall entrance, I realized that I would never be able to forgive her. Ever.

Later on that afternoon, I pulled into my garage, collected up a half dozen shopping bags, and stepped into my kitchen.

An aroma of roasting meat mingled with a fresh pine scent greeted me. I turned the corner into the living room and saw Maria standing in front of a decorated Christmas tree.

I stopped when I saw the look on her face.

It was filled with love and happiness. For me.

I dropped the bags on the floor and walked towards her.

She smiled at me. "I wanted to do this sexy thing for you, C.J. You know, open my robe and show you my naked body. And I wanted to make love with you right here on the floor, in front of the tree. But look," she said as she opened her robe. "This big old belly of mine kind of kills the mood, doesn't it?"

"Look at you," I breathed as I stepped closer to her. "You are so beautiful."

"And then I was thinking, maybe I'll just tie a red bow around me and ask you to unwrap me. But," she said as she glanced down at her belly, "it's still here. Six months of baby."

"Six months of baby," I murmured as I lay a palm on her belly. "And a very, very sexy lady." I kissed her, then let my hands explore her nakedness.

We slowly dropped to our knees in front of the tree. I slid her robe over her shoulders, guided her gently to the floor, and let her watch while I undressed.

I came with such force and such intensity that tears sprang into my eyes as I climaxed. Maria lingered between my legs as my moans subsided, delivering soft, warm kisses as my insides contracted again and again on her fingers. Then she slowly slipped out of me, urged my head into her lap, and wrapped her arms around me. She gently rocked me until my trembling ceased.

When I caught my breath, I told her about my last Christmas with Debbe.

"I'm sorry," I said after I finished my story.

"What are you sorry about?"

"I shouldn't be talking about Debbe when I'm with you."

"Why not?"

"Because I'm with you, not her."

"But she's one of your memories, C.J. I want you to share your memories with me. The good ones, but most especially the bad ones. It helps me to learn about you, to understand you, to care for you."

I took Maria's hand in mine and kissed it. "You're so wonderful to me, Maria. And look at all you've done. The dinner. The tree. The way you greeted me tonight. All of this is so—"

"C.J.?"

"Mmm?"

"I love you."

Later on that night, as Maria lay next to me in my bed, she took my hand and rested it on her belly.

"Do you feel that?"

I pressed my hand against her stomach.

"Wait for a bit. She's moving around, kicking and punching. I want you to feel it."

I grinned. "What have you got inside there? A mini-kickboxer?"

"It's sure starting to feel that—"

"Wow!" I exclaimed. "I felt that! That's amazing! Will she do it again?"

"Oh, she'll do it all night. She's a bit of a night owl. She gave me a roundhouse kick to my ribs last night."

"She did? Maybe we should name her Jet Li. Or Jackie, after Jackie Chan."

Maria laughed. "Chantelle says—oh, there's another one—Bruce Lee."

"For a girl?"

"Chantelle says with my baby, anything is possible."

"But think of the ribbing she'll get being called Bruce. We have to think about the ramifications of what we name her. After all, she'll be stuck with her name for the rest of her life."

"Yeah. And think of all the calls I'm going to be getting from school principals about Bruce Lee Hernandez and the disruption she's caused on the playground."

"Well, I'll be proud of her. She'll be able to defend herself."

"She'll be a bully."

"No she won't. I'll teach her when it's right and when it's wrong to fight."

"C.J.?"

"Hmm?"

"You're saying *we* a lot."

"How do you mean?"

"Well, you're talking about when *we* name the baby."

"Oh."

"Which is fine. But I want to ask you a question."

"Shoot."

"What happens after the baby is born?"

"What do you mean?"

"Well, I'm just wondering what you're going to do . . . what you're going to *want* to do . . . you know . . . after the baby is born."

I gently rubbed Maria's belly. "I'm not going to breast-feed her, if that's what you're asking."

"Be serious."

"Okay. I'll get up with you in the middle of the night and I'll help you take care of her. Is that what you're asking?"

"I'm asking if you want me to stay after the baby is born."

I sat up. "Of course I do. Why wouldn't I want you to stay?"

"Well, it's you and I who are . . . who are sleeping together. Not you, me, and a baby."

"There's a potential baby in there, Maria. I've been making love to you and your baby, as far as I can see it."

Maria reached up and touched my face. "But do you want me *and* the baby, C.J.?"

"Yes, Maria. I want you and the baby."

"But this isn't what you signed on for when you asked me to live with you."

"Maybe it was."

"What do you mean?"

"Well, I didn't think we'd get together once you moved in. This has been completely unexpected—and wonderful. But I did think about what it would be like having you and your child living here with me. I thought that it would be a wonderful thing. I hoped that once you moved in, you'd stay. And after I saw how Lars had made the basement so nice for you and your baby, I felt it could work out. That you could be comfortable here."

"I am comfortable here. Although I really haven't spent much time downstairs."

"We can spend the night at your place sometimes if you want. But I hate all that packing and the long drive in traffic."

Maria laughed.

I placed my arm across Maria's chest and lay my head against her shoulder. "I'm falling in love with you, Maria. There's no way I'd want you to leave after you have your baby. I know I can try to be a good partner to you. You'll have to help me with the rest, with being a good caretaker to your child. Say, you know what I was thinking we could do?"

"We," Maria murmured, then kissed the top of my head. "I like that word."

"The *we* word?"

"The *we* word. It makes my heart sing when you say it, C.J."

"Well, do you know what I think *we* can do?"

"No. What can *we* do, honey?"

"Honey. I like that."

"Honey, honey, honey," Maria said as she rubbed my shoulders. "Tell me, honey, what we can do."

"We can make the guest room into the baby's room. And then we can move the guest room into your digs downstairs."

"Uh, oh."

"Uh, oh, what?"

"Are you . . . are you asking me to move in with you, C.J.?"

"Yes, Maria. I'm asking you to move in with me."

"Don't you think we're rushing things?"

"Well, perhaps. But just to be on the safe side, why don't you keep your own place for a while. That way, if we don't work out, you'll have a place to go to."

"I don't know. The rent there is awfully expensive."

"Well, we can try it out for a little while."

"Okay."

"I love you, Maria."

"I love you, C.J."

"Good night, little K.B."

"K.B.?"

"Kickboxer," I mumbled, then fell asleep in Maria's arms.

Thirteen nominations for L-TV prime-time shows were not only more than we had hoped for, but also more than we could've dreamed of receiving for our first season as a cable network that openly catered to an alternative audience. Our nominations, along with a slew of nominations for other cable and network shows, which had recently been announced by the editors at *TV Guide,* signaled what many in the television industry termed the beginning of prime-time television's "winning season."

The season officially began in February, when entry forms for the coveted Emmys were sent out to people in the arts and entertainment industry and the networks then lined up at the starting gate and began jockeying in earnest to call attention to their shows in a variety of illegal, though commonly accepted, ways. Hard-to-get courtside basketball playoff tickets, Rolex watches, and dinner reservations at prestigious restaurants often showed up on the desks of those who voted for award-winners. This year, rainbow-jeweled silver bracelets had been one of the many gifts received by the voters, courtesy of Debbe Lee on behalf of L-TV.

The Emmys capped off the prime-time winning season, which was officially kicked off by the *TV Guide* Awards in March, followed by the People's Choice Awards and the Creative Arts Awards. But since the Emmy nominations were announced in July and the awards ceremony was telecast in September, most industry insiders felt that the outcome of the *TV Guide* Awards gave a pretty good indication of who the winners would be from the Emmy nominees.

Madame President had scored big with *TV Guide,* earning four nominations, including best drama series, best supporting actress (Meryl Streep), best actress (Stockard Channing), and best writing (me). Both *One Big Happy Family* and *The Body Farm* had received nominations for best reality series. *Can't Let Go* had been given the nod in the newly created category best action-adventure series, with T-Rex earning a best actress nomination. She had told us, as we waited at Logan Airport for our flight number to be called so we could head out to the *TV Guide* Awards ceremony, that receiving the nomination "was an honor, that's for sure, but I mean—my God!—Stockard Channing is going to win. She's a *real* actress. This is just my first acting gig."

The group of us had neither agreed nor disagreed with her statement. I had told Maria the moment that we had found out about the nominations that I was rooting for Stockard, hands down, despite my feelings for Chantelle or T-Rex, and Maria had agreed with me.

"After all, Stockard is not just a natural, not just someone who has years of acting experience under her belt, but she really makes that character of the first woman president work," Maria had told me as we undressed for bed that night. "And you've written great story lines for her. She's had to handle both personal and national crises. She has as good an on-screen presence as Martin Sheen had in *The West Wing*. All T-Rex does, all she seems to do, at least to me, is a lot of eyebrow furrowing and running in slow motion from week to week, don't you think?"

"She is kind of one-dimensional," I had responded. "I mean, that's perfect for Chantelle's show."

"Right," Maria agreed as she uncapped the toothpaste tube as we stood side by side in the bathroom. "But that might be all she's capable of. She doesn't strike me as, well—"

"Multidimensional?"

"Exactly."

As we sat in the airport waiting area, Chantelle had leaned towards T-Rex and whispered something in her ear that had elicited a quick kiss on the cheek.

"And who knows about the fickle acting industry anyways," T-Rex had then said to the group. "I'm thinking, depending on how long Chantelle's show lasts, of maybe getting back into being a personal trainer. I don't like being away from my honey for a very long time, but that's what you have to do when you're in acting. I want to be . . . well . . . more grounded."

I glanced up from the magazine on my lap, met Maria's eyes, then quickly returned to the magazine.

"Well, isn't that your first love?" Maria asked. "Being a personal trainer?"

"Yeah," T-Rex replied. "I think it is. Acting's fun and all, but sometimes I find it really hard. I don't know how Stockard does it, but she's as believable as president of the United States as she was being Rizzo in *Grease*. One person being two different people is a hard concept for me to grasp."

"Well, it is to be an honor to be in nominations," Samata told her. "You will hear your name read in front of millions of people, in the company of Stockard and all the other actresses in your category. I have heard once a great acceptance speech by Michael Caine at the Academy Awards. Instead of talking about himself— going blah, blah, blah 'my agent this, my wife that, the crew they are so awesome, the director he is so brilliant, genius even'—he instead talks about each of the people he is been competing with for the award."

"I think he won for best supporting actor, for his role in *The Cider House Rules*," Meri added.

"I remember that speech," Taylor said. "I thought what he said was really classy."

Samata nodded. "So to be in a group with so many wonderful names, where your name is as well, that is sometimes as good as winning. I feel this way about my show, and maybe it is true for others too, yes?"

Each of the writers' shows had been nominated for best new series of the season, and they had all nodded their heads at Samata's statement. But rather than any one writer secretly harboring feelings that her show would win over someone else's at L-TV, from what I could gather there was little to no competitiveness in our group or even an ounce of jealousy over the recognition our individual shows had been given. Quite simply, we were all hoping to receive as many awards for L-TV as we could.

"To an outstanding first season!" Meri declared. "A season in which we're all winners!"

"I hear that," Chantelle agreed.

We toasted each other with cups of steaming coffee and cinnamon buns before our flight was called and discussed what we hoped would be the mistaken superstitious belief that thirteen was an unlucky number.

Several minutes later, as I sat on the airplane with Maria by my side, waiting on the runway to be cleared for takeoff, I thought back to the holidays. Christmas had flown by. Maria and I had spent some of the break from L-TV together and had celebrated our own Christmas on December 21, then had separated for a few days to visit our families. The greeting Maria told me she had received from her family members, who saw her suddenly six months pregnant when she walked through the door of her childhood home, was better than she had expected, particularly when she told them that she had separated from Jesse and was now in a relationship with me.

"She was not for you, not the person I wanted my daughter to be with," her mother had confessed to her when Maria was helping to prepare dinner for a house full of people. "I am not happy with your choice of life, my chica—this I know I have made clear to you on many occasions—but that Jesse did not seem to have her heart with yours when she came here to meet us. She seemed more focused on herself. Do you remember? She didn't want to do very much with you or the family, but wanted to go to the beach and go out drinking all the time. She was, well, she seemed almost bored with you. This type of person does not deserve to be with my daughter. You are exciting and beautiful and generous in your heart and soul."

Maria and I had set up a camera at home before we had left for our family celebrations and, using the timer, had taken several pictures of ourselves in front of the Christmas tree. Her mother had hugged Maria and then walked to the refrigerator. She tapped a finger on one of the pictures Maria had given her, which she had stuck on the front of the fridge. "Look at her! Look at how she looks at you with love and adoration! Yes, this is the one for you. You can see her love, you can feel it coming through this picture."

Maria had put her arms around her mother.

"What will make me most happy," her mother had then said as she gently took her hand and brushed her daughter's hair from her face, "is to know that you have someone who loves you and wants to be with you and your baby. This C.J. has a big enough heart for you and a baby. I can see this."

Maria's father had openly shed tears of joy in front of everyone at the family's holiday gathering over the knowledge that he would soon become a grandfather. He had risen from his chair at the dinner table and offered a toast to his beautiful daughter and the baby that he said he knew would also be beautiful. Then he had dropped to his chair and sobbed in sadness that he would never "walk my little girl down the aisle," to which Maria's youngest brother had responded by telling his father to "Face it, Papa. She loves women, and I don't see anything wrong with that. Women are beautiful. They should be loved."

"This doesn't freak you out, does it C.J.?" Maria had asked as we drove home from the airport after I had picked her up.

"Not in the least," I told her as I had taken her hand in mine and held it on my lap as we negotiated through traffic. "This separation from you has only made me realize that I fall in love with you more each day. And I can't wait to see your baby, can't wait to be there with you and her. Your family sounds wonderful, and I'd be honored to meet them."

The last time the writers had gathered together as a group before production of the second half of the television season was at a New Year's Eve party that had started with dinner at my house and then ended at Alley's for a raucous stroke-of-midnight celebration. It was then that Maria and I had officially come out to them as a couple, not because we had made a conscious decision to do so but because we simply couldn't keep our hands off of one another.

"If I wasn't as drunk as I am, I'd swear you two were an item," Britta had said as she downed the rest of her cocktail and watched as Maria and I slow-danced together near the table we had claimed in the crowded bar.

Maria had smiled at Britta and then placed her lips on mine for a long, lingering kiss.

"I think they're an item," Taylor had remarked during our kiss.

"Maria?" Chantelle had asked as she leaned closer to us. "Is there something I should know that I don't know?"

"I'm pregnant, Chantelle!" Maria had shouted.

"I know that, girlfriend."

"And I'm in love with C.J. In love, in love, in love!"

"Thank God that secret's out now," Meri sighed as she leaned back in her chair. "It took you guys long enough to let everyone know."

"You knew they were together?" Taylor asked her.

"I caught them kissing at Thanksgiving in the kitchen," Meri confessed.

"Holy shit!" Taylor exclaimed. "You *can* keep a secret."

"Of course I can," Meri responded. "I'm a very trustworthy person."

"Well, I wouldn't trust my virginity with you," Taylor replied.

"If you were a virgin, I wouldn't either," Meri laughed.

"There is to be a long life of happiness for both of you, Maria and C.J.!" Samata had exclaimed and raised her glass in the air.

"And baby makes three," Meri had added.

Maria, who was now in her ninth month and due to deliver ten days after the awards ceremony, had argued for making the overnight trip to attend the awards—against my protests. She had assured me that her doctor was pleased with her progress, and I knew that she had followed the book for ensuring her and her baby's best health because I had been one of her most vocal enforcers. She had gained the right amount of weight, was making up for the sleep she was losing at night by cutting back on her workdays or taking naps in her office during the day, had attended all of the childbirthing classes with Chantelle, and was listening to guided meditation tapes whenever production of her show became stressful.

Plus, she had reminded me, if her labor were to start early, birthing coach Chantelle would be with her.

The pilot cut into my thoughts with the announcement that we were fifth in line for takeoff.

"I hope he puts enough distance between us and the fourth airplane," Taylor muttered. "I hope he's not going to take off right after and then ram into the back of that plane."

"He's not going to do that," Meri assured her.

"Well, we're taking off much later than was scheduled," Taylor pointed out. "He might just try to pass the other airplane when he's in the air."

"Will you just chill out?" Meri asked her.

"I'm not a very good flyer," Taylor said.

Meri raised her eyebrows and turned to look at her. "Oh? Really?"

Maria suddenly gasped, then took my hand in hers and squeezed it hard. She clenched my hand for several seconds, took in several slow deep breaths, then slowly released the grip on my hand, exhaled, and flashed me a smile.

"Braxton Hicks," she told me.

"Who was he, and why did they name contractions after him?" I asked as I shook my hand to restore the circulation after Maria's vise-like grip.

Maria grinned. "I have no idea."

"Now the book says that you should—"

"I can't get up and walk around or lie down until we're in the air," Maria cut in.

"See? This is exactly why I didn't think you should take this flight. You should be at home, taking it easy. The book does not recommend traveling after the eighth month."

Maria took my hand in hers and brought it to her belly. "No way. We want to be there when you win your awards, C.J. And you *will* win. I'm sure of it. *Madame President* is a great show, much better than the others you're up against in the category. And anyway, you've seen all those pregnant actresses show up at the Academy Awards."

"But they didn't have to sit on an airplane for hours. They got limo service from their front door in L.A."

"I'll be fine, C.J."

"What's going on?" Chantelle asked as she leaned forward in her aisle seat in front of us and peered around the corner at me.

"Is something going on?" Taylor called over to us with an edge of panic in her voice.

"Braxton Hicks," we said in unison.

"Is he the pilot?" Taylor asked.

"Who's Braxton Hicks?" we heard T-Rex ask Chantelle.

"They're contractions," she told her.

"There are contractions?" Samata asked as she quickly unbuckled her seat belt and pulled back on my seat in order to stand up.

"Sam, what are you doing?" I asked.

"What's going on?" Britta questioned Samata.

"She is to be having contractions," Samata said. "There is to be a baby now!"

"Good! Then we don't have to fly," Taylor said. "Let's get off of this damn airplane. There's not enough air in here anyway."

"I'm not—" Maria began, but the rest of her words were drowned out when the airplane's engines began to rumble. The sound built in intensity.

"What's that sound?" Taylor yelled at Meri.

"The engines," she answered.

"What's wrong with them?"

"Taylor, there's nothing wrong with them," Meri said. "We're getting ready to take off."

"Meri, I don't think I want to go. I think I want to get off the plane. I think I'm going to be sick."

"Taylor, will you just relax? Take deep breaths. Go to your happy place."

"My happy place is on the ground."

"Please should I to be finding boiling water?"

"Sam, sit down!" Meri told her from across the aisle. "We're taking off."

"Do you know more airplanes crash on takeoff than on landing?" Taylor asked as she clenched the arm of her seat.

"Thanks for sharing that," Meri said.

"I will alert the stewardess," Samata said as she reached an arm up for the call button.

"Good. Tell her I want to get off the plane, Sam."

"Sam, it's nothing," Maria called over her shoulder. "These are normal contractions. Braxton Hicks happen from the—"

At that moment the pilot gunned the engines and the airplane began to shoot down the runway.

Samata fell back in her seat at the acceleration.

"Buckle your seat belt, hon," Britta told her.

"OhGodohGodohGod!" Taylor muttered loud enough for everyone to hear.

"As soon as this plane is airborne, I'm switching seats," Meri announced.

After we had paired up and checked into our respective hotel rooms, we rested until late afternoon. Then I called everyone's room and, when the phone was answered, I simply announced, "It's showtime!" An hour later, we were dressed and met up in the hallway outside our rooms.

"Well, don't we all look so fine," Chantelle exclaimed as she surveyed our outfits.

"Meri in a dress. I thought I was dreaming when she stepped out of the bathroom," Taylor told us.

"Yeah, well, it's a first and, probably, a last," Meri sniffed.

"You got legs, girl," Chantelle remarked with a grin.

"You look wonderful, Miss Wiggins," Samata smiled. "It is to be a beautiful color on you. It matches your eyes."

"Don't get used to it," Meri replied as she tugged at the dress. "I can't wait to get this off and get back into sweatpants. I never knew dressing like a chick took so much time. The underwear, the pantyhose, the slip. All that before you even put the damn dress on. And, as an aside, I don't know how Tina Turner can prance around in those heels. I'm having a hard enough time in these, and they're not even an inch."

"Just think of them as a fancy pair of sneakers," Britta suggested.

"That's easy for you to say, Miss Lipstick Lesbian," Meri told her.

"She is to be wearing sexy lingerie as well," Samata grinned.

The elevator then arrived, and we boarded it and rode down to the lobby. At the sound of the bell, the elevator doors opened, and for a moment we remained on the elevator, silently taking in the chaotic scene before us.

Camera bulbs flashed, reporters with microphones in hand were bathed in bright lights, and a low hum of excitement sent waves of electricity through our bodies.

"I don't think we're in Kansas anymore, Toto," Meri muttered as she took in the scene.

"This is what we've all been working for, people," I said as I made the first move to exit the elevator. "Come on."

We slowly weaved our way through the crowd of gowned and tuxedoed people in the lobby of the hotel, then found the entrance doors to the massive ballroom where we'd be served dinner and dessert prior to the announcement of the *TV Guide* Award winners.

"I have the butterflies that are in my stomach," Samata said.

"Me, too," Britta replied as she took Sam's arm.

A hostess met us at the door and, after I told her we were from L-TV, led us through the maze of round tables set for dinner. We advanced towards the front of the ballroom. She stopped at a table, then consulted her clipboard and held up her hand as we began to pull out chairs.

"Sorry," she said. "I thought you'd be sitting up here, but I see that you were moved further back."

We turned and followed her in a single-file line to the back of the ballroom.

"Here you are," she said as she indicated the L-TV place card on a table that was stationed nearly at the back of the room.

I peered at the stage from the table. "This certainly seems like a long walk to the stage," I told her.

She shrugged her shoulders. "I'm only following what this seating chart says. You had been up here," she said as she tapped a sheet of paper on the clipboard, "but then were moved back here. To this table."

"So what . . . so what happens if one of us wins an award?" Taylor asked her. "I mean, how would we get up there to the stage to accept it?"

The woman shook her head. "I dunno. I only do seating and then serving dinner. You'll have to talk to someone else about that."

"This doesn't seem right," Chantelle said as she pulled out a chair and sat down. "You can hardly see the stage from here."

Meri put her things on a chair, then consulted her watch and left the table. We watched as she strode up a narrow aisle on the left-hand side of the ballroom and made her way to the stage. She bounded up the stairs, and then walked to the podium. "Thirty-five seconds!" she shouted back to us. "Wherever you are out there."

"That's a long time," Taylor muttered. "Are they really going to wait for us for that amount of time?"

"I guess we just have to keep our acceptance speeches short," I said.

"Maybe this means we're not going to win anything," Maria offered as she pulled out a chair and sat down.

"I don't think anyone knows who won until the envelopes are opened," Britta replied as she took a seat with her back to the stage, and then tried to turn her chair around. "When this room is full, it certainly is going to be hard to see anything."

"There is to be just enough chairs for us," Samata said as she took a seat next to Britta. "Where is Debbe Lee to be sitting?"

"She's certainly not going to like sitting way back here," I said.

"Then she'll be sure we get us moved closer to the front," Britta remarked. "Debbe will take care of it."

Dinner crawled by at a snail's pace, and we picked at the food that was served in a wave of plate clearing between several courses. Conversation was limited.

From time to time each of us looked around the ballroom, trying to spot Debbe Lee.

"I can't believe she's not here yet," Britta said as she consulted her watch. "She flew in last night and called me from her room, so I know she's got to be here."

"Maybe she's waiting to make a grand entrance," Taylor suggested. "You know how much she loves the attention."

"I've got to get up and walk around," Meri announced as she dropped her napkin on the table and stood up.

We watched her disappear into the crowded room.

Maria then stood up and asked Chantelle to come with her to the ladies' room.

"What's wrong?" I asked her.

Maria placed a hand on my shoulder. "Nothing. I just want to talk to Chantelle about something that really doesn't make for interesting dinner table conversation."

I took her hand in mine and kissed it. "Are you sure?"

"I'm sure."

"You look tired."

"I am a bit. But I'm fine."

"Do you want me to come with you?"

"I'll be with her, C.J.," Chantelle said. "You stay here."

Maria gave a quick rub to my shoulder. "I'll be back soon." Maria then took Chantelle's arm and walked slowly out of the ballroom.

"Maybe this trip was a bit much for her," Britta said as she watched Maria walk away.

I nodded. "I think it has been. She hasn't been getting much sleep lately. And the Braxton Hicks contractions are getting more frequent and more painful."

"What are those?" T-Rex asked.

"It's like the uterus is flexing its muscles, limbering up in preparation for real contractions," I answered. "They start out as a tightening sensation in the uterus and only last a short time, but then as the pregnancy progresses, they get more frequent in duration and sometimes more painful. At nine months, the pregnancy book says it's hard to tell when the contractions are Braxton Hicks and when they're true labor contractions."

"Do you think she is to be starting labor?" Samata asked.

I shrugged my shoulders. "I don't know. I hope not."

"Are you excited, C.J.?" Taylor asked.

"I'm really more nervous than excited. I just want everything to go okay."

"It will," Britta assured me.

T-Rex sighed and sat back in her chair.

"So what about you, best actress nominee?" I asked T-Rex. "Are you nervous?"

She shook her head. "Not nervous. Just . . . just feeling edgy, I guess."

"That is how I feel as well," Samata said. "It is not excited. It is not stressed. It is not how there is a word to describe."

"You know, C.J., we really should think about having a comedy series next season at L-TV," Taylor suggested. "We don't have any."

I nodded. "I thought about that, too. Do you have any ideas?"

"Well, Meri and I were kicking around a couple. Is it okay if we work together on it, maybe flush something out for you before the summer begins?"

"Sounds good."

"Comedy—it is very hard to write," Samata said. "The thing one person laughs at is not to be what another thinks is funny."

"That's what we're finding out," Taylor said. "One's a little off-beat—that's Meri's idea, of course. And then mine is a little more run-of-the-mill, more of a sitcom. We thought that if we could find a way to bring our ideas together, we could—"

"C.J., I just saw the son-of-a-bitch," Meri announced as she returned to our table. "I saw her. The Dragon Lady's sitting up there, way at the front," she said as she waved her arm in the air. "She's sitting at a table with Stockard Channing and Meryl Streep and some other actresses."

"The actresses? Then why isn't T-Rex sitting with them as well?" Britta asked.

"I don't know," Meri snapped as she yanked out her chair and sat down. "And so I walk up to the Dragon Lady and lean over to talk to her—she clearly sees me coming—right?—but instead turns right away from me and starts chatting it up with Meryl. And she waves a hand in the air at me like I'm some sort of annoying gnat when I come up to her. So I say to her, 'Excuse me, Debbe, but I have a quick question for you,' and so she says to me, 'Not now, Meri. Can't you see I'm busy?' So I say to her, 'Debbe, we're stuck in no-man's-land in the back of the room,' and do you know what she does? She keeps talking to Meryl. Like I'm not even there. Meryl even looks up at me and isn't even looking at Debbe at that point, being her very nice self, showing me that it's okay with her if I have to interrupt. So then Debbe notices Meryl's paying no attention to her and whirls around at me and hisses in that reptilian tone she gets, 'Meri, get the hell out of here, will you?' And so I did. I got the hell out of there. Who the fuck is she? I mean, who the FUCK is she?" Meri yelled, causing the conversation at nearby tables to stop for a moment.

Taylor reached out for Meri's hand. "Cool it. Just cool it."

Meri tossed aside Taylor's hand. "But she made me *so mad*. She embarrassed me *in front of Meryl Streep!* She treated me like SHIT!"

"Okay, let's take a walk," Taylor said as she stood up. "Let's go outside the hotel. Then you can scream and shout and curse and do whatever you want."

"I don't *want* to go outside," Meri said, lowering her voice. "But I want to know why she's sitting *up there* and we're all the way *back here,* when *we're* the ones who are up for the awards. Not her. Her name isn't on *our* awards. They're ours. She should be supporting us right now, not treating us like we're second-class citizens."

"Let me see if I can talk to her," Britta said as she pushed back her chair.

At that moment, the lights flicked on and off three times, and David Letterman, the emcee for the evening, strode onto the stage. The room erupted in applause.

"Here we go," Taylor said as she raised her hands in the air and crossed her fingers.

"We must all break our legs," Samata said.

"We probably will, walking a mile and a half to the stage," Meri muttered.

Several minutes and several award presentations later, Martin Sheen's name was announced and he walked out to center stage. The applause swelled and then gradually died down.

"Dramatic series are just that," he said as he began reading from a cue card. "They're filled with drama rather than comedy, high tension rather than nonstop action, tight plots rather than funny gags, and strong characters and emotions. This year's nominees are terrific examples of the genre, and it is with great pride that I will momentarily announce the winner. In the category of best drama series, this year's nominees are . . ."

As Martin Sheen announced the list of nominated shows, I turned and looked at the closed doors of the ballroom.

"She's okay, C.J.," Taylor assured me.

"I just wish she were here right now," I told her.

"Maybe she was tired and went up to your room to lay down," Britta suggested. "She can watch the show there, on TV."

"Oh, that is such a good point," Samata said. "I bet that is where she is. And Chantelle is there with her, too."

"This is it, C.J.!" Meri broke in.

"And the *TV Guide* winner for best drama series is . . ." Sheen paused as he fumbled with the envelope, and then pulled out the card inside. He read it, and then announced, "The winner is *Madame President!* Produced and written by C.J.—"

"You won!" Meri said as she stood up.

"Get up there!" Britta urged me.

I stood up and started up the narrow lefthand aisle of the ballroom.

I was halfway up the aisle when I heard Sheen's voice say, "Accepting the award tonight is the CEO and president of L-TV, Debbe Lee."

I stopped and stared at Martin Sheen, who had turned to his left with the award in his hand.

Debbe Lee walked across the stage, accepted the award from Sheen and gave him a quick kiss on the cheek, and then stepped up to the podium.

"Thank you all *so much,*" Debbe gushed breathlessly into the microphone. "Wow! It's been an unbelievable ride this year at L-TV, and I am so proud to have been the one to dream up such an awesome show. *Madame President* is something I'm very proud of, and I'm sure all the people who work on the show from week to week know how very, very happy I am with their professionalism and skill. And, of course, there's Stockard Channing and Meryl Streep, who bring to my series a—"

As Debbe's voice droned on, I turned and walked back to the table.

I pulled out my chair, then slowly took my seat.

A woman who was sitting at the table in front of us—someone I didn't even know—turned around and met my eyes. "What the fuck is *she* doing up there?" she asked me.

I shrugged my shoulders.

"She pulled that same shit at the network I worked at," the woman went on. "Believe me, I wasn't sad to see her sorry ass get kicked out on the street."

I nodded, then picked up my spoon and began to play with the food that was left on my dessert plate.

The awards ceremony slowly ticked on. Then the category of best reality series was announced.

"What if Maria is to win?" Samata asked me.

"You accept the award, C.J.," Meri told me. "You accept it for her."

The announcer listed the nominees, then broke open the envelope. "And the winner for the best reality series is *The Body Farm*, produced and written by Samata Naroff."

Britta threw her arms around Samata and gave her a quick kiss.

"Okay, I must go to accept this," Samata said as she stood up.

"Accepting the award tonight," the announcer said, "is CEO and president of L-TV, Debbe Lee."

"No!" Samata cried out. "That is not to be right! She is not the one to be receiving this award! It is to be my hard work!"

Britta immediately stood up and took Samata's arm. "Let's go."

"But this is to be *my* award!" Samata argued.

Taylor nodded to Meri, who then pushed out her chair and took hold of Samata's other arm. "Come on, we're blowing this popsicle stand," Meri told her.

I stood up and headed for the ballroom doors in advance of the others.

I laid a palm hard against the door, and it immediately swung open.

"I will have to be killing her!" Samata yelled as the door closed behind us. "She is to be strung up and covered with honey and a thousand army ants will be led to her."

"Sam!" Britta snapped at her.

"What?" Samata replied as she wrestled her arm out of Britta's grasp. "That is to be too nice? Okay. I get more graphic for you. I be to putting her head under a—"

"I don't want to hear this," Britta cut in. "Don't you let her do this to you. Don't you let her make you so angry. It'll get you nowhere."

"Let's just kidnap her and take her to a state that has the lightest sentence for first-degree murder," Meri suggested. "We'll do the crime, we'll do the time, and then write a book about it and be millionaires."

In spite of my anger and frustration, I laughed at Meri's comment. "Will you wear a dress to her funeral?" I asked her.

Meri rolled her eyes. "A dress? Aw, geez! Do I have to?"

I tossed my arm around Samata's shoulders. "Come on. Let's get Chantelle and Maria and go find a greasy spoon. We'll order chili dogs and grilled-in-lard hamburgers and buckets of fried clams. Then we'll find the coolest gay bar in the area and dance and drink ourselves silly."

"Now that sounds like a plan," Meri grinned.

We headed for the bank of elevators.

As I was about to press the Up button, elevator doors slid open and Chantelle and Maria slowly walked out. Maria was leaning against Chantelle, and her face was ashen.

"We're heading for the hospital," Chantelle said. "We just called a cab. She's starting labor."

"My bag . . . it's in . . . the . . . room," Maria told me. "You . . . need—"

"I'll get it," I told her as I rushed onto the elevator.

"Taylor and I will stay with C.J.," Meri said. "Sam, you and Britta ride with Chantelle and Maria."

"I'll call a cab and wait for you guys outside," T-Rex told us.

Fourteen long minutes later, a cab pulled up at the front of the hotel to take us to the hospital. As we piled into the backseat, T-Rex told the driver the name of the hospital and asked him "to step on it."

"Lady, have you seen the traffic tonight?" he replied as Taylor squeezed herself into the backseat and slammed the door shut. He flipped up the meter and inched the front of his cab into a long line of cars. "Some damn awards ceremony has created gridlock since early this afternoon. I'll do the best I can."

"Yes, it *was* a damn awards ceremony," Meri muttered.

I sucked air between my teeth as I peered ahead at the traffic, then glanced at my watch.

"Maria's going to be fine," Taylor reassured me as she patted me on the leg. "Chantelle wouldn't let anything bad happen to her."

"That's right," T-Rex agreed. "Chantelle will take care of everything. After all, they've rehearsed for this, right?"

I nodded as I clutched Maria's overnight bag between my legs, sandwiched in the back of the cab with Taylor, Meri, and T-Rex. "But she's early," I told them. "She's ten days early. She never should've made the trip here. I told her to stay home."

"Then you'd be here and she'd be there," Meri pointed out. "Would you want that?"

"Not really," I said. "But I'd rather that she be in Boston at Brigham's, with her own doctor."

"I'm sure the ob-gyns at this hospital are just as good as her own," T-Rex told me.

"I guess," I replied. "This just wasn't the way we had planned it."

"Ten days ahead of schedule isn't at all unusual, C.J.," Taylor said. "Due dates aren't cast in stone. My sister's first baby was three weeks ahead of schedule, and she and the baby were both just fine."

"Really?" I asked.

Taylor nodded. "I'm not just saying that."

"Do you know what Chantelle told me, C.J.?" T-Rex asked as we sat in traffic, making forward progress at a snail's pace. "That Maria was okay when she left the ballroom, just tired, but having some of those contractions that you told me about. So Chantelle suggested that they go up to Maria's room and watch the ceremony on television. They watched the show, with Maria lying in bed with her feet up and relaxing. Then Martin Sheen announced your award and Debbe Lee accepted it and went on and on in her speech about how *Madame President* was her show. Maria started swearing at the television and spouting off about what Debbe Lee had done. Chantelle tried to calm her down. That's when the contractions started up again. So Chantelle isn't sure if this is—how did she say it?—true labor or just a result of Maria being stressed over the awards."

I gripped the overnight bag hard in my hands. "If anything happens to Maria or the baby because of the stunt that Debbe pulled tonight, I'll kill her. I *will* kill her."

"No, *I'll* kill her," Meri said.

"If it's just false labor, then that's okay," Taylor told me. "I think that happens to a lot to women with a first pregnancy."

"Your friend's at the best hospital," the cabbie told us as he peered into the rearview mirror at me. "My wife gave birth to my son and daughter there. The doctors are great."

I forced a smile at him.

"I'm gonna take us on a shortcut, too. I think we'll cut away from some of the worst traffic."

"Thanks," I mumbled.

"You know, it had to have been Debbe who relocated us to that table at the back of the ballroom," Taylor said. "Britta told us that she had flown in last night. I bet she saw to it that we weren't going to be anywhere near that stage. My guess is that she knew what she was going to do before we even got there."

"But why would she do something like that?" T-Rex asked, then promptly held up her hand. "I know, I know. You're probably all going to tell me, 'Because that's what Debbe Lee does.' Believe me, Chantelle has filled me in on the evil woman's doings. But think about it. Your contracts are up at the end of next season. If you guys jump ship then, what's she going to do? Hire new writers? From where? All the best writers in the industry were at the show tonight. Do you think Debbe's actions went unnoticed? Who's going to want to work for her?"

"You have a point," I told her.

"But maybe she's not looking beyond two years," Taylor suggested.

"What do you mean?" Meri asked.

"Well, maybe she just wants to make a quick hit in the industry, create a successful network, and then sell L-TV to the highest bidder," Taylor answered. "She gets two great years out of us, and then we get a new boss. And Debbe walks away with armloads of cash."

The cabbie made an abrupt left-hand turn in front of three lanes of ongoing traffic at an intersection. "Hold on," he told us, but we had already been forced hard to our right as the vehicle shot ahead of the honking traffic and headed down a one-way street.

"Hey, this is a—"

"Hold on," the cabbie told us again as he negotiated a sharp right-hand turn in front of an approaching car that was flashing its high beams at us, sending us sailing to the left in the backseat.

"Okay. Clear sailing now," the cabbie said as he steered down a nearly deserted street. "I'll have you there in a few."

"Phew!" Meri exclaimed.

An hour passed as we sat, paced, or idly scanned through dog-eared magazines in the waiting room area outside the delivery room. Then the operating room doors clicked open and Chantelle emerged from behind them.

I sprang up from my chair. "How is she?"

Chantelle lowered the paper face mask she was wearing and beamed at me. "She's doing great, C.J. Everything's fine. She's in active labor now. Her contractions are stronger. The hospital staff is continually monitoring the baby's condition. Maria's blood pressure is great, and she's got a lot of strength left to take her into the advanced stage of labor when she'll need to be pushing the baby out. It's just going to take awhile."

"Can we see her?" Taylor asked.

Chantelle shook her head. "It's probably best to keep her stress level to a minimum. It'll be less confusing, you know? And there's really not a whole lot of room in there. She's relaxed right now, and I'd like to keep her that way."

"Does she want to see me?" I asked.

"You know she does, C.J.," Chantelle told me. "But I think seeing you will only get her upset about how you weren't able to accept your award tonight. She was so angry at what Debbe did. I don't want to get her all worked up again."

I nodded. "I understand."

"So do you think that the stunt Debbe pulled at the awards had anything to do with her going into labor now?" Meri asked.

"It sure didn't help," Chantelle answered. "Stress can certainly accelerate things. But who knows? Maybe this was supposed to be her time. The good thing is that we're all together, and she's not at home doing this alone. She's going to be so happy when I tell her that you all are out here rooting for her." Chantelle gave me a quick hug, then rubbed my arms. "Listen, I gotta go back in there now. Don't worry. I'm there with her, and she's doing just fine. And I'll come back out here and let you know what's going on whenever I can."

"Tell her that—"

"I will, C.J.," Chantelle cut in. "And she wanted me to tell you that she loves you, too."

By dawn the next day, Maria was still in labor. Chantelle checked in with us nearly every hour, reassuring us about Maria's progress and telling us that everything was going along the way it was supposed to.

"She's even doing this without any pain medication," she grinned. "My sister screamed for the pain medication six minutes into each of her labors. But Maria is handling this so well. I'm so proud of her."

Samata and Britta brought us cups of coffee and stale doughnuts from the hospital cafeteria, and we passed the slow advance of time by hunkering down in the uncomfortable plastic molded chairs and taking catnaps. At 7 A.M., we clicked on the television in the waiting room to catch the morning shows, but when we saw that each of their lead stories was about the *TV Guide* Awards, we immediately shut the television off.

Then, at a little past 10 A.M., Chantelle emerged with the announcement that mother *and* baby were doing just fine. She told us that Maria was going to get some much-deserved rest after her long night and morning and would be staying in the hospital for a couple of days—"nothing to worry about, just something that new mothers do" she told us—and so we trooped out of the hospital, hailed a taxi, and returned to the hotel to extend our room reservations until the end of the week.

Meri stopped in her tracks and grabbed my arm after we had cleared the revolving entrance doors of the downtown hotel. "Debbe," she hissed in my ear.

"Just walk by her, C.J.," Chantelle advised me. "Go up to your room. I'll take care of the reservations."

I clenched my teeth and then lurched away from them.

"C.J.!" Taylor shouted as I ran towards Debbe. "Don't!"

At the sound of my name, which echoed in the high-ceilinged lobby, Debbe turned her attention away from papers she was signing at the checkout counter and looked at me.

I flew up to her.

"C.J.! What a relief! I've been just worried sick about—"

"What the fuck . . . who *the fuck* do you think you are?" I yelled at her as I pushed her hard against the checkout counter.

"My goodness! Where is all this rage coming from?"

I grabbed the front of her silk blouse and pulled her face towards mine. "How *dare* you embarrass us in front of everyone in that ballroom last night! How dare you take our awards away from us!"

The others came up behind me.

"Could you kindly release your grip on me?" she asked, then turned to the clerk behind the desk. "Would you mind calling security for me, darling? I believe there may be an unpleasant scene here in front of your guests."

The clerk reached for a phone, but T-Rex slammed her fist down on the marbled counter in front of the clerk and said in an even voice, "If you make one move, I will personally jump over this counter and rip the phone out of the wall. And you don't want to know what I'll do to you."

The clerk raised her hands in the air and slowly stepped back from the counter.

"Go ahead, C.J.," T-Rex told me as she kept her eyes fixed on the frightened clerk.

I tightened my grasp on Debbe's blouse.

"C.J., this is imported silk you're ruining," she informed me.

"This will be a worthless rag when I'm done with you," I hissed at her.

"*The Body Farm* is not your show," Samata shouted at Debbe from behind me. "The *Madame President* is not your show. You have to be so mean to us at the office, but you have to be so mean to us in public is not to be excused."

"Listen, I have your awards," Debbe said. "They're in my suit-case. I'll get them for you right now, if you'll just unhand me, C.J."

"Unhand you?" I hissed at her. "You're lucky I'm not strangling you right now."

Debbe turned to the clerk. "Miss? I *asked* you to call security."

"I wouldn't even think of it," T-Rex told the clerk.

Debbe glared at the clerk. "I'll have you fired."

"Don't worry," I told the clerk. "She says that to everyone."

"Right now is not when we want the awards, Debbe *Asshole* Lee," Meri snarled. "We wanted them last night, when they were awarded to us. Not you."

"That is right," Samata said. "I was to be accepting my award. For *my* show, which is not yours."

Debbe gripped my hands in hers and swallowed. "But when I saw how far away from the stage you guys were last night, I just thought—"

"And who put us there?" Meri cut in. "We were *supposed* to sit at a different table, a table that was closer to the front of the ballroom. But *someone* apparently changed that at the last minute."

"Now who would've done that?" Debbe asked.

"You were here a day ahead of us," Britta pointed out. "You had every opportunity."

"But that doesn't matter," I said. "The fact of the matter is that you didn't even let us accept our own awards."

"It was taking you *forever* to get up to the stage," Debbe answered. "You know, every second of an award show is sched-uled. You can't dilly-dally. And so I thought it would be best if I just—"

"What you did wasn't based on a spur-of-the-moment deci-sion," I snapped as I pushed the back of my fist against her throat. "Martin Sheen *knew* you would be accepting the award. He read it from a cue card. Now how would he have known to do that, un-less someone had clued him in?"

"Martin knows me. He knows that I'm CEO and president of—"

"Martin Sheen doesn't know you anymore than he knows the thousands of women Charlie Sheen had sex with," I cut in.

"Then I don't know why he did that," Debbe answered. "All of a sudden, I heard my name announced, and so I—"

"All of a sudden, my foot," Meri cut in. "You were moving up to the stage the minute the award was announced. I know. I saw you."

"Okay, okay. You know—what*ever*."

I tightened my hold on Debbe.

Debbe gasped. "C.J., I . . . I can't breathe."

"Then turn blue, would you?" I hissed at her. "But before you pass out, why don't you just admit that *you* were the one who re-located us to the back of the ballroom and *you* were the one who arranged to accept those awards yourself."

"Is that what you want to hear?" Debbe choked out.

"Let's just hear the truth," Taylor said. "Then C.J. will let you go."

Debbe locked eyes with mine.

"Say it," Meri said as she glared over my shoulder at Debbe.

"I did what I felt was best," Debbe gasped.

"Why don't you tell that to Maria?" I asked.

Debbe's eyes darted around the group of people behind me.

"No, she's not here, Debbe," I informed her. "She's at the hospi-tal. The stunt you pulled last night sent her into early labor."

Debbe swallowed.

"So why don't you tell me again what your explanation is for how we got stuck way the hell in the back of the room and the an-nouncers knew to call your name to accept our awards for us."

"How is Maria?" Debbe asked.

"Terrible," I cut in before anyone could say anything.

"Because of—"

"Yeah, because of what you did last night."

"Listen, I never meant any harm," Debbe said. "Just let go of me, C.J. I'll explain everything. We can have coffee. Or breakfast. Yes, that sounds like a great idea, doesn't it? I'll treat you all to break-fast. We'll sit down and just talk this over—"

"I do not be wanting food from you," Samata informed her. "I would not be wanting to share any meal with you. I would be appreciating the truth."

"Okay, okay. I did it," Debbe confessed. "Now let go of me, C.J., or I'll call the cops myself."

"Tell me what you did, Debbe. Tell us *all* what you did. Then I'll let go of you."

"I was doing what I felt was best, C.J."

"That's not the answer I want to hear."

"Miss?" Debbe said as she turned to the clerk.

"I'm busy," the clerk said as she leaned against the wall behind the counter.

"Good answer," T-Rex told her.

"Alright! I moved you guys, and then I let it be known that I'd be accepting your awards. Now will you just let me go, C.J.?"

"Then why let us even fly here?" Taylor asked. "Why not tell us to just stay home?"

"You wouldn't have," Debbe said.

"So you just decided to blindside us?" T-Rex asked. "What kind of sick game is that? And tell me something, now that you're suddenly being honest. I was supposed to sit at the table with Meryl Streep and Stockard Channing, wasn't I?"

Debbe nodded. "But I thought you'd want to sit with Chantelle."

"Why didn't you ask *me* what I wanted?"

"Because I'm the boss, and I get to decide what's right for L-TV," Debbe answered. "And, anyway, you aren't in their league."

T-Rex stared at Debbe.

Chantelle stepped past me and delivered a swift punch to Debbe's belly.

Debbe cried out and doubled over, causing me to release the grip I had on her.

Chantelle bent down to Debbe. "That's just one ounce of the pain Maria has been going through for the past eleven hours," she informed her. "And that's how I feel about your comment that

T-Rex isn't in the same league as Meryl and Stockard. She wasn't nominated for best actress because of anything you've ever done, Debbe. She was nominated because of the work she does. On *my* show. You disgust me. You've brought shame to L-TV because of what you did. You think you're so high and mighty, but let me tell you something. You're not."

Debbe slowly straightened up.

"And let me tell you something else," Meri said as she stepped up to Debbe. "All those things you told C.J. about our supposedly lurid pasts could easily be used in a lawsuit against you. Defamation of character is what I think it's called."

Debbe met my eyes.

"Don't look at me," I told her. "You made up the stories and led me to believe them."

"How about this," Debbe said as she leaned against the counter and rubbed her belly. "I'll talk to the press. Or, better yet, I'll issue a statement in which I admit I was out of line to accept the awards on your behalf."

"What's that supposed to do now?" Britta asked her. "Samata didn't get to give her acceptance speech. She didn't get the recognition she deserved from her peers. Neither did C.J. To say anything now wouldn't make them feel better. And it would only make them look worse."

"Then I don't know what I can do to rectify this situation," Debbe answered. "I can only offer you my heartfelt apologies."

"That would be nice, except you don't have a fucking heart!" Meri spit out.

"Then I'll give you all more money," Debbe offered. "A thousand dollars each. Right now. Cash. How's that?"

Chantelle tipped her head and put her face in front of Debbe's. "You think a thousand fucking dollars is going to make any of us feel better about what you did? Do you think a thousand fucking dollars is going to make Maria and her baby feel any better?"

"She had her baby?" Debbe asked. "That's so wonderful! What hospital is she at? I'll send her a nice big bouquet of fresh flowers right away."

"I'll tell you what," I said as I grabbed Debbe's purse from her and opened it up. I flipped through her wallet, then extracted several charge cards. I distributed a card to each person. "For the emotional suffering we have each been through, we get to go on a shopping spree, courtesy of Debbe Lee. You don't mind that, do you, Debbe? Because, after all, that's how you feel any problem can be resolved."

"C.J., you're talking about a lot of money," Debbe said as she looked at her charge cards.

"She's just going to call in and cancel them," Britta said as she placed the MasterCard she had been holding on the counter. "I don't want her money. I just want her out of my sight."

One by one, the writers placed the cards on the counter.

Debbe reached for them.

I quickly swept my arm across the counter and sent the cards sailing to the floor.

"C.J.!" Debbe yelled in protest. Then Debbe turned to the clerk. "A little help here, please?"

"Let her get the cards herself," T-Rex told the clerk.

"I'm not doing anything for anyone," the clerk said.

As Debbe bent down and began to pick up her cards, we turned and walked away from her.

"I've never hit anyone before in my life," Chantelle said as tears slid down her cheeks. T-Rex placed an arm around her shoulders as we rode the elevator up to our floor. "What kind of person am I to have done that? That's not me. I'm not someone who does something like that."

"I know you're not," T-Rex told her.

I shook my head and sighed. "I've never been that angry with anyone. Even when Debbe did the things she did to me in our relationship, I never once felt that kind of . . . that kind of rage. That's what it was. Flat-out rage. I literally felt that I could kill her."

Samata nodded. "There is to be no reasoning with her, and there is to be no remorse from her actions. You get to be so blind-white mad that you do not know what is to be done. I have felt this way, too."

"We all did," Taylor added.

"I am so sorry I hit her," Chantelle sobbed.

"It's okay," T-Rex comforted her. "It's been a long night for you. What you did is something you don't have to apologize for."

"But I hit her!" Chantelle exclaimed.

"She deserved it," Meri said. "And much more."

I shook my head. "No, she didn't deserve anything we did to her. We shouldn't be thinking that way about her, or about anyone else."

"I agree," Britta said.

"But she is to make us so mad," Samata argued. "And to take away from us our acceptance of our awards. *Our* awards!"

"They're just awards, Sam," I told her in a tired voice. "They're just lumps of plastic and metal. They shouldn't mean so much to us that they get us to act this way."

Taylor nodded. "Debbe took us down to her level by what she did. We were as mean and angry to her as she's been to us."

"But she is to be pushing and pushing at us," Samata said. "It was only to be a matter of time before there was to be an explosion."

"We've got to find a better way to channel our anger and frustration at her," Taylor added.

The elevator doors slid open, and we slowly stepped out of the car.

"Let's all get some rest," I suggested as we stood in the hallway. "Then we'll have lunch together and go to the hospital to see Maria."

"And we won't say a word to her about what just happened in the lobby," Chantelle advised. "We need to be happy when we see her."

"And the baby," I added. "Hey, you guys. Maria just had her baby." I smiled at them. "Let's not forget that we've got a lot to celebrate. We were given a lot of awards for our hard work at L-TV. And Maria had a healthy baby girl."

Slowly, smiles began to form on everyone's faces.

I lay in the queen-size bed in my hotel room, staring up at the ceiling. In my mind, I replayed the scene in the lobby with Debbe. What if the clerk had called the cops? I wondered. What if I had been arrested for assault? What if Chantelle had been arrested for punching Debbe?

Was the clerk on the phone now, talking to the police? Had Debbe called the police on her own?

No, that wasn't a good thing I had done, I realized with a deep sigh. My taking Debbe hostage in the lobby had sent the wrong message to the writers. I was supposed to lead them, to show them that all of us should be able to handle things professionally, no matter how badly we may have been treated. I had acted no better than a school-yard bully in front of them. My threatening actions may have forced a confession out of Debbe, but they had also fueled the frustration and anger everyone had felt since the ceremony.

I had allowed that to happen. Shame on me, I chastised myself.

And, I wondered, had anyone else seen what we were doing to Debbe? Were we the only ones in the lobby?

I thought back to the awards ceremony, about how proud and excited I had been to hear that *Madame President* had won the award for best drama series. *Best.* It had felt like I was walking on a cloud as I moved through the ballroom to accept the award. It had felt just like the first time I had kissed Maria. But then I had fallen hard back to earth—crashed like a sky diver who was wearing a faulty parachute—when Debbe Lee had bounded up on the stage to accept the award.

The feeling reminded me of how I had felt the first time I had learned that Debbe had cheated on me. It was as if someone had punched me in the stomach.

And poor Chantelle! I thought. The woman who had helped my partner to give birth to a child I would be helping to raise had been driven to a point that had stunned her, causing her to feel sadness, guilt, and shame.

I have to do better, I told myself. I have to first put this whole sorry episode behind me and then help the writers to put this incident behind them as well. I had to somehow find a way to rally them together again.

But how? I asked myself.

The problem was, as long as Debbe Lee was our leader, we would have to put up with her antics and her treatment. We would have to endure them for however long we worked for her. Though maybe Taylor would be proven right. Maybe Debbe would sell the network after the next season.

But that thought didn't sit right with me. Although I didn't want to work for Debbe one minute more, I also didn't want to work for someone else who might come in to head up the network. Though it had always been Debbe's brainstorm and Debbe's dream, the writers had made L-TV happen. Without us, we would not have had as strong a prime-time lineup as we did. Without our shows, we wouldn't have increased the viewership across the nation.

L-TV had become ours, and yet we had no say in how the network was run.

I sat up in bed, and leaned back against the headboard. Then maybe that was the answer, I thought. *Ownership.* Not a partnership with Debbe—hell, no!—but ownership of the network by the writers. Each writer would own a piece of the network. But how could we do that? I wondered. Could we buy our way into ownership, with each of us shelling out enough dough to purchase a percentage of the network?

Debbe certainly wouldn't allow that to happen right now, but if she put L-TV up for sale, then perhaps the writers could buy the network.

My mind began to whirl with possibilities. Now I just had to figure out how to make the possibilities happen.

"Hey," I said softly to Maria as she slowly opened her eyes and focused on me.

"Chica," she whispered, then licked her lips and reached out a hand to me. The plastic tube of the IV that was connected into her arm followed her.

I moved closer up on the bed to Maria and clasped her hand in mine.

"Did you see her?"

I smiled and nodded. "I saw her. I went to the nursery after everyone left and just stared at her. I lost all track of time. She's beautiful. Absolutely beautiful. How are you?"

"Tired."

"I know. But your legs have been shaking the whole time I've been sitting here watching you."

"That happens. It'll stop. The strain . . . you know. It's a lot."

"I know." I raised her hand to my lips and kissed it. Then I gently rubbed my fingers against Maria's cheek.

"I must look a wreck."

I shook my head. "Not to me. Never. You're even more beautiful."

"I feel like a wreck."

"You feel soft and warm."

"I held her in my arms, C.J. I held my Katrina April Hernandez in my arms, and she let out the most enormous cry you've ever heard."

"Oh, I'm sure I'll get to hear that pretty soon for myself. At all hours of the day and night."

Maria nodded. "Look what you signed on for."

"I know. I'll have two beautiful women in my life to love. How many people can say they have that?"

"I love you, C.J." Maria's eyelids fluttered.

"Go to sleep, my love."

Maria mumbled something, and then her breath settled into a slow, steady rhythm.

I kissed her softly on the lips and felt an incredible wave of peace and serenity settle into my heart.

Fifteen clandestine after-work meetings in a month, in addition to end-of-the-season production of our shows at L-TV, Maria and I learning what it took to care for a new baby while tending to our blossoming relationship, and some of the writers struggling to balance work with enjoying and growing in relationships that were still in their infancy, were clearly taking a toll on us. When Maria came back downstairs and joined us in the living room of my house for what we hoped would be our last out of the office meeting, her expression conveyed to the group both fatigue and frustration.

"Listen, you've got to keep your voices down," she said as she rejoined us. "I'm placing this baby monitor right here, near me, and the next time Katrina even makes a peep, this meeting is adjourned."

"Sorry, Maria," Britta said. "Maybe we should leave and just do this another time."

"No way!" Meri yelled at her, then clapped a hand over her mouth and glanced at Maria. "Sorry."

Maria raised an eyebrow at Meri, picked up the baby monitor, and held it to her ear.

"It won't happen again, Maria. I promise," Meri said.

Maria placed the baby monitor back on the coffee table.

"We have got to all be agreeing with this plan by tonight, or it is out of the window," Samata told us.

Taylor shook her head and sat forward on the couch. "I know we do. But it just sounds so . . . so risky. What if she figures out what we're doing? What if she—"

"What if, what if, what if," Meri cut in. "You've been what-ifing us to death on this since the get-go. It's *going* to work, Taylor."

"It's not going to work if she doesn't take the bait," T-Rex said.

"I've told you guys again and again, Debbe confided in me she's in love with Britta," I explained. "When Britta tells her she wants to go away with her, that she's really in love with her and not Sam, she'll have her bags packed in five minutes."

"But what if Britta isn't convincing enough?" Taylor asked.

"Again with the what-if," Meri said as she threw her arms up in exasperation.

"Taylor, I can be a very convincing liar," Britta told her. "Remember, I was in deep trouble for years with the debts I owed to some pretty nasty people. I had them convinced for a long, long time that I'd be repaying my debts."

"I can believe what she's sayin' there," Lars interjected. "Addicts is damn good at bein' convincin'. My ex, hell, I had her fooled that I wasn't drinkin' no more even though I stank a liquor when I came home at night. Anywho, you're dealin' with a pro here when it comes ta buildin' a convincin' set. And the pictures C.J. gave me are damn good. There's no way Debbe's not gonna believe she's at her beach house at Amelia Island."

"But what I'm most concerned about is getting her to sign the new contracts," Maria said. "All this planning and scripting of what we're going to do and the hours and hours we've spent going over every detail of this plan aren't going to matter if we can't get her to sign the new contracts."

"I know," I said. I nodded at the woman who was sitting next to Lars. "Sheila, tell these guys what you told me before they arrived tonight."

"But Sheila was Debbe's lawyer during your split with her, C.J.,"

Taylor argued. "And you told us last week that Debbe fired her when she learned how much you had been given in the breakup."

"You're right, Taylor," Sheila responded as she stood up. "Debbe Lee wants nothing more to do with me, even though I followed exactly what she had told me to do back then in her breakup with C.J. She told me to give C.J. whatever C.J. wanted, and I did. When I called her to go over some of the terms of the agreement, the only thing she nixed was the Lexus. And then she signed the papers."

"And fired you," Taylor added.

Sheila nodded. "And fired me. After she had pretty much guaranteed me the job of head of the legal department at L-TV. That's why I'm on board with you guys one hundred percent. I quit a very good job at a law firm in Boston to come to L-TV. And when Debbe told me I wouldn't have a job because I had, quote, screwed her, end of quote, in the breakup settlement, I was left high and dry. My old firm didn't want me back, and Debbe bad-mouthed me to all the big firms in the city, which effectively slammed some lucrative doors shut to me. That's why I had to hang out my own shingle, and it hasn't been easy building up a solid client base. I've been making nowhere near the salary I was pulling in at the law firm." Sheila paused, then sighed. "But, hey, that's neither here nor there. I'm just reminding all of you of how easy it was for me to jump at this opportunity to get back at Debbe when C.J. called me. And remember, she's never going to see me. She's never going to know that I was the one who drafted the new contracts. But what I told C.J. earlier is that the current head of legal services at L-TV, Janette Garrison, is more than happy to help us out. She can't stand working for Debbe, and so she's going to hand in a letter of resignation for Debbe to sign while we take her on her fantasy vacation to Amelia Island. After Janette's had her picture taken standing next to Debbe when she signs the new contracts, Debbe will then sign Janette's letter of resignation. It'll be a done deal."

"But what if," Taylor began, then shot a look at Meri and said, "I still can't believe she's going to sign anything."

"She's going to be pretty out of it at the time," Chantelle said. "Even though my aunt said she doesn't want to get involved in our scheme—after all, she'd be fired from her job as a home nurse and lose her license if anyone found out where certain, uh, supplies went—she's assured me that the stuff we'll be giving Debbe is going to keep her pretty high and happy until she signs the new contracts."

"I just do not be really secure with that part of this plan," Samata said. "C.J., she is being having no allergies to medication, right? We are not going to be killing her, are we?"

"That would be plan B," Meri grinned.

"That is not being funny," Samata responded.

"My aunt has given me really good instructions," Chantelle reassured her. "It's not like we're giving her a narcotic. What we'll be using is a little stronger than the laughing gas a dentist gives you. She'll still be awake, but she won't be really grounded. And she'll be very, very happy."

"How long will it take to wear off?" T-Rex asked.

"The minute we take off her oxygen mask or turn off the gas tank even with the mask on, she'll stop breathing in the gas and oxygen mixture," Chantelle said. "She'll come out of it right away. Though the beauty of using this is that she's not going to remember very much of anything. It's all going to be kind of a blur to her."

"And I'll take care of filling in the details for her later on," Britta added.

"Our costumes have got to be really good," Maria said. "And we've got to keep those OR masks on the entire time we're with her."

"And use different voices," T-Rex added.

"But won't Debbe have a problem with Janette, once she finds out she signed the new contracts in her presence?" Taylor asked.

"She'll certainly be pretty pissed off at her," Sheila answered. "But Debbe will have no real legal basis of an argument with her because Janette will no longer be representing L-TV. And since

Debbe's signature will be on both the new contracts and Janette's letter of resignation, that will prove that she was aware of what was going on. There will be no indication that she signed the new contracts under duress."

"And that's going ta be when we hafta switch the sets to the one of her office," Lars broke in. "When she's signing them contracts."

"Since she's never leaving Boston anyway, why do you have to build another set?" T-Rex asked Lars.

"We don't want no one seein' us," Lars answered. "We take her in the buildin', even late at night, and someone's sure ta see us."

"We're never going to leave L-TV's studio warehouse," I added. "That's the only place that's secure. And that's the only place that no one will suspect anything if they see us going in and out of the building."

"To get back to your question, Taylor, the new contracts will be dated prior to Britta and Debbe leaving for their trip to Amelia Island," Sheila said. "Debbe will have no recollection of signing them, of course. But, there her signature will be. And there's no way she can challenge the signature because she'll be signing the documents."

"She's going to be so mixed up, she won't know what's going on," Meri grinned. "Oh, this is a great plan!"

"Okay," Taylor said as she stood up and began pacing the room. "Okay. I know you guys are going to get really upset with me with what I'm about to say, and so let's just remember to keep it down so we don't wake up the baby."

Meri rolled her eyes. "Don't tell me you're not going to go along with this now, after all this planning. Don't tell me you're pulling out now."

"No, no," Taylor said as she held up her hand. "No, I'm in on this. I am. But can we go over this plan, step-by-step, one more time? Just so I'm clear in my mind."

Low groans issued from everyone.

"I'm sorry," Taylor responded. "But what's it going to hurt if we go over this one more time?"

"C.J.?" Maria said as she looked at me. "Give us the plan, and then let's call it a night."

I stood up and cleared my throat. "Britta is going to tell Debbe that she's in love with her and not Sam. She's going to beg and plead with her to take her away so they can be together. She'll mention the beach house on Amelia Island. She'll tell Debbe that she heard about it from me when she told me how much she regretted not going to Aspen with Debbe. Debbe will only be too happy to agree to go."

"But she told you she was being in love with Britta four months ago, C.J.," Sam pointed out. "Perhaps she no longer is to be feeling this way."

"Even if she isn't still in love with Britta, Sam, Debbe will jump at the opportunity anyway," I answered. "I know her. And her ego can't resist knowing that she's been chosen over someone else. She likes to win. She *always* likes to win."

"Let's hope that's how she feels," Taylor mumbled.

Meri shot her a look.

"Okay, okay," Taylor responded. "Go on, C.J."

"On the limo ride that Debbe will believe is taking her and Britta to the airport, which will really be just a couple of trips around the block—"

"I'll be driving the limo in disguise," T-Rex broke in.

"Right. On the ride Britta will put a cloth that's been soaked in chloroform over Debbe's mouth—"

"Rendering her unconscious for about an hour," Chantelle added.

"And that is to be safe?" Sam asked.

"Absolutely," Chantelle answered. "She'll have one hell of a headache when she wakes up, but that's all."

"During the time that Debbe's out," I resumed, "we'll put both of Debbe's legs and her left arm in what will look like casts. But we'll be able to take them on and off in a matter of seconds. They're just stage props."

"My aunt helped us with those," Chantelle added.

"That's when we set her up at the Amelia Island locale," Lars said, and then grinned. "To her bood-wow-er."

"And when she wakes up, I'll explain that we had a terrible accident while we were out boating," Britta said. "That will provide her with the reason for the casts she'll be wearing and the headache she'll be experiencing from the chloroform. And I'll tell her that she complained so much about being in the hospital that she ordered me to take her back to the beach house and hire 'round-the-clock care."

"That's when some of us are going to be assuming the roles as her caregivers," I went on. "Sam is the doctor. Maria and Chantelle are the nurses."

"And I'm the one who will be serving her the terrific hospital meals," Meri added. "Just call me Betty Crocker."

"I have everyone's costumes ready," Chantelle said.

"And do you have our nametags, too?" Maria asked.

Chantelle nodded. "It's taken care of."

"I have the lightin' worked out," Lars said. "The person who's gonna be operatin' that is fine with this. She works for me on my show."

"Good," I told her. "Now, in Debbe's mind, this entire episode is going to take place over the course of ten days. It'll actually be only about five or six hours, tops, with the light on the set changing every two hours to replicate the passage of time from sunrise to sunset. Once we get her settled in for one of the nights, the casts will be removed and she'll be placed in the set that duplicates her office."

"I got them video cams set up, too," Lars added.

I nodded. "Right. Remember that Debbe's office is outfitted with a video camera that records everything that goes on in her office, twenty-four, seven. That's when Janette will show up with the contracts and her letter of resignation for Debbe to sign."

"And she'll still be getting the gas then?" Taylor asked.

"Well, that's when things are going to get a little tricky," Chantelle answered. "We obviously can't film this with her wearing an oxygen mask."

"Janette's going to have to work fast at that point," Sheila said.

"Right," Chantelle nodded. "I'm going to increase the gas before we get her to the office set, then take her off of it. If she starts coming around, we'll stop filming and replace the mask until she gets to her happy place again."

"And then, after she's signed the new contracts and Janette's resignation," I continued, "we'll put her back in the limo and settle her in at her home. I have the key."

"One more dose of chloroform in the limo," Britta said, "and she'll wake up in her own bed and see me getting dressed to go home."

"And all the things that she packed for the trip will have a nice ocean smell, thanks to Boston Harbor," I finished. "Remember. I'll be directing what goes on all the time, and Taylor and Meri will be making sure we follow the scripts we've been writing over the past few weeks, detailing what we're supposed to say and do. But we have to be ready to improvise."

"And if I'm not giving her enough gas to keep her loose," Chantelle said, "Maria or I will step on the button that will activate an alarm on the machines we'll have set up near her bed. We'll say something like, 'Her blood pressure's dropping,' and then I'll increase the gas."

"It'll be like one a them soap operas," Lars grinned. "Anythin' can happen, you know?"

"Well, let's hope that everything goes according to plan," I answered. "We don't need any surprises."

"That's right, we don't," Taylor agreed.

"I know, I know," Lars said. "I was jus' sayin', is all. Everythin's gonna go jus' fine."

"And then we'll all be part owners of L-TV?" Britta asked.

Sheila nodded. "Debbe will end up owning forty percent in total. The writers will have in their new contracts that they each own ten percent, with a clause that should anyone leave L-TV, her percentage of ownership will be equally divided among the remaining writers. A separate agreement that all the writers except C.J. will sign states that you each agree to give one percent of your ten-percent shares to Sheila, Janette, T-Rex, Lars, and Britta for a period of three years. Which will compensate us for our time involved in this project."

"And the buildin' supplies?" Lars asked.

"They're coming out of the budget for *Madame President*," I answered.

"And so Debbe can't sell L-TV now, can she?" T-Rex asked.

"Not without a majority percentage," Sheila answered. "That means that at least two of the writers have got to agree to a sale."

"So we will end up owning more of L TV than Debbe?" Maria asked.

"Together, yes," Sheila said.

Maria smiled. "I am *so* into this plan. After what Debbe did at the *TV Guide* Awards, and then to have the audacity to show up at the hospital and try to convince me that that's what you guys wanted—"

"After what she's done all season," Britta added.

"She's getting just what she deserves," Meri concluded.

We nodded our heads in agreement.

I held open the bed covers for Maria, then draped an arm around her as she snuggled next to me.

"How's Katrina?" I asked.

"Sleeping. Like a baby."

"Well, at least she's doing what she's supposed to be doing. Thank God she isn't sleeping like . . . well . . . a walrus."

Maria chuckled. "And thank God she doesn't look like a walrus."

"She's beautiful, Maria."

Maria sighed. "Yes, she is. Even if she is my baby, I think she's the most beautiful baby I've ever seen."

"And so are you."

Maria gently rubbed her fingers against my face. "You always say such nice things, C.J. You're so wonderful to me. You're so wonderful *for* me."

I stroked Maria's hair. "I feel the same way about you, love. I never thought I could be in a relationship that was so relaxing, so exciting, so passionate, loving, gentle, and open and honest. With Debbe, things were never that way."

"I know. I feel the same way about my relationship with Jesse. Maybe that's why things are so wonderful for us. We know what it's like to be with someone who falls so short in so many ways, who has treated us badly. After Jesse and I ended, I made myself a promise to never, ever, get involved with someone who was a lot of work, with someone who couldn't be nice to me all the time. And then I looked at you one day at a meeting and I thought to myself, 'Now that's the kind of person I should be looking for. Someone like C.J.' "

"Well, have I come close to this C.J. person you just mentioned?"

Maria laughed. "Yes, dear. You fit her to a T."

"I'm actually her clone."

"You mean there's an even better model walking around somewhere?"

"Um, I take that back. I'm the real thing. No need to look any further."

We held each other in silence for a few moments.

"C.J.?"

"Um?"

"You're okay with this plan, aren't you?"

I took in a deep breath. "The honest answer is yes. And no. I don't like being duplicitous. I don't like to be vengeful. I don't like to break laws. That's something I really, *really* don't like to do. I've always been someone who tries to do the right thing. I always try to think about how my words and my actions will affect someone else. What we're doing is so deliberate. It kind of scares me sometimes if I think about it too much. But then I think back on all the things Debbe has done to me over the years, both when we were a couple and at L-TV, and I wonder why I haven't done something bad to her in the past. Like let air out of her tires or charge up a storm on the joint credit cards we had when we were together. And then sometimes I wonder, will I be happy or proud of myself after Debbe signs the new contracts? I don't know. That's the part that worries me the most. It's not how I feel right now about what we're going to do in two days. But how I'll feel afterwards. About myself."

"I know what you mean," Maria said. "I feel those things, too. And I'm sure everyone else does, at least at some level."

"Except for Meri."

"Yeah. Except for her," Maria chuckled. "But I think even Meri knows deep down that what we're doing isn't really the best thing. Maybe it's not even the right thing to do. We're all going to have to work through our own moral dilemmas after this whole thing is behind us."

"There's something to be said about a group mentality, though."

"What do you mean?"

"Well, I think it's easier to do something like this when you have the support of others. Maybe it helps us to justify what we're doing. Maybe it helps to give us courage to carry out the plan. I know that I couldn't do something like this alone."

"Nor could anyone else, C.J. But if we don't do this, I'll tell you what will happen to our lovely, tight-knit group at L-TV. One by one, we'll all end up leaving. We'll go our separate ways. And I don't know about you, but this is the first time since leaving home that I've felt like I'm part of a family. I love everyone in this group, and I'd be so sad to see us go to different jobs or different geographical locations."

"I hadn't thought about that, hon. But you're right. We can't keep working together at L-TV as long as Debbe has all the power and constantly uses it against us. And who knows what she'll do when next season is over and our contracts are up. She may not renew them, and then we'll all have to leave. When this is over, when she's signed the new contracts, I know she's still going to be the same old bitch she's always been. But we'll have a level of control. And we'll have a lot more security."

"And we'll have our dignity," Maria added. "She can't keep kicking us around and threatening to fire us all the time. She's abusive and manipulative. It's too nerve-wracking working for someone like that. Like you said, she'll still be Debbe when all this is over. But we'll have some control over her actions. We'll be able to guide L-TV in the right direction. And we'll make sure that everyone is treated well. We'll make it a much better working atmosphere."

"And probably get more respect in the industry," I added.

"That, too."

Maria yawned. "C.J., I'm so happy. I never thought my dreams could come true. But they really have with you."

"I feel the same way. I never knew a relationship could be so good. I love being with you. Holding you is like . . . well . . . I feel like I'm home when I'm with you."

"It's happened so fast."

"It has."

"But it's good."

"It is."

"Good night, C.J."

"Good night, love."

I was drifting in a boat on a calm ocean, with Maria in my arms and lines from the Prince song "When Doves Cry" running through my head. *Animals strike curious poses, they feel the heat, the heat between me and you . . . you and I engaged in a kiss . . .*

"C.J.? C.J.?"

I slowly left the ocean and opened my eyes.

Maria was sitting up in bed next to me.

"What?" I asked her.

"Did you hear that?" she whispered to me.

I listened.

"That! Did you hear that?" she asked, then squeezed my arm.

"Ow! That hurts."

"Sorry," she whispered as she released her grip on me. "But I think there's something outside the house."

I rubbed my eyes. "Yeah. It sounds like a raccoon just tipped over the trash barrels."

"I don't think it's a raccoon."

"Then maybe it's a skunk."

"Listen!"

I slowly sat up.

"I think someone's outside," she whispered to me.

"It's just an animal."

"No, it's not! Did you hear that?"

"Okay, okay," I said as I threw back the covers and slid my legs over the side of the bed. "I hear something, too. I'll go check it out. But I'm sure it's—"

I was interrupted by the sound of pounding on the front door.

"*That's* not an animal," Maria said, breaking her whisper.

The doorbell then started ringing. And ringing. And ringing.

"Who the hell is here at this hour?" I asked as I pulled on my slippers.

"I don't know," Maria snapped as she jumped out of bed. "But all this racket is going to wake up the baby."

"I'll go down and see who it is."

"Take the pepper spray," Maria told me.

I slid open the top drawer of the nightstand and took out the canister.

"Maybe we should just call the police," Maria suggested. "It's two in the morning."

"I won't open the door," I told her as I slipped on my bathrobe. "I'll just look out and see who it is. Then I'll call the police."

A few minutes later, I looked out on the front porch, pocketed the pepper spray, then opened the door.

"C.J.!" Debbe shouted at me.

"What the hell are you doing here at this time of night, Debbe?" I asked as I squinted my eyes at her.

"Oh, I was just out driving and thought I'd stop by," Debbe said as she pushed past me, then stumbled down the hallway with an unopened bottle of champagne dangling from one of her hands.

"Debbe, you're drunk."

"C.J., I'm feeling just fine. *Just fine.*"

"Do you know what time it is?" I asked as I closed the door and followed her down the hall.

"Does anyone really know what time it is?" she sang between giggles. "Does anyone really care? ABOUT TIME!" she bellowed out.

"Debbe, keep your voice down."

Debbe whirled around, lost her balance, and leaned against the wall. She gave me a lopsided grin. "So, my sexy little ex. Aren't you going to invite me in?"

"You are in. Now why don't you just go home and sleep this off."

"Sleep? Sleep? How can I sleep in my big old empty bed? No. No! I can't do that. I tried already. So I decided—do you know what I decided?"

I crossed my arms across my chest. "What did you decide? To wake up everyone you knew?"

"I decided to find out how the other half lives, so to speak. You know. The other half as in those people who *are* sleeping with other people tonight. As opposed to me. Who *isn't* sleeping with anyone. Do you see what I'm saying?"

"Yes. You wanted to make an ass of yourself in front of an audience, as opposed to just staying at home and making an ass of yourself alone."

"Well, now, no! THAT'S NOT FUCKING WHAT I'M SAYING!"

I stepped up to Debbe. "Keep your voice down," I hissed at her. "I don't want you to wake the baby."

"WAKE THE BABY! WAKE THE BABY! WAKE THE BABY!" Debbe chanted in a loud voice as she skipped down the hallway and into the living room. "Say. You know, I've never been here before. At this house. At this house that *I* bought you." Debbe made a slow, unsteady circular turn. "Fireplace. That's good. Kitchen there. Good. Nice furniture. Good, good, good." Debbe placed one hand on her hip and waved the champagne bottle around in the air. "I'd say you've done all right for yourself, there, ex-girlfriend. Yes, indeedy. I'd say you were pretty well taken care of. Don't you?"

"Well, I don't have my Lexus," I pointed out.

"Well, I don't have my Lexus," Debbe echoed in a whiny voice, then raised the champagne bottle in the air. "FUCK THE LEXUS! AND FUCK YOU, C.J.!"

Sounds of a baby crying came from upstairs.

Debbe lowered the champagne bottle and stepped towards me. She placed a finger over her mouth. "Shhhh. You'll wake the baby."

"Listen, Debbe, if you want to you can just sleep this off downstairs. But I've got to get back to bed."

Debbe grabbed the front of my bathrobe. "Does this remind you of anyone, C.J.?" she snarled, then quickly released her grip on me. "Okay, okay. I didn't come here to be nasty to you. Believe it or not. I came here because I wanted to see that you're happy. I really want you to be happy, C.J."

"Oh, good Lord, Debbe. You've never wanted me to be happy. Why don't you just go downstairs and get some sleep. And let the rest of us get to sleep, too."

"The baby's still crying, C.J."

"I know. Thank you."

"You're welcome!" Debbe boomed. "Now where is that lovely wife of yours? She is not my beautiful wife. This is not my happy home. Home, home on the range," Debbe sang, then stopped. "Tell me, C.J. Where is that hot Latino number named Maria Hernandez? Maria!" Debbe bellowed out as she stepped towards the staircase. "Yoo-hoo! Maria! Maria! I've just met a girl named Maria," Debbe sang out as she began to walk up the stairs. "And suddenly that name, will never be—"

The door to the nursery opened and Maria walked out with Katrina in her arms. "Debbe, get the hell out of here. C.J., call the police. NOW!"

"Aw, now come on, Maria. I'll be quiet. I promise I will," Debbe said as she slowly advanced up the stairs. "I just wanted to see the baby. And your happy home. Your happy, happy home. I wanted to see one big happy family here—ha!—that's the name of your show, isn't it, Maria? I've just met a girl named Maria."

"C.J.?" Maria said as she raised her eyebrows and looked at me.

"What am I going to tell the cops?" I asked her as I shrugged my shoulders. "And what are they going to do?"

"They can take her the fuck out of here so I can get Katrina settled down."

"I'll tell you what," Debbe said from midway up the staircase to the second floor. "You don't call the police. No, no, no. You don't do that. I'll settle down. I promise. Cross my heart. In my Cross My Heart bra. I just need this bottle of champagne opened up. We'll all have a drinky-poo, and then I'll go to sleep. I promise I will." Debbe stood on a stair, then leaned against the wall as she fumbled with the champagne bottle. "Now I got the wrapping off and that little piece of metal wiring, but I can't seem . . . I can't seem . . . how the hell do I get this damn cork out?"

I started to walk up the stairs behind her.

Debbe turned around. "Oh. C.J. There you are. Be a love and open up this bottle, would you?"

Debbe tossed the bottle high into the air in my direction.

I quickly reached a hand up, but the bottle sailed over my head, hit the wall at the bottom of the staircase, and then began to roll down the rest of the stairs and into the dining room.

"Oh, shit!" I cried out. "Maria, MOVE!"

Maria looked at me as she held the baby in her arms.

"MOVE!" I screamed at her.

At that moment, a loud pop signaled the release of the cork from the bottle of champagne. Like a bullet, it ricocheted from the dining room to the staircase wall to the wall at the top of the stairs where Maria was standing. Then it sailed back to the first floor and hit the chandelier above the dining room table, shattering glass and scattering shards all over the table and rug.

For a few moments, silence reigned eerily in the house.

"Well, that was something, wasn't it!" Debbe exclaimed, then burst into laughter. "It went bam, bam, bam, CRASH!" Then she sank to the stair. "But now look what you did, C.J. My expensive champagne is leaking all over your floor. All over your floor. Oh, what a world. What a world."

I raced up the stairs past Debbe and down the second-floor landing to where Maria had been standing.

Maria had slid to the floor. Her face was ashen, and she clutched Katrina tightly in her arms as the baby emitted loud wails.

I kneeled down to her. Maria began to cry.

"If you hadn't . . . if you hadn't . . ." she stammered and then began to sob.

Katrina's crying mingled with Maria's.

I slowly raised my head and looked at the wall above her. I stood up and stared at the wall.

A depression about two inches deep had been gouged into the plaster from the force of the champagne cork.

I swallowed hard. If Maria hadn't moved, she would've been hit on the head by the cork. Or Katrina would have been nailed. Maria might have ended up with an aching bruise. But Katrina would have been killed by the force of the cork.

I clenched my fists, then carefully pried the baby from Maria. Maria looked up at me with tears in her eyes.

I held Katrina out from me and surveyed her head. Then I cradled the baby in my arms. "She's fine, Maria. She's fine."

I turned and glared at Debbe, who had passed out on the stairs.

I clenched my jaw, then touched the hole the impact of the champagne cork had created.

"We are never having this hole repaired," I said to Maria in a soft but determined voice. "Because I never want to forget this night. *Never*. And about our conversation before we went to sleep. I have absolutely no doubts. No second thoughts."

Maria slowly nodded at me. "Me neither."

"*Sixteen* Godzilla in about sixteen seconds to your location," I said in a low voice into the two-way communicator as I stood behind my slightly open office door. My message was being transmitted to T-Rex, who was sitting in the driver's seat of the limo parked outside the front entrance at L-TV. I peered from behind the door into the hallway and watched as Debbe followed Britta onto the elevator.

"Hurry up," Debbe snapped at two of her assistants who were staggering under the weight of several pieces of luggage. "I haven't got all day."

The elevator doors started to close on one of the assistants.

Britta reached out to take one of the suitcases, but Debbe grabbed her arm.

"You're not lifting a finger, sexy," she said as she pulled her close to her. "This vacation is going to be total pampering of you. *Total*. And just so you know. I'm going to make love to you so hard that you're going to scream. And then beg for more. I'm going to be doing things to you that no one's ever done before. I promise you that you will never forget this trip. *Never*." Debbe ran a tongue over her lipsticked lips, then leaned forward to kiss Britta.

Britta pulled her head back from Debbe's.

Debbe giggled. "Oh, I love it when you play your little hard-to-get game, Britta baby." Debbe ran her manicured fingernails down Britta's cheek and then grinned. "But I'm going to be getting you pretty soon, aren't I? Every part of you." She turned her attention away from Britta and scowled at her assistants. "Move it, you weaklings! Christ, if I can lift them, you can."

The assistants finally boarded the elevator with Debbe's assortment of luggage. The doors squeezed shut.

I pulled open the door to my office, raced down the hallway, and threw open the door to the stairwell. "Godzilla has company," I said into the communicator as I raced down the stairs. "Repeat. Godzilla has two handlers."

"Copy that," T-Rex said. "They won't be a problem. The trunk is open and we're ready to rumble."

I stopped on a stair, consulted the list I had taped on my arm under my sleeve, and switched channels on the communicator. "Godzilla is leaving the zoo. The keeper's ready to put her in the cage."

"We're all set for guests," came Chantelle's voice over the communicator from the L-TV production warehouse located about a mile away, on a Boston Harbor dock. "The noontime sun in Florida is shining right now."

I switched to the channel that linked me with Maria. "Gentlewoman, start your engine."

"Engine is revved," Maria's voice said to me as I cleared another stairwell.

I switched back to T-Rex. "Let me know when you have a visual."

"Copy that."

I raced down the remaining stairs, then peered through the small glass window of the stairway exit door. I watched as Debbe and Britta walked by, followed by the assistants and their load of luggage. The group exited through the front entrance of the building.

"Godzilla in sight. Signing off," T-Rex said in a hushed voice.

I pocketed the communicator and opened the door. I hugged

the walls in the lobby entrance and watched as T-Rex loaded the luggage into the trunk of the limo. As the assistants reentered the building, I dropped out of sight behind an empty security check-in desk, which the guard had readily surrendered earlier that morning when I had handed him twenty dollars and told him to take a long breakfast break. After I heard the assistants pass by the desk to the bank of elevators around the corner, I rose and watched as T-Rex strode to the passenger door of the limo and held it open for Debbe and Britta.

T-Rex kept her cap low on her forehead and her head down as they slid into the backseat of the limo. Then she slammed the door and trotted around the back of the limo to the driver's side.

The limo surged away from the curb.

I raced through the doors after the limo had made a right-hand turn, then jogged around the corner of the building. I opened the passenger door to my car, then got in.

Maria turned to look at me.

"Are we ready?"

"Let's do it," I told her as I buckled my seat belt.

Maria shifted into drive and pulled away from the curb.

We followed at a safe distance behind the limo as it slowly eased through early morning traffic. The bright sun blazed in our eyes.

After we had circled the block twice, the communicator crackled.

I pressed T-Rex's channel. "Repeat," I said.

"Godzilla is sleeping."

"Good work," I replied, then switched the channel. "The pilot has been cleared for landing," I announced.

"Copy that," Chantelle responded. "We're ready for arrival."

I slipped the communicator into the pocket of my jacket and leaned my head back against the headrest.

Maria placed a hand on top of mine. "This is it, C.J."

"Yup," I replied, and then swallowed. "I just hope Chantelle is right about the chloroform. And that Debbe buys that she's in her Amelia Island beach house. Lars did a good job following the picture I gave her when she built the set, but it's a few years old. I took it when I was down there with Debbe. What if she's changed something since that time?"

"Well, that's out of our control now, C.J. And hopefully she'll be so woozy with the gas Chantelle will be giving her that she won't notice anything that's out of place. I just hope the gas really does work. And that none of us blows our lines and says someone's name."

"I know."

Maria squeezed my hand. "We're doing the right thing, C.J. Keep thinking about Debbe accepting your award for you. About her coming to the house that night. Keep thinking about that champagne bottle that exploded."

"I am. Believe me, I am."

We drove in silence for a few moments.

Maria broke the silence with a chuckle.

"What's funny?"

"Well, I guess I really am a criminal. Just like Debbe told you."

"We're only criminals if something goes wrong and Debbe gets wise to what we're doing. Then we're in deep doo-doo."

"And probably out of a job," Maria added. "But we'll still have each other."

"What if we don't share a jail cell, Maria? Or have adjoining cells?"

"C.J., we're not going to jail. But we're being bad, honey. Very, very bad."

"I know," I replied, then looked at Maria and smiled. "It's kind of exciting, isn't it?"

"Yes, it is. Maybe this is going to be the start of a life of crime together."

"But what kind of parents will we be to Katrina?"

"We'll be the lesbian criminals with a baby."

"There's certainly not many of us out there, are there?" I asked.

"A life of crime, huh? Now that's a career path I've never thought of pursuing."

"We could be the lesbian version of Bonnie and Clyde."

"Butch and Sundance."

"Harley Davidson and the Marlboro Man."

We pulled up to a stop sign and then turned and looked at each other.

"Are you thinking what I'm thinking?" she asked me.

I grinned and nodded. "A new show for L-TV. Lesbian partners in crime."

Maria nodded. "Partners in crime. I like that. That could be the name of the show."

"And the two women don't do anything violent."

"No. It's like a modern-day Robin Hood. They rob banks—"

"And leave the money off for shelters and soup kitchens," I finished.

"They ride motorcycles from town to town across America—"

"Always staying one step ahead of the law."

"Are they lovers?" Maria asked.

"No. But there's sexual tension between them. You know that they love each other—"

"But it never happens," Maria finished. "There's always that moment when you think they're going to kiss—"

"And yet they have love interests in whatever towns they stop in."

"And you can see the jealousy, *feel* the jealousy whenever that happens—"

"That's what keeps the viewers interested," I said.

"This is a *great* idea, C.J."

I nodded. *"Partners in Crime.* A new series from L-TV."

The communicator crackled.

I reached into my pocket and pressed a channel. "Say again?" I answered.

"Godzilla's in the house. Let's go. It's time for a day in paradise," Chantelle urged.

"Put the pedal to the metal, Thelma," I told Maria.

"Okay, Louise."

We headed for the warehouse.

"It was just terrible, Debbe," Britta said as she sat next to Debbe on the edge of the queen-size bed. "One minute we were zipping along the water, and then we were upside down. If those teenagers hadn't been jet skiing near us at the time, I don't know what would've happened. You'd broken so many bones and hit your head. I could barely save myself. You would've drowned my . . . uh . . . love."

Debbe's eyes fluttered as she listened to Britta. "My . . . head . . ." she mumbled from behind the oxygen mask that was positioned over her mouth and nose.

"I know, I know," Britta said in a soothing voice as she patted Debbe's hand. "The doctor said you have a mild concussion. You're going to feel woozy for awhile. That's why you're on oxygen."

"Doctor?"

"Yes."

"Hospital?"

"Oh, God, no. Not anymore. You raised such a stink in the emergency room when they wanted to check you into a room and keep you for a few days. You wanted to come back to the house. You told me to hire people to take care of you. That's what I did. We have a full staff of personnel to make sure you're okay. We're here at your beach house on Amelia Island. Don't you recognize it?"

Debbe's eyes wandered around the set that Lars had built, then squeezed her eyes shut and nodded. "Why can't I move?"

"You have broken bones, Debbe."

"My legs?"

"Yes, uh . . . honey. They're both broken and in casts."

"Huh?"

"Yes. And your left arm, too."

Debbe slowly raised her head and looked down at her body. Then she dropped her head to the pillow and groaned. "How long before the casts . . . how long before I can—?"

"Well, I don't know," Britta answered. "That depends on how much you help in your recovery."

"But this was supposed to be a hot time with you, baby. Why would I have wanted to go out on the boat? I'm sure that wasn't my idea. I wanted to spend every second in bed with you."

"Yes . . . well . . . so did I. But you insisted. We didn't even have a chance to unpack. I think . . . well, I think you wanted us to make love on the boat."

Debbe gave a crooked grin to Britta. "That makes sense. I've had some hot times on *Clarissa*. I would've made you take off your clothes and we would've laid on the deck nude, drinking champagne and fucking, fucking, fucking."

"Well, perhaps when you're better—"

"I'm not waiting until I'm better. Come into bed with me now. Take off your clothes."

"I don't think that's a good idea, Debbe. Considering your condition."

"Hell, a few broken bones isn't going to stop me. I've got my right hand, and my tongue's still in working order. And so is yours. So get in here with me. I want to lick you all—"

"And so I see the patient is awake, yes?"

"Oh, here's the doctor now," Britta said as she released herself from Debbe's grip on her arm and stood up.

"Good afternoon, everybody!" Samata boomed as she strode into the room clad in blue hospital scrubs, a paper cap, and paper mask. "And how is you to be feeling today?" she asked as she stood next to Debbe's bed and looked down at her.

"Like crap," Debbe answered.

"Ho, ho, ho! Yes, well, that is to be expected from the ocean plunge you have taken."

"I don't remember taking the boat out," Debbe said. "I don't even remember boarding the airplane. I don't . . . I think the only thing I remember is the limo ride."

"Well, we're here on Amelia Island . . . honey," Britta reassured her.

Debbe looked around the room again. "I know. But I don't remember taking the boat out or how I even got here."

"Well, we did go out on the boat," Britta told her.

"That's what you've told me. But why can't I remember anything?"

"You hit your head pretty hard."

"Yes. You are to be having a concussion," Samata cut in. "Sometimes with a concussion such as yours, the memory fades in and out. Perhaps at some point, you will recall. It is a condition known as temporary amnesia. But now is probably not when this will happen."

"I want to talk to a doctor," Debbe said.

"I *am* a doctor. I am Dr. Vaishayne."

"I want a *real* doctor."

"I am as real as they be getting, Miss . . . Lee," Samata said as she glanced at the clipboard she was carrying.

"I don't want a foreign quack," Debbe snapped. "Get me someone who is American."

"Ah, you want an American doctor."

"That's what I said."

"I see. Well, I am American and I am being a doctor. That is what INS tells me. That is what Harvard Medical School tells me. That is what my internship at Johns Hopkins tells me. I am one of the best orthopedic surgeons in the Americas. If you being to want a quack called in, I can certainly see about getting you one. I know of several who would gladly take your money. But please do not ever plan to walk again without a limp. Or maybe even with the assistance of a cane. Perhaps in old age you will be confined to a wheelchair. Maybe never use your left arm again. Would that be fine with you?"

"No."

"Okay. So you are to be stuck with me, then. I am one of the—"

"Yeah, yeah. Harvard. Johns Hopkins. I heard you. Now when the hell can I get out of bed?"

"Well, that is to be depending upon you. Upon your body chemistry that is to be healing. On how good a patient you can be. A patient patient. Ho, ho, ho!"

"But I have a business to run. Do you know who I am?"

"You are my patient. A Miss Debbe Lee is from what I read on your chart. That is all I need to know about who you are. How you are, however, is to being my business."

"Look at me, you quack. Don't you watch television?"

"Ah, television. The great American way to waste time. Turn on the channel and eat. Gain weight. Get obese. Make your mind turn to Jell-O. No exercise except for a finger."

"Listen, you idiot. My shows have won awards. And I am a very rich, very famous person."

"Rich and famous, maybe. But here you are in a bed under a doctor's care. So? What is your point to be?"

Debbe sighed. "There's no fucking point."

"Okay, then. I leave you in the care of these fine nurses. I will be back tomorrow."

"You're not coming back until tomorrow?"

"This quack has other patients, Miss Lee. A rich and famous baseball player with a wrist injury is for one. He is to be nice to me. Maybe when I come back, you be nice to me, yes?"

Samata turned to exit the room as Chantelle and Maria entered clad in nursing attire and wearing paper face masks.

"Ah! Nurse Rodriquez and Nurse Moreland. Please to be taking care of this patient. I will check in with you tomorrow."

"Yes, Doctor," Maria and Chantelle said in unison.

Samata exited the bedroom.

"Okay, that went fine," I said to Taylor and Meri as we watched the Amelia Island bedroom scene being played out on a television monitor in a soundproof booth located a short distance away from the set. "Time for you to serve Debbe some lunch, Meri."

Meri nodded, then tucked her hair under a blue paper hospital cap.

"Don't forget this," Taylor said as she placed a paper mask over Meri's mouth and nose, then walked behind her and tied the strings behind her head.

"What's for lunch?" Taylor asked.

"A tuna sandwich on whole wheat, a carton of milk, and green Jell-O," Meri replied. "It's what she'll be getting every day. Because I can guarantee you she's not going to eat this."

"Let's hope," Taylor said. "Or we'll have to go out and get more food for her."

"It's good to know that you're still thinking positively about this whole plan, Taylor. You know, I think I'm going to start calling you Eeyore. After that depressed donkey in—"

"Go," I cued Meri.

"Just don't make the food sound appealing to her, is all I'm suggesting," Taylor told her as she opened the door to the booth.

"Hush," I said as I saw Meri place her hands on her hips and start to reply to Taylor.

Meri shook her head, then picked up the food tray and left the booth. Several seconds later, she appeared on the monitor.

"Who the hell are you?" Debbe snapped at her as Meri entered the bedroom.

"I'm from the hospital kitchen," Meri mumbled in a deep voice. "Brought ya some lunch."

"Do you want to sit up . . . dear?" Britta asked Debbe.

"I'm not hungry."

"Well, you have to eat something. You didn't eat anything on the plane, and it's been—"

"Don't push it, Britta," Taylor told the monitor.

"What the hell are you trying to make me eat?" Debbe asked Meri.

Meri shifted the tray to one hand, then stuck her fingers in her mouth and touched the tuna sandwich. She licked her fingers, then touched the sandwich again and shrugged her shoulders. "I dunno. It's . . . uh . . . geez. I can't tell if it's tuna or chicken or what it is. And there's some sort of green liquidy stuff in a bowl that's—"

"Take that crap away," Debbe ordered Meri.

"Thank God," Taylor sighed.

"No, thank Meri," I told her.

"Fine by me," Meri replied, then turned on her heels and walked out of the room.

"Help me up out of bed," Debbe told Britta as she struggled to rise up on her right elbow.

"You can't leave the bed, Debbe."

"I have to go to the bathroom. Help me up."

"The bathroom?" Taylor asked me as she watched the monitor. "That's not in the script."

"Damn," I replied.

"Um . . . Nurse!" Britta called out as Debbe started to remove the oxygen mask.

Chantelle and Maria quickly moved towards the bed.

"Lie back down, Miss Lee," Maria told her as she raced to one side of the bed.

"You have to keep the mask on, ma'am," Chantelle said as she squeezed by Maria, slammed a hand hard against Debbe's chest and pushed her back to the bed, then replaced the mask.

"Don't push me around!" Debbe yelled at Chantelle.

"She has to go to the bathroom," Britta said as she looked first at Chantelle and then at Maria. "That wasn't . . . um—"

"Don't say anything else, Britta," I cautioned the monitor.

"Okay," Chantelle said as she walked off the set, then returned moments later with a silver metal bedpan in her hands. She handed it to Maria.

"Thank God she brought that along," Taylor said as she rubbed a hand across her forehead.

"What are you giving me this for?" Maria asked Chantelle.

"I'm not doing it," Chantelle told her. "I was hired to monitor the oxygen, remember?"

Maria stared at Chantelle.

"Oh, shit," Taylor moaned.

"One of you do it," I told the monitor.

"I have to go to the bathroom NOW!" Debbe yelled at Maria.

Maria extended the bedpan towards Chantelle.

Chantelle pushed it back to Maria.

"Come on, come on," I pleaded to the monitor.

"I don't care who puts that damn bedpan under me," Debbe snapped. "But I gotta pee. And why the hell is everyone who comes into this room wearing a mask? I want to see your faces. I want to know who the hell you incompetent people are! I'll have you fired. Do you hear me?"

"Again with the threat of firing," I sighed.

"We're wearing masks to prevent the risk of infection," Chantelle told Debbe in a calm voice.

"How the hell can I possibly get an infection?" Debbe challenged her. "I have broken bones, you clod. Not an open wound. Now take off your damn face masks. It's annoying the hell out of me!"

"Honey, you've got to calm down," Britta told Debbe.

"Increase the gas," Taylor pleaded to the monitor.

"Don't you tell me to calm down!" Debbe shouted at Britta.

"If you don't calm down, we'll . . . we'll . . ."

"We'll what, Britta?" I asked the monitor.

"We'll what?" Debbe asked her.

"We'll . . . we'll never . . . make love again," Britta finished. "And I . . . I want to . . . I want you to make love to me again and again. I have never been . . . so turned on by anyone as I . . . was with you. In the airplane. Yes, in the airplane. You were awesome!"

"Alright," I said as I breathed a sigh of relief. "Now you've got her attention, Britta."

"I was?" Debbe asked. "When?"

"Uh, what did you call it after we, you know? That I was now a member of the mile-high club?"

"What's that?" Taylor asked me.

"Having sex in the bathroom on the airplane," I told her.

"Who has sex on an airplane?" Taylor asked.

"People do," I answered.

"What people?"

"A lot of people."

"The pilot?"

"No, not the pilot. Passengers."

Taylor stared at me. "You? Have you done that before, C.J.?"

I nodded.

"You have?"

"Yes."

"When?"

"With Debbe."

"Oh, my."

Debbe smiled up at Britta. "We did it? On the airplane?"

"Yes . . . baby. We did it," Britta told her. "And it was amazing."

"How the hell do you make love in that cramped little smelly place?" Taylor asked me.

"Some other time, Taylor," I told her.

"Roll over," Maria told Debbe.

Debbe held out her right arm to Britta. "I haven't done it on an airplane in a long, long time. Let me see your breasts, woman. I can't remember what they look like. I want to put my mouth on your—"

"Not in front of these people, Debbe," Britta answered as she pulled Debbe towards her.

Maria lifted the satin sheets and slipped the bedpan under Debbe.

"Then as soon as they leave," Debbe said as she rolled onto the bedpan, then howled. "Christ! This thing is cold!"

Chantelle pulled two tissues from the box on the nightstand, then handed the tissues to Debbe.

"What are these for?"

"Wiping," Chantelle told her.

"You do it," Debbe answered.

"Listen, sister, you're not paying me enough money to wipe your rich white—"

"I've got it, Ch—" Maria started to respond.

"Don't!" Britta cut in.

"Don't what?" Debbe asked her.

"Oh, my God! Look at that sunset!" Britta exclaimed as she quickly turned on her heels and looked at the closed shutters of the bedroom window.

"What sunset?" Debbe asked as she tried to sit up. "I don't see a sunset."

"Yes, it's lovely, isn't it?" Maria agreed.

"It's fine," Chantelle commented.

"I don't care about the goddamned sunset," Debbe grumbled. "I've really got to pee."

"Then go, lady," Chantelle told her. "You're on the bedpan."

"I know I'm on the bedpan, you idiot! But I can't go."

"That's not my problem," Chantelle said.

"Just relax," Maria told Debbe.

"Yes, honey, just relax," Britta said. "Imagine that you're sitting on the toilet and then just let go."

"Visualize," Maria told Debbe.

"Will everyone please shut up so I can pee!" Debbe snapped.

"C.J., it ain't time for the sunset," Lars' voiced boomed into the soundproof booth.

"Don't worry about it," I spoke into the microphone that connected me to Lars. "Britta said that just to distract Debbe."

"So how is the patient to be doing?" Samata asked as she entered the room.

"What's she doing on the set?" Taylor asked as she frantically flipped through the pages of her script.

"I don't know," I answered.

"C.J.?" Lars' voice came over the intercom. "Sam ain't supposed ta be on the set till tomorrow. You know what I mean. In a couple a hours."

"I know, I know," I answered. "I don't know what's going on."

"What the hell are you doing here?" Debbe asked Samata.

"I am to be checking up on my patient."

"You said you weren't coming back until tomorrow," Debbe told her. "It's not tomorrow."

Samata stood at the foot of Debbe's bed in silence for a few seconds. "Yes. I see. Well, I am to be here now because . . ." Samata began, and then stopped. "Your body is on the bed quite strange."

"That's because I'm trying to pee into this stupid bedpan," Debbe answered her. "But I can't do this. There's too many people in here. I want to get out of bed and go to the bathroom."

"Yes, okay," Samata answered. "And that is to be why I am here. The nurses called me and said you were trying to get out of bed."

"How could they call you?" Debbe asked. "They haven't left the room."

Samata stared at Debbe.

"Well?" Debbe asked her.

Samata stood silently looking at Debbe.

"You're not a flipping doctor," Debbe exclaimed. "I don't know what the hell is going on here, but I intend to get to the bottom of this. I want everyone to take off your masks right now. *Right now!* I mean it!"

"Aw, hell," Chantelle said, then turned the valve on the tank next to Debbe's bed.

"What is going on here?" Debbe asked. "This seems . . . like . . . it doesn't . . . there's something . . ." Her voice trailed off as her eyelids fluttered, and then shut.

"This is getting so messed up," Taylor said as she flipped through the pages of the script. "I don't know where we are in this or who's supposed to be doing what."

"Get out of here, Sam," Britta told Samata. "You're not on yet."

"Don't say her name!" I yelled at the monitor.

"I apologize," Samata told her. "But I am to be getting mixed up."

"I'm running low on the gas," Chantelle said as she tapped a finger against the gauge on the top of the tank. "I didn't think we'd go through the gas so fast."

"Is there any more?" Maria asked.

Taylor tossed her script down. "C.J., this is so fucked up! I told you this plan wouldn't work!"

"Not now, Taylor!"

"C.J., what's going on?" Meri asked as she entered the booth.

"I don't know," I told her.

"It's a major fucking meltdown!" Taylor exclaimed.

"Do we have any more gas?" Maria asked Chantelle.

Chantelle nodded. "In the trunk of my car. There's another tank. But it's not full. My aunt gave that to me to use as a backup. Just in case."

"Well, it's now just in case. We've got to get it in here," Maria told her.

I pressed the microphone. "Lars?" I said.

"I hear ya, C.J. I'll go grab the tank."

"Before you do, go to midnight on the lighting," I told her. "We'll have to pick this up from there."

The lighting behind the windows on the set immediately blacked out.

"What's happening?" Britta asked.

"We must be going to night," Maria said. "We have to move ahead on the script."

"But she's still on the bedpan," Chantelle answered.

"Then get her off," Britta said.

"Can she hear us?" Maria asked Chantelle as she slipped her hands under the bedcovers.

"I don't know. I don't think so."

"Come on, people," I told the monitor. "I can't coach you now."

Taylor began to pace the booth. "This is getting all screwed up, C.J. I didn't want to be involved in this. I really, really didn't."

"Oh, shut up, Taylor!" Meri scolded her.

"Will you two be quiet?" I cut in, then took a couple of quick deep breaths and pointed to the monitor. "Everyone's doing fine. We'll get more gas. We'll get back to the script and continue with the plan. And look at Debbe. She's out like a light."

"Let's hope," Taylor muttered.

I crossed my fingers and stared at the monitor.

"**Seventeen** times?" I asked Janette Garrison as she stood facing me in the now crowded soundproof booth overlooking the Amelia Island set. The set was cloaked in darkness, save from the light provided by a lamp on a nightstand. Maria and Chantelle were sitting in chairs next to the bed, watching over the slumbering Debbe Lee. The rest of the writers, Lars, and T-Rex were standing around in the booth.

"She has to sign her signature seventeen times?" I asked Janette again, then shook my head before she could answer. "I don't know that we have enough gas in the spare tank Chantelle just hooked up to keep Debbe feeling high throughout the time it's going to take her to sign her name seventeen times."

"You're right 'bout that, C.J.," Lars cut in. "Chantelle said we have jus' enough left in the tank to get her from now till you give the word ta move her to the office set."

"I thought she only had to sign a new contract for each of us," I said to Janette. "That's only a handful of signatures. That was doable. But this—" I raised my arms in the air and shook my head.

Janette held up a large yellow envelope. "I told you already, C.J. She has to sign each of your new contracts. Then she has to sign individual agreements that invalidate your previous contracts. She has to sign her new agreement, which I've drawn up delineating her portion of the ownership of L-TV, and originals have to be attached to your contracts. And she has to sign both my letter of resignation and an agreement that terminates our relationship. With a generous severance package, I might add. That's something I'm requesting for myself, for services rendered and annoyances endured. Why all this, you might ask? Well, if there's one thing I know about Debbe Lee, it's this. She's a stickler for making sure everything is legal."

"That's because everything else she does is illegal," Meri scoffed.

Janette shook her head and turned to face Meri. "That's not true. Debbe may be a jerk, an asshole, a bitch—whatever you want to call her. She may be the most supreme manipulator of people that I've ever met. But I can assure you that from day one, L-TV has been and is being run by the books. So if we're going to get you guys part ownership of L-TV, then we have to do this right. Or Debbe will have grounds on which to stage a fight against your new contracts. And that's a fight that I'm sure you'll lose."

"Perhaps she is not being illegal in what she is being doing," Samata cut in. "But she is always being breaking the rules for how to be treating other people."

Janette shrugged her shoulders. "Unfortunately, there's nothing I can do about that. Except get the hell out of my job and out of her sights, which I'm doing. But you guys want to stay on. So you'll each have a really sweet deal at L-TV once Debbe signs your new contracts."

"*If* she signs the contracts," Taylor said. "And that's a big if. She's going to wake up with all that signing she has to do, that's for sure. And then we won't be able to put her back under."

"Why did we not be thinking this out better?" Samata asked me.

"I didn't know there was so much paperwork," I answered. "We didn't know we would go through the gas so fast. I don't know what to tell you, Sam. I thought we had everything covered."

"The best-laid plans," Meri began, and then stopped. "Are something, something, something. I can't remember the rest of the phrase."

"We are clearly not to be committing the perfect crime after all," Samata mumbled.

"There is no perfect crime," T-Rex told her.

"Now what do we do?" Taylor asked. "Take Debbe back to her apartment and just forget the whole thing?"

I shrugged my shoulders. "I don't know."

"It will be fine," Janette reassured us. "It's not going to take all that long for her to sign all the documents I've drawn up. It just sounds like it's going to take a long time."

"But what if she starts questioning what she's signing?" Taylor asked Janette.

"Good question," Meri said.

"We'll just have to handle it," I said as I tossed the script we had written on the console.

"What are you going to say to her?" Taylor asked Janette.

"I don't know," she answered. "I really wasn't planning on saying much of anything to her. The plan was that if she started asking questions, she'd get another hit of gas."

"Which can't happen now," Taylor pointed out.

"Taylor, I think we know that," Meri told her. "Would you stop being so pessimistic."

"Perhaps you have an idea you'd like to share with us, Meri," Taylor countered. "Something that could handle Debbe once the gas wears off and she starts wondering what the fuck she's signing."

"Maybe you could come up with a brilliant idea of your own instead of being so down on this whole thing," Meri snapped at her. "From the get-go, you were—"

"Guys," I cut in. "Now's not the time. We have to think of some way to deal with Debbe so she signs the contracts. And then we're done with this whole thing."

"I could distract her," Britta suggested. "You know. If she starts to ask questions."

"How?" Meri asked.

Britta shrugged her shoulders. "I don't know. I guess . . . I guess

I could . . . well . . . I could show her my breasts. It seems to be what she's most interested in."

"You will be doing no such thing," Samata snapped at her.

"Sam, I'll be doing it for us. For all of us," Britta told her. "She's not going to touch them. But maybe if she thought she was *going* to touch them, she'd breeze through signing. You know that she wants to get me into bed."

"Yes, that I know," Samata answered. "But I did not think that in the plan you would be revealing your breasts to her."

"It's just an idea, Sam," Britta told her.

"It's not a bad idea," I said. "It would definitely grab Debbe's attention."

"Mine, too," Meri agreed.

Samata shot a look at Meri, then turned to me. "Maybe this is not being a very good plan after all, C.J."

"What Britta would be doing isn't part of the plan, Sam," T-Rex said. "It's improvisation. It's doing what we have to do to get what we want."

"Well, I do not like it. Not if it means Britta must be—no! I must be counting out of this type of plan."

"So what are you saying?" I asked her. "Do you want to give this all up now?" I looked at each person in the booth. "I'll do whatever you guys want. If you want to call it quits, just say the word. We'll put Debbe in the limo and take her back to her apartment. And then life will go on at L-TV. Just the way it did before."

"Well, I don't want that," Meri mumbled. "Why don't we just give it a try? The worst that could happen is that Debbe doesn't end up signing the new contracts. We may not have gained anything by doing this, but what have we lost?"

"I agree with Meri," Taylor said.

"Well, there's a first," Meri told her.

"I'm just trying to be supportive," Taylor answered.

"I'm glad," Meri said, then flashed Taylor a smile.

"I do not want the horrible Dragon Lady to be accepting any of my awards or taking credit for the work I have been done on my show," Samata said. "But I also do not be wanting Britta to be baring her breasts to her. They are beautiful breasts, and I am the one who is to be seeing them."

"They're just breasts, Sam," Taylor told her.

"Okay. So are you to be baring your breasts to the Dragon Lady?" Samata countered.

"She's not interested in my breasts," Taylor answered.

"We could all bare our breasts," Meri suggested, then giggled.

"Oh, I'm sure you'd like that," Taylor snapped.

"Can we get focused, people?" I asked. "Now what do you say? Are we going ahead with this plan or not?"

"I'm in," Meri told me.

"Me, too," Taylor said.

"Let's give it a try," Britta suggested.

We looked at Samata.

"I want to just be getting this over with," she sighed. "I will vote with the majority. But I am not liking the breast thing."

"Duly noted," I said. "Then here's what we'll do. We'll move Debbe to the office set now, while she's still sleeping. Are you ready, Lars?"

"I'm all over it like a cheap pair a underwear, C.J."

"I'll help Lars move Debbe there," T-Rex added.

"Great," I answered. "Britta, do whatever you have to do to keep Debbe signing those agreements. Sorry, Sam. But we're almost done with this whole thing. And try to move Debbe along with the signing, Janette. Do the best that you can."

"I'll try," Janette said, then tucked the envelope under her arm.

Britta gave a quick kiss to Samata, and then followed Janette out of the booth.

Debbe's head rested on an exact replica of her desk on the set of her L-TV office that Lars had constructed. Janette stood next to her, holding a stack of legal-sized documents. Maria and Chantelle had joined the group in the booth, and we peered at each of the two monitors on the console. One gave us a full view of the set, from offstage. The other was positioned directly on Debbe's desk, as the one in her office was, and was hooked up to a VCR so we could record Debbe and Janette and later add the tape to Debbe's collection of security tapes.

"Debbe?" Janette asked. "Debbe?"

"What?" Debbe mumbled, her head still on the desk.

"I'm still waiting for your signature on these documents."

Debbe slowly raised her head, then ran her hands over her face. "What documents?" She slowly looked around the set of her office. "How did I get back here?"

"What do you mean?"

"I was . . . I thought I was still on Amelia Island."

"No. You came back from your trip. You've been back in the office for a few days now."

"I have?"

"Yes." Janette stared at Debbe. "Are you okay? You don't look so good."

Debbe rubbed her face with her hands, then ran a tongue over her lips. "My mouth is really dry. I feel so tired. So out of it."

Janette nodded. "It appears that you are. You've been nodding off on me. Maybe you're coming down with something. Or maybe it just means you had a really good time on your trip."

Debbe shook her head. "I don't think so. I think I was in an accident."

"Yes, honey, you were," Britta said as she entered the set. She walked over to Debbe's desk, then placed a hand on her shoulder and kissed her on top of her head.

"I am not liking this," Samata said as she watched the monitor.

"She's just playing a part," Maria told her.

"When did we get back from our vacation?" Debbe asked Britta.

"I told her a few days ago," Janette quickly interjected.

Britta nodded. "That's right, hon."

Debbe looked down. "Weren't my legs in casts? And my arm? I thought they were broken."

"Well, here's the thing, Debbe," Britta began. "Do you remember that doctor who was treating you? The one who you thought was a quack?"

"Vaguely."

"Well, it turns out that your legs and arm really weren't broken. You just had bad muscle strains. And the doctor didn't have all those fine degrees she bragged about. She really was a quack."

"That's what I thought," Debbe said. "There was something not quite right about her."

"There is to be something not quite right about *you*," Samata told the monitor.

Britta patted Debbe's hand. "The one good thing, though, is that by the doctor immobilizing your legs and arm in casts, your muscles got a chance to heal. You're almost one hundred percent now. But this is why you wanted Janette to prepare these papers she has for you. We discussed this already."

"We did?"

"Yes, honey. You were so furious when you found out that your legs and arm weren't really broken and that . . . and that our vacation was ruined. So . . . so you asked Janette to draw up papers . . . to draw up papers, um, so you won't have to pay any member of the staff I hired to take care of you. They all turned out to be incompetents—the lot of them. I'm so sorry. It's all my fault."

"I don't understand," Debbe said as she flexed her left arm. "How did we figure out my arm and legs weren't broken?"

Britta opened her mouth, then closed it.

"Uh, oh," Meri mumbled.

"Janette?" Debbe asked as she looked at her lawyer.

Janette raised her eyebrows and began to tap a pen against the desk.

Britta rubbed Debbe's shoulder. "Oh, dear. They said this would take a while, and I'm afraid they were right. You still really aren't very clear in the head, are you honey?"

"Well, no. No, I'm not. And so that's why I'm asking you. How did we figure out my legs and arm weren't broken?"

"It's just going to take time for you to . . . for your head to start clearing, I guess."

"Fine. So it will take some time to clear. But I'm feeling a little better now. And I want to know how we figured out my legs and arm weren't broken? Did I go to another hospital?"

"Her mind's clearing up," Taylor mumbled. "Isn't there something we can do?"

"We're nearly out of gas," Chantelle told her. "And there's no way we can get on the set now."

"Come on, Britta," I coaxed the monitor.

Britta stood up from the desk and began pacing near Debbe. Then she stopped and faced Debbe. She placed her hands on her hips. "How long do I have to keep telling you the same things over and over again? Huh? How long? I'm just getting so tired of this, Debbe."

"Tired of what?" Debbe asked.

"Yeah, tired of what?" Taylor echoed as she watched the monitor.

Britta crossed her arms. "You know, all I wanted was a little bit of attention from you, Debbe. Just a little. I thought you were interested in me. But all we've been talking about, all you've asked me over and over again, is what happened." Britta suddenly slammed a fist on the desktop, startling Debbe, Janette, and everyone in the booth. "Day in, day out, you ask me, 'What happened? What happened?' You're like a broken record. It's driving me . . . it's driving me nuts!" Britta leaned closer to Debbe. "Now I know that you got a bump on the head in the accident. I know that at least one diagnosis was correct. You *are* having a hard time remembering things. Now I've tried to be patient with you. I've answered your questions time and time again. But it's not sticking in that head of yours. So let's just let it go, would you? Let's get on with being close and making love. That's why I left Samata for you, Debbe. So we could get something going. All I got was a little . . . a little action on the airplane. And that was nice. It really was. But clearly, well, clearly you're not interested in me. Why don't you just sign all those documents so we can move on? Or maybe you want me to go back to Samata? At least she didn't ask me the same questions over and over again. At least she showed some interest in me."

"She's good," T-Rex commented.

"I love her," Samata said.

"We know," Meri replied.

"But will Debbe buy it?" Taylor asked.

We held our breath in the booth.

Debbe took in a deep breath of air, then looked up at Britta. "Okay, okay. Listen, I don't want you to go back to Samata. And I do want to pay attention to you. I can't even remember doing anything on the damn airplane. But—okay, okay. My head will eventually clear up." She turned to Janette. "What do you want me to sign?"

Janette slid the first document towards her and handed her the pen. Then she tapped a finger against the bottom of the page. "Sign here."

"Here we go," Maria said as she watched the monitor.

"One down!" Meri exclaimed.

Debbe finished signing her name, and Janette took the document away and replaced it with another.

Debbe signed again, and Janette repeated the process.

Debbe poised the pen to sign, then set the pen down on her desk and picked up the document. "I want to read this."

"Red light," Taylor groaned.

"You don't need to read it," Janette said. "It's just a standard termination of work-for-hire agreement and refusal to pay for services not delivered."

"Well, I should still read it."

"Don't you trust me, Debbe?" Janette asked her.

"Trust is not a word in my vocabulary," Debbe told Janette. "You should know that by now."

"Just sign it, Debbe," Britta told her.

"I would like to know what the hell I'm signing," Debbe answered.

"Then I'm out the door," Britta said as she turned away from Debbe.

"Wait."

Britta turned towards Debbe.

"Just give me a few minutes here to figure these documents out. I just need to know—"

"Figure this out, Debbe," Britta told her, and then stepped out of the range of the camera that was positioned towards Debbe's desk. She reappeared seconds later on the set monitor.

We watched as she slowly peeled off her shirt over her head. Then she reached behind her, deftly unhooked her bra, and dropped it to the floor.

Debbe's eyes latched onto Britta's chest.

All eyes in the booth were riveted to the monitor, glued to Britta's bare back.

"Is that a tattoo?" Meri asked as she squinted her eyes.

"It is to be a birthmark," Samata answered. "But you do not all have to be watching this, do you?"

"We're not looking at her breasts," Chantelle pointed out.

"Which is a damn shame," Meri muttered.

"Sign here," Janette said as she slipped a document under Debbe's hand.

Debbe picked up the pen and signed her name.

Janette slipped another document under Debbe's pen.

Britta's hands moved to the front of her pants. Slowly, she eased the pants over her hips.

"Now that's nice," Debbe grinned as she hastily signed her name.

"Oh, I cannot be watching this!" Samata moaned.

"She's doing it for us," Taylor told her.

"I'll say she is," Meri agreed.

Debbe signed another document, and Janette deftly slipped a new one under her pen.

Britta's pants dropped to the floor.

"Sexy," Meri mumbled.

"Shut up!" Taylor said as she jabbed an elbow into Meri's ribs.

"She is to be stripping, is she not?" Samata moaned from a corner of the booth.

Britta's hands went to the elastic of her underpants.

Debbe looked at Britta, then vigorously scrawled her signature on another document.

"This was a great idea!" T-Rex exclaimed.

"Are you almost done?" Britta asked Debbe in a sexy voice. "Because I am getting *so hot* for you, Debbe. I want you to touch me *all over*."

Debbe grinned at her, then signed her name to another document.

"Please to be done. Please to be very done, very soon," Samata said as she pushed her fingers in her ears.

"Hurry up," Debbe snapped at Janette as she scrawled her signature once more.

Britta slowly stepped out of her underpants, tossed them on the floor, and then raised her hands above her head and began to slowly sway her hips from side to side.

"Hubba, hubba," Meri grinned.

"Would you shut up?" Taylor asked her. "This is killing Samata."

"I'm only human," Meri answered.

"No. You're only horny," Taylor snapped.

"This is the woman I am being with that you are making lusting noises about, Meri," Samata scolded.

"Sorry, Sam," Meri replied. "But she's got a great body."

"I'm getting *wet* for you, Debbe," Britta said.

"Oh, please to be over," Samata moaned.

Debbe signed another document.

Britta continued her sexy dance, now thrusting her hips back and forth, while Debbe continued to sign.

"Turn around, turn around," Meri whispered to the monitor.

"Meri, I am hearing everything you are to be saying. And I will be killing you if you continue to look!" Samata exclaimed. "All of you! Please to be taking your eyes off the monitor. No one has to be watching this striptease. Except for you, C.J."

Reluctantly, everyone in the booth except me turned to face Samata.

"I wish I was C.J. right now," Meri muttered. "You know, I don't think I can be celibate for much longer."

"You are keeping your eyes on Debbe, aren't you, C.J.?" Maria asked.

"Yes, love," I answered as I kept my eyes glued to Britta's dance and rubbed the back of my neck.

"C.J.!"

"Right," I answered as I leaned closer to the monitor aimed at Debbe's desk.

Janette pulled the last document away from Debbe, picked up her briefcase from the floor, and then opened it.

She pushed the documents into her briefcase.

"Stop the taping now," I told Chantelle, who hit the STOP button on the camera that was filming Debbe's office.

Debbe started to rise from her chair.

Janette quickly removed a cloth from a plastic bag, and then stepped towards Debbe and placed it over her mouth and nose.

"What the—" Debbe began.

Janette turned her head towards Britta, and then dropped the cloth onto Debbe's lap.

Debbe's eyes fluttered open.

"Janette!" Britta yelled at her.

"What?"

"Take care of Debbe, would you?"

Janette turned away from Britta, quickly picked up the cloth, and replaced it over Debbe's face.

"Show's over, folks," I announced as soon as I saw Debbe slump forward in her chair.

I watched as Britta picked up her clothing from the floor. Then she turned, flashed a thumbs-up sign to the camera lens, and exited off screen.

"We didn't happen to tape that, did we, C.J.?" Meri asked as she turned back to the monitor.

"Meri, you have no sensitivity whatsoever," Taylor said.

After we helped carry Debbe out of the office set and into the limo, T-Rex and Britta left for Debbe's apartment. We thanked Janette, who assured me that I'd be getting copies of the signed documents for my files.

"Good luck to you guys," she said as she zipped up her briefcase and then walked to the warehouse exit.

Maria and I followed behind her.

At the door, Janette turned and shook my hand.

"We couldn't have done this without you," I told her.

"I was happy to help, C.J. Getting back at Debbe Lee has been one of my fantasies. I don't like people like her, and I like working for them even less. Now you're stuck with her, and she's stuck with you. I know that was your choice. I just hope you get what you want." Janette pulled out her cell phone. "I gotta run now. But you know what the really sad thing is about people like Debbe? They always land on their feet. *Always.* It's like you can never bring them down, never get the better of them. Legally, she can't do anything to you or your writers. I've made sure of that. But emotionally, well, lawyers aren't supposed to deal in emotions. All I'm saying is she's not going to let up with you or your writers. She's still going to be the same person she's always been. Maybe even nastier."

"Maybe," Maria agreed. "But at least we'll have some say about things at L-TV. At least we'll have some leverage now."

"You will," Janette nodded, then turned to me. "Tell me something, C.J. Why is it that you can't walk away from this woman? Most people I know would get the hell out of Dodge if they had to be in the same room with an ex. I can't imagine working with my ex."

"I think you feel that way if you still have feelings for someone," I answered. "I'll admit, it was rough for me for awhile at L-TV because seeing Debbe made me remember both the love I once had for her as well as the hurt. She ran over my heart, and then backed up and ran over it again and again. But now, well, I just don't have those feelings anymore. Maria and I are in love. We have a family and share a very happy home together. I'm relearning that love can be a truly wonderful feeling, if you are lucky enough to find the right person."

"So love conquers all, is that what you're saying?" Janette asked.

"It certainly makes life more manageable," I answered. "But my personal feelings for Debbe aside, she's a smart businessperson. Perhaps the smartest in the television industry. Who knows where the road leads now that my writers and I are partners in the destiny of the network? But in one season, we've made our mark. We're now in the same league as HBO and Showtime. And that's not a bad position to be in."

Janette nodded. "I agree with that. Debbe Lee is a fearless risk-taker. There's not many lesbians like that. Well, I wish you and your writers well. If you ever need any other help, give me a call. I'll be working with Sheila now. So you'll have two lawyers who will always be on your side."

"Can you guys handle an adoption?" Maria asked, then turned to me and took my hand. "C.J. and I haven't really discussed this yet, but I want C.J. to be Katrina's parent as well. If that's okay with you, C.J."

"I want that more than anything, Maria. But I don't know how easy it will be."

"I'll check into it," Janette said, then started dialing her phone. "I gotta run. I'll give you a call next week and we can talk about this more."

I locked the door after Janette left.

"C.J., I know we didn't discuss this yet," Maria told me as she took my arm. "So I hope I didn't blindside you. But it's been something I've been thinking about since you first kissed me and held me in your arms."

"What's to discuss?" I asked as I pulled her towards me. "I love you, I love Katrina, and I want to be with both of you for the rest of my life. You are the greatest thing that's ever happened to me. I mean that. I want to grow old with you. I want to see who Katrina will be."

Maria turned to me and pressed her body against mine.

I put my arms around her. "Hey, I can hold you close to me now. There's no basketball in the way."

"It feels good, doesn't it?"

"Hmmm," I murmured, then placed my lips on hers.

"It's your kiss, C.J. Your kiss just drives me wild."

I kissed Maria again.

Maria touched my face, then hugged me. "It's, um, it's okay if we do something now," she whispered in my ear.

"Really?"

"Really. All systems are go."

"Well, I'm ready."

"So am I."

"How about tonight?" I asked.

"It's a date," Maria said, then softly kissed my neck.

Maria and I joined the others to help break down both of the sets. Lars had rented a Ryder truck to cart away the furniture that had been purchased for both the Amelia Island bedroom and Debbe's office, and the plan was for her, Meri, and Taylor to make stops at Salvation Army stores in Providence, Rhode Island; Manchester, New Hampshire; and Springfield, Massachusetts, to donate what we had collected. We figured that dividing things up would make it harder for anyone to trace what we had done.

We loaded up the truck, and then watched as they drove off. Then Chantelle gathered up the costumes and gas tanks, loaded them in her car, and left to return them to her aunt.

Maria, Samata, and I surveyed the warehouse one more time, making sure that we hadn't forgotten anything. I tucked the videotape we had made of Debbe signing the contracts under my arm. Then we locked the warehouse and headed out to the parking lot.

"I am to be going home now," Samata said as she pulled out her car keys.

"Thanks for all your help, Sam," I told her, then gave her a quick hug.

"I am just being glad this is over," Samata said, then looked at the tape I was carrying. "You did not be making a tape of Britta as Meri wanted, did you?"

I shook my head.

"Well, that is to be a relief. And so now I will go home and wait for Britta to return. And then we can get on with our lives, can we not?"

"We can," I assured her.

That night, after Katrina was asleep, Maria and I pulled the bedcovers over our naked bodies and made sweet, passionate, lingering love. We spent hours touching, tasting, caressing, fondling, penetrating, licking.

After we were satisfied, we were both still wide awake.

"I want you again, C.J.," she said as she shifted her position and lay on top of me.

"Oh, all right," I answered as I spread my legs and wrapped them around her. "If this is what you really want."

"Well, it's okay," she said, then ran her tongue down my neck to my breastbone.

"Only okay?"

She ran her tongue across my lips, then inside my mouth. "Well, better than okay," she said as she kissed my nose. "Much, much better."

I stared up at Maria. "God, woman, you turn me on."

Maria smiled, then dropped her head to my chest. Her mouth

engulfed a nipple and she began to suck hard, pulling my nipple into her mouth. She massaged my other nipple with her fingers, then began to play with it harder. She pushed her hips into me, and I responded by pushing up against her.

Maria moved her fingers from a nipple, raised her hips up slightly, and then slipped one of her hands between my legs.

"So wet," she sighed as she felt me. Then she pushed inside me, groaned, and arched her back.

"You feel so good inside me, Maria."

"I want to be inside you all the time, C.J."

I watched her breasts sway above me, then cupped one of her breasts in my hand and brought it to my mouth. I massaged her nipple with my tongue as her fingers pushed deeper inside me and began a pleasurable rhythm.

"I can't get enough of you, C.J.," Maria panted.

I let one of my hands travel down her back, across a hip, and then under her belly. I found her wetness and warmth and moved my fingers in it in small circles. I heard my heart pound a steady beat in my ears as Maria's sighs turned into low moans. I slipped inside her, and she cried out and thrust her hips into me. My insides tightened on her fingers.

"Look at me, C.J.," Maria gasped as she lifted her head.

I opened my eyes.

"For as long as you can, I want you to look at me. I want to see your beautiful brown eyes. I want to see your love for me. Can you do that for me, baby? Can you?"

"Yes," I gasped as I pushed my hips up.

"I'm coming, C.J."

"I feel you."

"Come for me, C.J."

"I'm coming."

I locked eyes with Maria's and kept them open.

As waves of contractions swept through me and against Maria's fingers, for the first time I saw what had been eluding me for years.

I saw the love I was feeling in my heart. It raced out of me and into Maria, and then raced back into me in waves of strength and hope and passion. It was exciting. It was scary.

I continued to look in Maria's eyes as I came for her again and again and felt her come in steady contractions against my fingers.

And then tears filled my eyes, and I saw them well up in hers. We fell into each other's arms, held each other close, and cried.

"Eighteen weeks until the Emmy nominations are announced," I told the writers as we met up in the conference room a few days after Debbe's journey to and return from Amelia Island.

The writers cheered and clapped their hands.

"Do you know the exact date in July when the nominations are made?" Taylor asked as the celebration died down and she took a seat.

"I think it's around mid-July," I answered as the rest of the writers settled in around the table. "But we won't know who won until the CBS telecast of the awards in September."

"It's going to be a long wait," Chantelle said.

"This time, we are to be accepting our own awards, is that not correct?" Samata asked me.

I nodded. "Yes."

"Damn straight," Meri commented. "There's no way that bitch is taking the stage on our behalf."

"Or claiming that our shows are hers," Maria added. "Those days are over."

"Let's hope," Taylor said.

"Yes, Eeyore, let's hope," Meri told her. "It might rain. It might be sunny. But let's hope it's sunny, shall we?"

"The battling Bogarts are at it again," Chantelle sighed, then turned to me. "Have you run into Debbe yet?"

I shuffled some papers in front of me. "No. But then I haven't really made myself available. I haven't left my office except to go to the ladies' room. And her door's been closed the entire time."

"The less that we be seeing of her, the better," Samata added. "I for one am wishing there is more distance that is put between us and what we have been doing to—"

"Don't say anything, Sam," Meri cautioned as she looked around the room. "Loose lips sink ships."

"What is that to be meaning?" Samata asked.

"It means we don't talk about *certain things* in the office," Meri replied. "If you know what I mean."

"I know what you be meaning," Samata answered. "But what does that have to be doing with ships?"

"Sorry I'm late," Britta said as she entered the room, then closed the door behind her.

"Have you seen Debbe?" Meri asked her as her eyes continued to search the ceiling and walls of the conference room.

Britta shook her head and pulled out a chair. "No. Thankfully. I came in early yesterday morning and cleaned out my desk."

"Does she be knowing what your new job is to be?" Samata asked her.

"I don't know. But personnel has completed all the paperwork. I'm now officially assistant to the writers. Debbe Lee will have to find someone else to kick around as her executive secretary."

"Congratulations!" Maria smiled at her.

"Thank you," Britta said, then uncapped her pen. "Is there anything I've missed that I should write down?"

"We're just starting," I told her, then cleared my throat. "Okay, back to business. We need to make the best use of this time between seasons to talk about next season's shows. I recommend that you hand the production of your current shows, which are all being renewed for a second season, over to your assistants. They can report to you on upcoming episodes and take over a lot of the work you did on them last season. You all need to shift your focus to new prime-time offerings. So let's brainstorm some ideas for new shows. Maria and I have an idea for a show that—"

"Well, well, well," Debbe pronounced slowly as she swung open the door of the conference room. "If it isn't my new part owners of L-TV, all gathered around the conference room table. Like it's business as usual. I bet you guys are feeling pretty high and mighty right now, aren't you?" she asked as she slammed the door shut behind her, then ran her hands down her red silk dress. "You're having a meeting without me, C.J.?"

"This is a writer's meeting, Debbe," I answered.

"Oh, are you still writers, C.J.? Is that what you still consider yourselves?"

"Yes," I said.

Debbe flipped her long black mane over her shoulders, revealing a dangling pair of diamond and gold earrings. "Writers, huh? I think not. Look at you. Look at the lot of you. Do you know what I'd call you? Not writers. I'd call you traitors. That's what I'd call you."

"You're welcome to join us, Debbe," I told her.

"What's that, C.J.?" Debbe asked as she cupped a hand behind one ear. "I'm *welcome* to join you? I don't need a welcome. I am still owner of L-TV."

"You are one of the owners of L-TV," I corrected her.

"Yes, so the contracts on my desk tell me. It seems much has happened since I left these offices for Amelia Island. A regular coup has been staged, hasn't it? Or maybe that was part of the plan. Some plan you bitches dreamed up to get me out of here so you could assume ownership." Debbe walked up behind Britta's chair, and then placed her hands on her shoulders. "Well, darling. It seems our little fling is over, isn't it? Your desk outside my office is empty, and I just received a memo from personnel informing me that your position should be posted. And you've been transferred to work with the writers—oh, I mean traitors." Debbe leaned down towards Britta. "Am I getting that right, darling?"

"Yes," Britta mumbled.

Debbe pulled out the empty chair next to Britta and sat down. She took Britta's hand in hers. "Don't you know you're just a pawn to them, Britta? Someone they used to get back at me? Look around the room at all of these miserable people. They didn't have the decency to confront me face-to-face with their demands for ownership, so they sent you to me. You were their sexual sacrifice. As much as I do like such sacrifices being made on my behalf, it just doesn't seem right now, does it? Tell me, you gorgeous Swede. Do you really want to work for these bitches?"

"Yes. Yes, I do."

Debbe released Britta's hand, then stood up. She slowly circled the table.

I followed Debbe's path around the table for a few moments, then opened my notebook. "Okay, everyone," I said. "Let's pick up where we left off."

"Yes, C.J., let's," Debbe cut in. "Just a few days ago, I was the sole owner of L-TV. That's where I left off. So why don't you fill me in on the details since that time."

"There's nothing to say, Debbe. You signed the contracts, and here we are."

"Yes, here we are. But the question that needs to be answered—that simply *begs* to be answered—is *how* did I sign those contracts?" Debbe stopped behind Maria, and then leaned towards her. "Have I ever told you that you have the most beautiful hair?" Debbe ran a hand over Maria's head. "So sexy. So kinky. So shiny."

Maria whirled around in her chair, grabbed Debbe's arm, and then stood up. "Leave me the fuck alone."

Debbe burst into laughter. "Oh, she's a feisty one, C.J. She's dropped the baby and getting back to her fighting weight. You know, I bet she's great in bed. Nice and rough. Full of—"

"Sit down and shut up," I hissed at Debbe. "If you want to sit in on this meeting, then sit in. But let us get on with it."

"I'll tell you what we're going to get on with, C.J.," Debbe said as she pulled out of Maria's grasp and stormed towards me. "We're going to talk about how I went from sole owner of L-TV to part owner."

"You signed the contracts, Debbe."

"I did sign contracts, C.J. That's certainly true. But not contracts which I believed would be relinquishing part of my ownership. No. I would have never done that. Because I've built this network. Me! You all have jobs because of me. Does anyone here dispute that fact?"

No one responded to her question.

"That's what I thought." Debbe crossed her arms and stood behind me. "So, C.J. Why don't you explain to me how *the fuck* I signed contracts that I never would've dreamed of signing?"

I shrugged my shoulders. "I don't know either, Debbe. But it is what it is."

"It is what it is?" Debbe echoed. "What the hell does that tell me? That tells me nothing."

"Well, I don't know what else to say," I told her.

"Of course you don't. But I have a lot more to say. Now let me tell you something. I have two plane tickets to Amelia Island. But the funny thing is, they're intact. What does that mean, you ask? Well, that means that the tickets weren't used. That means I didn't go to Amelia Island. What do you have to say to that, C.J.?"

I felt my pulse begin to race. *Have we thought of everything?* I remembered asking Samata and Maria as we did our final sweep of the warehouse.

"I'm waiting for a response, C.J."

I can't think of anything we've forgotten, Maria had told me.

And yet we had, I thought as I looked up at Debbe.

Debbe leaned towards me. "I didn't go to Amelia Island, C.J. I *know* I didn't. Are you hearing what I'm saying to you?"

There's no perfect crime, I heard T-Rex's voice in my head.

She's right, I thought as I kept my eyes on Debbe and the room grew uncomfortably still. I heard fresh air blowing into the room but felt like I couldn't pull in a deep breath. *Somehow, things always get fucked up. A bloody glove is left behind. Phone records are examined. Receipts for the purchase of murder weapons are dug up.*

"I didn't get on the airplane," I heard Debbe say.

It's always something, I recalled Gilda Radner once proclaim.

I knew that everyone sitting at the table right now was thinking the same thing. *Why didn't I think about the airline tickets? How could I have been so stupid?*

"And if I didn't go to Amelia Island, C.J., then I'm wondering, where *the hell* did I go?" Debbe pursued. "There are some things I remember from wherever I went. Or was taken to. Some things that are just not making sense. I have a videotape in my office that shows me that I signed documents in Janette's presence, but there's certainly something very weird about that. I'm not really focused on what I'm doing, and Janette seems hell-bent on getting me through the signing without really telling me anything about what I was signing. But, that aside, let's get back to the tickets, shall we? When I called the airline, I was informed that I never showed up at the terminal. So I'll ask you again, C.J. If I wasn't on Amelia Island, then *where the fucking hell* was I?"

We should've thrown the airline tickets away, I thought. *Then Debbe's credit card would've shown the purchase of the tickets, and she would have assumed she got on the airplane.*

"WHERE THE HELL DID I GO?" Debbe shouted. "I didn't walk to Amelia Island. I didn't take a bus. I didn't take a train. Because I checked. I never went to fucking Amelia Island!"

"As far as we knew, you did," Meri said.

Everyone else nodded.

"Well, I didn't, Meri Maid!" Debbe yelled at her. "I didn't, and you know it." Debbe swept an arm around the room. "All of you know it!" Debbe marched over to Britta and turned her chair around. "So we didn't have sex on the airplane, did we? And yet that's what you said on the videotape. Why don't you tell me, Britta? Why don't you tell me where the fuck I was?"

Britta slowly stood up and put her face near Debbe's. "We were at your beach house on Amelia Island," she said. "I know. I was there with you. And you had an accident. Perhaps that's why you don't remember anything. We took the limo to the airport. We raced through the terminal because we were late. We were the last ones to board. We made it just in time. All the other passengers were sitting down with their seat belts buckled. And then we sat down and took off moments later. I don't know anything about the airline tickets. No one asked us for anything once we were on the plane."

"Oh, I find that hard to believe," Debbe scoffed. "Someone would've taken our boarding passes from us. It's called a fucking security system. And airlines have to know who boarded a flight and who didn't. Just in case the plane crashes. They need an accurate manifest. So there's no way we could've gotten onto that plane without someone handling our tickets."

"Well, they didn't."

"They should have."

"They didn't!" Britta shouted at her. "They didn't, they didn't, they didn't! And now you've gone and . . . and . . ." Britta turned to Samata. "Oh, Sam! I'm so sorry I didn't tell you I went away with Debbe. I just . . . well . . . we weren't getting along. You were still so mad at me for sleeping with Debbe when I was with you. Nothing I told you about how I felt about you would convince you that she didn't matter to me. And so . . . and so I just decided to get back at you. And yes, Debbe and I did have sex in the airplane bathroom. But that's the only time. And she meant nothing to me. Nothing! I swear." Britta turned and glared at Debbe. "I thought I could keep our little trip a secret. I thought Sam wouldn't find out. But now, thanks to you, she knows. And now I have to do a lot of damage control." Britta pushed past Debbe and walked over to Samata.

Samata turned her chair to face Britta. "Yes. Okay. Well. Why did you not be telling me this? I know that we were being in arguments all the time. But why did you have to go back to her? I thought it was done and finished with her."

"I didn't go back to her, Sam," Britta answered as she dropped to her knees. "It was a mistake. It was just . . . I was just trying to get back at you."

"Well, certainly you have done this getting back at me good. I have been blinded on the side by you."

Debbe began to clap her hands. "Oh, this is wonderful. Wonderful! Positively brilliant. You are a damn quick thinker, Britta. I keep forgetting that you've had years of perfecting your knack for fabricating stories with all the gambling troubles you've had. Addicts really do make the best storytellers." Debbe turned to me. "C.J.? Is she telling the truth?"

"How do I know?" I answered. "I didn't go to Amelia Island with her. I didn't know that she and Sam were having problems. What the writers do on their own time is their business, not mine."

Debbe grinned at me. "So it just is what it is, right?"

I shrugged my shoulders. "I don't know what to tell you, Debbe."

"How about the truth."

I raised my head and locked eyes with Debbe. "I've always told you the truth, Debbe. You didn't seem to care for the truth very much when we were together, but you always got the truth from me then. It was you who lied to me. I never lied to you."

Debbe stared at me. "You hate me, don't you, C.J.? And you'd do anything to get back at me, to give me a taste of my own medicine, isn't that right?"

"If that was the case, Debbe, then I would've cheated on you, like Britta is admitting she cheated on Sam. But that wasn't in my nature. All I wanted was for us to work out. Back then. I didn't think that playing any game with you would make that happen."

"Well, you have played a game now, C.J. You know it, I know it, and everyone in this room knows it. Because airlines don't just let people board without checking their tickets."

"Maybe they did," I said.

"Oh, okay. Let's go along with that, shall we. Maybe Britta and I did board the airplane." Debbe swept her arms in the air. "So I'll go along with this, everyone. I'm on Amelia Island. There I am. Close your eyes. Picture the palm trees. The bright white sandy beaches. Feel the balmy breezes. See the sparkling clear ocean. Is that image fixed in everyone's heads? Now tragedy strikes. Uh oh. I got into some sort of accident. The funny thing is, though, that none of the hospitals have any record of me being admitted to their emergency rooms. Isn't that strange? Isn't that curious?"

Shit, I thought. *Yet another detail we had forgotten. If we had only taken care of the plane tickets.*

"And here's another funny thing, C.J." Debbe interrupted my thoughts. "Since we're talking about the past, do you remember, when we were together, about my boat?"

The boat, the boat, the boat, my mind chanted as I stared at Debbe.

"I don't know what you're talking about," I answered. *What about the boat?* I asked myself.

"Don't you remember?"

"Remember what?" *Remember what?* my voice screamed in my head.

"The boat needs gas, honey bun. The boat needs to be checked in and out of the marina, sweetheart. So I'm told that I got into an accident on my boat on this fantasy trip to Amelia Island. Well, do you know what I did? I called the marina and talked to Juan. Don't you remember Juan, dear heart? The one who would prepare the boat whenever we'd go down to Amelia Island? He'd stock the refrigerator for us, check the engines, fill up the tank and a spare can with gas. I chatted with Juan. And, lo and behold, he tells me he never saw me. Now don't you think that's a bit odd? Especially if I took the boat out and had *a goddamned accident* in it."

Let me just call Juan and make sure everything's ready, I remembered Debbe saying to me as I unpacked my bags on our last trip to Amelia Island.

Fuck! I thought. I heard Meri's voice say, *The best-laid plans— something, something, something.*

"Well?" Debbe asked me. "I didn't get on the airplane. I didn't go to a hospital. I didn't go out on my boat."

"I'll tell you what happened, Debbe," Britta began.

"Oh, I'm sure you will, Britta," Debbe cut in. "I'm sure you've got a very entertaining and almost convincing story. But I'm not going to buy whatever you tell me. Because I know that I never went to Amelia Island. It sure looked like Amelia Island, but it wasn't. And so I know that this new ownership agreement was done without my full knowledge. I was manipulated into signing your new contracts." Debbe surveyed the room, glaring at each of the writers. "So I'll tell you all what I'm going to do. I'm not going to give up getting to the bottom of this. I will keep after it and keep after it and keep after it. And when I come up with something, when I find out what really happened to me, I'm going to break those contracts. I assure you all of that."

Debbe grabbed the handle of the conference room door, blew it open, and stormed out of the room.

I let the dust settle for a few moments.

"Not one word," I cautioned everyone. "Not one word. We're fine. The contracts are solid."

"But what if—" Taylor began.

I held up my hand. "The only thing we will discuss in this office is L-TV business. *The only thing.* This room—everywhere at L-TV—is not safe. The walls have eyes and ears. Does everyone understand this?"

The writers nodded their heads.

"No e-mails," I continued. "No telephone conversations. No whispered exchanges in the elevator or the ladies' room about anything Debbe has brought up. And unless and until Debbe finds a way to break those contracts, which I doubt she will despite everything she's told us, we are part owners at L-TV. She has no proof, and the contracts are ironclad. And that's all the discussion we're going to have on this subject. Now let's turn our attention back to next season."

I turned on my desk lamp as the late spring afternoon sun disappeared behind nearby skyscrapers, then resumed my work.

My e-mail alert went off, and I opened up a message from Maria, who had returned home after the meeting, as she was still on maternity leave.

Katrina hasn't taken one nap today, so I know she'll crash early tonight. Dinner? Then maybe we could watch Sweet November *again. I love that movie. Don't you?*

I smiled. Maria and I had worked out a code to communicate personal messages between us that we didn't want anyone who might be accessing our e-mails to figure out. *Sweet November,* a sappy recent remake of an older movie, had reduced us both to tears one night on the living-room couch. Maybe it was the fact that the characters had finally found true love, only to have death end their relationship. Maybe it was the haunting tune sung by Enya that kept playing whenever something melodramatic was happening. Or maybe it was because Maria and I had fallen in love in November. Since we had watched that movie, whenever we wanted to make love we'd say, "Let's watch *Sweet November* again." Because we had first kissed and made love in November. And we were truly, madly, deeply in love. Just like the characters in the movie.

I hit the Reply key, then wrote, *I've got about another hour or so left of things to finish up. Leftover lasagna? Yes, let's watch the movie again. Maybe a couple of times. If you're up for it.* I grinned and pressed the Send button.

"Ownership requires long hours in the office, doesn't it, C.J.?" Debbe asked as she entered my office, then closed the door behind her.

I turned away from the computer. "What brings you to my neck of the woods, Debbe?"

"An off-the-record visit," she said as she took a seat in front of my desk.

"I didn't think anything with you was ever off the record."

We stared at each other for a few moments.

"Well?" I prompted her.

"I have to hand it to you, C.J. You're pretty damn smart after all."

I leaned back in my chair.

"All those years together, and I thought you were just a pushover. Just a sweet, innocent, do-gooder with big, brown puppy-dog eyes who kept wagging her tail no matter what happened to her."

"That about sums me up," I said.

"Oh, I think not. There's a whole other side to you that I've never seen before. I'm quite certain that you had a major role to play in this whole takeover of L-TV."

"It's not a takeover, Debbe."

"Well, I went from CEO and president of L-TV to part owner."

"You still have those titles."

"But not the clout."

"No. You apparently decided to sign that away."

Debbe flashed me a smile. "So how did you do it, C.J.? I know you weren't acting alone. I know everyone else was on board with your scheme. Just how did you pull it off?"

"I'm not a schemer, Debbe. I am exactly what you think I am. Just a darn nice person. A puppy dog."

"This whole thing has happened because of how I treated you when we were together, isn't that right?"

I shook my head. "This," I said as I leaned forward in my chair and raised one hand, "is you and me and what we once had as lovers. This," I paused as I raised my other hand, "is you and me working together at L-TV. Two separate issues. And, as far as I'm concerned," I finished, lowering the first hand I had raised, "our past relationship is a dead issue."

"Because now you and Maria are together."

"No, because you and I are over. We've been over for quite a while now."

"And now Maria has you."

"Yes, she does."

"I don't know why I let you go, C.J."

"Please tell me you're not hitting on me, Debbe."

"No, I'm not."

"Good."

"But if you were single—"

"I still wouldn't be interested. You've had your chances. Three, the best I can recollect. That was my limit."

"I wasn't a good lover to you, was I?"

"Debbe, I really don't want to journey down memory lane with you."

"I'm sorry."

"Now what did you want to talk to me about?"

"I said I'm sorry."

"Okay."

"No, C.J. You don't understand. I'm telling you that I'm sorry. I'm sorry for cheating on you. I'm sorry for treating you so badly when we were together. I'm sorry for hurting you. I never told you I was sorry."

"No, you didn't."

"I am now."

"Okay."

"Aren't you supposed to say something back?"

"What would you like me to say, Debbe? I'm glad that you're sorry? I'm glad I'm finally hearing those words?"

"It's not an easy thing for me to say, C.J."

"Well, I'm not going to congratulate you for telling me you're sorry, if that's what you're looking for. You said it. I heard it."

"But do you accept it?"

I stayed silent for a few moments before I spoke. "There's not much that you do that I accept, Debbe. You're a beautiful woman who has a lot of nice qualities. You really do. Deep down inside, there's a nice person just waiting to come out. I got to see this nice person from time to time when we were together. But never for very long. You didn't treat me very well when we were together, that's for sure. But what I've realized, since I've been working here with you, is that you really don't treat anyone very well."

"So is that why you decided to trick me into signing your new contracts?"

"Debbe, you signed those contracts. That's all I know. And I really don't want to discuss this anymore with you. Would you please leave?"

"Not yet, C.J."

"Well then I'm leaving," I said as I stood up from my desk.

"Please sit down, C.J. I just want to ask you something."

I sighed and sat down. "What?"

"Do you think this will work out? Do you think we can continue building L-TV by working together? With the writers being part owners?"

"Yes, I do. You have a lot of talent here, Debbe. You've gotten things off to a great start. I'm certain that all of us can continue to make L-TV better and better. You've just got to let everyone do their jobs. Take their own credit for the work they've done. You've got to trust that we're all in this together."

"Ah, there's that word again. Trust."

"Yeah. I know you hate it. But there it is. At some point in your life, Debbe, you're going to have to learn how to trust."

"You don't trust when you've been burned, C.J."

"You're wrong about that, Debbe. If you've been burned, then you don't trust the person who burned you. Like, for example, I no longer trust you. But you can still trust everyone else. Especially the people working here at L-TV. They're good people."

"Who have burned me now."

"Who burned whom first?" I asked her.

Debbe stared at me.

"Stop playing games with people, Debbe. Once you do that, you'll find that people won't play games with you."

"I got burned at the network, C.J."

"I know you did. But this isn't the network."

"Do you know why I got fired?"

"No. You've never wanted to tell me."

"Because I slept with the wrong person."

I rolled my eyes. "Why doesn't that surprise me?"

"She was someone I trusted at the network. And then she got

me fired. She used me. Because she wanted my job. Which she now has."

I sucked air between my teeth. "You're going to get no sympathy from me about that episode in your life, Debbe. But what happened to you there didn't have anything to do with trust. It was a lapse in judgment. On your part."

"She was at the *TV Guide* Awards, C.J. The woman I slept with at the network. And so I wanted to show her up. That's why I accepted your awards."

"You didn't show her up by doing that, Debbe. You burned your own writers. In fact, you used us and the work we had done to get back at her."

Debbe stared at me for a few moments. "Boy, don't you have an answer for everything, C.J."

I shook my head. "When are you going to learn to take responsibility for the things that you do, Debbe?"

"What do you mean by that?"

"*You* slept with the woman at the network. *You* accepted the awards at the ceremony. No one else did that, Debbe. You did."

"But I told you, I was trying to get back at—"

"That's the excuse you're using so you don't have to take responsibility for what you did," I cut in. "And you know something? It sounds way too familiar. Do you know how many times you told me, when I'd catch you sleeping with someone else, 'Oh, C.J., I wasn't interested in her. She was dogging me.' That was the excuse you used to justify cheating on me." I tapped my fingers against the desktop, then stopped. "Maybe your way of thinking makes you feel better. But it leaves everyone else feeling miserable."

Debbe thought for a few moments. "Well, okay. Let's say I buy into what you're telling me. Yes, I did sleep with the woman. But she burned me and—"

"And so then you chose to try to get back at her by screwing your writers. The ones who have created award-winning shows for you. Tell me again, Debbe. Who's screwing whom? Do you think that woman you slept with gave a rat's ass about you taking credit for our awards at that ceremony? But don't you think the writers cared a great deal about accepting their own awards and getting the recognition they deserved? Instead, you cheated them out of that."

Debbe sat in silence for a few moments. "I didn't mean to do that to the writers."

I showed Debbe a slight smile. "I'm sure that's true. You didn't mean to. But you did. And that's my point. You need to start taking responsibility for the things that you do instead of offering up excuses that you think will cover your behavior. Since you've already said you're sorry once today, you might want to think about saying it again, sometime soon. That might go a long way with the writers." I glanced down at my wristwatch. "Listen, I've got to go."

Debbe stood up. "I know, I know. You've got your honey at home. And your baby. A regular little family."

I rose from my chair.

Debbe walked to the door, then turned to me. "Listen. Maybe we could get together sometime after work. You know, just for a drink or something."

"Oh, Debbe—"

Debbe held up her hand. "I'm not asking you out, C.J. Really. It would just be, you know, a friendly type of thing. Maybe you could help me start learning about that whole trust thing. And that responsibility stuff you just told me about."

"Debbe, I'm not your therapist."

"I know, C.J. It's just . . . well. Okay. I know you have to go. It was, uh, good talking to you. That's all. It just might be nice to talk again sometime."

"Let's just see how it goes here at work with us, Debbe."

"Sure." Debbe opened the door, then walked out of my office.

I watched as she slowly strolled down the corridor. She stopped in front of one of the framed posters that was hanging on the wall, then turned and looked at me.

"This show of yours, C.J.," she said, pointing to the poster in front of her.

"Yes?"

"It's dynamite. It really is."

"Thanks," I said.

Debbe turned away from me and continued walking. "They're all good, C.J.," she called over her shoulder. "All of them. You tell your writers I said that, would you?" She tossed a hand in the air and waved. "See you tomorrow."

I waited for Debbe to turn down the corridor to her office, then put on my coat. I shut off the lights to my office, then closed the door. I traced Debbe's steps down the hallway and stopped in front of the promotional poster for *Madame President*. I blew a kiss at Stockard Channing and Meryl Streep, then turned to the elevator bank and pressed the Down button.

I thought about the ride home. The commute wouldn't be bad at this time of night. I'd probably pull into my driveway in about fifty minutes. The lights in the house would be lit, welcoming me home.

I thought about walking through the door to my house and being greeted by Maria. She'd throw her arms around my shoulders and pull me close to her. I'd breathe in her spicy, sweet scent and bury my nose in her hair.

I thought about holding Katrina in my arms and breathing in her soft baby scent, then watching her fall asleep in her crib.

I thought about the "sweet November" Maria and I would soon be sharing together.

I smiled. The elevator door opened, and I stepped into the car.

What happened next . . .

Collectively, the L-TV writers walked away with a hefty armful of Emmys for their shows in September. C.J. accepted a total of five awards for *Madame President,* including Best Dramatic Series and Best New Show of the Year. Samata was awarded three Emmys for *The Body Farm,* Maria took home four for *One Big Happy Family,* and Chantelle earned two for *Can't Let Go.*

Debbe sat in the back of the auditorium at the awards show and, between spurts of clapping and cheering for the awards L-TV was getting, successfully put the moves on an attractive executive from HBO who sported Tina Turner legs. She missed the return flight back to Boston and spent three days enjoying room service with her new fling.

She never offered an apology to the writers.

T-Rex starred in a second season of *Can't Let Go,* but negotiated her on-screen death in a flurry of FBI gunfire at the end of the season so she could work on a new L-TV daytime entry, a fitness show called *Bulking Up with T-Rex.*

Chantelle moved out of her sister's apartment and bought a condo in the South End with T-Rex.

Britta and Samata moved in together and spend their vacations in both Egypt and Sweden. Samata still struggles to grasp the intricacies of the English language. Britta attends weekly Gamblers

Anonymous meetings and has become an outspoken opponent of the Massachusetts Lottery.

Lars fell in love with Katrina. She fashions intricate wooden toys for her and has become her regular babysitter.

Sheila and Janette's partnership worked out so well that they now have a growing law office.

Maria and C.J. endured a long adoption process with Janette's help. Each of the writers provided affidavits that attested to their loving partnership. C.J.'s petition for adoption was heard in Suffolk Superior Court, and the judge granted her adoption of Katrina several months later.

Meri and Taylor started dating after the Emmy awards but continue to argue endlessly about who actually made the first move, among other things. Meri calls Taylor Eeyore, and Taylor calls Meri Piglet.

Please turn the page for
an exciting sneak peek of
Elizabeth Dean's
newest novel
BETWEEN GIRLFRIENDS
coming in July 2003 from Kensington Publishing!

1

It's Not My Party (So I'll Criticize It If I Want To)

World-famous author Gracy Maynard decided that this year she would take time off from her hectic, international book tour to stand alone at the most boring party in the world, tucked into a corner of a room, a pathetic wallflower with whom no one was interested in engaging in a lively conversation—

I broke off my spiraling-downward-into-the-depths-of-depression-on-New-Year's-Eve thoughts by taking a sip of some liquid I had ladled out of a container in the crowded kitchen shortly after I had entered the house. I had slopped the drink into a cup, smiled at women who clearly had no interest in returning my smile, let alone a halfhearted nod, then squeezed my way out of the tight gathering of estrogen and into a corner of the living room. There I had pitched a tent, lit a campfire, and settled down for what I knew would be a long night.

I swallowed whatever was in my plastic tumbler, but still couldn't fathom what the concoction was. I sighed and glanced at my watch. A full two minutes had ticked by since I had last checked the time. The stroke of midnight was still as far away as Mars. I was bored, tense, edgy, lonely, and sad. I was going to have a stroke just trying to make it to the new year.

Just another typical New Year's Eve in my life, I thought, then gave myself a sound mental scolding. *Don't go there. Just finish your drink and exit, stage left. No one will miss you. After all, no one even knows that you're here.* I cursed my cousin, immediately regretted taking out my bad evening on her and removed the curse, then turned my attention back to the only entertainment I had found enjoyable.

Three women, who were standing about an arm's length away from the spot of the wallpaper I had claimed as my territory, had been chatting together for a while. From what I had been able to gather in observing them and listening in on their conversation (translation: eavesdropping), they knew no one at the party and had just met one another as well. A large woman—in height, width, and the design of her hairstyle—who was wearing a jewelry counter's worth of gold bracelets and rings and was femininely and fashionably attired, had introduced herself to the others as Parker Lowell. Standing next to her was an African-American woman, who was a shade above five feet tall and a little bit overweight, but who was really cute and had a beautiful, ear-to-ear smile. She had straightened dark brown hair that was held back from her face with a clip and was wearing a black and off-white herringbone wool skirt, an off-white sweater, and a string of pearls. I had heard her introduce herself to the others as Blair Brown.

Blair kept her head perpetually skewed to one side as she listened attentively to Parker and Lindsey Tompkins, a woman who stood stiffly in front of them sporting a tailored pin-striped gray pantsuit and black silk tie, an outfit which matched her short, salt-and-pepper wavy hair. I pegged her as a funeral director because I hadn't seen anything other than a furrowed brow and a tight, tense smile displayed on her face.

I took another sip of my drink, then tuned back into their conversation.

"Honey, this isn't a party. Not in the truest sense of the definition," Parker declared as she sipped her drink, then grimaced and secreted the plastic cup behind a flourishing Wandering Jew that was set on a table behind her. "I mean, plastic cups? And this drink that some butch in the kitchen informed me was a mocktail? What the hell is a mocktail? It sounds like some species of animal that men hunt down in the fall. 'Hey, Ed. I hear dem mocktails is running this year. We gonna bag us some?' "

Lindsey chuckled.

Parker flashed a smile at her. "Let's just call a spade a spade, shall we?" she asked, then picked at an invisible speck of lint from her deep purple silk shirt that was unbuttoned to reveal a generous line of cleavage from her enormous breasts. "This isn't a party, and this drink isn't even close to a cocktail. This is a gathering of women—and I use that term loosely as well—who are clearly en-tertainment-challenged. And this drink is—"

"Delicious, I think," Blair cut in with a bright smile, then raised her eyebrows and lowered her voice. She leaned in closer to the other two. "You see, I think there are no alcoholic beverages here because a couple of the women may be recovering alcoholics," she whispered with a concerned look on her face.

Parker leaned toward her and kept her voice low. "Oh? Really? There are *lesbian* alcoholics? What do they look like? I don't think I've ever seen one before."

Blair shrugged her shoulders. "Parker, they look just like you and me." She nodded her head knowingly. "But they have a prob-lem with alcohol. Which makes them alcoholic. So they have to stop drinking. Alcohol, that is."

"Really!" Parker exclaimed. "So if they don't drink anymore, why aren't they called nonalcoholics? Like this damn drink."

Blair tipped her head to the other side, then shook her head. "That's a really good question. I don't know the answer to that."

"Cut it out, Parker," Lindsey hissed with a scowl, then looked at Blair. "She's teasing you."

Blair glanced at Parker, then smiled and blinked her big brown eyes. "Oh. Well, that's okay. People do that to me all the time. They tell me I'm naive." She took a sip of her drink, then another. "It's really not so bad. It's, well, refreshing."

Parker let out a loud snort. "Refreshing? My guess is that it's Diet Sprite and cranberry juice, which some butch poured into a spaghetti pot shortly before we arrived." She crinkled her nose and sniffed. "Refreshing would be a martini in a chilled glass. Refreshing would be a Manhattan or a gin and tonic, or even a simple rum and Coke. Refreshing would be any drink but this."

"It's a holiday punch, I think," Lindsey clarified as she pulled out a pair of glasses from the breast pocket of her jacket, brought her drink up in front of her eyes, and closely regarded it with an intensely serious look. "It *is* a bit festive-looking."

"Just because it's red doesn't mean it even qualifies to be called punch," Parker argued, then shook both of her arms so the dozens of bracelets embracing them jingled like sleigh bells on a Clydesdale. "And just because it's served in a pot and there's a ladle—"

"I think you're being way too critical, Parker," Blair cut in. "I for one think it's important for lesbians to address the issues that confront them. The difficulties each one of us faces in—"

"Knowing that we'll never be able to hold a candle to gay men when it comes to throwing a party?" Parker broke in. "Honey, Martha Stewart was born into this world solely to give gay men a reason to get up in the morning. Several theories are being kicked around that she's really a gay man in drag. Perhaps that's why straight people simply can't wrap their brain cells around her ideas. Only gay men can see her visions."

"So do you disagree with lesbians being PC?" Lindsey asked Parker as she picked up a paper plate from a table next to her. "I think I'm going to go ahead and try some of this," she said as she shoveled a plastic fork into a mound of pasta and scooped a healthy forkful into her mouth. "I mean," she continued as she chewed and then swallowed, "don't you agree that we need to be sensitive to the particular issues that each lesbian faces?"

"If PC stands for plastic china, then yes, I disagree with lesbians being PC," Parker answered. "I mean, have you ever been to a party thrown by gay men? Their subscriptions to *Martha Stewart* get used. They plan their parties for weeks. They're very much *events*.

They lay out fancy table settings. There's delicious food. And alcohol. Lots of alcohol. Not the cheap stuff, either. And honey, there are the richest, most mouthwatering desserts you could ever imagine. But the most important part of their parties is what gay men do best. They always have a theme. When they're not fucking or playing out some high drama or trying on women's clothing—and don't they look great in it, by the way?—they're using all of their creative energy to come up with *a reason* to gather people together. A white party. A diva party. A favorite literary figure party. There's always some sort of theme that unifies everything. The theme of this, well, whatever it is," Parker said as she waved an arm in the air, then shook her head and dropped her arm on her lap, "is, I believe, chaos."

"This is a New Year's Eve party," Blair said. "That's the theme."

"Then where are the noisemakers?" Parker countered. "I mean, other than the loud dykes in the den? Where are the party hats and favors? The decorations? Is there any indication in this house that this is, in fact, a New Year's Eve party?" She ran a tongue over her teeth and then sucked air between them. "Party? Ha! I wouldn't use the word party to describe this, unless you put the word pity before it," she concluded as she balanced a large hip on the edge of an overstuffed chair and crossed her ample legs. Her slit skirt opened to reveal a large, muscled calf and a foot housed in a black heel.

"A party can be defined as a gathering of people," Lindsey said as she shoved her plate on a side table, wiped her face with a napkin, then tossed the wadded napkin onto the plate. She pulled up the sleeves on her blazer and tucked her short hair behind each ear. "People are gathered. Thus, it's a party. I think you're being way too critical."

"Me, too," Blair agreed. "But, I mean, I'm not trying to be critical of you in saying that."

"What do you think?"

I listened to the pause in the conversation and waited for the answer. When none was offered, I shot a quick glance in their direction and noticed all eyes were on me.

"Yes, you," Parker said as she nodded at me. "You're not the hostess, are you?"

I shook my head. "No. A reluctant guest. I really don't want to be here."

"Neither do we." Parker smiled, then waved an arm noisily in the air. "Come. Come join the joyless club. I'm Parker Lowell."

"Blair Brown," Blair introduced herself as I stepped next to Lindsey. Blair extended a hand to me, and then shook mine. "It's a pleasure to meet you."

"She's the polite one in the group," Parker said. "I think we'll call her Miss Manners."

"There's nothing wrong with manners," Blair sniffed.

"I'm Lindsey Tompkins," Lindsey said as she turned to me. "I'm an attorney in Boston. Here's my card."

I stared down at the embossed card she extended to me, then took it and slid it into a pocket.

"Lindsey is going to sue for defamation of the character of this, well, I don't know what it is," Parker said as she looked around the room. "An excuse for me to get out of the house, I guess. Since Bob and Tom broke up this summer, there's no New Year's Eve party at the boys' house. Which is usually where I go."

"Gracy Maynard," I said as I nodded at the group. "So, do you all know each other?"

Heads shook.

"I guess we're the outcasts from the party." Blair frowned.

"Honey, we *are* the party," Parker pointed out.

"I was invited here through friends of friends, who haven't shown up yet," Blair continued. "I don't know a soul here. So I just stuck myself in this corner of the room and gave myself a time limit for how much longer I was going to stay."

"And I came over and asked Blair what time it was," Lindsey cut in. "I've been meaning to pick up my watch from the repair shop, but I never seem to get out of work in time. I don't know a soul here either. One of my coworkers told me about it. I think one of the women here is her ex. She advised that I get out of the office and do something social. I kind of, well, work hard. And for some reason tonight they closed the building where I work."

"It's New Year's Eve, honey," Parker said. "Although you wouldn't know it from this party."

Lindsey shrugged her shoulders. "I had a ton of work to do tonight. Briefs. Cases to review. Some dictation, too. Seems like I have to work double-time to earn my keep, compared to the men in the firm. I mean, if I'm going to make partner some day . . . anyway, I won't bore you with job-talk. I heard that the party was potluck, so I thought, *Looks like a free home-cooked meal for me.* I don't think I've used the stove once in my apartment. I usually order out. I eat out of containers in front of the television when I'm home. Or at my desk at work. You know, the food here isn't that bad."

"I haven't tried it," I told her. "I'm not really hungry, I guess. Or maybe I'm just a little nervous." I met Parker's eyes. "And so your story is . . . ?"

"Well." Parker shifted her weight and recrossed her legs. "I joined this little group because these women were the only ones in this house who were not wearing jeans and a flannel shirt. The kitchen brigade looks like they're putting on a fashion show for Woolrich, Dockers, and Levis." She glanced down at my jeans. "At least you ironed yours, honey. And that jacket is to die for. I love a girl in leather."

"She's not a girl," Blair corrected her. "I teach girls in my school."

"I hope you teach them how to dress well," Parker countered. "You dress nicely, Blair. You dress like a girl."

"Woman," Blair corrected her.

"The paralegals and secretaries in the office hate being called girls," Lindsey said. "And yet the men keep doing it."

"The point I'm trying to make," Blair continued, "is that a girl is a young female. The people here are women. And I think they would object strenuously to being called girls."

"Of course they would," Parker snorted. "That's because most of them would be shocked if you told them they were women. 'You gotta be shittin' me!' they'd probably exclaim."

"I think they know they're women," Lindsey said. "They're just not girly-girls. They're more butchy. Dykey."

"Don't we call that 'soft butch' nowadays?" I asked.

"They looked like hardasses to me." Parker chuckled. "Did you see the Arnold muscles on the one who was wearing—"

"Maybe we should call them tomboys," Lindsey suggested.

"No!" Blair protested. "And you shouldn't call them girls, either. How would you like it if I called you a girl, Parker?"

"I'd love it," Parker replied. "Because I *am* a girl. And so are you, Blair. And you, Lindsey. And you, Gracy. Girl, girl, girl, girl."

"Wasn't that the name of an Elvis Presley movie?" I asked with a grin.

"I remember that one!" Lindsey smiled. "I once dressed up as Elvis for an office Halloween party."

"It's just not politically correct," Blair told Parker.

"To dress up as Elvis?" Lindsey asked her. "Gay men dress up as women all the time. Why can't I dress up as a man?"

"I'm not talking about you, Lindsey," Blair said, then let out an exasperated sigh. "All I'm saying is that it's not politically correct to say *girl* when you mean woman."

"Well, tough titties, Blair," Parker said as she placed her hands beneath her breasts and jiggled them. "I'm the most un-PC lesbian you'll ever meet. I'm here, I'm queer, but I have a lot of problems with most things here and queer. Like this sorry excuse for a party, for instance. Potluck! Can you believe it? Only in the lesbian community do women invite other women over to their homes with the request to bring food. Don't lesbians shop? Is no one in the lesbian community capable of cooking for a group? And there's no alcohol served because of"—Parker raised both hands in the air and then shot two fingers from each hand up and down—"alcohol issues. Issues. God, I love that term. It seems like everyone in the lesbian community has some sort of issue. Even if it's not an issue, they make it an issue. And there's no smoking. Sure, I know it's dangerous to your health, but how else can you drink? And there's not one woman here wearing a skirt besides you and me, Blair. Here's my opinion. Take it for what it is. Girls cook. Girls entertain. Girls get drunk. Girls smoke. Girls wear skirts. Girls wear makeup. Honey, while most of these dykes here are out camping in the wilderness— which to me is a very scary place to be and why the hell anyone thinks that's fun is beyond me—I'm enjoying a makeover at Filene's counter. Or trying on clothes at Lord & Taylor. I enjoy being a girl. And I like girls who are girls."

"I shop at Lord & Taylor," Lindsey said, then opened her palms in front of her. "This suit."

"Love it!" Parker smiled. "Very snappy. But why not a skirt? Lesbians do have legs, you know. Or perhaps you're not into shaving."

"I think you're getting too personal, Parker," Blair said.

Parker raised an arm over her head and nodded at her bare underarm. "See? Shaved. Not braided. I don't have shaving issues." She lowered her arm. "And here's another thing that drives me nuts. I spell woman w-o-m-a-n. Not w-i-m-m-i-n or w-o-m-y-n. I love being a woman, and I love to be with women who love being women. There, Blair. I've said women several times. Are you happy?"

"I'll tell you what I don't like about these parties," Lindsey said as she pushed her hands into the pockets of her tailored pants. "Everyone here is a couple. Every party you go to in the lesbian community, it's couples, couples, couples."

"Except for us," Blair pointed out.

"Who wants to be in a couple?" Parker asked. "There's way too much to choose from out there. Who wants to get tied down? Except in bed, of course."

"I wouldn't mind being tied down," Blair said.

Parker beamed a broad smile at her. "I didn't think you were the type."

"Not for that—for what you're thinking," Blair quickly added. "But for being in a relationship. A lasting, true love. Forever and ever."

"I bet you read a lot of fairy tales when you were growing up," Parker said.

"There's nothing wrong with wanting a happily ever after," Blair answered as she played with the string of pearls around her neck. "I've liked being in relationships. Waking up with the same person every morning. Talking about the day you've had in the evening when you come home. Deciding what to do for the weekend or where to go for a vacation."

"I bet you just rope 'em in as fast as you can." Parker snickered, then turned to me. "I gather you're the shy, quiet type, Leather."

I shook my head. "Not really. I just, well, I'm not into the party scene. I used to go out all the time. With, you know, whoever I was with at the time and all of her friends. Now that I've been single for a while, I just can't seem to get too excited about trying to meet someone again. In a social situation like this. It's all too . . . too—"

"Painful?" Blair suggested.

"Problematic?" Lindsey offered up.

I paused to search for an answer.

"Honey, you're not going to find anyone with potential at this, well, at this," Parker said. "Unless you're into lumberjacks."

"So where do you meet women?" Lindsey asked. "I've done the bar scene. And I've dated friends of friends. It's not easy finding a soul mate. And I work too damn hard. I don't think I have time anymore to be on the search, let alone try to make something work. But I hate coming home to an empty apartment."

"Well, this is certainly not a very upbeat conversation," Blair pointed out.

"You want upbeat, go into the kitchen," Parker responded. "They may be making another batch of Hawaiian Punch. Woo-hoo!"

"Well," I said as I glanced down at my watch. "I think I'll head out."

"Don't go!" Blair begged as she reached for my arm. "Okay. I don't like to be critical or judgmental—"

"Except with me," Parker cut in.

"—but you guys are the most interesting people I've met in a long time," Blair continued. "I mean, you women can actually hold a conversation."

"But you've disagreed with everything I've said," Parker pointed out.

"That doesn't mean I don't think you're interesting," Blair answered. "You're a very different person from anyone I've ever met. Before I came over to this corner of the room, I tried talking to the people in the kitchen. But they're all—"

"Couples, talking about couple things they've done together," Lindsey finished. "When *we* went to Yosemite. When *we* played for the championship softball game. When *we* decided to add on to our house last fall. What happened the last time *we* went to the gynecologist because *we're* trying to have a baby."

"Exactly!" Blair exclaimed. "And I'm sorry, but I think that's rude. I mean, how can you meet new people or hear different points of view or—"

"Find out common interests or even things you don't know about," Lindsey added.

I nodded. "I did try to engage some of the kitchen people in conversation. And then I got this look from a few of them—you know, it's a look that's kind of off-putting, a look that tells you—"

"—to butt out, it's none of your damn business," Lindsey cut in and frowned.

"Well, not so much that," I answered. "But like, well, I think Margaret Cho said it best in her one-woman show, *I'm the One that I Want*. She talks about going on an Olivia cruise with hundreds of lesbians and experiencing firsthand the lesbian drama that plays out whenever a new face shows itself on the scene. Except on that cruise, just about everyone on the cruise was a new face. So she said that each lesbian started questioning her lover, asking, 'Are you interested in her? In her? In her? In her?'"

"That's exactly how I felt when I went into the kitchen!" Blair exclaimed. "Everyone's looking at me like 'Who is she?' and then I could sense the couples pulling closer together. Like I was going to steal one of them away."

Lindsey nodded. "The new lesbian sighting syndrome."

"Circle them wagons, Alma!" Parker cried out. "Thar be a new lezzie in town, and ah'm thinkin' she gonna be stirrin' things up for the rest a us. Ah'll go git ma gun."

"Which totally puts a lid on the possibility of making a new friend," I pointed out. "I mean, I'm not looking for a potential partner here tonight, although everyone in the kitchen probably thinks that I am. I just wanted to get out of the house and have a good time."

"I'm having a good time with you guys," Blair said. "I really am."

"That's because we're way too good for anyone in the kitchen," Parker sniffed. "We've got class. We've got brains. We've got wit and charm."

"And yet they all have what we want," Lindsey added.

"A battleship-gray Saab convertible with heated seats?" Parker asked Lindsey, then laughed. "Sorry. That's what *I* want. Listen, honey, having someone doesn't mean you *are* someone. And having someone doesn't necessarily guarantee happiness. When you're in a relationship, it just means you have someone to go to the movies with. All the time. It takes a long time to find a lifelong partnership with someone that lasts. You have to do a lot of work and go through some rocky times as well as some good ones. It's fucking hell. Which is probably why I'm not in a relationship because I don't have the patience that's needed to process or to go deep and get heavy. I just want to be in bed with a woman. As much as I can."

"And then after bed?" I asked.

"Well, then, we usually go the kitchen and make a snack together," Parker answered with a smile.

"I was thinking about trying to meet someone through the personal ads," Blair said.

"Uh-oh," Lindsey answered, then shook her head. "I tried that once. Not a good experience. You have to read the fine print—"

"Spoken like a true attorney," Parker interjected.

"What fine print?" Blair asked.

"What someone writes in an ad is usually very different from who or what that person really is," Lindsey answered. "I tried that route myself. I responded to an ad that was written by a woman who said she was slightly overweight. We talked on the phone a few times, then we decided to get together. She was the size of a house. Another wrote that she wasn't into the bar scene. So where do you think she wanted to meet me?"

I grinned. "At a bar?"

"Affirmative." Lindsey chuckled.

"I used to read the personals all the time," I said. "I never responded to any of them, but I got to playing this game whenever I'd read them. I'd try to look beyond what was written to get to the heart of what was really meant. So if I read that someone liked long walks on the beach, I'd think to myself, 'Uh-oh. There's someone who can't relate to people.' Someone who would write that she liked fine wines—"

"Is a lush, honey." Parker chuckled.

"People usually write the opposite of what they really are because they'd like to think that that's how they are," Lindsey said. "Someone may say they're sane, grounded, spiritual, strong, centered, and so on, but more likely than not they're none of those things. That's just how they'd like to be. And they think if they attract someone like that, those things will rub off on them. I found looking through the personals all too frustrating."

"I took out an ad once," Parker said with a sly grin. "Here's what I wrote: *I want to meet other lesbians for casual sex. All I want to do is come, come, come. So come with me. I want to suck you and fuck you. Must be feminine and sexy.*'"

"Oh, my!" Blair exclaimed.

"That's pretty clear," I said.

"I thought so," Parker answered. "And I got responses. I decided that I was going to meet each and every one of these women. So I told them all to show up at a certain place at a certain time."

"At the same time?" Lindsey asked.

Parker nodded. "The designated meeting place was at a restaurant near a women's bookstore in Boston. I sat in my car in the parking lot and watched woman after woman walk into the place. And several men as well. There was not one sexy, feminine woman in the lot. So I figured, why bother going in? They're each going to think one of the others took out the ad, and maybe a few of them will decide to hook up. That's the last time I took out an ad."

"So where the hell do you meet single women?" Lindsey said. "Wait. Let me clarify that. Where the hell do you meet single *quality* women?"

"Define quality," I told her.

Lindsey thought for a moment. "Someone like me. I think I'm a quality person. I'm looking for someone who's professional. Kind. Respectful. Honest. With a brain. And with good looks and charm."

"You want the whole package," Blair pointed out.

"Exactly," Lindsey answered.

"This small group of women right here in front of me is looking pretty good," Parker said. "You all seem to have those qualities. As do I. So let's go to bed and make wild, passionate sex."

Blair stared at Parker.

"Oh, for God's sake, I'm joking, Blair," Parker clarified. "You're the first group of women I've met that I haven't wanted to take to bed. No offense. I'm not saying that you all aren't attractive. But I actually would like to talk more with each of you. For the first time in my life, I've met some nice-looking, put-together, quality lesbians and just want to talk with them. What an eye-opening experience!"

"I agree," Blair answered. "I mean, with wanting to continue talking with you guys."

"So," Parker began, and then looked at us. "What do you say?"

"What do you say to what?" Lindsey asked.

"To all of us meeting up again," Parker suggested. "For drinks. Or coffee. Or dinner. We can go out and talk and enjoy each other's company. No strings attached."

"Sounds good to me," Lindsey said.

"Me, too," Blair chimed in.

I nodded. "Me, three."

As I headed home that night, I thought about the conversation I had had with Parker, Lindsey, and Blair, and about Lindsey's question, Where does a single lesbian, with quality, meet another single lesbian who also has quality? When I reached my apartment building, I bounded up the stairs, threw my jacket on the floor, raced to my computer, then sat down in front of the blank screen.

After a few minutes, I began to type.

Single lesbian. Lonely. Looking for love. Please send directions . . .

Where do single lesbians meet other single lesbians?

The hardest part in seeking a definitive answer to this question—or at least some suggestions—is that every single lesbian approaches meeting another single lesbian with a certain set of expectations in mind, a certain itinerary, a certain plan for an outcome. Some want to meet just to have sex. Some want to meet to begin a friendship that may possibly develop into what the personal ads identify as LTR—long-term relationship. Some want a companion to join them for hikes up mountains, days on the beach, and nights at the movies, but with no thought of sex or intimacy—kind of like a date without potential. And some truly want to meet someone to begin a committed, long-lasting relationship—something they haven't been able to find in the many social avenues available to single lesbians: the bars, the discussion and book groups, the parties, the sports teams.

How does a single lesbian approach such a search without feeling that she may once again be setting herself up for defeat? That she's once again pining all her hopes and dreams on another person in the attempt to create something that may start out with a whole lot of potential and then, for a multitude of reasons that most often begin with, "It's not you, it's me," end in heartbreak?

The single lesbian is one of the gay community's most perplexing dilemmas. Because there are a lot of single lesbians out there. There are far less than six degrees of separation that keep single lesbians apart. Each day we pass by them unknowingly or even interact with them as we go about our daily business. Sometimes we don't have to work hard to find a lifelong partner. But more often than not we have to go through a series of heartbreaks in the search for our true soul mate.

But how does this happen? Where does the single lesbian begin her search?

I wrote for hours that night without realizing that one year had ended and another had begun. As I composed the last paragraph and then reread my words, I realized that I was just seeing the tip of the iceberg in the lesbian community. There was so much more for women to talk about, so many other things that were important to lesbians, and so many other, as Parker called them, *issues,* that affected lesbians in their pursuit of love.

I began writing down other questions I wanted to have answered.

I stared at the list as I printed the article I had just written. It didn't matter that I didn't know the answers. Because I knew Parker, Lindsey, and Blair could help me—and other lesbians—to find those answers.